Swimming Monkeys
Genesis

by

Steve Hadden

TELEMACHUS PRESS

This book is a work of fiction. Names, characters, places and incidents are either the product of the author's imagination or are used fictitiously. Any resemblance to actual persons, living or dead, or to actual events or locales is entirely coincidental.

SWIMMING MONKEYS: GENESIS
Copyright © 2012 by Steve Hadden. All rights reserved, including the right to reproduce this book, or portions thereof, in any form. No part of this text may be reproduced, transmitted, downloaded, decompiled, reverse engineered, or stored in or introduced into any information storage and retrieval system, in any form or by any means, whether electronic or mechanical without the express written permission of the author. The scanning, uploading, and distribution of this book via the Internet or via any other means without the permission of the publisher is illegal and punishable by law. Please purchase only authorized electronic editions and do not participate in or encourage electronic piracy of copyrighted materials.

The publisher does not have any control over and does not assume any responsibility for author or third-party websites or their content.

Cover Design by Pete Garceau

Published by Telemachus Press, LLC
http://www.telemachuspress.com

Edited by Winslow Eliot
http://www.winsloweliot.com

Visit the author website:
http://www.stevehadden.com

ISBN: 978-1-938135-45-3 (eBook)
ISBN: 978-1-938135-46-0 (Paperback)

Version 2015.11.13

10 9 8 7 6 5 4 3 2 1

Read the Swimming Monkeys Trilogy

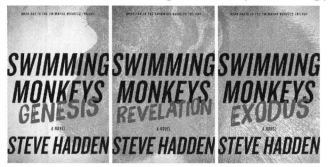

Also by Steve Hadden

Genetic Imperfections

The Sunset Conspiracy

Dedication

For my children,
thanks for going along for the ride.

Acknowledgements

As always, this book would not be possible without the help and support of my wife, CJ, who was with me at the genesis of this crazy idea. Special thanks goes to Winslow Eliot, who once again did a wonderful editing job and provided great words of encouragement. Thanks to Steve and Terri Himes, Steve Jackson, Mary Ann Nocco, and the entire team at Telemachus Press. I'm grateful for the assistance of the team at The Editorial Department including Liz Felix, Jane Ryder, Peter Gelfan, and Julie Miller along with the great cover design work by Pete Garceau.

Swimming Monkeys
Genesis

CHAPTER 1

RYAN WEBSTER STARED at his iPhone. The text arrived at 12:01 a.m.

Come now and don't tell anyone else.

He reread the message, hoping its meaning would magically change. It didn't. He jammed the phone back into his jeans. Getting messages at midnight on Saturday wasn't unusual. At seventeen, he looked forward to late-night texts and weekends that tested total irresponsibility. But it was the sender that made this message so strange. It came from the only person for whom he'd drop everything, including his girlfriend Sarah. And it signaled an end that he didn't want to come—and a beginning he didn't want to face.

Despite the hammering thunderstorms pounding South Florida, he made it to the parking lot of Saint Paul's Hospice in ten minutes. He cruised past the few cars in the lot and parked his pickup next to the steps leading to the front doors. The wipers stopped, and sheets of rain soaked the windshield. Saint Paul's Hospice was the place to go for end-of-life care and spiritual and emotional support. At least, that's what the brochure sitting on his dashboard said. A bolt of lightning exploded above the trees and provided a brief snapshot of the building. They'd done a great job making the hospice look like someone's sprawling ranch home. A long porch ran the entire length of the building. White wooden rocking chairs added to the deception. But the place always had a haunting glow at night, and the sheets of rain blurring Ryan's view made it even more unsettling.

He shook his head. He'd rather be anyplace but here. The man had done so much for him. He opened the door and got out. Immediately drenched by the warm Miami rain, he pivoted around the railing and bounded up the steps, three at a time. Then he waited at the glass double doors until the night attendant spotted him. Ryan was no stranger here. Six hours earlier he'd made his daily visit to Phineas Barnum Webster.

The magnetic lock clicked, and Ryan stepped inside, pushing back his wet hair and dripping water on the tile. He was sure he looked like he'd just finished his training session for the 4x100 freestyle.

"Thanks, Maggie."

He'd grown friendly with Maggie while coming here each evening for the past two weeks. She was younger than his mom, but not young enough to stir any romantic interest.

"Hi, Ryan. I didn't expect to see you back so soon."

He remembered the text. Still, he thought an explanation for his return was in order.

"Grandpa looked a little worse than usual this afternoon, so I thought I'd check in on the way home."

"That's kind of you. Your mother must be proud to have such a good son."

His jaw tightened, and he looked toward the entrance to the ward. He was always uncomfortable with compliments. Maggie pressed the magnetic release and the door quietly vibrated. He eased it open.

Ryan crept down the hall. Pale green wallpaper attempted to hide the sterility of the place, but the white linoleum floors, bright fluorescent lights, and smell of disinfectant reminded him this was the ass end of a glorified hospital. The last stop before you crap your pants then check out for good. Most doors were open, and the rooms were dimly lit. He tried not to look inside but couldn't help himself. Some patients lay on their inclined beds with their mouths open—asleep, he hoped. Others were awake and stared at the silent TV mounted on the wall. One of the residents offered an expressionless stare as he passed. He looked ancient to him. He consoled himself with the fact the man had lived a full life and this was just part of the process. But then he passed a child with a shaved head and tired, sunken eyes. He hung his head and cursed every childhood disease he remembered.

He stopped at the end of the hallway. The intersection formed a T. He scanned the hallway to his left and then turned right. He slowed his pace and approached his grandfather's door. The lump in his throat took up more permanent residence.

For a moment he stood in the doorway and looked at his grandfather. He lay on the bed with his eyes closed. Despite the ravaging cancer inside him, he was still an imposing figure. Ryan knew he got his rugged square jaw and chiseled cheekbones from his grandpa. And despite living under fluorescent lights for the past two weeks, his grandfather still held a tan. Ryan assumed all of the adventures as a zoologist for the Smithsonian in jungles, deserts, and tundra around the world had tattooed his skin.

His grandfather had lived seventy-four years and seen more beauty and tragedy than anyone else Ryan knew. He'd spent hours telling Ryan about the modern discoveries he'd made and the expeditions that resulted in identifying and cataloging hundreds of new species. He'd built natural history exhibits around the world to share his love of animals with those who did not have the good fortune to see them thriving in their own habitat. Along with his father, Ryan's great-grandfather, he'd started the most successful wild animal park outside of the San Diego Zoo, the Webster Primate Park, and made his fortune on that business. But as far as Ryan was concerned, the greatest accomplishments of his life weren't the discoveries, the awards, the dinners with heads of state, or the fame. They were those years he'd spent mentoring and encouraging his grandson.

"I can feel you burning a hole in me with that stare, Ryan." Phineas never opened his eyes.

Ryan chuckled. Grandpa always had a sixth sense. "You always know when I'm around, Grandpa. You're kinda scary."

They both laughed.

"Not scary, Ryan. It's a gift. A gift you have, if you choose to develop it."

Ryan just grinned.

"What's up with the midnight text message? I didn't know you even knew how to text, let alone after midnight."

"Never too late to learn."

Phineas smiled and opened his eyes. Ryan thought about how little time his grandpa had left to learn, and the lump in his throat choked off his reply.

"Come sit here next to me on the bed. I have something very important to tell you, and I can only do it once. You'll want to listen closely."

He certainly had Ryan's attention now. Ryan maneuvered past the IV stands and monitors and sat at his grandfather's side. The rhythmic traces of his grandfather's heart appeared on the monitor across the room as if they were some morbid countdown. "Okay, Grandpa, shoot."

His grandfather turned and gazed at him with bright blue eyes. They flickered with life and excitement, as always.

"What I'm about to say you can't share with anyone. Understood?" He wheezed and coughed. "Your great-grandfather wanted it this way."

Ryan nodded and leaned in a little closer. He recalled the hours of stories his grandpa had told him about how his great-grandfather had explored the world from 1910 until his death in 1976. He'd described how Zachariah Webster had encountered new species, scoundrels, and geniuses, but his most prized encounter was when he was a young boy and met P. T. Barnum. In honor of that man, he'd named his only son Phineas and made Barnum the family middle name, carried by three generations of Websters.

"In 1926 your great-grandfather made a discovery. He knew the world wasn't ready for it to be revealed. We would have destroyed it. So he kept it secret until he was on his deathbed and then he passed the clues on to me."

"What was it, Grandpa?"

His grandpa's wheezing got louder and Ryan leaned in closer. "He'd told me that there would be a Webster who had the right abilities and who would know how and when to share it with the world. He said I would recognize that individual, and when I did, it was my responsibility to pass it on to that person. He made me promise. Those were the last words my father spoke before he died."

Ryan was momentarily distracted by a thunderclap and glanced at the rain pelting the window.

"So who is it?"

Ryan was convinced it wasn't him. After all, he'd been barely pulling a B-minus average in school and had been sent to the office enough to know what each of the principal's family members looked like.

A lightning bolt flashed and the lights flickered. His grandfather grabbed Ryan's forearm.

"It's you, Ryan. It's you."

Ryan pulled his arm back.

"No. No! It can't be me."

His grandpa yanked his arm closer.

"You and I both know the gift you have."

Ryan stiffened. "But that's not a gift. It's a curse. And you promised never to tell anyone about it."

"I didn't and I won't, but you need to know it's not a curse."

"I don't want anyone to know—they'll destroy me at school."

"Don't worry—you'll only have to use it if you succeed."

"Succeed. I have no clue what to do to even get started."

"Ryan, I've told you before to rely on your intellect. You can figure this out and I know what that gift can do."

He decided his protests were useless, and he felt guilty arguing with a dying man. He cut his eyes to the window as a bright flash of lightning lit up the room.

"What did he discover?"

"Monkeys."

"Monkeys?"

"Not just any monkeys—swimming monkeys."

Ryan glanced at the IV and wondered if the morphine drip had Grandpa high. They'd told him his grandfather's mental faculties might falter just before the end, and now he was convinced it was here—the old man had lost it.

"Okay, Grandpa."

Phineas's eyes flashed.

"Don't patronize me, boy! I'm not loopy. You'll want to hear the rest of this. Don't let your youthful impatience get the best of you. You have an obligation here."

Ryan refocused on his grandfather.

"I don't understand."

"These monkeys *learned* how to swim," Phineas explained.

"But the Java monkeys in the park wade and dive in the water."

"Did you ever see them do the Australian crawl?"

"The what?"

"Boy, for someone who holds the state record in that event ... the freestyle!"

Ryan immediately had an image: a monkey swimming like one of his teammates. He chuckled. His grandpa had always been a jokester.

But Phineas remained silent, and his glare intensified. Ryan saw it was no joke. He remembered all the time he and his grandfather had spent in the New World monkey exhibits. He'd never seen a monkey swim like a human. They certainly had the physical attributes and strength. He stopped smiling and squirmed on the bed.

"Not so funny now," Phineas said. He gave Ryan a grin. Ryan had seen it a hundred times before when his grandpa knew Ryan had learned some abstract scientific point.

"There's something else. Something your great-grandpa said would change the world forever, if and when we were ready for it."

Ryan stopped squirming. "What is it?"

His grandfather released Ryan's forearm, rolled onto his back and searched the ceiling for an answer.

"I can't tell you," he said.

"Can't tell me?"

Phineas turned back to him and scowled. "Not here and not now."

"Why not?"

Phineas opened his mouth to answer, but then wagged his head in frustration. "Because the world may not be ready now, and besides, you never know who's listening."

Ryan quickly scanned the room. No one was listening, except him.

"Not ready?"

"That's what I said. My father said that because of what was going on in the world at the time of the discovery. When my father told me what I told you, he said we still weren't ready."

"What was going on?"

"The year before his discovery, in 1925, the State of Tennessee vs. John Thomas Scopes was happening."

"What?"

"You saw *Inherit the Wind*, didn't you?"

"Uh, I remember the title. I think we saw it in junior high."

"What do they do in the schools these days?"

Ryan shrugged, as he always did when asked that question.

"Well, the movie is about what the papers at the time called the Scopes Monkey Trial. John Scopes was a high school teacher who intentionally violated a law on the books there called the Butler Act. Essentially, it made it unlawful for anyone in a state-funded establishment to teach any theory, such as evolution, that denies the story of divine creation in the Bible. Scopes taught a chapter from *On the Origin of Species* by Darwin."

"So? They teach that stuff all the time now. I remember you and me discussing Charles Darwin and his work on the Galapagos Islands."

"That's true, but back then this was a very divisive issue in the US. Divine creation versus man from monkeys."

"So that's why Great-grandpa Webster didn't want to announce his discovery?"

"Yes, partly. He thought the evolutionists would've used it to prove they were right, and some might have taken it as far as trying to prove there is no God. The radical Christians would have tried to destroy the monkeys to protect their literal view of man's creation."

"And now they're ready?"

"No. There's more. He said that there were two aspects of the discovery that would cause many people to do anything to get at the monkeys. Lie, cheat, even murder. He didn't want to be part of that and said the world was not ready, so he put everything in a notebook for safe keeping."

Ryan's head was spinning. How could something that sounded as ridiculous as swimming monkeys have that effect on mankind? What was *he* supposed to do with this?

"Why are you telling me this?"

"Because it's time, and you have the gift."

"Why is it time?"

"Your great-grandfather did tell me they were in a rainforest. And I received a cryptic message from one of his old friends that said their rainforest was being destroyed to make room for some pipeline. The squatters following the pipeline were burning the jungle along the route. He said they won't be around much longer."

"So it's time to tell the world?"

"I didn't say that. It's time to be sure they're safe and ensure they survive. You'll have to decide if it's time to share them with the world."

Ryan dropped his shoulders. There was the punch line. *He* was the one expected to find them and to make a decision that could change the world forever. He barely kept gas in his truck. How would he do this? Grandpa always expected more of him than he felt he had, and usually he delivered. But this was too much.

Ryan looked at the rain on the window again. "I can't do it."

Phineas raised himself on one elbow and grabbed Ryan's arm. "You have to. There's no one else."

"But I'm just a kid. I have no money and no idea where to start."

Phineas rolled on his back again, and Ryan heard his breathing getting labored.

"You'll have a little help."

"From who? Not Dad. He can't stand to help me. The only thing he hates worse than helping me is the Primate Park. You know how he is. Everything by the book. Get through school, get into college, get a degree, and get out of the house."

Phineas coughed uncontrollably. Ryan adjusted his pillows. Finally, the attack subsided, and Phineas drew in a short breath.

"He loves you, I'm sure. It's me he doesn't care for. He's always been jealous of the time I spent away building my career and the park. You know I love him, but he's of no use here."

"Then who?"

Phineas began to cough again, and a nurse appeared in the doorway with a syringe. Ryan moved from the bed, and she injected the clear liquid into the IV. More morphine. In seconds the coughing stopped, and the excitement in his grandfather's eyes disappeared.

"Mr. Webster, it's best if you give your grandpa a little time to sleep."

Ryan hovered and looked down at his grandfather. Phineas waved him away from the bed.

"We'll talk again soon," he said softly, and closed his eyes.

Ryan looked back at the nurse, and she motioned him outside. He squinted as his eyes adjusted to the bright lights in the hallway. His legs felt much heavier than on the way in, and he stared at the floor as he trudged down the corridor. He opened the double doors to the reception area and passed by Maggie without looking up.

"Goodnight, Ryan."

He waved his hand but kept walking. Outside, it had stopped raining. He opened the door, got in and started his truck. He hesitated and looked back at the rocking chairs on the front porch of the hospice. He knew his grandpa was dying, and this was his last wish. He'd given him the love, time, and guidance that his father never did. Now, he'd be gone. Ryan felt more alone than he ever had. He jammed the truck into gear, turned out of the parking lot, and drove slowly toward home. In his side view mirror, he noticed a dark sedan in the lot turn on its lights. At first, it didn't move. He drove to the corner and turned right and kept his attention split between the passenger's side view mirror and the street ahead. Remembering his grandfather's warnings, he slowed, looked back toward the hospice entrance, and saw the car race from the lot. He pulled behind a dumpster adjacent to the convenience store on the corner and turned off his lights. The sedan turned the corner and slowed. The two occupants' heads swiveled left and right. He slipped down in the seat as they passed. The passenger slammed his fist into the dash and the car accelerated out of sight. Convinced they were gone, he pushed himself upright. Maybe they'd visited someone in the hospice and were lost—maybe it was a coincidence. He didn't want to believe the alternative. Still, he pulled the truck forward and decided to turn left—take another way home—just in case.

CHAPTER 2

CYRUS SCHULTZ GNAWED on a Cuban cigar and his nerves tingled with anticipation. The evening with the children at the hospital lasted longer than he'd planned. But it was time well spent—anything for the children. Somehow helping them made his own childhood seem more tolerable. He gazed out the window in his oceanfront town home in South Beach. The rain pelted the windows and gave an eerie glow to the lights of the freighters anchored outside of the Port of Miami. He winced at a flash of lightning from a wandering thunderstorm, but he continued to stare into the black night. The storms roamed across the horizon, and he grew more impatient with each minute. He'd waited over thirty years for this night.

He noticed the reflection of the green and red indicator lights on the three computer screens stretched behind him and then detected the hulking shadow just over his shoulder.

"Good evening, Karl."

"*Guten Abend.*"

"You have some good news, I trust?" he said without turning.

"*Ich habe gute Nachrichten!*"

"In English, Karl. You left Germany a long time ago, and besides, I've decided I don't need any reminders of my father, including his native language."

Karl stepped into the light. Cyrus saw his reflection and found it more haunting than meeting him face-to-face. Karl's head was thick and capped with a white flattop. His forehead, trimmed with white brushed eyebrows, cast a deep shadow over his eyes. His face glowed white and his black long-sleeved pullover stretched over his chiseled six-four frame. Still, he had an apologetic look as he replied in forced staccato English.

"Yes, sir. Sometimes I miss the old days. I have good news. The boy has left, and we're following. Phineas Webster told him about the targets but gave no location other than the rainforest. We think there will be more, but not tonight."

Cyrus corralled his disappointment and flicked his cigar. He faced Karl. "Stay on it. I want you to be on the boy twenty-four seven. The old man won't last the week, and he'll have to pass on more detail to the kid."

Karl stared back with his dead black eyes.

"We have two of our best men on him, and they won't let him out of their sight."

Karl made a rare attempt to smile. "Did you enjoy your time with the children?"

"I did. They hold a special place in my heart."

Karl lost the smile. "I won't let you down, sir."

"I know you won't. The Websters are about to move. When they do, we'll be ready. Do whatever is necessary to find the location of the targets. They hold the key to everything my father spoke about before he died. And I suspect they hold the key for those children, too."

Karl remained silent, as he usually did.

Cyrus turned back to the window and tracked another storm across the water. He needed to relax. He'd waited most of his adult life, and he could wait another few days. He tried to wash the thought of his father from his mind, but his vindictive nature wouldn't let it go.

He puffed the last of the cigar and headed to the makeshift command center. Karl had returned to his post, pacing behind the three men at the computer screens. Cyrus joined him and stopped at the third screen as it showed the F-150 pickup maneuvering the rain-slicked streets.

"The boy has no idea?" Cyrus asked as he looked to Karl for confirmation.

Karl grinned and wagged his head in agreement.

"Good, keep it that way until he has the information we need." Cyrus returned his attention to the screen. "The Webster family's time is coming, and when it arrives, I want to deal with them personally."

Despite living in extreme wealth from the empire he'd built on his father's work, Cyrus's family had suffered at the hands of the Webster clan long enough. They'd selfishly held him at bay. But their time was coming, and he'd return the favor.

CHAPTER 3

MOST SUNDAYS AT 9 a.m., Ryan was fast asleep. Under his mother's protection, he'd snooze until 11, after his parents left for 10:30 mass, so he could miss the lectures from his father on sleeping the day away.

But not today. He was wide awake. He'd been that way most of the night, wondering what the hell the swimming monkeys had to do with anything. He'd always trusted his grandfather, and he didn't want that to change now. But his trust was being tested by the partial revelation he'd had last night. He committed to get back to the hospice today and glean the rest of the story from Phineas. After lying in bed for what seemed forever, Ryan ripped off the covers, showered, dressed, and made an unusual early morning appearance at the breakfast table.

"Ryan." his mother said, as if surprised.

At the sound of his name, Emma and Abby scrambled from a dead sleep in their beds in the den and headed into the kitchen. Abby, his three-year-old black Labrador Retriever, snagged her stuffed bear and greeted him with her morning offering. She nuzzled against his leg, wagging her tail like a windshield wiper in a downpour. Emma, his nine-year-old yellow Labrador, eased in past Abby, squinty-eyed and protecting herself from the relentless flicking of her sister's tail. They took turns getting the usual ear massage from their best friend. Ryan patted them both and headed toward the stove.

"Hi Mom," Ryan said, and gave her a customary hug on his way to the table.

His mother's face lit up.

"You're up early. Are you planning to go to church with me today?"

She held a smile as she awaited his reply. It was a full-court press. Ryan decided to sidestep the issue.

"I'd love to, Mom, but Sarah is coming by later to take me to her church. I may drop by the Sunday night mass, too."

"Be sure you go, one way or another." She kept smiling but turned and opened the refrigerator. She grabbed the sage sausage, eggs, biscuits, and milk, and began to make his favorite breakfast.

He flipped on the flat-screen TV tucked under the cabinets and found SportsCenter. Abby and Emma took their usual positions flanking him. They stared at him as if they were sending subliminal messages to slip some of the impending feast their way.

His father appeared in the doorway dressed in a white shirt, red tie tied in a full Windsor knot, perfectly creased tan slacks, and a blue blazer. "Well, I need to go get the camera. No need to go to church today, dear, Jesus must be coming here."

Ryan crossed his arms and shook his head. His father was a man on a mission, all the time. This morning was just more of the same. He'd been on Ryan's case ever since the day Ryan had decided he'd had enough of his father's bullying and came to his mother's rescue. While his father was just over six feet tall, Ryan now topped six-two and enjoyed the silent victory of looking down on his father.

"Hi Dad. Nice to see you, too." Ryan said, without missing the replay of the Marlins' walk-off homer in the bottom of the ninth.

"Where were you last night?"

He knew the tone. The interrogation was starting. "Sarah's."

"And then where?" His dad raised one eyebrow. If they were playing the world series of poker, that would be his father's "tell." It meant he already knew the answer, and the trap was set. Lie and risk a lecture and grounding. Tell the truth and get the lecture anyway.

"I went to see Grandpa afterwards." Ryan pet Emma's head.

"I know. I saw him this morning, and Maggie told me you stopped by. What did you talk about?"

"Nothing." Ryan kept watching SportsCenter and rubbing Emma's head. Less was better, and it was his typical response when he didn't want to engage in conversation. He was sure his grandfather's request to tell no one applied to his father.

"But you never go by late on a Saturday?"

"Just thought I'd drop by and see if he was awake." While guilt rarely worked on his father, he thought he'd give it a try. "I figured he doesn't have much time left, and I just wanted to see him."

His father didn't take the bait. "So what did you talk about?"

The eyebrow was raised again, but it was a bluff.

"Nothing. They had to give him a shot, and I had to leave right away."

His father paused, then reluctantly gave up on the line of questioning. "Okay. Your mother and I are headed to 10:30 mass. You going?"

"No."

Still no eye contact.

"Then I expect you to get the chores done early today. One more year and then it's on to college. No time for slacking off now."

Ryan ignored the comment and inhaled the sweet smell of sage sausage and eggs over easy.

His father raised his voice.

"You got it?"

"Yes Dad."

His father shot a glance in the direction of his mother, who'd kept her attention on the stove the entire time.

"We leave at 9:45," he said, and then vanished.

She ignored him.

Ryan shook his head. If the time ever came, he'd never treat his wife that way. He'd never figured out why his mother put up with his father, but he never commented. It would be too demeaning. She rattled a few plates and appeared at his side with the feast. He leaned into her and gave another hug; this one much longer. He knew she needed it.

"Love you, Mom."

"Love you too, Ryan." She leaned in and kissed him on the head. Ryan picked up his fork and dug in.

She returned to the stove, threw the dishes in the sink, and scurried out of the kitchen. Ryan inhaled the meal before the commercial break. He dropped his egg yolks in Emma's and Abby's bowls, dumped the dishes into the dishwasher, flipped off the TV, and headed out the door to his pickup. He jumped in and spotted the hospice brochure on the floor.

"This is bullshit," he growled to no one.

He cranked the volume of his satellite radio as Eric Clapton's "Layla" hit the guitar solo. Five miles later, he turned into the Webster Primate Park, perched on the edge of the Everglades.

There was one other car in the lot. He immediately felt better. Uncle Thad was always there. It was hard to believe his uncle came from the same gene pool as his father. He was certain his grandfather would agree. He pulled in next to the ancient VW bug. His uncle had turned him on to the classic rock still blaring on his radio—Ryan hoped his uncle's advice on how to deal with his grandfather's request would be just as good.

CHAPTER 4

BEFORE HE COULD leave the truck, Ryan's iPhone played the chorus of The Fray's "How to Save a Life"—Sarah's tone. He yanked the phone from his pocket, turned down the radio, and answered.

"Hey, Sarah."

"Everything okay? You left a little early last night."

"Just had to take care of something for Grandpa."

"Is he okay?"

"He's okay."

"Well, Mom and I were wondering if you'd join us for Sunday night service?"

Ryan felt the clamps coming down. Despite the fact he was a cradle Catholic under his mother's watch, Sarah and her mother were on a crusade to get him to accept Jesus Christ in their church. Sarah was the hottest girl at Heritage High, so he went along to a degree. And sometimes, attending their service made him feel a little better. It also made him feel like a traitor to his mother and the Catholic Church.

"Okay." He folded. For some reason she was his kryptonite.

"Then we'll see you at four."

He wondered if it was the chance to get another convert notched into her pew that kept her with him.

"See you then." He jammed his finger into the phone to end the call.

Ryan jumped from his truck and glanced at his watch. It was just after eleven in the morning. The service entrance to the park was well concealed

by the heavy jungle foliage that had overtaken the chain-link fencing surrounding the perimeter of the park. The palms, plants, and trees had been
imported from the Amazon in the late 1920s, '30s and '40s to provide a
natural equatorial habitat. South Florida's sixty inches of rain each year were
supplemented by a complex irrigation system to simulate the 180 inches of
rain required in the Amazonian jungles. With the heavy foliage chopped
away, the employee gate was the only visible evidence of the fence.

He unlocked the door, stepped inside, and was refreshed by the cool
breath of the artificial jungle. He was always more comfortable with the five
hundred inhabitants here than in the world outside. A few steps down the
walkway, he entered the gray cinderblock maintenance building, stopped,
and grinned at the sight before him.

"Hey, Uncle T."

His thirty-five-year-old uncle sat dressed in hiking shorts, a tie-dyed
tank-top shirt, and high-top Converse tennis shoes Ryan was certain were
time-transported from the 1970s. Thad fumbled with a banana and engaged
in a staring contest with a capuchin. The capuchins had gained fame as "the
organ grinder monkeys" in the 1900s, and both competitors looked equally
intelligent in this contest.

Ryan couldn't contain his laughter.

"What the hell are you doing, Uncle T?"

Thad held up his right hand without breaking his stare, silently asking
for a moment. He slid his right foot forward and a banana slowly descended from the ceiling directly over the monkey's head. The capuchin's
attention remained locked on Thad. Fishing line connected to Thad's foot
was strung through a rafter and tied to the dangling fruit. Ryan covered his
mouth to choke off a full belly laugh. The banana touched the capuchin's
head and he jumped, screeched, and then seemed to realize what had happened. He grabbed the banana, spun, and sat down facing Thad. He
jammed the first bite into his mouth. Thad laughed out loud, and Ryan
swore the monkey was laughing with him.

"I was just testing the little guy," Thad said as he took a bite of his banana, stood up, and grinned.

"For what?"

"Well, they say these guys are the smartest of the New World monkeys, and I thought I'd test their concentration. He wanted to win that staring contest, even though I know he smelled the banana. Now, because he could see the one I was eating, he may have thought that was the banana he smelled. He really wanted to win that staring contest. But I outsmarted him."

Ryan shook his head.

"So, what's up?"

"Here to get the chores done, I guess."

"You're a little early."

"Yeah, I got something I gotta do later."

"Go see your grandpa, I'd guess."

Thad kept smiling and Ryan froze. He trusted Uncle T, and knew his grandpa trusted him too. Thad recognized the hesitation.

"He just called me this morning. Said he told you about the monkeys."

Ryan felt a sense of relief. At least he wasn't alone with this mystery. "He told you too?"

Thad finished the banana, tossed the peel in the trash can in the corner, and brushed his hands together. He walked up to Ryan and put his hand on his shoulder.

"I've been hearing about them for years now."

"What?" Ryan's stomach knotted.

"Look, Dad started talking about this hidden new species of monkeys with me again ever since I got back from Iraq. He said there would be a time when he'd ask me to help. When the time was right, and he was certain that he'd find someone with what he called 'the gift.' And check this out, I understand that's you, dude."

He pulled Ryan close and gave him his trademark '70s soul handshake.

Ryan still couldn't believe his ears. "What?"

"He wants us to go see him as soon as we can. He'll tell us more when we get there. He's very worried about some bad guys your great-grandpa came across in his time who got some of his notes from the 1920s. Thinks they may be close."

Thad patted Ryan on the back, picked up the capuchin, and headed for the door into the park. The knot in Ryan's stomach eased a bit, knowing his Uncle T would help.

"Did he tell you about what they can do?" Ryan asked.

"What who can do?" Thad said, pausing at the door.

"The hidden species of monkeys."

Thad pet the capuchin's head, and they both looked back at Ryan.

"He didn't tell me everything, but he said they could learn to do things like swim."

Ryan noticed Thad's serious demeanor. He believed. And now Ryan had no choice either.

"We need to take care of the critical chores and then we're out of here," Thad said.

"Okay. I'll take care of the feeding."

Thad gave a thumbs-up. "Let me get this guy back to his kin." He turned and disappeared behind the door.

Ryan heard the howler monkeys roar in the makeshift jungle through the steel door. He knew it was probably Thad stirring the largest of the monkeys they had at the park. But part of him wondered if something else was setting them off. He knew if they sensed new groups of people potentially threatening their territory, they'd warn them off with a roar. And Thad had said someone was close; someone who'd kill for the secret. Ryan's stomach twisted as if he'd chugged two Red Bulls as he felt the weight of his grandfather's last request again—and he wondered if it would be worth dying for.

CHAPTER 5

RYAN WRESTLED THE heavy plastic bags of fruit into the large rectangular plastic tray sitting just outside the caged walkway, which kept visitors confined while the monkeys roamed free. Billowing gray clouds occasionally gave way to intense sun, and he welcomed the shade of the sixty-acre jungle. In just minutes he'd already sweated through his polo shirt. A troupe of squirrel monkeys had been tracking him in anticipation of the afternoon feast. The tiny fuzzy gray pocket-sized monkeys sprang from branch to branch, squeaking, and wrestled for the prime position. He surveyed the area and noted the group numbered in the seventies. Perched higher in the dense jungle understory, a few capuchins formed a perimeter and awaited the delivery. He loved these animals. He related closely to the squirrel monkeys because for ten months out of the year the guys hung out together. The females were dominant, and any adventurous male was quickly beaten down if he attempted to join the girls, except during the two months of mating season. Then the boys bulked up, mingled, and mated, only to be tossed out again for another ten months. Not much different than high school.

Ryan sliced open the bag with his pocket knife, tossed the fruit into the tray, and quickly stepped back. The squirrel monkeys swarmed the tray and jammed the fruit into their mouths. They grabbed what they could in their tiny hands and scattered to various positions in the shrubs and trees to consume their bounty. Occasionally, the much larger capuchins would swagger in, and the squirrel monkeys dispersed, giving them a wide berth.

Once the capuchins had their fill, the squirrel monkeys descended back on the food. They clustered in groups and seemed to chat, turning to each other while chomping the fruit. The scene made Ryan stop and think of the new monkeys Phineas had mentioned. He imagined these little guys learning how to swim as humans do, taking instruction on each kick and stroke, and modeling the freestyle perfectly. He shook his head and quietly laughed: no way.

Thad exploded from the vegetation behind him, and Ryan's heart nearly jumped out of his chest.

"We ready, dude?" Thad said, smiling. "My guys are good to go."

"Jeez, you scared the crap out of me."

Thad grabbed Ryan by one shoulder, spun him around, and surveyed his backside. "I don't see any. Let's go." He laughed.

Thad headed through the open gate to the caged walkway leading out of the jungle. Ryan grabbed the plastic bag, locked the gate, and trotted to catch up to his uncle.

Thad's phone rang and he answered. "Hi Dad." He jammed his index finger in his ear and strained to listen. His usual grin drained from his face. "We'll be there right away, pop. I love you."

Ryan braced for bad news. "So Grandpa's not doing well?"

"Nope." Thad didn't look at Ryan. "He said he wasn't sure he had much longer. We gotta go now."

Thad pivoted and started to trot. Ryan kept pace. They passed the maintenance building and headed to the parking lot.

"Let's take yours, I'm low on gas," Thad said.

"No problem."

His uncle was always low on gas. He wasn't absent-minded, but it just wasn't a priority. Ryan would see his uncle deeply immersed in a book when he wasn't surfing or drinking beer with friends. And everyone was his friend.

They climbed into the suffocating heat of the truck. Ryan started it and sped out of the parking lot, coaxing cool air from the vents. The park sat twenty miles southwest of Miami, in the flat hardwoods at the southern tip of the state. The area was home to large nurseries, but not many people. An occasional bar or makeshift convenience store constructed of painted cinderblock provided support for the largely immigrant workforce in the area. Probably no cops on a Sunday. He accelerated to seventy.

The temperature inside the truck had reached a tolerable level, and Ryan had questions.

"Hey, Uncle T, do you know what this is all about?"

"No more than you, dude. All I know is that Dad needs us. He's always been there for me, even after Iraq. I figure whatever he wants, he gets now."

"Do you think we're in danger?" Ryan probed.

"I know your grandpa doesn't make those kinds of things up. And he's been telling me and your dad bits and pieces of this story since we were your age. But he's never given us the charge to go find them."

"I've never heard my dad talk about it."

Thad swiped at the air with both hands in frustration.

"He won't. He tells us it's bullshit—it doesn't make any sense and won't lead us anywhere. He's warned your grandpa and me more than once not to fill your head with this crap."

"What do you think?"

"I think it's real."

"Why?"

"I got to spend some time with your great-grandpa. He was a stud, man. He went to places you can't imagine, back in the days before first-class air travel, vaccines, and generators. He'd travel to the deserts and jungles for the Smithsonian to build their exhibits and shows. He started the park too."

"So why does that make you think it's real?"

"Well, he was one of those 'your word is your bond' types, you know. No nonsense and no lies."

"He also thought P. T. Barnum was a genius. That's how we all got stuck with our middle names," Ryan said.

"Yeah. I asked him why he and my dad did that. Especially since I'm saddled with Thaddeus Barnum Webster."

"What did he say?"

"He said Phineas Taylor Barnum was the greatest man who ever lived. He was a businessman, promoter, entertainer, congressman, philanthropist, and animal lover. Said he introduced America to animals through his circus, and actually started the first aquarium in the US."

"But Barnum was credited with the phrase 'there's a sucker born every minute,' wasn't he?"

"Probably. But I read a book about him. He denied it to his death. Your great-grandpa said when it came right down to it, he did more in a lifetime than any dozen men. But I'm telling you he wouldn't make this up. He was smart, brave, and a man of his word. So's your grandpa."

Ryan wasn't sure if that was a comforting thought or one that simply piled on more responsibility. He glanced at his uncle, who deadpanned and turned up the radio, indicating enough talk for now. Ryan welcomed the view of the entrance ramp to the Florida Turnpike and raced north toward Doral and Saint Paul's Hospice. He reached the Doral exit, signaled, traversed the ramp and turned right toward the hospice.

***

Six cars back, the old faded Impala followed. Its two occupants' haircuts probably cost more than the car. But it was good cover, and their instructions were clear: Don't take your eyes off that boy.

CHAPTER 6

RYAN SPOTTED HIS father's pearl-white Lexus 460 in the lot and cut a glance at Thad.

"He's got the nurses under strict orders to call him if they think the end is near. It is. This is bad, man," Thad said. "This oughta be a hoot."

Thad stared straight ahead. Ryan saw his perennial smile had disappeared. His throat tightened as they stepped out of the truck and trudged up the steps to the front door. Ryan forced the tears back, but wasn't sure he could do it much longer. He'd never faced death before, especially of someone he loved so much.

Thad beat him to the front door and the magnetic lock buzzed. Thad opened the door and put his arm around Ryan's shoulders as they walked down the hallway and past the front desk. It was nice to know he was not alone. He knew his uncle had seen too many people die. Ryan watched Maggie, expressionless, buzz them into the ward without a word. His friend had said in the hospice business, the entire staff knows when the end is near, and no words can relieve the dread of the inevitable.

This time, he refused to look into the rooms as they passed them. He couldn't face their dying tenants today. He looked up and counted the fluorescent lights instead. Sixteen lights to the T and then a right turn. Ryan stopped, surprised, when he spotted an unfamiliar orderly standing just outside Phineas's door. The orderly glanced at Ryan, then retreated hastily down the hall.

Ryan walked to the door. He prepared himself to look in. He didn't want to see his grandpa die, but he knew he had to be there. Thad joined him, and he glanced at his uncle. Thad's eyes brimmed, ready to overflow. He lowered his head and placed his hand on Ryan's back. Ryan took a deep breath and stepped into the room.

His father sat on the far side of the bed and his mother hovered at his father's shoulder. Ryan listened for the monitors, but they were faint. His grandfather lay silently in the dark with his eyes closed. He looked much older than he had last night. Under the white sheets, the outline of his body looked skeletal. Ryan had easily lifted him from the bed several times, assisting the nurses over the past few weeks. While his grandfather had been well over two hundred pounds most of his life, Ryan guessed he'd withered down to one-twenty now.

His father, John, looked up and glared at Ryan.

"It's about time," he said in a whisper.

What an ass.

Phineas opened his eyes and slowly rolled his head toward Thad and Ryan. A weak smile followed.

"Glad you two are here. I've been waiting for you."

Ryan knew what he meant. He'd been holding on just to speak with them.

"Now, Dad, you need to be quiet," John said.

Phineas rolled his head back in John's direction and managed a scowl. He turned back to Ryan and Thad.

"Come closer, you two. It's not contagious," Phineas wheezed. The smile returned.

Ryan held back his tears. He knew his father would call him weak, and he didn't want to upset his grandfather. But he couldn't swallow. He bent over and hugged Phineas.

"I love you, Grandpa," he said.

Ryan heard Thad say, "I love you, Dad."

Phineas gently rubbed Ryan's head.

"It's fine, boys, it's okay. I love you guys too. Now, I have something to tell you."

Ryan rose up and wiped his eyes. He could see his father's look of disgust, but he didn't care. Ignoring John on the other side, Phineas motioned them closer.

"The monkeys. I've got to tell you about the monkeys."

"Oh, Dad, don't start," John said. "Don't fill his head with that crap now."

Phineas cut his eyes in John's direction and whispered, "He never understood. He doesn't have the gift. But you do. I know it."

He tugged Ryan's hand closer. John huffed, folded his arms, and looked away.

"There are just a few clues. My father, your great-grandpa, did it this way to protect them. Cyrus Shultz is the son of the man who tried to steal your great-grandfather's work in the sixties. He will kill to get the secret of the swimming monkeys. Follow the clues and then follow your heart. And let your soul be the ultimate decision-maker."

Ryan looked at Thad. This wasn't making sense. Too much morphine? He knew at the end, the dose was raised to near lethal levels to ease the pain and make the transition smooth.

Phineas must have seen Ryan's doubt. He nodded for Thad to get closer and then continued. "The notebook is the key, and it sits on a cliff overlooking five stars. The five stars are near a castle made of newspapers." Phineas looked at Thad. "You know the place. All that you need is there. But be careful. The secrets are powerful, and the world may not be ready." His voice faded and his eyes squinted. He spoke more slowly. He was nearing the end.

"You must hurry. The deforestation may kill them, and with their death goes mankind's fate. Find them, Ryan. Find them."

Phineas let go of Ryan's hand and grabbed Thad. Tears were running down Thad's face, and tears escaped from the corners of his grandpa's eyes.

"Forgive your brother. He's well-intentioned, but he can't see or feel things like we can. Trust yourself and your abilities. You've been a great source of joy to me. You're a great man. I love you, son." A tear spilled out of his weak, tired eyes.

"I love you too, Dad."

Phineas reached toward John on the other side of the bed and took his hand.

"Son. I love you. I know we never saw eye to eye, but I did what I thought was best for the family. Please don't be disappointed. There is much more to life than what we own. You're a good man. Find yourself."

Phineas released John's hand and returned to his back, trying to look at both sons. "You protect him." He nodded toward Ryan. "You both protect him." He closed his eyes and gently sighed. "Now, it's time."

The room became still. The only audible sound was the faint ping of the heart monitor that slowed along with Phineas's breaths. Thad stood still, his eyes locked on his dad, and held his hand. Ryan's mother covered her mouth but didn't make a sound. Even John stared, holding his father's other hand, and for the first time in Ryan's life, he saw his father's tears. Ryan shut his eyes tight. Tears streamed down his cheeks.

His grandfather's breathing slowed and became shallow. Ryan froze, as did everyone else, as Phineas drew in his last breath and let it out with a long sigh. In that moment, Ryan sensed a gaping emptiness in a place deep inside him, unlike anything he'd felt before. He felt a debt to this man he might never repay. He'd never experienced a moment like this. It was spiritual, strangely peaceful, and tragic at the same time. Phineas Barnum Webster was gone. But the boy he said had the gift remained. And in that moment, Ryan committed to do whatever it took to grant the last request of the greatest man he'd ever known.

CHAPTER 7

KARL AND CYRUS sat in opposing white leather chairs in the South Beach condo-turned-command-center. The condo provided a secure location with direct access to state-of-the-art communications, and the cover of the pricey neighborhood drew little attention to the high-end equipment being delivered.

"Play the tape again," he said, staring at Karl.

Karl obliged and Cyrus listened intently as the voice on the tape gave the clues to the notebook's location.

Karl halted the recording and gawked at Cyrus. Cyrus glared back at Karl.

"I have no idea what the old bastard is talking about."

"Sorry, sir," Karl replied in his thick German accent. "Didn't your father say anything about the stars or the castle when he told you about the legend?"

"He told me that Zachariah Webster had made a discovery that would shock the world. And that the selfish bastard had kept it to himself because he didn't think the world was ready. He said in 1961, after Webster refused his offer to pay him for his discovery, he'd ransacked his office and found nothing other than just a couple of notes that referenced Juan Ponce de León and the fountain of youth and a marked-up copy of Darwin's *On the Origin of Species* cross-referenced to the Bible. There was nothing about five stars or a castle."

Karl waited for direction.

"We've got nothing here. Stay with the kid and that goofy-assed uncle. They'll get the notebook and then we can get what we need."

"Yes sir." Karl edged toward the door.

Cyrus waved him from the room. "Go."

He knew Karl could snap his fat neck with one hand. But Karl was loyal to his paycheck, and his paycheck was as fat as Cyrus's neck. As far as Karl was concerned, Cyrus knew his money bought loyalty. But with the scale of the operation expanding, he needed more than just Karl and his gang of mercenaries. He needed a partner with a vested interest in finding the monkeys, someone with the resources to track the boy and his uncle across the country.

Cyrus headed to the garage, jumped into his Bugatti Veyron, and headed to his mansion on Key Biscayne.

As he sped across Rickenbacker Causeway and onto Key Biscayne, he wondered why he'd spent thirty million on a home on an island that could be washed away in an instant by a hurricane. But the thought faded quickly. He was preoccupied with the idea of getting a partner. He passed the end of the causeway and flipped on the satellite radio to the Patriot station. The commentator was lamenting the rise of a book to the *New York Times* bestseller list written by Charles Grandby, a professed atheist. The book was titled *Evolution and the God Myth*. Grandby was well-known for disproving God's existence through the parade of scientific findings supporting evolution. Over the years, his argument had gained traction and his fame was reaching star status. The commentator described how he'd made millions from his books and speaking engagements and how he'd formed a cult-like organization that covered the world looking for evidence that supported his principle: Science shows God didn't create the world and all religion was a fabrication, a means to control the masses.

He killed the radio and commanded the car's digital concierge to call Karl.

"Yes, sir."

"I need you to get me everything you can find on Charles Grandby."

"The scientist?"

"Yes."

"I'll find out everything I can."

"Do it quietly?"

"What's our angle?"

"The creatures could be the proverbial missing link and drive another scientific stake into the heart of the world's organized religion. He'd kill to be a part of that."

"And he has something we need?"

"Yes indeed. Call me as soon as you have it."

He ended the call and turned up the radio. If the legend of the monkeys was true, he'd hoped it was enough to recruit Grandby—and defeat the one thing he feared the most—his own death.

CHAPTER 8

RYAN WAS FED up with sitting around and stifling his sadness, listening to his father gripe about his grandfather. He complained about being stuck with the park, called Phineas a deluded old man, and scoffed at the bullshit about swimming monkeys. Ryan simply wanted to mourn with his mother, but his father would call him weak and tell him to man up. After a shouting match with his father, Ryan went to his room and punched the closet wall. He missed his grandpa more than he'd imagined. It felt like a part of him had died too.

He wiped his face, looked at Emma and Abby, curled up in their beds, and chuckled at the hole in the wall. As he imagined the bitching his old man would hurl at him when he discovered it, he smiled and nodded at the dogs. "This will be our little secret for now."

He closed the closet door and swore he saw a grin on Abby's face. He rubbed her head on the way to his desk.

His cell phone had been rattling in his pocket most of the evening, catching texts from his friends telling him how sorry they were to hear the news. The Fray rang out in his pocket, and just like a trained monkey, he answered immediately. As he pulled the phone out, he scolded himself and promised he'd change.

"Hey Sarah."

"Ryan, I am so sorry. I know he meant a lot to you."

"Thanks, Sarah. I'm okay."

"Well, my mom and I would like you to come over here and let us share a few moments of consolation and God's word with you."

Ryan's face soured, and he pulled the phone away from his ear. Seeing Sarah would be better than what was going on downstairs, but he hated her mother's transparent attempts to convert him. The lesser of two evils, he thought. At least he might get some sympathy.

"Give me half an hour and I'll be there."

"Okay," Sarah replied in the soft Tennessee accent she'd picked up from her mother.

He stuffed the phone in his pocket and grabbed his keys, then headed downstairs and explained to his mother where he was going. She understood, and she'd probably go with him if she could. On the way out, he gave the front door a little extra yank, knowing the slam would piss off the old man. It felt good for a moment, but then the guilt took over. He wondered if his mother would pay for that one. He lingered at the door and listened. It was quiet.

He trotted to the pickup, jumped in, and turned the key.

It was Sunday evening and the remnants of the sun created an orange aura around the thunderheads in the dusky sky to the west. Ryan leaned forward over the steering wheel and scanned the horizon. His grandfather was there somewhere, he hoped. For some reason, grand scenes of nature's beauty made Ryan think about God. He wondered about Heaven, and secretly deep inside, he wondered if it existed. He believed in God, or at least he thought he should. But there were so many religions and interpretations of who or what he was. His Catholic upbringing was strong. His mother made sure of that. But some of the rules seemed too controlling or created too much guilt to make sense. Today, he forced the doubts from his mind and prayed the Act of Contrition for his grandfather for what seemed like the hundredth time today. He made the sign of the cross, looked over his shoulder, backed out of the driveway, and headed to Sarah's.

Sarah Costa lived in the most exclusive neighborhood in Coral Gables. Her father made sure of that. When Ryan first met him, Luiz Costa described how he was the son of Brazilian immigrants, and how he saw firsthand the struggle his parents endured to carve out a little piece of the

American dream. They told Luiz they would not let the same thing happen to him. Under his parent's strict and watchful eyes, he attended private high school and earned a scholarship at Duke. Six years later he returned with a law degree and joined Lambert and Cole, one of Miami's most successful law firms. Proudly, he said the firm was now called Lambert, Cole & Costa.

Ryan assumed that as the firm's managing partner and the handsome son of Brazilian immigrants, he was the perfect face for the firm. Ryan noticed some of the excitement in his eyes disappeared when he said he'd met his wife, Hanna, at Duke and was instantly smitten by her beauty and Tennessee charm. It was at her insistence they bought the Coral Gables mansion. Ryan liked him and actually felt sorry for him. Mrs. Costa was a handful, and if you weren't on her side, you didn't exist.

Ryan pulled down the neatly manicured drive to the call box in front of the towering iron security gates. While he was partly attracted to the Costa's wealth and social stature, it intimidated him. Sometimes he felt like the help. A voice spoke from the brass call box.

"Hi Ryan. I'll buzz you in," Sarah said.

"Great. I'll—"

Before he could finish, the box beeped, and the gates parted. He drove along the pastel-pink stamped concrete drive, illuminated with landscape lights every four feet or so. The ferns and palms were so thick it reminded him of the deepest part of the rainforest at the park. The white stucco mansion quickly appeared, its orange tiled roof bathed in soft lighting. As instructed on previous occasions, he pulled past the front entrance and parked his pickup truck in a side lot hidden from street view, where the gardener and housekeeper parked. As Sarah greeted him at the service entrance, he remembered Eric Clapton's "Back Door Man" and chuckled.

"Ryan, I am so sorry," she said with a smile. She was dressed in a short silk dress that clung to her firm figure in all the right places. Her glossy dark-brown hair dipped over her dark eyes, curved over her ear, and curled gently against her neck. Ryan wanted to thank her mother for Sarah's features and her father for the glistening smooth brown skin. She was a little taller than other girls and could easily kiss him on the cheek. Ryan inhaled the light fresh scent of her perfume. He could never identify the fragrance, but it was as sweet as any flowers he'd smelled. He knew she was going through the motions to look good, but Ryan didn't care. She stirred an irresistible primitive hunger inside him no girl ever had. He'd tolerate all the other bullshit just to be with her.

"How are you?"

She barely got the words out before she grabbed his hand and dragged him through the gourmet kitchen like a found stray.

"I'm doing fine," he lied.

She led him across the polished marble entrance and down a few steps toward the back of the house. They dropped down into the game room with a sprawling view of the pool and Intracoastal Waterway. From here, the house appeared to be made of glass, with floor-to-ceiling windows. The light-tan marble floor was divided into areas by the largest, most expensive rugs he'd ever seen. One, Sarah mentioned, cost more than her father's Lexus. A billiards table was tucked at the far end of the room and a full-service bar sat in the center. The most radical home theater system he'd ever seen occupied the other end. The entire room was furnished with white leather. He told his friends their decorator must have been from the North Pole. Ryan immediately spotted Sarah's mother watching CNN on the huge flat-screen framed in the wall. Ryan knew the Sunday night ritual. Hanna Costa had just returned from Victory Baptist Church, the sprawling monument she'd helped Pastor Smith build into one of the largest churches in the South. Sometimes Ryan wondered if Hanna was the leader of the flock and Pastor Smith a mere disciple. Although in her mid-forties, she still stirred urges Ryan tried to ignore. Her brown hair, light makeup, nails, toes, dress, and matching sandals sent the message that she was in control. As she flipped off the remote and patted the long leather sofa, he braced himself for the greeting.

"Ryan, you poor child. Come here and let me comfort you," she said in her Southern drawl.

Ryan reluctantly released Sarah's hand as she turned him over to the master. *Let the games begin.* He stepped around the silver-framed glass coffee table and dropped onto the sofa next to her. Sarah flanked him on the other side. Tonight it would be the squeeze play. Hanna wrapped her arms around Ryan's neck and gave him a hug. Considering what he'd been through, it actually felt good, but the punch line wouldn't be far behind.

"So can we pray with you?"

Ryan sheepishly nodded in agreement. Hanna took his left hand and Sarah took his right. He pulled his right hand away and made the sign of the cross. Both women seared him with their eyes, and he quickly returned his hand to Sarah's.

Hannah prayed, "Heavenly father, please give this young man the strength and the grace to accept this as your will and to seek out your son, Jesus Christ, in all aspects of his young life. Grant him the peace that comes with knowing you, and bless the soul of his grandfather so that he is with you forever. Amen."

"Amen," Ryan said. He knew the prayer was just another reminder that Hanna thought he was some kind of heathen for being Catholic, and that the only true way to God was through Victory Baptist Church. She probably thought this was a moment of weakness when Ryan would be the most vulnerable. She was close to being right.

"Ryan, how's your family?" Hanna asked.

She seemed sincere, so Ryan opened up a little. "We're doing okay; it was hardest on my uncle Thad and me."

"I know that. You spent lots of time with him at the park."

"We were very close," he said.

"I'm hoping he'll be accepted into the Lord's arms. I've been praying he'll be forgiven for professing all that disgusting man-from-monkey evolution garbage."

Ryan leaned back. "He was a great man and no matter what you think, he's in Heaven."

She'd never showed an interest in the park and he was pretty sure she hated anything to do with monkeys. She'd pounded on him several times about creation and the evil people who espoused any link between man and monkey, but this insult was too much.

She didn't react. Instead, she just smiled. "I understand why you couldn't join us today for Sunday services, but let's make it a point to get you to the Wednesday night service this week to pray. I'll have Pastor Smith make it part of his service. You know *we* don't believe one needs a priest or a Pope acting as a middle-man. We will give you a direct line."

She patted his hand and rose, making it clear she didn't expect a reply.

"I'll leave you two alone to talk and pray," she said as she left the room. Praying and talking were the last things on Ryan's mind.

He turned to Sarah. "I don't need her BS."

"Never mind her."

Sarah leaned in and gave him a long warm kiss. It was followed by two short pecks and then Ryan pulled Sarah closer. He could feel every inch of her body through the thin dress and immediately felt the surge of blood and hormones in all the right places. It drove him crazy and Sarah seemed to enjoy that. When the session got to the "get-a-room" point, Sarah pulled back. Ryan always had enough character to respect a girl and call off the jam when she did.

She turned on the TV and found a repeat of *Entourage*. They watched for a few minutes, then Sarah excused herself to powder her nose and touch up her makeup. She returned looking fresh as ever and dropped back onto the sofa, leaned her head on Ryan's shoulder, and took his hand.

"So you'll go with us on Wednesday?"

"No," Ryan replied. "I may have to go out of town for a little while."

"Out of town?" She dropped his hand. Ryan knew he'd made a mistake.

"Where are you going?"

"I have to do something."

"What do you have to do? Your grandfather just died and you need to mourn. You need to pray too, and we can help."

He turned to look at Sarah. "It's something important."

Her eyes flashed and widened. "What can be more important than prayer?"

"Can we not talk about this now?"

"No, Ryan. I want to know, what can be more important?"

He considered telling her it was none of her business, but he feared that would be the end. With the surge of hormones still pulsating through his body, he decided he needed to say something.

"It's my grandfather. He asked me to do something for him."

Sarah's tantrum escalated. She moved further away. "What? What did he ask you to do?"

"Find something."

He remembered his grandfather's warnings. He didn't want to say anymore. Sarah grabbed the remote, turned off the TV, and stood up, crossing her arms.

"Ryan, you stop being evasive and tell me what's going on or you're going home."

"Look, if I'm still here I'll go with you on Wednesday, but this is important to me. It was his dying wish, and no matter what, I have to do this. I know you may not understand, but that's the way it is."

For the first time, he put his foot down. He sighed and a wave of relief swept over him. Sarah froze for a minute, probably pondering her next move. She sat down next to Ryan again.

"Okay. But if you go, you'll have to let me know all about it."

He thought for a moment. He'd already said too much, but agreeing would stop the conversation.

"Okay."

Sarah flipped the TV back on and leaned onto Ryan. He wrapped his arms around her and hoped it would lead to another session. His mind wandered back to his grandfather's hospital room and remembered the warning he'd been given.

"Tell no one."

Those words echoed in his head and he felt a sinking weight pulling him down. It was a feeling he'd felt as a kid when he knew he'd done something wrong. He called it the *uh oh* feeling. He'd already let his grandfather down a little, and it hadn't even been twenty-four hours. This was not going to be easy.

CHAPTER 9

THE PUNGENT SMELL of cigars and leather told Ryan this place was old. The sagging hunch-backed posture of the wiry, white-haired man sitting at the thick mahogany desk made the place ancient. The office of Robert Franklin was exactly what Ryan had expected for the venue for reading his grandfather's will. They called it the reading of the last will and testament, but Ryan couldn't see how a dead guy could testify. The dark-red carpet hugged the mahogany shadow box paneling that covered three of the walls and ceiling. The wall behind the desk was the largest floor-to-ceiling bookcase Ryan had ever seen. Old oil paintings of more old guys were strategically spaced around the room. Three high-back mahogany chairs with matching dark-red seat cushions faced the desk. There were no windows and the only light came from a dark-green shaded lamp on the desk. A huge grandfather clock kept time in the corner. Ryan watched the polished gold pendulum swing with each tick of the clock. He jumped when the chimes rang out, followed by five gongs.

Ryan stood with his father and Uncle Thad just inside the doorway, waiting for the old man to finish organizing the files on his desk. They'd each received the invitations and had compared the identical notes. No one else was present, and with three side chairs, Ryan guessed this was it. The old man behind the desk extended his bony hand toward the chairs and forced a weak smile.

"Please take a seat, gentlemen."

John sat in the first chair, followed by Ryan in the middle and Thad on the end.

Ryan noticed his father and Robert Franklin locked in a stare.

"Mr. Webster," Franklin said with a nod.

"Mr. Franklin," John nodded back.

They clearly didn't like each other.

Thad sprang to his feet and extended his hand.

"How ya doin', Bob?"

Franklin smiled, leaned across the desk, and shook Thad's hand.

"Good to see you, son."

Franklin turned his attention to Ryan, smiled, and extended his hand. "This young man must be Ryan."

Ryan stood and shook his hand. It was cold and felt like a bag of bones.

They both returned to their seats as Franklin said, "I've heard a lot of good things about you from your grandpa, young man. Please call me Bob."

Ryan immediately liked him.

"Okay," said Franklin, "let's get to the business at hand."

He pulled a file from a thick brown accordion folder in front of him. He opened it, removed three envelopes and set them to the side. Ryan listened as Franklin read some legal gibberish and then paused. He looked up at John and then back at the page.

"To my oldest son John, I want you to know how much I love you. I think you're a good man, who needs to learn that how much you have doesn't define you. Please read the letter I've given to Bob when you're alone and know it came from my heart. I do hereby leave you one-third of the Webster Primate Park and a one-third share of the Phineas Webster Trust."

"One-third!" John yelled as he stood. "What the hell is going on here?"

"Mr. Webster, please sit down and be quiet. This is your father's decision."

"You son-of-a-bitch. You told him to do this."

"Mr. Webster, I assure you this is your father's last will and testament—not mine. And if you continue your tantrum I will ask you to leave and not hear the rest of the will. I suggest you take this letter and abide by your father's wishes."

Franklin handed the letter to John. John snatched it from his hand, dropped back into his chair, and rubbed his jaw. Ryan caught his father's glare and knew it wasn't the last he'd hear of this.

Franklin continued. "And to my son Thad, you are a kindred spirit and a great man. Don't let your memories of what you've seen and done in this country's honor steal your joy. Please read the letter I've left with Bob when you're alone and know it came from my heart. I do hereby leave you a one-third share of the Webster Primate Park and one-third of the Phineas Webster Trust."

Ryan glanced at his uncle and saw the tears running down his face as Thad looked away. Ryan reached over and wrapped his arm around his uncle's shoulders. Thad glanced back, smiled, and patted Ryan on the leg. Ryan knew he couldn't speak. The same grief was building in Ryan's throat.

Franklin read on. "Finally, to my dear grandson Ryan, I want to extend an apology. I know you're young and shouldn't have to bear this responsibility. The request I've made of you will raise more questions and self-doubt than you'll ever experience the rest of your life. But you have the gift we discussed and with that gift comes the responsibility to use it to its fullest potential. You literally have the chance to change the world, and there's no person I'd trust more to do that. I leave you my copies of the Bible and Darwin's *On the Origin of Species*." Franklin reached into the accordion folder and pulled out the two tattered books. Ryan noticed one of the pages of the Bible had a red tab marking its place.

"Oh no. Not that monkey bullshit again," John said.

Everyone ignored him. Franklin shook his head and continued reading. "Please read the letter I've left with Bob when you're alone and know it came from the heart. I do hereby leave you a one-third share of the Webster Primate Park and the income from a one-third share of the Phineas Webster Trust until your twenty-fifth birthday, when you'll get full control over that one-third of the Phineas Webster Trust."

Ryan felt his father's stare but looked straight ahead. He never paid much attention to his parents' finances, let alone his grandfather's. He'd hear his father talking about the trust on many occasions as if it were the

Powerball jackpot. He knew the park was very valuable and ranked behind only the San Diego Animal Park. With that kind of money, he'd never have to worry about gassing up his truck or buying that new pair of Jordans. Franklin handed him the envelope, and Ryan stood and shook his hand.

His father smiled. "Well, since Ryan is still a minor, I guess I'll have control over his assets."

Franklin shook his head and pointed his bony finger at the page. "No, the income and his share of the Primate Park are his, and I will remain executor of his share of the trust until he's twenty-five."

John shot up. "Are we done here?"

"Yes we are." Franklin scowled.

John drove his knee into his son's leg.

"Let's get out of here!"

Ryan rubbed his thigh, rose, and shook Franklin's hand. Franklin winked at him and said, "Read the letter."

Ryan turned to Thad, who remained seated. John was already out the door. When he was gone, Thad stood up and shook Franklin's hand.

"Thanks, Bob. I'll see you at the poker game?"

"Looking forward to it."

Ryan waited for Thad, and they left the office together. It would be a long ride home.

CHAPTER 10

RYAN PARKED BENEATH one of the halogen security lights in the parking lot of the Primate Park. He picked up the envelope from the passenger's seat. He stared at his name scrawled on the envelope in his grandpa's handwriting. Gently, he ran his fingers over his name. He took a deep breath, but still felt himself getting sucked into the black hole of despair he'd become so familiar with these days.

He opened the center console and found his pocket knife, slit the envelope at the top, and carefully removed the neatly folded pages. They were covered in his grandfather's neat cursive. He read the words of love and encouragement from his grandfather. He slid the first page behind the second. The second page was not a series of paragraphs like the first. Instead, it was a note.

Ryan,

This is critical to your search. It was passed to me by my father in the same way. This, along with the location of the notebook, will lead you to the most remarkable discovery in the past two thousand years. I didn't want to speak about it when I was alive because I was not certain who could be listening. Guard them with your life.

When you find them, use your gift. Zachariah also asked me to memorize this quote. Please do the same.

Psalm 100:3

"Know ye that the Lord he is God: it is he that hath made us, and not we ourselves, we are his people, and the sheep of his pasture."

Ryan folded the paper and looked through his windshield at the moonlit sky. He'd never read the Bible from front to back. He'd never seen the need. He'd read the passages in catechism class at Sunday school and occasionally would listen to the readings and the gospel at Sunday mass. He enjoyed the stories and sometimes would look for the hidden relevance to his life. As a teenager, he found few. He remembered his grandfather's words about deciding if the world was ready.

Ready for what? Swimming monkeys? He read the verse again, and it sent a quick shiver through him.

The Scopes Monkey Trial, the Bible verse—the world wasn't ready. He recalled his biology class and the theory of evolution, and he looked at the tattered books on his seat. He picked up Darwin's *On the Origin of Species*. He remembered Hanna Costa's rants about the blasphemy of the theory of evolution.

He punched the steering wheel. "Shit." It started to make sense now.

Evolution, swimming monkeys, and the Bible—did his great-grandfather stumble on the missing link? He felt trapped, privileged, and scared shitless at the same time. He needed to think. He stuffed the letter inside the Bible, stacked it atop Darwin's tome, and slipped out of his truck. He hurried to the side gate and fumbled for the key. He was eyeballing the jungle when he heard a rustling behind the thick underbrush just beyond the fence. The combination of moonlight and the artificial glow from the halogen lights in the parking lot cast multiple shadows across everything. Unnerved, he refocused on the key and jammed it into the padlock. The lock sprang open, and he slipped into the park, locking the gate behind him. He was quickly down the path, past the cinderblock maintenance building, and on the main path heading toward the pond.

He'd never been afraid in the park, and he didn't like the feeling. Usually he ignored the rustling in the canopy of the artificial jungle at night. Now he focused on every click, crackle or shuffle. Ryan had visited the park at night with his friends and knew the monkeys weren't nocturnal. They'd be fast asleep. On one occasion though, they had startled the howler monkeys and all hell broke loose.

He pushed the sounds from his mind and made it to the bamboo-covered sitting area next to the pond. The pond was rimmed on three sides with large gray rocks and boulders stacked to form a natural barricade behind it. In the center, a waterfall chattered, dumping fresh water into the rock-strewn pond. Ferns and thick deep-green-leaved tropicals draped over the rocks and down to the water's edge. Across from the pond, the bamboo-and-thatch-covered sitting area completed the grotto. Ryan sat at the center table under the security light mounted on the pole behind him. The dark pathway to the left led out of the grotto, to the orangutans, gibbons, and Charlie, the sole gorilla. The path to his right led to another caged walkway that wound through the jungle toward the entrance. Ryan laid the two books on the table and opened Darwin's first.

As he let the yellowed pages flutter past his thumb from back to front, he noticed many passages were underlined and marked with numbers in the margin in old black ink from a quill pen. Halfway through the book, the howlers let loose with ear-splitting roars and barks. Someone was in the park. Ryan slammed the book shut, grabbed the Bible, and stuffed both books under his arm. He stood up and drifted into the shadows at the edge of the pathway leading deeper into the park. He knew it wasn't Thad or anyone else who worked there. They knew not to disturb the howlers.

He leaned further into the darkness of the pathway and listened. The howls and barks died down and were drowned out by the waterfall.

He heard shuffling on the pathway coming from the entrance across the grotto. He peered in the direction of the sound. Nothing. He kept his glare locked on the entrance. Still nothing. Then he saw it. It was just a slight movement in the inky darkness, but someone was coming fast. He spun and darted into the blackness. He used his memory to follow the path deeper into the jungle. When the path turned to the right, he looked back and accelerated. Before he returned his attention back down the path, he was knocked off his feet and hit the ground hard. He thought he'd hit a wall. Pain ripped through the right side of his face. He wiped it with his hand to check for blood.

Then he heard him.

"This has been a long time coming, boy."

Ryan shoved his hand behind him to get up, but a huge black boot stomped on his chest and pinned him against the wood-chipped path.

"Let me up, you asshole." Ryan shouted.

The boot nearly crushed his ribcage and a huge silhouette leaned over him. The thug was dressed in black, and a balaclava mask covered his face. Ryan could only see the whites of his eyes. Their intensity scared the shit out of him. Then he spotted something else. It was black and glistened in the light coming from the grotto. The biggest gun he'd ever seen. It replaced the boot on his chest.

"Get up!"

Ryan stood. The man smelled like cigarettes. He grabbed Ryan's right arm and twisted it behind him, followed by the left. The books fell to the ground. His wrists burned when the zip ties were yanked tight. He was shoved back toward the grotto, and he spied a second man, identically dressed, waiting with another big gun. He was shoved the last few feet and the other thug caught him.

"What do you guys want?" Ryan said. He was doing his best *Die Hard* imitation, but it wasn't working.

"You, boy," the masked thug replied, and pressed duct tape over his mouth. Ryan struggled to breathe and twisted from side to side.

They spun him toward the pathway leading to the entrance.

"Relax and breathe through your nose, kid."

They pushed him down the path and followed behind him. It was about one hundred yards to the maintenance shed, then a right turn past the snack bar and another fifty to the entrance. While the path was caged with chain link throughout the Amazonian forest, it opened to the jungle at the shed. Ryan wondered how they'd gotten in. The security system would've caught them at the main entrance and the electrified fence on the perimeter would prevent climbing it. He approached the turn at the shed and started to the right.

"No, kid, other way."

That led to the employee entrance. He wasn't going to let them kill him, at least not here. He sensed they wanted him for what they thought he knew. He felt surprisingly determined. He turned to the left, heard the chirp of a squirrel monkey, and immediately knew what was coming. The squirrel monkeys were asleep. He sped up then turned and head butted the nearest thug. He spun in time to see Thad let go of the second thug as he fell to the ground next to the other.

Shocked but strangely confident, Ryan stared at his uncle. Dressed in bleached-out ripped jeans and a tie-dyed tank top, he stood over the bodies. His tattooed biceps glistened with sweat.

"You okay, dude?"

Ryan shook his head, and Thad pulled out a knife, turned Ryan around and cut the ties. Ryan hugged him. Thad grabbed Ryan's shoulders and pushed him back a bit.

He looked into Ryan's eyes, ripped the duct tape from Ryan's mouth, and said, "This is for real, Ryan."

"No shit!" Ryan said, rubbing his face.

"We need to get these guys out of here. They'll wake up in a little while, but we'll be gone. Help me get them into the truck."

"But shouldn't we call the police?"

Thad stepped in close, "Hell no! Didn't you listen to your grandpa?"

Ryan froze.

"We can't go to any authorities," Thad explained. "This is about the monkeys. We'll have to do a bunch of shit, most of which may not be legal, to get to them. If the feds get wind of this, they're toast, and we won't be able to do what we promised."

Ryan trusted his uncle more than anyone in the world. He felt a bit alone, but with Thad on his side, he'd give it a shot.

"Okay."

Thad quickly bound the thugs, and Ryan picked up the books. They dragged them to Ryan's truck and rolled them into the bed. Ryan looked across the bed of the truck at Thad.

"What now?"

Thad nodded to the cab and said, "We'll dump these guys in an alley."

"Hang on."

Ryan remembered the car that had followed him from the hospice and the strange orderly at the hospice. He checked the front wheel well. He'd found a tracking device planted by a teammate's paranoid parents the same way.

Nothing. When he checked the back he found it. He yanked off the transmitter and showed it to Thad across the bed.

"Awesome, dude," Thad said.

He dropped it on the ground and stomped it into pieces.

Ryan walked to the cab and got in. Thad jumped into the passenger's seat. After they silently checked the cab for bugs, Ryan said, "I'm ready to go find them. How 'bout you?"

"I'm in, dude—besides," Thad said, looking at Ryan with a grin. "I know where we're going."

CHAPTER 11

CYRUS LOVED A grand entrance with a big audience, and the Fountainebleau Hotel in Miami Beach provided both tonight. He downshifted his Bugatti Veyron into second and let the growl of the sixteen-cylinder engine announce his arrival. He thought about the arrival of others on this stage over the decades: Frank Sinatra and Dean Martin in the fifties, the Beatles in the sixties, and the cocaine cowboys of the seventies who pumped tons of booger sugar into the US through Miami and spawned the onslaught of Versace T-shirts and pastel jackets made famous on *Miami Vice*. As he brought the car to a stop at the entrance, he noted the over-the-shoulder glances from the tuxedoed crowd making its way into the lobby. With a nod to the valet, he stepped from the car, tugged on the sleeves of his tux, and paced around the car. His wife, Charlese, tightly wrapped in a blazing-white sequined dress, smiled and took his arm. He knew this was an act; she paid no attention to him. But he was well aware of the jealous glances tossed in their direction.

The Miami Pioneers Society raised money from elite South Floridians for popular causes that drew lots of press: homelessness, battered women, and underprivileged school children were the favorites. Coverage was ensured by including the principals from every media outlet in the city. The excuse for the get-together was to induct one of their own or a local star into the Pioneer Hall of Fame. The crowd included the most rich and powerful, along with a host of wannabes mingling like pilot fish around a deadly shark's mouth.

Cyrus feigned the required chit-chat in the lobby, lubricated by the open bar, but his mind was elsewhere. It was past nine and he'd heard nothing about the mission. He glanced at the corner where Karl stood, stiff as a board in a black tux. Karl nodded toward the door and Cyrus quickly dispensed with the congressman who'd been boring him for the last ten minutes. As he darted through the crowd, the smell of coconut oil and perfume filled his nose. He spotted Charlese with a tanned thirty-something he'd noted at a few other events and bristled at the thought of the affair he'd tried to ignore. But she was occupied, and he had business.

Cyrus pointed to a vacant conference room off the marbled hallway. Karl followed and shut the door behind him.

"What's going on, Karl? Any word yet?"

Karl looked like he'd eaten a grenade. "No sir. No word from the team and we can't reach them on their coms."

Cyrus stepped closer. "What the hell does that mean?"

Karl looked at his shoes. "It means the mission was not executed as planned."

"How do you know that this early?"

"Their coms are independent—on two separate channels. We can't reach either. We sent the backup into the park, and they found nothing. The last report we had was that the boy was in the park, and we were closing in."

"So where the hell is he?" Cyrus asked.

"We don't know."

Cyrus leaned into Karl's face. "You don't know. What happened to the GPS on his truck?"

"Someone disabled it."

"Shit. I knew this might happen. I don't know what the hell I pay you for."

Cyrus shoved Karl aside and drifted to the window. The curving lines of the pool wound around the palms and the luxurious cabanas. His money gave him anything he wanted, except the one thing he wanted the most. He'd scoured his father's notes for years and knew every word, every reference to Zachariah Webster's discovery, and yet he still couldn't solve the riddle. The key to his lifelong quest was in the hands of a seventeen-year-old. And his methods were proving ineffective. Time was running out. Once revealed, they'd be protected or destroyed. Either outcome was not good for him. He turned back to Karl.

"Get Grandby's people on the phone now and set up a meeting."

"But sir, we can handle this."

"Like you handled it tonight?"

"But why Grandby and why now?"

"We need an ally who is committed and can quietly muster an army of followers so committed nothing else matters, not even their own lives."

Cyrus stomped out of the conference room. He didn't want to elaborate. His father's notes had contained a reference that even Cyrus found hard to believe. He hadn't shared it with anyone. It was all he wanted. He didn't care about the atheists' religious implications. But he'd use their zeal to get what he needed. He'd ensure that a crusade would begin that would make the middle ages look like a tennis match. He'd recruit Grandby and give the Godless a head start.

CHAPTER 12

THE G5 TOUCHED down at Westchester County airport two hours after leaving Miami. For once, Cyrus was impressed. Thirteen hours after giving the order to set up a meeting with Grandby, they were on the ground and headed to Grandby's secluded farmhouse. This was good news. Grandby must have been intrigued by the teaser Karl had carefully conveyed to his assistant, and on that basis, he'd cleared his morning to meet with Cyrus. While he had an army of followers, Cyrus had great interest in the rumors of a covert network of highly skilled investigators, scientists, and mercenaries dedicated to scientific discovery that undercut religious folklore. He knew it would be a tough sell to get Grandby to engage a network he officially claimed never existed, but it was his only chance to secure the prize he craved.

The sleek private jet taxied to the entrance of Mercury Jet Service.

"Let's go, Karl."

Cyrus bounded down the retractable steps and was into the black Suburban before the engines stopped spinning. There was no time to waste. The boy had a head start. Karl followed, hauling the black briefcase that rarely left his side. He pulled out his Blackberry and ducked into the SUV.

"What's the latest on the boy?" Cyrus asked.

Karl covered the phone with his meaty palm. "Still looking, but we'll get him soon."

Cyrus shook his head and then stared straight ahead. "Useless."

Karl turned his attention back to the phone, and the driver maneuvered through the security gate and headed out of the airport. An unseasonable fog hugged the low-lying valleys and gave a haunting glow to the struggling daylight. They were quickly in the wooded rolling hills that provided refuge and anonymity to Wall Street's cover boys, the political elite, and successful artists and actors. The winding road was lined with rock walls built during the infancy of the country.

"Karl, you see these walls along the road here?"

"Yes, sir."

"It probably protected a few of the patriots fighting your British neighbors for our independence."

"We studied the history of the United States in school. 1776."

"Did you also know the average life expectancy back then was in the 40s?"

"No, sir."

"So you and I would most likely be dead."

Karl seemed to ponder his own demise. "Do you think their spirits still roam the hillsides?"

Cyrus shook his head. "No, Karl. I don't."

It was a firm reply, but there was doubt. It was a doubt he continually pushed deep into the back of his mind. What if he was wrong and his mother was right? Would he be roaming the Earth for eternity in his own version of hell? Or was his father right in his belief that there was life on Earth, and then nothing? Cyrus quickly convinced himself of the latter and focused on the monkeys. Charles Grandby would help him, and he'd taste the closest thing to immortality anyone on Earth ever knew.

The driver turned into the huge entry, stopped at the iron security gates, and spoke into the call box framed in stone and mortar. The gates drifted open, and Cyrus spotted the renovated barn cradled in the hollow below them. A large pond in front of the barn emptied through the paddlewheel of an old gristmill and then streamed toward the back of the property. Steam drifted off the water and added to the mist that partially concealed the structure. Huge round rocks formed the foundation and the walls. Whitewashed clapboard framed most of the windows, except those framed by stone in what used to be a silo. He counted at least three floors. It looked like the castle of a Godless man. It was cold, intimidating, and arrogant.

They stopped at the front entrance. What used to be the barn door parted, and a servant scurried to the car and escorted Cyrus and Karl inside.

Cyrus stopped in the immense entry and gawked at the sixteenth-century artwork and antiques that graced the walls.

"Mr. Schultz, it my pleasure to welcome you to my home."

Cyrus looked up at the spiral staircase and spotted Charles Grandby. He was even thinner than the photos on the back flap of his controversial books, almost gaunt. His light-gray suit was perfectly tailored and complemented by a thin black tie on a bright-white shirt. His eyes were dark brown or black, with no evidence of a pupil. He moved down the steps with the grace of unshaken confidence. With eighty percent of the world professing a belief in a God, Cyrus expected as much.

Cyrus stepped forward to greet him.

"Thank you for seeing us on such short notice," he said, shaking Grandby's hand. He couldn't help but think about shaking hands with the devil.

"If what your assistant conveyed is true, the pleasure is mine." Grandby smiled but it came out like a grimace. "Let's move to the study and get comfortable. Eli, can you bring tea and whatever else these gentlemen would like?"

Cyrus almost chuckled at the thought of a person with such a biblical name working for this man. "Thank you. We're both fine with tea."

Eli opened the double pine doors to the left and stepped aside. Cyrus and Karl followed Grandby inside. The room was at least as big as half a basketball court. Rough-cut wood planks ran across the entire floor. Two-story bookcases ran along two of the walls up to a steeply pitched ceiling. A massive window framed a bulky antique desk at the far end from the door. Persian rugs made a feeble attempt to warm the room. Three high-backed side chairs faced the desk and were separated by polished antique end tables. Grandby stepped behind the desk and extended his hand.

"Have a seat, please."

Cyrus took the seat in the middle. Karl sat in the seat next to him.

"So, you may have a discovery of some interest to me?" Grandby folded his hands on the desk.

"Mr. Grandby, I think we have an opportunity to work together to advance both our causes considerably."

Grandby leaned forward. Cyrus continued.

"I have evidence that there may be an undisclosed species of monkey that may prove the evolution of man from a common ancestor of Old and New World monkeys."

Grandby rubbed his narrow chin and raised an eyebrow.

"Mr. Shultz, we already have evidence that a chimpanzee's mitochondrial DNA matched 98 percent of that of a man. Darwin's work has been verified through archaeological discoveries that show the split of man and other hominids about five million years ago. So what's new here?"

"As you know, there are still many in the world who support divine creationism and point to the lack of fossil evidence to make a direct link. Those who drift toward evolution a bit still claim intelligent design by a creator. It's my hypothesis based on thirty years of study and evidence secured by my father that these monkeys will confirm evolutionary theory because they have traits never seen in Old World monkeys and apes."

"What traits are we talking about here?" Grandby leaned back and crossed his arms.

Cyrus sensed his disbelief and decided to share something he had never shared with another person. He'd hold back the most important fact, though, to protect his interests.

"These monkeys have learned to swim like human beings. They are much more social in their behavior, a major deviation from the behavior of chimpanzees. My father uncovered evidence that they bury their dead and communicate through drawings. I believe these traits show a third evolutionary path that more closely follows that from the first Hominins to Homo sapiens."

Grandby sat up and cleared his throat, obviously concealing his shock. Cyrus had hit pay dirt.

Grandby leaned closer. "Where are these monkeys?"

"Well, that's the catch. We have evidence they're in a rainforest, and we're following a couple of descendants of their discoverer who are on the way to find them, but we don't know yet where they are. That's where we need your help."

"Why not just turn the information you have over to the authorities and the scientific community?"

While Cyrus had anticipated this question, he had to answer carefully.

"First of all, the authorities and scientific community could destroy them. I have a very specific use for them, and they have to be alive. I understand there may be just a few left, and they are of no use to me dead. Secondly, the Webster clan had some kind of blood oath to keep their existence a secret, and they are the only ones who know where they are and have irrefutable evidence."

Grandby looked suspicious. "What is your use for them?"

"I can't tell you at this point. But I think I am correct that your interest could be served greatly with such a discovery?"

"Yes, that's right. More irrefutable evidence confirming Darwin's principles of natural selection as related to humans will further expose the lie of religion. If our evolution is proved, then the thought of a personal God becomes unsupported."

A little brown-nosing at this point might close the deal. "I'm impressed. I've followed your work closely."

"So what do you need from me?"

"We believe you have an extensive network of scientists—let's call them mechanics—dedicated to your cause. We assume they are spread across the globe, and they are well-connected and financed. While I have financial resources, I can't build the necessary network for a global search in time. You can, and time is running out."

"I don't have such a network. I'm sorry you and your colleague came so far for nothing." Grandby stood and pressed a button in the phone. "Eli, our guests are ready to leave."

Karl rose and looked confused, but Cyrus remained seated. Grandby stepped next to Karl and extended his palm toward the door. Eli opened the doors. Grandby looked directly at Cyrus. "I think were done here."

Still seated, Cyrus looked straight ahead. "You get to reveal the discovery to the world at the appropriate time. You get full credit, you can control the data and information flow and shape the story. You essentially get to hold the dagger that puts the fatal wound in the world's organized religions and proves beyond a doubt what you've claimed all along."

Grandby remained still, then walked back to the desk and sat. "How do I know this is true?"

Cyrus nodded to Karl, who opened the black briefcase at his side and passed an envelope to Cyrus. Cyrus pushed it across the desk.

"This should be sufficient. It includes copies of the evidence my father uncovered and the work I continued after his death."

Grandby pulled an old dagger from his desk drawer and sliced the envelope. He flipped through a few of the documents. Cyrus thought he detected a smile.

"Who discovered them and who are these descendants?"

"It's all in there. We need your help to find them, track down the monkeys, and get them safely into the country undetected. Time is of the essence."

"That's a tall order, Mr. Shultz."

Cyrus smiled. The hook was set. "That's why we came to you, sir."

"All right, I'll look at this material and if I'm interested, you'll be contacted before the end of the day."

Grandby stood up. The meeting was over. He shook both men's hands and led them to the door of the study.

"Eli, show these men to their car."

Once in the car, Cyrus looked at Karl. "Get our men ready."

Cyrus knew the call would come. He looked over his shoulder at the farmhouse shrinking in the distance. The trap had been set and the seventeen-year-old boy would be no match for the Godless army about to descend on him. With Grandby involved, not even Heaven could help him—it didn't exist.

CHAPTER 13

RYAN KNEW THIS route well. It came in useful on late nights when his return home was better undetected by his parents. He wiped the sweat from his face with the bottom of his T-shirt and walked next to the tree-lined wall that snaked along the drainage ditch on the backside of his neighborhood. The swamp-fed palms and mangroves on the far side of the ditch, which stretched for half a mile before it ended at the interstate, provided the cover he needed. The salty smell of the brackish swamp water hung in the thick air. Vigilant for any signs of a stray gator or snake, he stepped carefully through the tall wet weeds. He didn't remember being so careful before, but tonight he was sober, very sober. He wished he had a cold Stella to quench his thirst and bolster his courage.

Whoever was trying to kidnap him would be watching from the front, but probably not the back. They wouldn't give up after the setback at the Primate Park, and they'd kill him before they let him go again. Thad had agreed to watch the street and warn Ryan if he spotted any sign of trouble. He'd dropped Ryan at the end of the swampy greenbelt nearly a mile away. Ryan checked his iPhone. The signal was strong.

Ryan counted the tops of the palms in each yard he passed. He stopped when spotted six. The cinderblock wall was painted white and capped with orange tile. Vines gripped the back of the wall and provided a makeshift toehold. He grabbed a vine with his sweaty hands and hoisted himself up. He struggled to find a firm foothold as some of the vines crackled and broke under his weight. He cringed, hung for a moment, and listened. If Emma and Abby were outside, they'd raise hell, alerting neighbors and any dirtbag watching the house. It was still quiet, except for the babbling water from the waterfall in the pool. He raised himself up again and climbed the laced vines. When he reached the top, he peeked over the tile cap and scanned the yard. The light drifted from the back of the house and reflected off the pool. He spotted his mother in the kitchen, probably seeking refuge from his father. While the white wood blinds were drawn in the den, he could see the flat-screen TV was on. The old man was probably watching CNBC.

Ryan slipped over the wall and dropped into the yard. He scurried to the far side of the house and looked through the wooden gate that faced the street. He scanned a few cars in the street. He saw movement in a car two houses down, opposite side of the street. It was a black Impala. The driver had slumped down, probably watching the house in his mirror. Four houses down, his uncle's rental curled into a spot. He jumped when his phone vibrated. He read the text.

Impala. One scumbag. Two houses north, east side. Be careful.

The rest of the street was quiet. Silently, he crept back to the kitchen door and attempted to turn the knob. It was locked. He tapped lightly on the white frame of the glass door. His mother recognized the rhythm and slid quietly across the white tile to the door.

"Ryan honey? Is that you?" she whispered.

Ryan saw her eyes peeking through the blinds. "Yeah Mom. Let me in."

The door swung open and his mother hugged him. He returned the hug but she held it much longer than usual.

"What's going on, Mom?"

She released him, and he saw a tear in her eye.

"I've been trying to reach you for two hours on your phone. I told your father you'd called and were headed back from Tyler's so he wouldn't get mad. But when I couldn't reach you, I called Tyler. He tried to cover for you, but he finally confessed he hadn't seen you. I was worried."

Sleepy from their evening coma, Emma and Abby swaggered in, managed to shake their tails a few times, and leaned against Ryan's legs. He sensed their concern.

"Sorry, Mom," he said, rubbing the dogs' heads. "When I called yesterday I couldn't tell you what was going on. Thad thought it was better that way."

"Thad? What does he have to do with it?" She put her hands on her hips and scowled. "What's going on?"

"Okay Mom. I'll tell you, but you can't get all freaked out here."

She stepped closer and wagged her finger in his face. "Ryan Barnum Webster, you tell me what's going on right now!"

"I'd like to hear that too, young man," his father said as he appeared in the doorway from the den.

Busted. Ryan hissed out a sigh and dropped into a chair at the kitchen table. The dogs dropped their heads and slinked back into the den. He was jealous they had that option. Now he'd have to tell his old man what he was doing, and the battle would be on.

His mother sat next to him, and his father strutted to the table with his arms crossed.

"Wellllllll …?" his father asked.

"Okay. But you guys have to be careful and not tell anyone what's going on."

"You don't make the rules in this house." his father said.

"I'm not making the rules—"

"Ryan, tell us what's going on," his mother interrupted. "We'll listen." She glared at his father, then looked back at Ryan.

"I was at the park …"

"What the hell were you doing at the park?"

His mother slapped the table. "Let him finish."

His father bit his lower lip and his face turned crimson. She'd pay for that one later.

"I was at the park," Ryan continued, and stared back at his father, "when two guys jumped me."

"Jumped you?" his mother asked.

"Yes. They tried to take me out of the park, but Uncle Thad was there. We kicked their asses."

"Were these some boys you pissed off somehow?" his father asked.

"No. These were men. Thad thinks they're some kind of mercenaries."

His mother covered her mouth. "Mercenaries?"

"Jesus Christ." His father threw both hands in the air.

"John, don't take the Lord's name in vain."

"Go on," his father said as he refolded his arms.

"They're after me because of the monkeys."

"Holy shit. I told you to ignore that crap."

"Kind of hard to do, Dad, when these assholes are trying to kill me."

"Why are they after *you*, Ryan?"

"I don't know. But I think it has to do with the fact that Grandpa said I was the one. The one who'd find the monkeys and decide if the world was ready. I already found a GPS transmitter on my car and I think they had the room bugged when Grandpa told Uncle Thad and me about the clues."

"Oh, here we go," his father said.

"What clues, honey?"

"Grandpa gave me a few clues about what the monkeys could do and where they are."

"I'll tell you where they are—nowhere. They're just a fantasy made up by my grandfather and embellished by your grandfather."

"I don't think so, Dad. Why would someone try to kidnap me for a fantasy?"

"Because they're as stupid as the rest of you."

"Bite me, Dad." Ryan shot up from his chair. "These monkeys are real. I know it. And Thad and I are going to go find them. It was important to Grandpa, and he never lied to me."

"You're not going anywhere, young man."

"You can't stop me. I have money from Grandpa's trust, and I can move out if I have to."

"Stop it. Both of you," his mother said. "We're not going to kick you out, and you talk to your father with a little more respect. John, you do the same. Now Ryan, why don't we just go to the police with this?" She took Ryan's hand and pulled him back into his seat.

"No, Mom. You can't do that. Please," he said. "If the cops get involved and they start snooping around, I won't be able to find the monkeys and get back here with them."

"Back here?" his father said. "How the hell are you going to get the monkeys back here? And then what are you going to do with them?"

"I don't know, Dad. I just know that it's important that no one else gets to them. Thad thinks he knows where to start, and we're leaving tonight."

"For where?" His father leaned across the table.

"He didn't tell me."

"That dumbass can't even hold a good job, and you're going to let him lead you on a wild goose chase?"

Ryan hugged his mom. "I'll call you when I can, but I'll be fine."

"Before you go, I have an offer for you to consider." His father's tone had calmed, and he was smiling. The old man was up to something.

"What is it?"

"I have an offer for your share of the Primate Park."

Ryan was caught off guard.

"I have a buyer. He wants controlling interest, so we need your share."

"And who is the buyer?" Ryan asked.

"Some LLC out of Miami."

"I don't want to sell the park," Ryan said. *Stay firm*, he told himself.

"Wait until you hear the offer, boy—five million dollars."

Ryan heard his mother catch her breath. *Five million dollars.* Just four days ago he was scraping for a twenty to fill up his truck. He immediately thought about a Corvette and season tickets to the Marlins. He'd skip college and buy a nice condo in South Beach. He inserted himself into the last episode of *Entourage*. Maybe he'd be an actor—

"Ryan?" his mother's voice broke the trance.

Ryan turned slowly to his mother, his mouth half open.

His father chuckled, "Looks like you have something to think about."

Ryan turned back to his father, still not knowing what to say.

"Well, don't think too long. The offer I have is only good until close of business tomorrow. Let me know."

Grinning, his father left the room.

CHAPTER 14

RYAN KNEW THIS was a bad idea.

His uncle reinforced his concerns directly. "Dude, what the hell have you been smoking? She's not worth the risk. These guys are playing hardball, and you're the ball."

But Ryan couldn't help himself. There was an intense gravity around Sarah that he couldn't describe. The closer he got, the stronger the pull. She was beautiful, hot, and popular, and for some reason he didn't understand, he worried that no other girl with her talents would give him a second look. He knew he'd already told her too much, and now she'd trapped him into his promise to tell her when he was leaving.

Despite his protests, Thad had helped him devise the plan to get in and out undetected. Ryan waited inside the 7-Eleven next to the coolers at the back of the store and read *People* magazine until he spotted Maria's Tahoe roll into the parking space next to the front door. He easily recognized the SUV he'd parked next to by the servant's entrance every time he visited Sarah. He was always polite and helpful, and they'd formed a quick bond. Maria held the title of governess at the Costa household. She did all of the household chores and had raised Sarah since she was a baby. She'd been brought to South Florida as an au pair from Brazil in her late teens and then "promoted" to governess by Hanna Costa upon Sarah's birth. Luiz Costa pulled a few strings at immigration and in a few years Maria took the oath and became a US citizen.

Ryan grabbed a gallon of milk from the cooler, paid the clerk, jogged to the passenger's door, and hopped in.

"Hi Maria. Thanks for helping me out here."

"Mr. Ryan, you are very welcome. You're a very nice man, and I'm happy to help. Besides, Miss Sarah says it's very important to her."

"Thanks, Maria. Sorry about the cloak and dagger stuff, but I have to jump into the back seat." Ryan pushed himself up on the console and squeezed between the captain's chairs.

"I'm not sure why, but it's okay with me," she said, glancing in the rearview mirror.

Maria maneuvered out of the parking lot and weaved through the streets of Coral Gables. After entering the Costas' driveway, she pulled behind the shrubs concealing the servant's entrance. Ryan felt the SUV stop. He peered over the seat and noted the porch lights had been turned off. The moonless night provided adequate cover.

"Okay, Maria, now."

They both opened their doors at the same time. Ryan slipped from the Tahoe and crept to the door behind Maria. Sarah met them at the door. Ryan was surprised. He'd rarely seen her anywhere near the servant's quarters. She smiled, cradled Ryan's face, and gave him a long kiss.

"I'm glad you're safe, Ryan."

She took his hand and led him down the hallway from the servant's quarters and into the main house. They made their way down another hallway and into her father's library. The oversized desk sat centered in the room, flanked by two deep-red leather chairs. Sarah pulled Ryan to the matching leather sofa that hugged the wall on the right.

She flashed a bright smile. "Okay, now tell me about what's going on. This is exciting." She held both his hands in hers.

Ryan was glad he had her attention, but her excitement made him a little uneasy.

"Sarah, this is serious. I need you to promise me you won't speak a word of this to anyone. It's not a game. People tried to kidnap me already tonight."

The smile drained from her face, but she kept his hands in hers. "All right. So you're getting ready to go?"

Ryan wondered how she could ignore his attempted kidnapping. "Yes. Leaving right after this."

"Leaving? To where?"

"It's better you don't know."

She dropped both his hands and frowned. "What do you mean? You don't trust me?"

Ryan knew that tone. It always sounded like a threat to him. *I am unhappy and if you keep it up, you're gone!* That damned gravity again. He twisted a little more to face her head-on.

"Look. This is very serious. The less you know, the better. These people could hurt you."

"What people?"

"The people trying to stop me."

Sarah shot up. "Look, Ryan, if you don't trust me enough to tell me what's going on, maybe we don't have any reason to be together."

He didn't want to take the next step, but he knew if he didn't, they were through. It was getting hot, and he felt the sweat drip down his face. He knew how Sarah and her mother felt about any talk of evolution, and he'd surely experience that wrath again if he told her the truth.

"Where are you going?" she repeated firmly.

At that moment, he decided nothing was as important as keeping his word, not even Sarah. He shook his head. "I can't tell you. But I came here to tell you that I'm leaving tonight." He stood up. Whatever Sarah would do was up to her. He wasn't going to say any more.

"I've gotta go. I just wanted to let you know I was leaving."

Sarah stood. "Ryan!"

She was playing him now, and Ryan could see it.

"Maria is waiting. Don't tell anyone. Not a soul."

"I won't, but you have to call me." She followed Ryan out the door and down the hallway.

He shook his head and left the room. He passed the entrance to the den and spotted Sarah's mother, Hanna, sitting in front of the TV. He ignored her, but swore he saw her eye him in the way he'd seen hawks eye their prey. He marched into the servant's quarters and stopped at the door.

To his surprise, Sarah hugged him and gave him a kiss.

"Call me," she whispered as Ryan followed Maria out the door. He slid into the back seat and lay on the floor in the darkness as he felt the SUV weave back to the 7-Eleven. One vision haunted him, and he couldn't push it from his mind. It wasn't the kidnappers or the scenes of his own death he'd obsessed about since the Primate Park. It was the haunting look of the woman who professed to be the best Christian she could be.

CHAPTER 15

JACOB REMINGTON DROVE along the winding parkway that edged the Great Smoky Mountains National Park. He marveled at the beauty of the thick green forest and mist that swept the rolling Tennessee countryside. This was truly the work of God. Just like his father and his grandfather, he made this trek to the secluded compound just outside of Gatlinburg to protect the Creator and his word. A threat had been detected, and the three-person council was called together for a special meeting to address it. The surveillance of Charles Grandby was finally paying a dividend.

He was proud to be the third-generation president of the society his grandfather had founded in 1926 on the heels of the Scopes Monkey Trial. While Opus Dei was started two years later by the Catholics and attracted most of the modern press's attention, the Society of True Believers had quietly grown a network of members and contributors that would dwarf the Catholics. Despite receiving so much press as a result of *The Da Vinci Code*, Opus Dei's membership was still reported to be approaching only 100,000 members. The Society of True Believers numbered five times that and had a strong funding base anchored by some of the wealthiest Christians across the globe.

He pulled to the gate flanked by high stone walls and swiped his passcard against the black reader. The heavy iron gates parted, and he waved to the security camera peering down on his Lincoln. The secluded ten-acre compound had been the Society's headquarters since 1968, the year after Tennessee was forced to repeal the Butler Act, which prohibited the teaching of evolutionary theory in schools. The action provided a huge surge in funding. Remington followed the wooded lane as it wound past the twenty cabins used to house members and trainees and pulled into the gravel lot in front of the main lodge that served as the headquarters. He parked and admired the sprawling log structure his father had designed. The eastern white pine logs blended with the natural beauty of the surrounding forest and created the illusion of a welcoming lodge. The offices, communications center, and underground weapons bunker were well concealed.

Remington grabbed his briefcase and marched to the double glass doors under the A-framed entry. With another swipe of the passcard, he entered the lobby and waved to the two security guards seated behind the large monitoring station. They waved back and the magnetic lock buzzed, releasing the thick redwood doors to the offices. He scurried down the hallway and entered the first conference room on the right. The other two council members were huddled in the corner with the intelligence officer, getting a pre-brief for the meeting.

"Gentlemen." Remington said.

He tossed his briefcase onto the large conference table with a thud. The huddle broke and David Smythe and Fortunatus Richman smiled and extended their hands.

"Hey, Jacob old boy!" Smythe shook Remington's hand first. He was in his sixties, heavy-set with an early seventies Beach Boy haircut. He was a blowhard, but the bylaws specifically said the council was to be made up of only the direct descendants of the original founders. He shook his hand and then looked past him to Richman.

"Jacob." Richman shook his hand and smiled as if both men shared the same thought about Smythe.

"It's good to see you, Fort." Remington thought it appropriate that one of the wealthiest men he knew would be named Fortunatus. His parents had named him in honor of the ambassador of the Corinthian church mentioned in 1 Corinthians 16:17, who returned with Paul's first letter to the Corinthians. While the Latin translation was blessed or fortunate,

Remington bet the abuse he must've taken as a child didn't make him feel fortunate. The wealth that followed must've delivered a sweet revenge.

He nodded across the room to Greg Blackmon, the head of the Society's intelligence group. "Hi, Greg. Let's get to work." He dropped into a chair. The others followed suit.

"Greg, what do you have?"

"We have reports that Grandby has mobilized his associates on a project that we think may be of great importance, judging by the number of people he's contacting and the nature of their talents."

"What do you mean by 'nature of their talents'?" Smythe was notorious for asking obvious questions.

Blackmon glanced at Remington. Remington faked interest in the question to appease Smythe, and Blackmon answered.

"He's mobilized six two-man teams of his best mercenaries, coupled with electronic surveillance specialists. He's also put out a broad alert to his intelligence cells around the globe."

"It sounds big," Remington said. "Do we have any intercepts yet?"

"We've done better," Blackmon said. "We have a couple of informants imbedded in a few of the cells who received the alert."

"Tell him what it said," Richman said, frowning.

"The alert was brief." Blackmon read from a sheet of paper from his black zippered folio, "We have been made aware of a potential opportunity to capture and reveal a discovery of great importance. Rumors of Mono Grande or Ardi-like species have been discovered—alive. Location only known to two targets we're currently tracking. Focus all resources on cultivation of sources and information possibly related to this topic, and transmit immediately."

Remington nearly choked. "What? Alive?"

"He said alive," Richman said as his face turned sour. "Even if there is no truth to this, it will erode the numbers of faithful on the fringe. And you know how many are on the edge already. The evolutionists have hammered us with these scientific discoveries for the past few years. Some of our believers are even questioning Genesis and its account of man's creation. Ardi was bad enough as a five-million-year-old fossil, but a living species means decades of scientific studies and attacks."

"Yeah. Most of our followers are too ignorant to understand. I hear them all the time asking why we can't have both the Bible's teachings and that jackass Darwin's natural selection."

Richman and Blackmon gaped at Smythe. While he always had a friendly and jovial demeanor in front of their followers, behind closed doors his arrogance and narcissism were overwhelming.

Remington turned to Blackmon. "I think I understand Ardi. The discovery was made in Ethiopia. Another missing link."

"Right, but rumor is they may be alive," Blackmon added.

"So what's this Mono Grande?"

"It's a myth and a hoax so far. Mono Grande is Spanish for large monkey. It was first reported in 1533 by a conquistador named Pedro Cieza de León, who was exploring and chronicling Peru for the Spanish. Later, Sir Walter Raleigh wrote about it, giving it further credibility. This myth spread and in 1920 a Swiss oil geologist named François de Loys brought back a photograph of this ape-like creature from the Amazon. This would mean that hominids—human's ape-like predecessors—were not restricted to the Old World of Africa and Eurasia. This would throw the prevailing 'Out of Africa' evolutionary theory on its ear."

"So why isn't that good for us? The more controversy about evolutionary theory, the better," Remington said.

"This is where it gets unbelievable." Smythe folded his arms. "Go ahead, Blackmon, tell him what you told us."

Blackmon's eyes grew wide and he lowered his head when he spoke. "Our informants say there are rumors of human-like behavior."

Remington slammed his fist into the table. "That's bull crap!"

Remington never swore in public. He had an image to uphold. He walked a tight line. He had to show the edge the more radical members expected, yet demonstrate the Christian values of the Bible. But there was no mistake from those who provided most of the funding: He was to do the dirty work. Eradicate any threat to the Bible with the force of the Crusades. A hit man for the Bible, just like his hero, Richard the Lionheart. And he knew its cornerstone was the account of Creation in Genesis.

"How reliable is the information?" Richman asked.

"We have it from at least two sources. Granted, they are still rumors at this point. But even a rumor of this magnitude could do serious damage to our cause."

"You bet it can." Remington sighed as he leaned back in his chair and regained his composure.

"Doubt attacks faith and faith in God is all we have. It is built on the teachings of the Bible. Grandby and his lot have driven a wedge of doubt into all organized religion, alleging they are creations of men trying to control the masses. And this attacks the accounts in Genesis and strikes at the heart of what each of our parents and grandparents sacrificed so much for." He rose and paced around the room. "The Society of True Believers gets its power from its members, but our charge comes from God himself. These Godless non-believers must be stopped." Remington surveyed the members around the table. "Are we all prepared to muster the resources of the Society to end this threat by any means necessary?"

He used these words carefully. It had been a code passed down for generations: *Shed blood in the name of God, if that's what it takes.*

"Yes," Richman nodded.

"We don't have a choice," Smythe added.

"Okay, Greg. It looks like if we can get to the sources and shut this down before any discovery or revelation, we can nip this in the bud. If they get to the species and they're for real, then we have to destroy them all, and that could get messy."

"Yes sir."

Blackmon gathered his notes.

"Then I'll expect you'll activate the teams and the appropriate Crusaders. We'll want a daily morning report and immediate notification of any developments. Agreed?"

"Agreed."

"I'll take up residence in cabin one."

Remington snatched the briefing material from Blackmon and stormed out of the conference room. He concealed his shock well. He'd heard of these rumors before on the back steps of his grandfather's house in Knoxville. Only a few knew of the rumor about a renowned zoologist who was holding back a discovery that would shock the world. They thought it was only a rumor started by the evolutionists during the Scopes Monkey Trial. But even as a young boy, he had wondered what such a discovery would mean for his family and the church. He didn't want to find out now.

CHAPTER 16

RYAN SURVEYED THE sprawling urban mass that cluttered the Los Angeles Basin. He'd dreamed of California in his early teens. He'd watched *The OC* and seen the luxury cliff-side homes of Orange County and the beautiful young tempests that roamed the beaches every Thursday night. His vision had matured now to where he expected the easy excess portrayed on *Entourage*. But, as the Boeing 757 closed on the runway, the miles of warehouses, cramped neighborhoods, small houses with no yards, and endless miles of concrete and asphalt quickly destroyed that myth.

He glanced back at his Uncle Thad, sitting six rows back. They shared a nod. They had to travel using their real names, due to the TSA requirements, and they could be easily tracked. Ryan shifted his focus to the carry-on stuffed at his feet, and hoped the plan would work. He thought about the notebook and wondered if it held the location of the monkeys. His uncle had said he knew where it was, but kept the location to himself as a precautionary measure.

The plane bounced as the pilot made a hard landing and seemed to roll halfway to the Pacific. Once at the gate, Ryan grabbed the small duffel and snatched the carry-on from the overhead. He wiped the sweat on his palms against his jeans and pressed the crowd ahead to move up the jetway. Once in the terminal, he followed his uncle's instructions to the T. He headed to the restrooms located in the opposite direction from the baggage claim. He was suspicious of everyone: The gate agent seemed to eye him a bit longer than necessary, the businessman leaning against the wall seemed to only pretend to read the paper, and even the shoeshine man ogled him.

Once in the restroom, Ryan entered the handicapped stall at the end and ripped open the duffel. He quickly changed into plaid baggy shorts and a USC gray-and-cardinal T-shirt. He slipped on a cardinal USC cap, dark Ray-Bans, and laceless cloth tennis shoes. He slipped his iPhone ear buds into his ears and jammed his clothes into the empty duffel. He was back in the terminal and headed to the Airport Bus desk in minutes.

His phone vibrated, and he took the call through his ear buds.

"Take the escalator to your right down to the lower level and turn right. Go to the desk and ask for a ticket to Bakersfield. Pay cash like we discussed. Don't talk to anyone and get on the bus when it arrives. I'll be behind you but don't look at me."

It was good just to hear his uncle's voice. After buying the ticket he stood outside under the Airport Bus sign and felt the cool air against his face. The thick smell of exhaust fumes made him cough a bit, and his dreamy image of life on the West Coast eroded even further. The bus maneuvered through the morass of cars and rental-car busses and crawled to the curb.

Ryan got on and took a seat halfway back. He counted twelve others board as the seats quickly filled. He squirmed a bit when a heavy-set Hispanic man dropped into the seat next to him, leaving only one seat near the front. If his uncle didn't arrive, he'd be on his own, headed to some place called Bakersfield, and his uncle hadn't told him their ultimate destination yet.

"I'm right here," his uncle said over the phone. His head appeared in the doorway and he climbed the steps. Thad wore dark slacks, tweed sports coat, white shirt, and a gold-and-blue tie. Ryan tried to conceal his chuckle. Only his uncle would think being dressed up was a disguise. Thad quickly dropped into his seat and out of sight, and the bus headed to the freeway.

The trip to Bakersfield took two and a half hours. Along the way, Ryan kept his attention out the window. No contact with anyone. The urban landscape gave way to the gentle rolling mountains covered by scrub as they drove through Tejon Pass and then descended into the San Joaquin Valley. A heavy layer of smog capped the valley. Halfway down the mountain, the layer broke and Ryan gawked at the flattest and most desolate land he'd ever seen. It seemed to be endless, dusty, and dry. Huge patches of green farmland sprung from the arid ground. Ryan spotted the irrigation channels that gave the land life. It was another world from LA.

The landscape gave way to small old ranches followed by houses cramped together like postage stamps, box warehouses, and strip malls. Dirt and dust covered everything, even the palm trees and shrubs in the center divider. The bus left the freeway and entered what appeared to be a downtown scene Ryan had seen in old black-and-white movies from the '50s.

The bus came to a halt at the station and Ryan watched his uncle hop off. He followed his seatmate up the aisle to the door. Despite his dark Ray-Bans, the blazing sun caused him to squint. He stopped halfway down the stairs when the blast of heat hit him. He remembered the blast of heat from the five-hundred-degree ovens at his first job at Pizza Hut—this was hotter.

"Let's go, kid!" the wiry man behind him yelled.

Ryan stepped off the bus and walked into the station. He waited for his uncle to reappear from the restroom. This time Thad was in khaki shorts, a Punisher T-shirt, and sandals. He motioned toward the back door of the station, and they headed out the back door.

"You did good, kid. I don't see anyone tracking us."

Ryan was sweating. The air smelled like an old attic and was hard to breathe. "What is this place? It feels hot as hell."

His uncle slapped him on the back. "Jerry warned me about the heat here in August. It's probably 105 in the shade. Drink this." He handed Ryan a bottle of Gatorade from his duffel. Ryan chugged it and pitched the bottle in the dumpster against the wall.

"Jerry left the car in the lot over here. He rented it at a local joint under his name. He's a good dude. He claims I saved his ass in Baghdad, but I was only saving mine." Ryan didn't believe his uncle was trying to save himself. He'd seen the medals and ribbons Thad kept hidden from everyone.

Thad stepped over a guardrail at the back of the lot, ambled up to a black Impala, and scanned the area. Satisfied he was not watched, he reached under the wheel well and recovered the keys.

"Okay, hop in, kid. Let's get this show on the road."

Ryan yanked open the door and jumped in. "Shit, Uncle T, this is like a blast furnace." Ryan was instantly soaked with sweat. Thad started the car. Ryan saw the sweat running down his neck.

"The air-con will kick in once we get going," Thad said.

Thad maneuvered out of the parking lot and retraced the bus's route to the base of the Tehachapi Mountains at the southern end of the San Joaquin Valley. The car had finally cooled to a tolerable temperature when he headed west on Hwy 166 toward the coast.

"So Uncle T, can you tell me where we're headed now?"

"Montaña de Oro State Park."

"Where?"

"Montaña de Oro. It's a state park just outside the town of Los Osos, and Los Osos is just to the south of Hearst Castle."

"The castle made of newspapers Grandpa mentioned?"

"Yep. The castle was built by the great Randolph Hearst. He was a publishing and media big shot, and built a castle overlooking the Pacific."

"So what's the other part of the riddle mean? Grandpa said the notebook sits on a cliff overlooking five stars, and the five stars are near this castle of newspapers."

"Montaña de Oro." Thad grinned.

"Why there?"

"It's a park on the coast full of tidal pools. In those pools are thousands of starfish. There happen to be five species of starfish there. Five."

"How did you figure that out?"

"Dad took me there a couple of times on a side trip when we'd visit the West Coast. He loved the place. It's so peaceful and undisturbed. We'd sit for hours and watch the sea lions play while the tide went out. Then we'd wade through the water, and he'd teach me about the sea urchins, starfish, and crabs that filled the tidal pools. He knew I'd figure it out. Your dad never wanted to go. Had no interest at all. He just stayed with Mom. I think by then he'd already given up on Dad—said he didn't care since he was leaving us all the time."

The road snaked along the foothills then began to climb into the coastal mountains ahead. The two-lane road was narrow, and he wanted to let Thad focus on driving.

Thad glanced at Ryan and grinned, then reached under the dash. He pulled out a baggie with four tightly rolled joints inside.

"Ah, Jerry is certainly a good friend."

Ryan shook his head. "Isn't that illegal?"

"It's for medicinal purposes." Thad said, chuckling.

Ryan had seen lots of pot. A few friends in Miami smoked, but he didn't. He'd tried it once and decided it wasn't worth the risk. Not only was it illegal, but he couldn't stand to ever disappoint his mother. Thad was another story. Ryan had seen Thad's struggles since he'd returned from Iraq. Based on the stories of what he'd seen and done, Ryan figured Thad had earned a little latitude. It seemed to melt the terror Ryan occasionally noted in his uncle's eyes.

The road zigzagged as they climbed the mountains. Along the right, a river tracked the road at the base of a deep rocky canyon. Ryan nervously eyed the edge of the canyon as his uncle lit up.

"You want me to drive, Uncle T?"

"Nope," he said, holding in his first toke.

The road steepened. They climbed to the peak and then began a long sweeping turn descending into a small valley. They approached a blind curve, hidden by a huge boulder. They both spotted the wreck at the same time.

"Shit!"

Thad jammed the brakes, and the car skidded sideways and lurched to a stop inches from the overturned pickup. He brushed the burning joint from his lap.

"What do we do?" Ryan said.

Ryan had spotted the man first. His torso was hanging outside the driver's side door with his shoulders and head resting on the pavement.

"Get out but don't move him. Just check for breathing or bleeding. I'll back up a little to warn any oncoming traffic, and I'll call 911."

Ryan jumped out and ran to the truck. Thad backed up the road about twenty feet and pulled his cell phone from his pocket. The man was in his forties with a stocky build. He looked strong. His color was good and his eyes were closed, but Ryan detected the rise and fall of his chest.

"He's breathing!" he reported.

"Damn. I can't get a signal down here," Thad replied as he exited the car and trotted toward Ryan.

Ryan returned his attention to the man on the ground. He had short sleeves with bulging biceps. He noted a tattoo on his left arm but saw no blood. His other arm was underneath him, and Ryan stepped over the man to get a better look. Then he saw it, but it was too late. The barrel of the gun was already pointed as his chest. He froze. The man pressed himself upright, never losing aim on Ryan's chest.

"Dude, what are you doing?" Thad asked as he stopped just a few feet from Ryan.

"We're eliminating a threat." The voice came from behind Thad. A taller man slipped from behind the boulder. He held a black pistol, targeting Thad's head.

Thad began to turn.

"Don't—don't move. Just turn back around nice and easy," the man said.

The shorter man moved behind Ryan and pressed the gun barrel against the back of his head. Now facing his uncle, Ryan quivered and felt sick. He thought he'd crap in his pants. He shivered, but he was sweating.

"Don't kill me," he said, trying to buy time. He didn't want to die. He thought about his mom and how she would cry. He didn't think she'd go on.

"What threat?" Thad said calmly. Ryan noted Thad was staring at him as if he was about to make his patented no-look basketball pass.

"Your threat against the Creator and all that is good."

Thad's eyes widened. "Would you like to meet him?"

Both men holding the guns shared a bewildered look.

"What?" The man behind Thad laughed.

Like lightning, Thad snatched his attacker's wrist from behind him and pulled the gun forward, firing a shot at Ryan. The shot burned by Ryan's ear, and he felt a spray of warm liquid on his face. His attacker's body fell away. Thad twisted the second man's arm, jammed it into his gut, and fired. The man fell off Thad's shoulders like a sack of monkey feed going down.

Ryan instinctively wiped his face with his hand. It was bright red. Covered in blood. His knees buckled and he hit the pavement.

"You okay, dude? You shot?" Thad asked, rushing to his side.

"I—I don't think so," Ryan said.

Thad checked Ryan quickly, then said, "Time to get it together, dude. We gotta get out of here."

Thad helped Ryan to his feet and shoved him back toward the car. Thad searched his attacker, grabbed a few clips and the pistol, then searched his pockets and found a folded piece of paper.

"Go ahead. Get in," he yelled at Ryan.

Ryan yanked open the passenger's door and slid into the seat. Thad jumped in the driver's side and started the engine.

Thad reached behind him, grabbed his duffel, pulled out a gray T-shirt, and threw it at Ryan. "Here, use this to clean up."

Ryan gawked at the two bodies as Thad sped past them.

"What's wrong with you, dude?"

"I almost died. They almost killed us," Ryan said.

"Almost." Thad grinned.

"I'm not sure I can do this."

Thad slammed the brakes and Ryan hit the glove box. Thad stuffed the shifter in park, leaned over, and pinned Ryan against the passenger door.

"Listen to me. You're in this now, and there's no getting out. Your grandfather gave you something he didn't give to anyone else, and now, like it or not, you're the man. You're the guy who has to step up here. These people are going to try to kill you, whether you do this or not. Our only hope is that we succeed and get to the monkeys first. You got that?"

He threw Ryan against the door and shoved himself back into the driver's seat. He jammed the shifter into drive and started down the road. Ryan looked at his uncle. He'd never talked to him like that before, let alone manhandle him. Ryan sucked in a breath and tried to relax. It didn't work. He thought about his grandfather's warning.

He was seeking the clues but they *were* trying to kill him. He shook off the shock. It was time to grow up—whatever that meant—and follow his heart, wherever that may take him. He looked back at Thad and began to wipe the blood from his face.

"Atta boy." Thad said. "Let's go find us some swimming monkeys."

CHAPTER 17

RYAN NEVER THOUGHT he'd find a truck stop shower re-freshing, but getting the dried blood off his skin helped put a little distance between him and the incident. He stuffed his bloody T-shirt into the trash barrel and squinted in the bright fluorescent light in the hallway. He opened the door and walked toward the front of the travel store. Thad was resting against the magazine rack, reading *The Enquirer.*

"Feel better?" Thad smiled and stuffed the paper back in the rack.

"Much better," Ryan said as he pushed the stenciled glass door open and headed into the parking lot. Once outside, he stopped and inhaled the cool, clean air of the Central Pacific Coast. He looked to the west and spotted the thick coastal fog hugging the gentle hills.

Thad passed Ryan and patted him on the back. "That's where we're headed."

Thad jumped in the car. Ryan trotted to the passenger's side and hopped in.

"Where are we?" Ryan asked.

"Just outside of Pismo Beach. We're headed to Los Osos. The park is on the coast just outside of town."

Thad pulled out of the parking lot and headed up the ramp to Highway 101.

"Who were those guys back there?" Ryan would've preferred not to talk about it, but he wanted to know who was trying to kill them.

"Have a look at his." Thad pulled the folded paper from his pocket and shoved it at Ryan. Ryan unfolded the paper and came face to face with a photo of him and his uncle taken with a cell phone from the Airport Bus counter in Los Angeles.

"They knew we were coming."

"How?"

"Flight records. These guys are connected and well organized."

"Why did they try to kill us instead of kidnap us?"

Thad shot a look at Ryan. "You sure you want to know?"

"C'mon, Uncle T."

"Okay. I don't think they work for the same people. Those guys at the Primate Park definitely wanted you alive and wanted information. Probably where the monkeys are. Those other poor souls wanted us dead—no questions asked."

"But why kill us?"

"Did you hear what they said? They said we were a threat against the Creator and all that is good."

Ryan watched the traffic ahead as Thad darted between a big rig and an RV lumbering up the steep coastal incline. He thought about the radical Christians his grandpa mentioned.

Thad glanced at Ryan. "Don't sound like those other guys—do they?"

"No. They sound like religious wackos."

"Bingo."

Ryan felt the sinking feeling in his stomach creeping back. It seemed to be happening a lot lately, and he pushed it aside. Now there may be two groups trying to stop him. All he had on his side was his uncle. What kind of Christian radical group would be willing to kill to protect the word of God? Murder was a sin, last time Ryan checked the Bible.

"You really think there are two groups after us now?" Ryan looked at his uncle, hoping for a denial. It didn't come.

"No—I think there are three."

"Three?"

"Yup. Those guys from the park, the guys back there, and the authorities, once they figure out who we are. We just left two dead guys on the road."

Ryan wagged his head and gawked out the passenger's window. "Shit."

Thad looked at Ryan and smiled, then returned his attention to the road ahead. They rode in silence until Los Osos.

Ryan longed for the peacefulness of the little town. The small homes and cottages appeared to be nestled in the city's ancient landscape. Most of the stores looked small, locally owned, and like they just put in enough effort to make surfing money. The town quickly gave way to organized groves of eucalyptus trees.

"This is it," Thad said. "I remember Dad telling me that these trees were planted here back in the day for the railroads, but they couldn't use the wood—too soft."

The road split a long hillside that dipped into narrow rocky canyons to the west. The trees were thick on both sides and strangely planted in rows. Ryan looked down the hill and caught a glimpse of the sea through one of the rugged canyons.

"Here we are."

The forest ended and opened onto a high plateau overlooking the rocky surf. It was low tide and the tidal pools stretched all the way out to the breakers. To the left, Ryan spotted an old white shack tucked up against the edge of the eucalyptus trees.

Thad nodded up the hill. "One of the old docents lived up there when I was here with your grandpa twenty years ago. He knew him somehow. I'm guessing that's the place to start."

Thad jumped out of the car and started up the hill. Ryan sprinted to catch up. The house had a few old untrimmed shrubs making a feeble attempt to hide the cracked foundation and peeling paint. An old bicycle, trimmed in rust, leaned against the small concrete steps leading to the front door. Ryan heard the bark of a big dog and stopped about ten feet from the front door. Thad glanced back but continued to the door and knocked. The barking intensified, but Ryan heard a familiar playfulness in the dog's tone.

The door creaked open and a large yellow Lab bolted past Thad and sat directly in front of Ryan. Ryan instinctively rubbed the Lab's ears and the dog nuzzled closer. Ryan smiled at Thad, who spun back to the doorway.

"I'll be damned," a scratchy voice said from just inside. "She doesn't do that for just anybody."

A wiry, white-haired old man, dressed in an untucked, short-sleeved khaki shirt and jeans stepped into the doorway. He was taller than Thad, and his hair looked like a wisp of white cotton candy. He extended his bony arms, and Ryan immediately noticed the age spots. The man had to be at least eighty. Thad shook his hand, but the man never took his eyes off Ryan.

"My name is Thad Webster. This is Ryan Webster."

The man's eyes widened as he continued ogling Ryan and the dog. Ryan walked up the steps and shook his hand. The lab followed and sat beside Ryan.

"Ryan Barnum Webster?" the old man asked.

Ryan's felt his mouth drop open. The old man knew him.

"Yes …" Ryan said slowly.

The old man grinned and rubbed his chin. "So you're the one—you're the one."

Thad gawked at the old man, then looked at Ryan and grinned. He patted the old man on the back.

"Yes, he certainly is."

"Well, boys, come inside. I've been waiting for you for a long time."

The old man kept his eyes on Ryan, and with his shaky hand, guided him through the door.

Inside, the small three-room house was simple: a couch, recliner, and small television in the living room, an even smaller kitchen with a gas stove Ryan guessed was from the fifties, and plain, water-stained olive drapes partially covering the windows. The bedroom door was open, and Ryan spotted the rumpled, unmade twin bed against the back wall. Two saw-horses supported a plywood plank covered in stacks of papers. Old books stuffed with torn papers marking the reader's relevant passages were scattered about, and the entire house was covered with a thick layer of dust.

"Have a seat, boys." The old man pointed to the couch. "I'm Jasper Krick."

The name meant nothing to Ryan. Still, he was intrigued. Thad sat on the sofa and Ryan joined him. The yellow lab sat at Ryan's feet. The old man looked at the dog and shook his head.

"You always been able to relate to animals that way, son?"

Ryan wasn't sure what the man was asking. "Yes. I think so," he said, looking back at Jasper.

"I thought so. Her name is Bailey."

"After the circus?" Thad asked.

"Yup. I couldn't work in the reference to Barnum since she's a girl."

Thad laughed. "I guess you know why we're here."

"You're damn right. This young man is going to bring the world its gift." The old man nodded at Ryan. Ryan tightened his jaw. Another big expectation.

"I'm assuming you're the young man I met with your dad?" he said to Thad.

"Yes, I am."

"Well, your dad and I go back a long way. We've been friends since we were crapping our drawers and spitting up on ourselves." He looked at Ryan and smiled. "Yes, I know it looks like I do that now—just the circle of life and all that bullshit."

Ryan relaxed. He liked the old man. He could see why his grandpa did, too.

"Our fathers were friends too. Your great-grandfather, Zachariah, traveled the world with my dad, John Henry Krick. He was a geologist for the oil and mining companies. Your great-grandfather was a great explorer and zoologist. Boy, they had some stories to tell."

The old man's eyes drifted to some distant place for a moment. Ryan looked at Thad for direction. Thad raised his index finger, indicating they should wait.

The old man's gaze drifted back to Ryan. He seemed to catch himself. "But you're not here to listen to an old man go on and on. Your great-grandfather gave my father a notebook in 1976. When my dad died, he gave it to me. The instructions were simple. 'Give this to no one and don't speak of it or its contents. At some point, you'll be contacted by one of the

Websters,' he told me, 'the one who has the gift. Then, and only then, you're to give them the notebook and anything else they need.'"

The old man stood and walked to the throw rug in the center of the room. He peeled it back and pulled a pocket knife from his pocket. He carefully pried up the boards. His hand disappeared into the floor up to his shoulder. He gently pulled up his hand and produced what looked like a steel strongbox from the old cowboy movies Ryan used to watch with his grandpa, and laid it on the floor. He pulled a handkerchief from his other pocket and brushed the dust from the box. He grabbed the box and started to stand, but struggled to get up.

"Can I help you?" Thad stood.

The man waved him off. He finally pressed himself upright and smiled. He shuffled over to Ryan. Ryan saw tears in the old man's eyes.

"Just as I promised my father before he died, and just as you promised your grandpa," he said as he handed the strongbox to Ryan. The old man was clearly crying now.

Ryan held his composure. Then the old man raised his index finger to the sky. "Wait!" He waddled into the bedroom and returned in a few seconds with an old key and a piece of paper. The key looked like something from *Harry Potter.*

"You'll need this, too." He shuffled back to the recliner, slowly folded into the chair, and started rocking.

"Do you know what's in there?" Thad asked.

"I made a promise to my father that I wouldn't look. But I know what he told me. There's a discovery so great that it could elevate men to heights they never imagined or destroy all we hold dear. That's all he said. His word was his bond, and he gave his word to Zachariah. And I gave my word to him."

The old man nodded knowingly at Ryan and a wrinkled smile drifted across his face.

"We can't thank you enough," Ryan said.

The old man's face turned serious and he stopped rocking. He leaned forward in his chair. "You won't thank me. There are people who will kill for that. The only thanks I need are for you to find them. Now you'll need to get out of here. There's not much time."

Ryan and Thad shared a puzzled look. "What do you mean?" Thad asked.

"Well. I've gotten word from one of Dad's old geologist buddies that the burning is getting close. You've gotta get there now. I asked him to help you, and he said he would."

"Where is he?"

"Houston. His name is Bill Martin. His information is all there. He'll help you get to where you need to be."

"You know where?" Thad asked.

"Read the notebook." The man stood and herded the pair to the door. He held Bailey by her collar and opened the door.

"Thanks so much, sir," Ryan said. Thad shook the old man's hand and then stepped onto the porch.

"Don't waste any time—there's not much left," the old man warned, and then he closed the door.

CHAPTER 18

RYAN WAS RARELY nervous when he flew. But this morning was different. The eleventh named storm of the season churned in the Gulf just two hundred miles southeast of Houston. Lisa had chased oil workers and fishermen from Destin to Corpus Christi, and it was growing. The plane shook and twisted through the thick clouds and sheets of rain coated the window. Ryan glanced at his uncle, who was reading the latest copy of *The Economist*, while propping his stockinged feet against the back of the seat in front of him.

The plane yawed to the right and then corrected. Ryan clamped down on the armrest and did his best to look unfazed. He squeezed the duffel between his feet and confirmed for at least the hundredth time that the notebook was still there. He'd read some of it on the trip down the coast to Los Angeles, but the thick notebook contained at least a thousand pages and chronicled most of the expeditions taken by his great-grandfather from 1920 until his death in 1976. There were many references to monkeys, but he had little time to read them in detail and discuss them in private with his uncle. They had to get to Houston.

The plane finally dipped and bounced on the flooded runway at Hobby Airport. Thad stuffed the magazine in the seat pocket and yanked on his Nikes. "Let's go." He nodded to the aisle as it cleared. Ryan grabbed the duffel and hugged it to his chest. They walked up the jetway, then through the empty ramps and hallways—no one with any sense was traveling with a category three approaching. In a few minutes, they were downstairs at the taxi stand. The air was heavy and smelled like wet carpet. The rain was falling in sheets.

"Where to?" the attendant asked.

The attendant hailed the taxi, and Ryan and Thad jumped in. Ryan thought it rained hard in Miami, but this was ridiculous. He'd never been to Houston and now he knew why. He squinted to make sense of the images distorted by the sheets of water surging down the windows. A bright flash announced the rumbling thunder that followed.

Ryan looked at Thad and unzipped the duffel.

Thad shook his head. "Not here." He nodded in the direction of the cabbie.

Ryan zipped the duffel and stared out the window as the cabbie wound through the surface streets, dodging the flooded underpasses on the interstates. The rain let up, and Ryan spotted an entrance to Rice University.

"Are we close?" he asked.

"Yes sir," the old cabbie replied in a thick drawl.

The area was an older section of town and magnificent oaks lined the streets. Small houses that looked like they were from the fifties were interspersed with large new brick homes straddling two lots. The cab pulled into a circled drive and stopped in front of two white columns framing the entrance to the two-story Colonial.

Thad slapped two twenties into the cabbie's hand and said, "This is it," as he exited the cab. Ryan followed with the duffel, getting drenched in the fifteen feet from the cab to the porch.

"You ready?" Thad asked.

"Yup." Ryan hugged the duffel and nodded.

Thad rang the doorbell. What was probably ten seconds seemed like an hour. Would Bill Martin be here? Would he help them? Would he even know who they were? Had he left because of the approaching storm? Another thunderclap made Ryan jump and nearly drop the duffel. Finally he heard footsteps and then the door cracked open.

"You fellas need some help?"

Ryan could only see a thick graying moustache and a pair of kind blue eyes framed by round glasses. He didn't discern an accent, certainly not one of a native Texan.

"My name is Thad Webster and this is my nephew Ryan."

The door opened wide. The gray-haired man extended his hand. "I'm Bill Martin. I've been expecting you."

Ryan guessed he was in his late fifties or early sixties. He was shorter than Ryan, but probably outweighed him by thirty pounds. His skin was tanned and he had a warmth that reminded Ryan of his grandpa. He directed Thad through the door and waited for Ryan to enter, patting him on his back as he stepped inside.

"So you're Zachariah's great-grandson."

"Yes sir, I am."

Bill led them down the long marble hallway lined with the most beautiful collection of minerals Ryan had ever seen. Each display glittered with bright colors and clean angles. They entered a study lined with dark, stained-wood bookcases. Rolled maps and mineral samples acting as paperweights were scattered about the room. A desk and drafting table, both covered with opened maps and aerial photographs, hugged the far wall. Bill pointed to an old brown sofa and side chair separated by an ancient coffee table on the opposite side of the room. Ryan followed Thad to the sofa. Bill eased into the faded side chair.

"You both look a lot like your great-grandfather," Bill said.

"Did you know him?" Ryan asked.

Bill grinned, and his eyes seemed to wander to a distant memory. "Yes. I knew Zachariah. He was quite a man." Bill's eyes twinkled. "I was mentored by John Henry Krick and Zachariah back when I was just a kid, a little older than you. John Henry had been traveling with Zachariah for years when I walked through his door looking for a job. The oil business was still growing back then, and he was doing consulting for the big guys and for a few mining companies." Bill paused. "Forgive my rudeness. Can I get you guys something to drink?"

"We're fine, Bill. We'd like to hear more about my grandfather. So you worked with him?" Thad said, leaning forward.

"Yes, I did. After John Henry hired me, I mostly did grunt work here in Houston while he traveled the world. I did mapping, cataloged samples he'd bring back, and prepared the material for his presentations to the companies. He traveled with Zachariah when he could, and they would go to South

America every year for a two-month expedition. When they would return, I'd spend the evenings listening to Zachariah and John Henry coach me about exploration and how to profit by taking risks." Bill sucked in a breath.

"South America?" Thad asked.

"Yes. He would never say much about the trip. They apparently found a few large oil and gas deposits up in the Amazon, but they were too isolated to be developed. But they spent at least two months a year there every year from the time I went to work in 1971 until Zachariah died in 1976."

"I assume you know why we're here?" Ryan asked.

Bill stroked his moustache. "I know when John Henry passed away he finally gave me information about where he was going every year with your grandfather. He told me no one else was to know until it was time, and that I'd know it was time when a Webster came to see me. Then I got the call from Jasper, John Henry's son in California, who told me you were on your way with some other information."

Ryan looked at Thad, and Thad nodded his approval. "We have my great-grandfather's notebook."

Ryan unzipped the duffel in his lap and placed the notebook on the table. He saw Bill's eyes widen as he stared at the scuffed leather binding.

"I also have these." Ryan pulled out the copies of Darwin's *On the Origin of Species* and the tattered Bible he'd received at the reading of the will.

Bill rubbed his moustache again and his blue eyes drifted from the book to Ryan, then to Thad. "I think we have some work to do."

Bill stood, walked to the drafting table across the room, and clicked on the overhead light clamped on the edge. It gave the room a yellowish hue. As Ryan followed with the books, he noticed his fatigue had disappeared, replaced by an electricity he'd never felt before. He was about to find out why all these men of their word rested their trust with him. He didn't understand what his grandfather meant at the time, but he was beginning to feel privileged, as if everyone else thought he had a gift, even though he kept it hidden because it had cost him dearly. And despite being nearly killed, he began to accept that privilege with pride and didn't feel so much like a kid anymore.

Bill sorted through the aerial photos and made a space in the center of the table. Then he looked up and gazed around the room. He darted to a panel in the corner of the study, pressed it hard, and it clicked open. A stack of rolled maps fell to the floor, and he plucked one from the pile. Returning to the table, he spread the map on the open areas with both hands, using a couple of rocks to secure the curled ends.

Ryan joined Thad leaning over the table. He recognized the area as the north half of South America. The map was yellowed and had been marked extensively with colored pencils. Thunder shook the overhead light and Ryan eyed Bill.

"Is this where they were?" Ryan asked.

"Yes. This was his map. It's topographic, so it shows the flood plain of the Amazon and where it may be dry. This is the area John Henry wanted me to monitor and report anything unusual to Jasper. He said when you showed up you'd have more information that would help us."

Thad studied the map for a few seconds.

"The Amazon. It's nearly four thousand miles long. Let's see if this can narrow it down," Thad said. He pointed to the notebook in Ryan's hand.

Ryan opened it on the table, and the three men began to study it. Ryan had carefully earmarked all the pages that referenced monkeys.

"The references cover three continents: Africa, Asia, and South America. I didn't have time to read them all in detail; I just looked at the time, date, and location noted in the heading of each entry."

"I think we can just focus on South America," Thad said, pointing to the map.

"Uh—right," Ryan felt stupid. He looked at Bill, who was smiling. "Sorry."

"I'm only smiling because you remind me of me when I was your age. You don't need to know everything. You're doing great."

Ryan immediately felt better.

Bill continued, "You might narrow it down further by only looking at the entries in the months of September and October. That's when John Henry traveled with your great-grandpa. It's the dry season in the area along the Amazon in Brazil."

"That's good," Ryan said. "These entries are all in chronological order. That makes it much easier." Ryan's hand quivered as he flipped through the thick book. "Here's the first entry, but it's in August 1926, way before 1976." Ryan was worried he was going too far back.

"That's the year after the Scopes Monkey Trial," Thad reminded Ryan.

Bill gave Thad a puzzled look. Ryan realized they hadn't told him what they were looking for, and he politely hadn't asked. Another clap of thunder shook the house and the light flickered. Ryan was reminded of the hurricanes in South Florida.

"We'll be fine here, son," Bill said, apparently seeing the expression on Ryan's face.

"We're looking for swimming monkeys." It sounded silly even as he said it.

Bill chuckled but stopped when Thad and Ryan didn't join in. "Really?"

"Yup," Thad added.

Bill looked at Ryan for confirmation.

"Yes. We're looking for a species of monkey that may change the way we look at ourselves and the world. My grandpa said they can swim like humans and do other things."

"I'll be damned." Bill rubbed the back of his neck.

Ryan turned his attention back to the yellowed page and read the notes scribed by his great-grandfather in blue ink.

"It says they found upright bipedal monkey-ape hybrids? What does that mean?"

"It means they walk on two legs like we do—keep reading," Thad said.

"It says they have rounded noses, gentle foreheads, and round eyes, and don't use their arms for locomotion. They're about five feet tall." Ryan looked up and saw Thad's mouth drop open. "What?" he asked.

"Bipedal hominids in South America. The only living hominids are humans and great apes, chimps, and orangutans. Except for humans, they have only been found in Africa and Asia. Their ancestors were in North America and Eurasia, but they went extinct everywhere except Africa and southern Asia."

"That's right," Bill agreed, "in the Oligocene era, about thirty million years ago."

"But what does that mean?" Ryan was confused.

"It means that if this is true, these monkeys may be hominids, ancestors of man that link us to monkeys and apes, and they are in the wrong place," Thad explained.

"It also means that the legend of Mono Grande and de Loys' monkey may not have been a hoax as first thought. These legends basically said ape-like creatures had been spotted in the South American jungle as far back as the 1500s," Bill added.

"Keep going, Ryan."

"'August 2nd—We have traveled with two Brazilian guides about 200 miles west of the City of the Mother of God.'" Ryan had no idea what that meant. He looked at Thad, who shrugged. They both looked at Bill.

"Manaus," he said matter-of-factly. "It translates to 'Mother of God.'"

Ryan's hand trembled as it drifted across the page. They were getting close to the location. "'My geologist says we are in a geologic phenomenon—an impact crater. We had to enter through a waterfall on the crater's rim. There is only one entrance and it's concealed by the falls.'"

"That's John Henry's report," Bill said. "Go on."

"'The crater is isolated from the rest of the jungle, and contains fruits and a plant species not yet cataloged. The geologist reports there are oil and natural gas seeps in the area, but too remote to develop.'"

"Hang on." Bill said.

He scrambled to the desk and grabbed a stack of aerial photos, then shuffled through the mess under the maps on the drafting table and pulled out a large color photo. Ryan could see the black-and-white aerial photos looked just like Google maps. But the colored map had various hues ranging from green to yellow to red, with arrows pointing to the red centers.

"What's this?" Thad asked.

"These are the maps of the area John Henry wanted me to monitor. I was supposed to keep his son in California updated on the encroachment of development. See these lines here?" Thad and Ryan nodded. "They're the new roads being built deeper into the Amazon. You can see the smoke plumes here and here along the road, as squatters move into the area and begin to clear the jungle to raise cattle and farm."

"So?" Ryan had to ask.

"See this area here?" Bill pointed to the corner of one of the photos. "It's about two-hundred miles west of Manaus and," he said, pulling the colored map forward, "this aerial survey shows hydrocarbon seeps in the same area. Now the crater is not as obvious, but the Iturralde Crater NASA identified a few years ago was not pronounced because of the jungle conditions and soft soil."

"So you know where this is?" Thad asked.

"Yes, yes I do," Bill replied and crossed his arms, smiling.

Ryan high-fived his uncle. They'd found the location. He was thinking about how they would get to Brazil, two hundred miles into the Amazon jungle. Then Ryan saw the next words on the paper, but didn't believe his eyes.

"Guys, listen to this." His voice shook as he read. He struggled to get the words out. "'August 4th, 1926—Camped on the south side of a lake in the center of the crater. Bathed and swam in the lake. The monkeys watched from a distance and then mimicked us. First the Australian crawl, then the backstroke. Every time, the monkeys entered the water and mimicked the stroke.'"

Ryan looked up and saw Bill and Thad, mesmerized like the young kids he'd tell scary stories to around the campfire at the summer camp where he volunteered. He grinned and read on.

"'The next morning, I spotted four of the monkeys cross from the north side of the lake and approach the perimeter of the camp from the west. I slowly approached them and left dried fruit about fifty yards away, then retreated another fifty yards. They slowly closed the distance and ate the fruit. They remained calm, as did I.'"

Thad and Bill were now leaning on their elbows on the table and cradling their faces. Ryan felt like he was reading a science-fiction novel.

"'September 14th—the encounters have grown more frequent, and we have begun to communicate through mimicking. Along the trails in the crater, we've discovered drawings carved into wood that seemed to mark the trails. The monkeys approached our camp last night and sat with us at the fire. We communicated with drawings in the soil. They were quite sophisticated.'"

"Holy shit!" Thad said. Ryan looked up. Bill was speechless.

"Sorry, go on, dude—this is getting good," Thad said.

Ryan read on. "'October 4th—we are readying for our return. The findings here are remarkable. We have noticed the monkeys favor a unique fruit, which I am unable to identify. It grows as a small plant like tomatoes, but it is yellow in color. It appears they actually cultivate it with rough tools. It is a staple of their diet. The monkeys are small in number, but a very hardy species.'"

Ryan stopped and rubbed his eyes. There was a little more to the passage. But the first sentence was underlined and enclosed in an emphatic square.

He said, "This part is underlined," and leaned in closer to the notebook. "'This species and my findings cannot yet be revealed to the world. They require further study and observation. Considering the events in Tennessee last year challenging Darwin's teachings, the world is not yet ready.'"

Ryan glanced at Thad, who smiled knowingly. Ryan knew that the words provided some satisfaction that they were on a worthy quest.

"Is that it?" Thad asked.

"No, there's a little more, but it's not underlined." Ryan followed the last lines with his finger. "'I am reminded of Darwin's observation that co-operation of individuals within a species is better than a well-equipped individual. I credit their survival to that trait and the isolation of the species in the crater. Revealing them at this point may bring their demise. Darwin wrote that forms which stand in closest competition with those undergoing modification and improvement will naturally suffer the most. I fear this will be the case with this species, if revealed and in close contact with man.'"

The passage ended, and Ryan stopped and looked up. The room was silent. A little dust floated in the light over the table, and Thad paced around the room. Bill's arms were still folded, and Ryan watched Bill's eyes tracking Thad. Thad pivoted and looked at the two.

"Bill, we need coffee, lots of it. We've got to sift through the rest of this and get a plan together."

"No problem. I'll assume you gentlemen will stay with us until the storm passes, and then we can head to Brazil. I was already planning my next business trip there."

"Thanks, Bill. That would be awesome."

Ryan wondered who Bill was referring to when he said "us." Bill strolled to the doorway. "Addy, dear, could you put some coffee on?"

"Yes, Daddy. Will they be staying for dinner?" a voice said from down the hallway.

"Yes, Addy." Bill looked back at Thad and Ryan. "My daughter thinks she has to take care of me now that her mother is gone. Gave up a great career in the Secret Service to do that. What can I do?" He raised his hands and smiled.

Ryan glanced at his uncle, who shrugged. He turned back to the notebook and read the last passage again. This time his stomach knotted a bit as the subtle became the obvious. He would be the one who would decide whether Darwin was right or not. Not about natural selection, but about the descent of man. And according to Darwin's theory, if Ryan decided to share the monkeys with the world, they would be in close competition with the deadliest species on Earth—man—and their extinction could be at hand.

CHAPTER 19

RYAN COULDN'T KEEP his eyes off her, and he didn't know why. It may have been the way she carried the tray loaded with four cups and a plate of cookies that exposed her well-defined but feminine forearms. She looked to be in her mid-twenties. Based on the way her brown eyes and dark hair complemented her naturally tanned skin, Ryan suspected the Martins had an Italian lineage. She moved with grace, and her gentle smile lit up the dark study. Despite every effort to return his attention to the notebook in front of him, Ryan's eyes tracked her across the room.

"Thad, Ryan, this is my daughter, Addy," Bill said.

Addy slid the tray onto the coffee table, grabbed two cups, and headed to the drafting table, where Bill sat on the stool. After kissing Bill on the cheek, she delivered a cup to Thad. Thad spun from the table to face her.

"Thank you, ma'am." He rubbed his hand on his jeans and then shook her hand. "Pleased to meet you."

Ryan caught a whiff of her light perfume and moved around the corner of the table to meet her as she delivered his cup, but he ran into the corner of the table with his crotch and doubled over in pain. Thad chuckled, and Ryan felt his face flush. He recovered as best he could, and grabbed the cup from her hand.

"I'm Ryan—uh, thanks for the coffee."

"You're welcome," she said, weakening his knees further with a smile. "You okay?"

He fumbled for a witty reply, but Thad cut in.

"He's fine. He does that all the time when he meets a pretty girl."

Now he was embarrassed. She laughed as she passed Thad and retrieved the last cup for her father. She returned to Bill's side, and her father hugged her. Ryan did his best to regain his composure. A gust of wind pelted the windows with rain, and the lights flickered. They all stopped and watched as the light steadied.

"The TV said Lisa will make landfall near Galveston around ten," Addy said.

Ryan had forgotten about the approaching hurricane. Bill apparently read his face again.

"We'll be fine here. We're on high ground, and we have a safe room and a generator."

Somehow Bill was a comforting presence, just like Ryan's grandpa always was. Ryan took a deep breath.

"What's this, Daddy?" Addy asked, pointing to the notebook.

"This is the notebook of Zachariah Webster."

Addy leaned back and looked her father in the eyes. "*The* Zachariah Webster?"

"The one and only." Bill looked at Ryan, his arm around Addy. "She also works as my assistant these days. She knows about my work with John Henry and your grandfather."

"So these are the people you were waiting for?" Addy asked as she smiled at Thad and then Ryan.

"They sure are. This young man is Zachariah Webster's great-grandson and this is his grandson."

Ryan plastered on his *Entourage* trolling grin.

"Will they be staying?"

"Yes, dear, they will."

"Then I'll get dinner ready." Addy kissed her dad's cheek and headed out of the study.

Thad checked his watch. "It's about five, so we should probably finish this." He nodded to the drafting table.

They spent the next four hours poring over the notebook and cross-referencing the entries with Bill's maps and the dog-eared pages of Darwin's book.

Finally, Thad grabbed a pen from the table. "What do we know?"

Ryan placed his palm on the notebook. "We know that Great-grandpa made annual entries on the subsequent trips, but only made short general references to the time and location. He wrote about the monkeys' strong social tendencies in the 1930s and estimated the population to be between sixty and one hundred. He also made several references to Darwin's work. He raised questions about Darwin's 'calculus of genetic change' in the 1947 trip, and talked about the risk of 'artificial selection,' where humans influence which species survive. In 1970, he reported he saw a group of about thirty bury a deceased monkey. He noted he'd not encountered any evidence of the death of any monkeys since their discovery, and he wondered about their age."

Thad stopped writing and looked at Bill. "What about location?"

"These aerial shots are only a few months old. Based on the aeromagnetic signature and the topography, we can tie it to the reports in the initial entries in the notebook. I think I can get us there."

"Into Brazil?" Ryan had no idea how they would get into another country, especially with all the security and customs checks he'd heard about after September 11th.

"It won't be a problem. I go there regularly to lead exploration work under contract to a few of the oil companies. I also have contacts who can get us all in on temporary work visas. Normally, I take a couple of people to help direct the seismic crews and surveyors. You two will just be part of my crew."

"How soon?" Thad asked. "We need to get there now. There are others who are not far behind."

Bill stared at his watch. "How 'bout in twenty-four hours, after this storm passes."

Thad smiled. "Dude—you must be connected."

"I've been doing this a long time."

"We'll reimburse you for everything."

Bill held up his hand. "No need. I've found two one-billion-barrel fields off West Africa and stuck big oil with a measly five-percent overriding royalty. That more than keeps the lights on around here. Besides, I made a promise to John Henry, and I intend to keep it." Bill stood. "All right then. I'll make a few calls, and the four of us will be out of here tomorrow night."

Ryan and Thad shared a quizzical glance, then Thad asked, "Four?"

"Yes, f—"

The lights cut off. No flicker or gusts of wind.

"Crap. That damn generator's supposed to kick on!"

It was pitch black in the house, but slivers of light leaked through the shutters from the streetlights. Ryan saw Bill's silhouette shuffle toward the door.

"Wait, Bill," Thad whispered, and pointed to the blinds.

Ryan noticed the lights were on across the street, and Bill froze when he spotted them.

Ryan shivered a bit as the hair on the back of his neck tingled. Every shadow was now a threat. Thad slipped through the darkness and stopped next to Bill at the door, never taking his eyes from the window.

"You have a gun in here?" Thad whispered to Bill.

Bill leaned into Thad and whispered something back. Thad nodded, and Bill moved to the old oak desk tucked against the wall opposite the window. He pulled a key from the lap drawer and unlocked the lowest drawer. Carefully, he laid a shiny black box on the desk. He pressed a few numbers on the keypad, lifted the lid, and slipped out a black handgun. Ryan had never spent much time around guns, but Thad knew them inside and out. Bill edged to a bookcase in the corner, reached to the top shelf, and pulled out a clip. Outside, Ryan saw a shadow slip past the window.

Thad saw it too. Bill ducked under the window and delivered the gun to Thad. The smell of baked chicken drifted into the room, and all three men shared the same reaction.

"Addy!" Bill yelled in a whisper.

No answer. Suddenly a dish shattered down the hallway, and Ryan heard a muffled scream. Thad spun with his back against the study door and disappeared into the blackness of the hallway. Bill followed, but stopped in the doorway.

"Drop it," a deep voice growled.

Ryan heard a clatter on the marble floor.

"Just take it easy, dude," he heard Thad say.

Bill raised his hands and backed into the study, then Thad backed in with his hands locked atop his head. A gun barrel was pressed against Thad's forehead, followed by the black glove holding it. The man was covered in black, including the mask hiding his face. He was much taller than Thad. He kept moving forward and shoved Thad into the study. Addy appeared with a black gloved hand around her neck and a gun pointed at her temple. The second asshole was much shorter. Ryan eased away from the table.

"Stop right there, kid. This is the end for you."

Ryan froze, and his stomach flopped. Instantly, the nausea and sweat roiled him. Shorty shoved Addy into the study and pointed the gun at Ryan. Only his eyes were visible through the mask, and they locked on Ryan.

"You've taken two of our faithful, and now we are going to do God's will," Shorty said.

Just as his eyes closed to fire, Ryan lunged sideways and heard two pops, each followed by the shatter of glass. Both attackers slumped to the floor. He scrambled to his feet and brushed himself off. His relief was short-lived, as two more intruders stepped into the room and aimed at the foursome.

"Don't try it, uncle. That sniper can hit you before you even think of moving." The German-accented voice came from behind the two men.

Ryan spotted a red dot on Thad's chest. So did Thad. The two men separated a bit, and a third, much larger man stepped in. His face wasn't covered. He was square-headed and sported a white flattop. He looked like an albino with black eyes. Ryan thought about all the movies where the victims always realized they would die because their attacker didn't conceal his face. The nausea and sweating worsened.

The albino pulled out a flashlight and walked to the drafting table. He shuffled through the papers and snatched the notebook. He turned to Ryan, and in one stride was face to face with him. He waved the notebook in Ryan's face.

"You and your little book are coming with us."

He shoved Ryan toward the door. Ryan stumbled and glanced up at Thad. Thad stood in front of one of the gunmen and cut his eyes across the doorway to Addy and the other assassin. Ryan remembered the look from the Primate Park, and he stopped, ready to act.

"Go, kid!"

The albino shoved Ryan again, and Ryan swung his elbow hard and caught the albino's jaw. Ryan heard breaking glass and a thud as the sniper fired. Ryan hit the floor. Three other muffled shots whistled above him. A crushing blow pierced his back, and for a moment, he struggled to breathe. Was this what it felt like to be shot? The pain disappeared, and he sucked in a deep breath as he lurched and lifted his head. The albino hurdled over his head and sprinted into the hallway. Two more shots echoed above him, and two shell casings bounced next to his face.

"You all right?" Thad yelled.

"I'm fine—go, go!" he heard Addy yell back.

He saw Thad's back as he sprinted down the hallway after the albino and heard a door bounce off its stop, then one more muffled shot. Stunned, he pressed himself to his feet, turned to the study, and scanned the room. Addy stood over two dead gunmen to his left, and another was sprawled facedown to his right atop the original attacker. Bill rose from behind the desk and hugged his daughter.

"You okay, Addy?"

"I'm fine, Dad. You all right, Ryan?" she asked.

Ryan fumbled for a reply. The room smelled like the firing ranges he visited with his uncle on occasion. The wind rushed in through the splintered blinds covering the broken window. Rain spattered on the floor. He remembered the sniper and jumped to the right.

"Don't worry about him. Your uncle took him out with one shot. I checked and it's clear out there," Addy said.

"What the hell happened?" Ryan said.

"Your uncle twisted his man into the path of the sniper's shot and then fired the guy's weapon back out the window at the sniper in the hedges."

"But what about him?" Ryan pointed to the man at Addy's feet.

"She kicked his ass." Thad said as he reentered the room, smiling proudly. "Where did you learn that?"

"My mom."

Thad and Ryan shared a puzzled look.

"Addy's mother had some very special skills, courtesy of the US Secret Service. Addy followed in her footsteps. Top of her class at the Service's training facility," Bill said.

"A freakin' Laura Croft!" Thad said.

"My mom said that if I wanted to travel with Dad I had to learn how to protect myself."

Ryan's head was spinning. A girl no more than five years his senior, who'd brought them coffee and cookies, had just helped take out two assassins and save his life. He rubbed his back.

The shutters rattled as another gust of wind blew in.

Bill stepped toward Thad. Bill was clearly shaken. "Who are these people?" He pointed to the bodies on the floor.

Ryan scowled at the dead men. "Based on the comments of these first two, I'd say they're part of the same fanatic religious group that tried to take us out in California. The other three seemed to be trying to take me alive, like the guys at our family's Primate Park in Miami."

Bill's face was panicked as he stumbled to the desk and picked up the phone.

"We gotta call the police."

"I'm gonna bet that's not working," Thad said.

Bill put the phone to his hear, then slammed it back in its cradle. He yanked a Blackberry from his pocket.

"Hold on, Bill. We need to think this through," Thad said.

"Think what through? I've got five dead bodies at my house that I can't explain."

"So if you can't explain them, why the police? They'll ask a shitload of questions, and if they don't lock us up for safekeeping until they figure this out, they'll tell us not to leave town. And they won't ever figure this out. They'll think it was a drug deal. Or worse yet, they'll run the background on these goons and think we're hiring mercenaries. And with the way the authorities are antsy about terrorists, we'll be lucky if we're not waterboarded, tossed into some remote prison, and left to rot."

Bill slipped the Blackberry back into his pocket and stared at Thad.

Thad surveyed the damage, then said, "We have to get to the monkeys. That's the only way to get these people off our backs. The storm was noisy enough to cover the gunfire. Looks like most of your neighbors evacuated. We'll clean this up and dump these guys, then head to the airport. It's the safest place for us now. We'll catch that flight to Rio tomorrow. Okay?"

Bill looked at Addy who nodded. He nodded back.

"Where's the notebook?" Bill asked.

Ryan remembered the albino had it.

Thad turned to Ryan. "I couldn't catch him. Sorry." He turned back to Bill. "That's another reason we gotta get going. It will take them a while, but they'll figure it out."

Ryan thought it couldn't get much worse. But then again, he'd thought that at least five times this week. He'd never been to Brazil—hell, he barely knew where it was—and now he would venture deep into the Amazon jungle with people he barely knew to find some swimming monkeys, if they even still existed. He thought about his pickup back home in Miami and wondered if it needed gas. He longed for the good old days.

CHAPTER 20

RYAN HUDDLED IN the dark corner of the bathroom and battled his fear. For the third time in less than a week someone wanted him dead, and they'd almost succeeded. He wasn't worried about himself now. He imagined what it would be like for Julia Webster to hear her son was dead. He felt her disbelief and the chasm of emptiness that would surely follow. His father would be of little comfort to her. That was Ryan's role in the family. He saw her face wrench in pain as the endless wailing left her curled in a ball on Ryan's bed. He longed for her hugs and the joy on her face when he returned them. He wanted to go home. He was just a boy, still only seventeen. And while he always tried to hide it, he still liked being close to his mother.

Despite the warning from his uncle, he grabbed the duffel from the floor, snatched one of the four prepaid cell phones, and ripped it from its packaging. He needed to call her. He glanced at his watch. It would be nearly 2 a.m. in Miami. He knew she would answer first, but worried about his father.

While wiping his nose with his other sleeve, he dialed the number and placed the phone to his ear. He peeked out the bathroom window and noted the rain and wind were diminishing. It rang twice, and then he heard his mother's voice.

"Hello," she whispered.

Ryan blew out a long breath. He felt better already.

"It's me, Mom."

"Oh, Ryan! I've been so worried. Are you okay?"

"Yes. I'm fine," he lied.

"Let me switch phones," she whispered. A few seconds later he heard a click and then, "Where are you?"

Ryan remembered his uncle's warnings. He'd said to only use these phones in an emergency, and even then be careful what he said. But this was his mom.

"I'm with Thad."

"But where, honey? When are you coming home?" she whispered.

Ryan hesitated. He could hear the distress in her voice, and the possibility of getting killed before he got to see her again made him want to comfort her.

"We're in Houston."

"Houston? Why?"

"One of Great-grandpa's friends is helping us."

"Helping you do what?"

"Find the monkeys."

"Where are they? You need to come home."

"I can't tell you. It's better that way."

Ryan heard a rustling over the phone.

"Give me that!" his father yelled. "Ryan. You need to get your ass back here right now."

"Forget it," Ryan bristled.

"You can say that, boy, but the offer for the Primate Park has just gone up."

"I'm going to do what Grandpa asked."

"Find those damned monkeys? You've got to be kidding me."

"We know they exist, and now we know where they are."

"That's a load of bullshit. It's a fantasy. In the meantime, your share of the park is now worth nine million."

Ryan pulled the phone from his ear and stared at it. *Nine million dollars.* Anything he wanted could be his.

"Did you hear me, son?"

"Put Mom back on."

"She's done talking to you, and so am I."

The phone went dead.

"Shit." Ryan closed the phone and stuffed it back in the duffel. He thought about his mother and the bullying she was surely getting from his father. He hated him. Not for what he did to Ryan—in a few years he'd be out of the house. He hated his father for how he belittled his mother. As soon as he was big enough, he'd stepped between them. That day marked the end of any hope of a normal father-and-son relationship. Then he realized nine million dollars would be enough to take care of his mother for the rest of her life, without his father. Ryan could be her savior and protector. He'd be proud. Then there was Sarah. Nine million would even get her attention. She'd be hanging all over him.

The reality of the situation washed away the pipe dream. These people, whoever they were, would not go away. They seemed committed to his death one way or another. He needed to be just as committed. The only way out was to find the monkeys. Seventeen or not, he was stuck. He wished there was another, someone else besides him. There wasn't—he was it.

He sucked in a deep breath and washed his face in the basin. He wiped his face with a towel and then looked at himself in the mirror. He looked older. Maybe he was growing up, or maybe he was just dragging. He stared at the man in the mirror and for some reason wondered what Sarah was doing. Was she waiting for him? He'd promised to let her know how things were going. He hadn't. If he went much longer, he knew she'd dump him. He turned back to the bag, pulled out the phone, and dialed her cell phone. He'd keep it short, and he wouldn't tell his uncle.

"Hello?" she said.

"Hi, Sarah. Sorry for waking you up."

"Ryan Webster, where have you been?" she said.

He fought the guilt and said, "I'm sorry. I don't have much time."

"Where are you?"

"I can't tell you."

There was silence on the phone and then, "Okay. Then where are you going?"

"I can't say!" he said.

Another long pause.

"Look, Ryan. You said you'd call and let me know where you were going. If you don't trust me enough to tell me, then maybe we aren't right for each other."

Ryan wondered why he called. He was trapped. He was certain she'd follow through with the threat, and Ryan would be left with nothing. He'd never find another Sarah. But now he wasn't sure he cared.

A knock on the bathroom door startled him, and he nearly dropped the phone in the sink.

"You okay in there?" Addy asked.

"Yeah. I—uh—I'll be out in a second."

"Okay"

"Who the hell is that?" Sarah screeched over the phone.

Ryan had to think quickly. "I'm in a unisex bathroom."

"You're calling me from a bathroom?"

He could hear her disgust peppered with some disbelief, and he felt strangely guilty. He wanted to distract her attention for some reason. He didn't want her to know about Addy.

"I gotta go."

"Ryan, you tell me where you're going or we're finished!"

"I really have to go. Gotta get on a plane," he lied again.

"You tell me where," she demanded.

"Bye." Ryan slammed the phone shut and leaned on the sink. He looked back into the mirror. He wasn't looking at a boy or a fool anymore—he was certain he was looking at a man—one who lived up to his promises.

CHAPTER 21

CYRUS JAMMED HIS finger into the button on his desk phone again and coiled, awaiting an answer. It had been ten hours since the breathless call from Karl exclaiming he had the notebook but he was waiting on the weather to clear enough in Houston. The last report said the G5 was one of the first to leave after Lisa had moved north, and the ETA was 11 a.m. in Miami. Cyrus glanced at the digital clock imbedded in the phone. It was 11:01.

"Yes, sir," a man efficiently answered.

"Where the hell is he?"

"We have them on approach, sir. Here in five, at your office in twenty."

"Make it fifteen. I don't care if you have to land that damned thing downtown. Get him here quickly."

Cyrus killed the speakerphone and shot up. His chair slammed into the wall behind him. He knew they were close. He also knew they'd missed another opportunity to secure the boy and control the situation.

He stormed to the plate-glass window and glared out over Biscayne Bay.

"Shit!" he yelled to absolutely no one.

He hated not being in control. The boy and his goofy uncle were headed to Brazil. They were getting close—close to the secret to his salvation—and he was playing catch-up again.

Cyrus paced. He looped by the desk to check the clock that crawled two minutes when he thought five passed. Each time he cursed and repeated another lap. Finally the door opened, and the haggard German entered. Karl grinned and victoriously held the notebook over his head.

"It's about time. How could you miss them?" Cyrus asked.

Karl's celebration was over. He lost the grin and trudged to Cyrus's desk.

"Let's see it."

Cyrus dropped into his chair and Karl stepped beside him, placed the tattered notebook on the desk and opened it to the first red-tabbed page.

Karl stuck his thick finger into the page and gave Cyrus the summary of the relevant passages. Karl paused. "So the story your father told was right."

Cyrus saw there were more tabs in the book. He desperately wanted confirmation of his father's reference to immortality.

"What else?" He pointed back to the book on the desk.

Karl reached down and flipped to the next marked page. "This entry shows they can swim and they learned strokes from the expedition team."

Cyrus slapped his knee. "I'll be damned. Swimming monkeys. It's true." The second most unbelievable part of his father's story was true. That bode well for the most important part of the legend. He felt relieved and vindicated for his obsession.

Karl flipped to the last marked entry. "They were able to communicate," he said tersely.

"Communicate?" Cyrus asked as he looked up at Karl.

"Yes, sir. Through drawings and mimicking."

Cyrus wanted to cheer. If they could communicate, then the last trait, the most important trait, was that much more likely. He waited for the good news.

"Webster reported they cultivate and eat a tomato like fruit. It says they bury their dead and use tools, and he questions their age. Then he warns that the species should not be revealed. He references Darwin—then the entries end in 1976."

Karl stopped, and Cyrus's euphoria disappeared into the pit of his stomach.

"What? He didn't verify the last thing my father told us about their longevity?"

"No, sir. The entries just stopped."

Cyrus was lost. He'd been certain the notebook would verify the key to his near immortality. His father's work had shown the transfer required the host to be alive and have the trait. All the money, the murder of his father, and thirty years of his life hinged on the confirmation of that trait. But it wasn't mentioned. Was that the one lie his father told as revenge against his ungrateful son? Had the old man reached out from the grave to stick it to him one last time?

Cyrus noticed Karl staring at him. He pondered his options.

"Get Grandby on the phone."

Karl walked to the opposite side of the desk, spun the phone around, and dialed. After clearing with the assistant, Karl offered the receiver to Cyrus.

"Put him on speaker."

Karl hit the button and slid the base toward Cyrus.

"Charles?"

"Yes, Cyrus. I hope you have good news. My people said your fellas had a run-in with a few Crusaders in Houston?"

"Charles, we took care of them. We have the notebook. It verified that there is a species of bipedal hominids that appear to be social and able to communicate in the Amazon."

"So you know where they are?"

"They're in Brazil, about two hundred miles west of Manaus."

"Great. Let's go get them and this thing will be over. I have a team of anthropologists staging with my extraction team, and they can be there Saturday."

"Sorry, Charles. We have the approximate location, but we'll have to trace them from Manaus. We need a little more help."

There was an uncomfortable pause on the other end of the call.

"You don't have the exact location?"

"No. How about that help?"

"The help is not the problem."

Cyrus glanced across the desk at Karl. Karl just shrugged.

"I just got a report from my source inside the STB. They have the inside track. They think they have someone on the inside, and they think they know the location. If they get there first, they'll destroy everything, especially these monkeys."

Cyrus didn't want to hear that. "Charles, that just can't happen. We have to get there first."

"I agree, my friend. But unless we have another angle to slow the STB down, it's a possibility."

"Look, can you have your point man talk to Karl and help us coordinate resources in Manaus? In the meantime, I have one other angle to work here. Neither you or I can afford to lose this discovery."

"I agree." There was another pause. "What's your angle, if I may ask?"

Cyrus looked at Karl again and said, "I share your belief and want to expose the fraud of religion." He smiled at the white lie, and Karl did too. Cyrus didn't believe in God. After all, God had never answered any of his childhood prayers and only brought him pain and misery. Once he abandoned his mother's religious beliefs and took matters into his own hands, things got much better—at least for him. But what others believed was of no concern.

"Okay. Karl, call the number we gave you yesterday. I'll be sure my men cooperate. But time is running out."

"Got it, Charles. We'll be back with you soon. With better news," Cyrus said.

"Great. Will you send me copies of the notebook?"

Cyrus saw the trap. He didn't want Grandby running to the press prematurely.

"We'll get them to you once we have the monkeys."

There was another long pause.

"All right."

CHAPTER 22

JACOB REMINGTON WAS devastated by the report. Three more Crusaders lost, and the boy was getting closer to a revelation that could destroy the foundation of the society his grandfather had prayerfully built. These Crusaders weren't the first to give their lives to protect God's word, and they certainly wouldn't be the last. After all, Richard the Lionheart led the holy warriors into battle to protect the word of God and reclaim Christianity's holy land. Yes they killed, but they did it in the name of God and earned a place at His side in Heaven. Still, Remington was the leader of the flock, and he felt the burden of that responsibility. He crumpled the report in his fist, knelt in the corner of his sparse cabin, and prayed for God to welcome their souls and to protect those he'd send after them. He asked for God's mercy on his soul and for the grace and wisdom to end this threat to the foundation of the Bible. He rose to his feet and walked to the door. He glanced back at the Bible on the nightstand and rededicated himself to protecting it, no matter what it took.

He opened the door and smelled the fresh pines that shaded him from the hot August sun. As he walked along the gravel path, he was vividly aware of every living creature in the forest. Squirrels scampered from branch to branch while jays squawked and chipmunks scurried in the underbrush. He thanked the Lord for reminding him that He created all things, and that His most precious creation was man—not a monkey. People were created in God's image, and they were not a product of some disgusting process of inbreeding and evolution. Darwin was inspired by the devil, and had admitted that his work resulted in abandoning the idea of a Divine Creator. The Society was righteous in its belief and chosen by God to defend his words with their lives.

Remington entered the log-framed headquarters and quickly made his way to his office. Blackmon paced just outside. He looked like he'd been to hell. His face was scratched and pale and the sling over his right shoulder suspended his left forearm. It was tightly wrapped in white gauze. His normally square shoulders sagged, and his eyes conveyed disbelief.

"You look like hell." Remington quipped. "Get in here." He marched into his office and leaned against the front of his desk, arms crossed.

Blackmon drifted in and closed the door. "They knew we were coming."

"Who?"

"I'm not sure."

Blackmon was not making sense. Remington knew he was always reliable, matter-of-fact, and never flustered. He certainly was now.

"Greg, take a seat and let's take it from the top."

Blackmon curled around the side chair and dropped into the seat. Remington listened as Blackmon described the botched mission in Houston and the mercenaries that killed his Crusaders.

"Who were they?" Remington asked. If there was another group involved, he needed to know what they were up against.

Blackmon rubbed his chin with his good hand. "They're not friendly with the boy," he said, thinking out loud.

"So what's your best guess?"

"The only group that tracks us closely is Grandby's."

Remington hated even mentioning the Godless man's name.

Blackmon shifted in the chair. "I think it's him. We've caught two of their people trying to infiltrate our ranks. They were all over us in 1994 when talk of Ardi first surfaced in Ethiopia."

"That would make sense," Remington said. "This discovery in the hands of the atheist could advance his efforts against organized religion and give his Darwinian colleagues more scientific fodder. But why protect the boy? It doesn't make sense."

"Because they don't know where he's headed. They want him alive so he can lead them to the discovery."

"So you think they're helping them?"

Blackmon shook his head. "No. I think they tried to kidnap him, but the uncle and that geologist somehow thwarted their abduction."

"His uncle and a geologist took down a band of mercenaries better trained than our Crusaders? That's ridiculous." Remington pushed himself away from the front of the desk and paced until he was behind his high-back leather chair. He leaned forward on his elbows and glared at Blackmon, awaiting his reply.

Blackmon squirmed. "I know—I know. The only people in that house were the boy, his uncle, the geologist, and his daughter. We checked out the geologist. He's around sixty, no military training, as mild-mannered as they come."

"So that leaves the daughter?" Remington asked.

"I guess so. The daughter and the uncle. We know the boy has no skills," Blackmon said. "If Grandby's in the picture, the threat is even larger. He could control the flow of information and shape it to his benefit. Remember his discovery of one of the lost books of the Bible?"

Remington didn't need to be reminded. He'd watched his seventy-year-old father battle Grandby on that one and lose. Just like Richard the Lionheart had turned back before reaching Jerusalem, his father had given up too soon. It had cost them twelve Crusaders in the process, and his father died two months later. Several of the most influential Society members thought he'd failed God's calling, and Remington saw that eat away at his father until it killed him. He wouldn't let that happen here.

"All right. I want all our resources on this one. Greg, you get down there and be certain this never sees the light of day. Destroy them—before they destroy us."

Blackmon left, and Remington stepped to the plate-glass window overlooking the green hills of the Smoky Mountains. He knew that if a living species of the great apes were found in South America, it would decimate his membership. The hard-core believers were dying off of old age, and the new believers were raised on cell phones and iPods, and were susceptible to scientific arguments. A live specimen would dominate the media for years to come. The Society of True Believers would go the way of the Knights of the Roundtable and disappear into a mythical world—and he would have failed God's calling, just like his father.

CHAPTER 23

RYAN STUDIED HER when she wasn't looking. Addy was myste-
riously attractive, and as he'd discovered in Houston, quite deadly. Her demeanor was kind and friendly, and yet below the smooth, tanned skin, dark
eyes, and soft black hair lived a deadly tempest. She was different than any
girl in school, and just watching her made him feel like a man, not a boy.

It had been a long eighteen hours since they headed to George Bush
International in the tail end of a hurricane and caught the first flight to Rio.
When they arrived, they'd hopped a private jet and were now headed for
Manaus. The jet was some kind of timeshare, but Ryan wasn't complaining.
He guessed Bill was Michael Jordan-rich, courtesy of the big oil companies
shoveling the cash to his accounts on a daily basis.

The Citation X had four leather seats in the forward section of the
cabin. Addy sat facing Ryan on the left side of the cabin and Bill and Thad
faced each other on the right. Ryan watched Addy survey the ground below.
She glanced at him and caught him staring. He froze for a moment, not
knowing what to do.

Addy grinned. "Look down there."

She pointed out the oblong window. Ryan leaned to his left and
looked out. The jungle was a deep green, with the treetops forming a continuous canopy. Thin, diffuse clouds seeped from the jungle and formed
scattered clusters of fog.

"You see, these rainforests create their own weather. Some of those treetops are over one hundred and thirty feet tall, and as the rainforest breathes, it sucks in CO_2 and exhales water vapor and oxygen."

"It's amazing." How stupid was that reply?

He watched as the jungle gave way to a huge river that stretched as far as he could see. The main body of the river was wider than any lake he'd seen in Florida, and it was flanked by countless ribbons of smaller tributaries that wound in and out of the jungle, forming thousands of islands. The water in the river appeared divided: black water in one half and blue water in the other. It was perfectly symmetrical, with no mixing of the two colors.

"It's the Rio Negro, the black river," Addy explained. "It enters just outside of Manaus and joins the Rio Solimoes to form what the Brazilians call the Amazon. They call the upper Amazon Rio Solimoes, from Manaus to the Peruvian border."

Addy smiled at Ryan again, and he relaxed and decided he'd not try to impress her like a high school boy. She had obviously been here before, and he was enjoying learning from her.

"Okay, guys," Bill interrupted, "we'll land, roll to the FBO, and wait on the cars there. Since we cleared customs in Rio, it will just be a brief check here. Remember, you two are part of my seismic crew here to plan our next shoot. My guys have already greased the right palms, so you shouldn't have any problems."

"Is anyone meeting us?" Thad asked.

"Paulo Machado. He's led all of my expeditions here. He's an ex-federal policeman too, so he doubles as my security."

"So we should be relatively undetected?" Thad asked

"As best we can. I asked Paulo to keep it quiet and not let our guides know where we're headed until the last minute," Bill said, glancing at Thad, then Ryan. "With the kind of people chasing you two, we need to take every precaution we can."

"Sorry about that, dude," Thad said.

"Look. I want both of you to know I owe my life to Zachariah. He took me under his wing and taught me how to be confident in my abilities and take the right chances. Worked out pretty good," he said, looking around the cabin. "I'm doing this because if he thought this was that important, it's important to me. No apologies necessary."

Ryan was impressed with Bill's reply. Bill was another man of his word, just like Ryan was trying to become.

"I've been thinking about those thugs at your house," Thad said. "They were obviously two separate, and apparently competing, groups."

"Competing for what?" Bill replied and crossed his arms.

Ryan saw Thad nod in his direction. He squirmed again.

"I think one group wants our friend here so he can take them to the monkeys." Thad leaned forward, looked Bill in the eyes, and whispered, "This other group seems to just want to kill him."

"No need to whisper, you jerk. I'm right here!" Ryan said.

Bill leaned across the aisle and grabbed Ryan's forearm.

"*This jerk* just saved your life, son. You may want to rephrase your comment."

Ryan shrank in his seat. "Sorry, sir."

Bill patted his forearm and leaned back in his seat. "That's understandable, son, especially since it's your young life. Who do you think they are?" he asked.

"Well, I am pretty certain the albino German and his team are working with a guy named Cyrus Shultz," Thad said.

"You know his name?" Addy said. "Why not just turn him in?"

"I wish it were that easy. My nephew and I promised to find the monkeys and protect them. I'm pretty certain the authorities would gum that all up, and we'd be answering questions for the next six months—maybe even get thrown in jail ourselves."

"Shultz. I've heard that name before," Bill said as he shook his finger in the air. Then his eyes widened. "Yes. I remember now. There was a Shultz Zachariah mentioned several times that he'd met in the sixties. He wasn't very complimentary. The guy would ride others' coattails, and then try to take credit for the work. Tried to steal Zachariah's work."

"I'll bet that's the dude," Ryan said. "My grandpa warned us about his son, and said he'd kill to get the secrets of the swimming monkeys."

"But why?" Bill asked.

"I think it has something to do with the Bible and evolution. The missing link and all that stuff."

Thad slowly wagged his head. "I think there may be something else."

Ryan looked at his uncle and waited. Bill and Addy stared at him, too.

Thad scanned the three of them. "Don't look at me like a tree full of young owls. I'm not sure what, but it's just a hunch. If you remember, the albino took the notebook first. There's something else they're after."

"What about the other guys at the house?" Addy asked.

"I think they're the same guys Ryan and I ran into in California. It may be some kind of radical Christian group."

"Why do you say that?" Bill said.

"Well, just before they tried to pop him," Thad pointed at Ryan, "they quoted some Bible verse or something."

Bill looked up in thought. "You know, there's a group called the Society of True Believers I've read about. They were formed just after the Scopes Monkey Trial in the twenties to protect the teaching of creation in the Bible. Zachariah would mention them sometimes in frustration. They'd try to slow his expeditions. Rumors were they had an extremist arm made up of individuals who called themselves Crusaders."

"Like the Crusaders in the holy wars?" Ryan asked. He wasn't good at history, but he remembered the stories. He knew the Crusaders had killed anything in their path in God's name, and now *he* was in their path.

"Yup."

"Oh shit," Ryan said.

"It's okay, dude. We got your back," Thad said.

"Yeah, Ryan, we'll take care of you." Addy reached over and touched his knee. Her touch electrified him. She touched him in a way that said more than *I'll help protect you*. He wasn't sure if that was true or if his mind wanted him to feel that way. Ryan looked back at Thad, who gave him a thumbs-up.

Ryan felt the jet bank to the left, and he looked to the western horizon. The river wound through the jungle to the edge of the Earth. He noticed several roads cut alongside the river. The road to the north terminated in a thick cloud of white smoke. He looked at Bill. "We need to get out there right away."

"We'll get there as quick as we can. Believe me, you don't want to be making that trip at night. We'll stay here tonight, and then we'll go as far as we can by chopper tomorrow."

One more night—another chance for something bad to happen. Ryan wanted to get there now. Surprised by his commitment, he thought about the boy who'd been striving for total irresponsibility just a week ago. That boy was gone, and he guessed this was what becoming a man was all about. He thought about the decision he'd face once he found the monkeys, and wondered if he'd be ready to make a decision on behalf of the world. Yes, becoming a man meant more than turning eighteen. It meant being accountable for the decisions he'd make. His eighteenth birthday would be spent in the jungles of Brazil. And his first decision as a man would be a decision *for* man.

CHAPTER 24

RYAN WAS JOLTED back to earth by the rough landing and to a reality he'd avoided, floating above the clouds: The people trying to kill him could be waiting. The sensation was similar to what he felt before each race in his high school swim meets, multiplied by about a million. As the jet maneuvered off the runway and headed to the FBO, everyone scurried to pack up, pull out their passports and other documents, and prepared to be boarded by local customs agents. No one talked, and everyone seemed to ignore Ryan.

He decided to follow suit, and rubbed the goose bumps from his arm. He pulled his passport from his duffel. The jet quickly came to rest in front of the glorified hangar, and the co-pilot hustled to open the door. Ryan hugged his duffel in his lap and propped up his right elbow, holding up his passport in anticipation of inspection.

Ryan felt a hand wrap around his forearm, and he jumped, nearly dropping the passport.

"Relax." Bill said. "You'll be fine. These guys will come on board, give you a serious scowl, glance at your passport, and mess up a page with their stamp. Then they'll send us on our way."

Bill released Ryan's arm. Ryan glanced back at Addy who was seated facing him. She smiled without comment, then looked out the window.

Two black SUVs pulled next to the jet. A pair of brown-skinned men in green slacks and white short-sleeved shirts marched from the FBO doors. The co-pilot met them at the bottom of the jet's stairs and Ryan carefully watched as they exchanged papers. He scanned the area and spotted a driver near the hangar leaning against his parked fuel truck. The driver was staring at the jet and talking into a cell phone. The goose bumps returned, and Ryan tried to rub them away again. He knew anyone could be helping the Crusaders. He continued to sweep the area, and spotted another man dressed in dirty, light-gray overalls walking just inside the hangar's open doorway. He tracked him across the doorway and assured himself: If he didn't look at the jet, he wasn't a threat.

"Welcome to Manaus."

Startled, Ryan looked at the brown-eyed Brazilian standing in the aisle of the jet. The man eyed him. Ryan took a deep breath and tried to hide his nerves.

"Passport, please."

The man extended his open hand without taking his eyes off Ryan's. Everyone in the cabin looked at him. Trying to steady his hand, he handed the passport to the agent. He'd gotten his passport for several family trips to Europe and Mexico, but at this point, he never wanted to go out of the country again. He pushed from his mind the vision of fighting for half a piece of bread in a dark prison cell and focused on the Brazilian.

The agent flipped through a few pages, then stopped and said, "What is your business here in Manaus?"

Ryan remembered Bill's instructions. "Just here to help Mr. Martin plan his seismic survey, sir," he said as he looked across the aisle at Bill.

"Mr. Martin, passport please."

Bill handed him his thick passport just as the shorter agent entered the cabin and smiled.

"Mr. Martin, it's good to see you, my friend. Here to find us another discovery?"

The agent mumbled something in Portuguese to his partner, who turned to Addy and Thad.

"Passports, please."

He gathered the documents and began stamping the passports in the galley of the plane.

"Emerson, my friend, it's good to see you too," Bill said as the shorter agent shook his hand.

Ryan exhaled and blew off the pressure. The taller agent returned, distributed the documents, and left. Bill continued his conversation with the shorter agent as they all gathered their bags and made their way down the stairway to the SUVs. The agents returned to the FBO as the driver and passenger doors of the SUVs opened in unison.

Two of the men were heavy-set and dressed in poorly fitting black suits—obviously drivers. The third man stepped from the passenger's side of the first SUV and advanced toward the group. He was a little shorter than Ryan and wore a black silk shirt that hung over his stocky frame past his waistline. His straight gray hair covered his ears and framed his tan face. Ryan spotted a bulge at his hip and knew why he wore an untucked shirt.

Bill stepped forward and the two men shook hands, then hugged. Addy stepped forward and hugged the man as well.

Bill led the man to Ryan. "Paulo, this is the young man I told you about," he said.

"A real pleasure to meet you, Ryan. I am Paulo Machado." His grip was firm, and Ryan thought he might not let go.

"And this is his uncle, Thad."

Paulo shook Thad's hand and nodded without comment. "We must go. Bill, I have you and Addy with me. We can conduct a little business on the way. Ryan and his uncle are in the next car." He motioned to the SUVs.

The luggage had been loaded, and they were quickly on the boulevard into town. The thick jungle flanking the road gave way to clusters of warehouses and assembly plants, occasionally separated by a barren sandy lot or a small plot of jungle. Shacks and apartments along with individual homes were scattered among the industrial sites. Many of the buildings looked old and in disrepair, but a few were modern and glistened in the tropical sun. As they moved closer to the city, they passed a sports complex with an ancient open-air stadium. The low-slung roof encircling the top of the stadium looked like a flying saucer and caught Ryan's eye.

"Not quite Sun Life stadium," Thad said as he looked up from the Fodor's Travel Guide he'd snagged at the airport in Houston.

"I think I'm missing it already," Ryan said.

"Yeah, I remember the feeling, dude. It will pass after a while. My first tour, I was homesick until I heard my first gunfire, then I was just scared shitless." Thad laughed as he finished the sentence.

Ryan faced Thad. "Do you think we can do this Uncle T?"

"Absolutely."

The fact that Thad's reply came without hesitation helped. Thad went back to studying the guide, and Ryan continued to assess the urban landscape. They sped past what looked like the center of a university, with manicured lawns, trees, and several tennis courts next to an Olympic-sized pool. Smaller skyscrapers were scattered about the skyline with a few cathedrals, and smaller, much older buildings in between. The architecture reminded Ryan of family trips to Europe, and he guessed some of the buildings were over 150 years old.

The road became six lanes, one-way, and banked around to the left as they caught a brief view of the docks along the river. They were jammed with multilevel boats and ferries. The river disappeared behind them, and they entered the guts of the city.

"Centro," Thad commented. "That's what they call this area."

The driver smiled and nodded. "Your hotel is right here, gentlemen," he said. He pulled to the curb and a doorman opened Ryan's door.

"Welcome to Manaus."

"Uh—thanks." Ryan didn't know what else to say.

"Obrigado," Thad said as he followed Ryan out of the Range Rover.

Ryan turned back and wrinkled his nose.

"It's *thank you* in Portuguese," Thad said, holding up his travel guide.

Ryan chuckled, but then remembered where he was. He surveyed the hotel entrance. The hotel was tucked snugly between two other buildings. Plate-glass windows ran from ceiling to floor and put the entire lobby on display for passersby. It reminded Ryan of the storefronts in New York City. To the right of the main double doors, the wooden front desk stretched half the length of the room. The desk and drop ceiling framed the clerks and the honeycomb of key boxes behind them. To the left of the doors, thick furniture completed the effort to mimic a cozy living room.

As he stepped across the sidewalk, Ryan's eyes burned, and he smelled the thick exhaust fumes. A couple of bellmen hustled by, and he noticed a man reading the paper in a high-back armchair in the lobby to the left.

Thad trotted past and entered the lobby first, eyeing the same guy. The man stood, and Thad stopped. Paulo appeared, waved to the man and directed Thad and Ryan to the desk. Bill and Addy followed. Paulo nodded to the desk clerk, who quickly produced a handful of envelopes. Paulo grabbed them and dealt them out like cards. Ryan slipped the envelope open and found a room key and a small cell phone.

Paulo looked at Ryan. "The phones are secure and you may use them to contact me or each other only. All the numbers are in the address book. Only use them if absolutely necessary. Do not call the States with them." He turned to Bill. "We're all on the same floor. I have two men who will be stationed on the floor all night."

"Thanks, Paulo. I'd like to go to the heliport immediately and review the flight plan and provisions for our trip tomorrow morning," Bill said, stuffing the phone into his pants pocket.

"I'd like to go along too, Bill. I have a little experience in critical missions, and think I could be of some help," Thad said.

Bill nodded. After Thad's actions at Bill's house, Ryan guessed Bill knew Thad had more than enough experience.

"Can I go too?" As soon as the words left his mouth, he wanted to swallow them. He sounded like a scared little boy. He shrank back from the group a bit and lowered his head, pretending he was checking his duffel. Bill cut a glance to Thad, who quickly answered.

"Dude, you'll be bored to death. You two stay here and get some grit. Two people can move around without drawing any attention."

Bill leaned in and Addy gave him a peck on the cheek. Addy turned to Ryan and gently touched his forearm. He thought he'd melt right there.

"Come on. I'll buy you dinner, and you can tell me about your last week."

Paulo nodded to the man in the lobby, who directed Ryan and Addy to the elevators.

"Leave your bags here and my men will get them to your rooms," Paulo said to Bill and Thad. He pointed to the lobby door. Another thick, square-jawed man dressed in an untucked silk print shirt appeared in the lobby and said something in Portuguese to one of the bellmen, who quickly snatched the bags and dropped them on his dolly.

Thad called over his shoulder to Ryan. "See you, dude."

Ryan cleared his throat and yelled, "Later, dude," trying to impress Addy.

She just grinned, shook her head, and stepped into the open elevator. Ryan slinked in after her with Paulo's man in tow.

They were quickly on the sixth floor. High enough to be inaccessible from the street, and low enough to escape a fire, Ryan noted. The door opened, and they made their way down the narrow hallway. Addy stopped at 605 and had a quick exchange in Portuguese with their handler.

She turned to Ryan. "I'll come get you in half an hour, and we'll have dinner in your room."

Ryan pushed from his mind erotic images of Addy in his hotel room.

"Okay?" she said, waiting for his reply.

Ryan's face warmed like a hot plate. "Uh—that's cool. Thirty minutes."

She disappeared into her room. Ryan could have kicked himself down the hall. What a stupid answer. She probably knew what he was thinking, and was laughing in her room right now.

Ryan dragged his duffel to 607, with the handler behind him. He opened the door and said, "Obrigado."

The stocky man smiled. "We will be just down the hall," he said, and pointed to two chairs against the wall by the elevator.

Ryan entered the room and probed for the light switch. The daylight had quickly disappeared, and the room was dark. He found the switch and popped it on. The room was a suite, with a dark wood parquet floor. What looked like antique furniture was assembled on a multicolored Persian rug and formed a sitting area along the left wall. To the right, a large round antique table and four chairs sat by a long, draped window. All the wood was polished and Ryan thought he smelled his mother's Lemon Pledge. Brass lamps and assorted knick-knacks accented the room. A dark stained door to the bedroom was ajar, and Ryan spotted the huge headboard of the lush king bed covered in white linens. Bill did have some bucks. Suddenly, dinner in his room was not nearly as frightening.

He unpacked, washed up, and carefully groomed himself in the marble bathroom. He did a quick check of the room and flipped on the TV. The only thing in English was CNN International. He left it on for a moment, then clicked it off, thinking that would be more mature. The knock at the door startled him and came much sooner than he thought. He checked his watch. Thirty minutes had passed like ten.

He stopped at the door, cupped his hand over his mouth, and checked his breath. Satisfied, he forced his best smile and opened the door.

"Hi Ryan. You ready for dinner?" she asked.

Ryan was caught off guard. Addy looked stunning. Her dark-brown hair lay gently on her shoulders and framed her smooth skin, red glistening lips, gently sloping nose, and her deep brown eyes. She too had taken a little time, and the light makeup softened her strong features. Ryan realized his mouth was open.

"Sure," he blurted.

Addy breezed past and the soft scent of her perfume filled his nose. He felt the surge of hormones, and fought back the animal urges they always fueled. Addy walked to the window and gazed at the lights of the city.

"I assumed you were a meat-and-potatoes guy, so I took the liberty to order for us."

"What kind of meat?" Ryan asked cautiously.

Addy turned and gave him a playful look. "You'll like it. Don't worry—no mystery meat. It's churrasco steak."

"I like the steak part. Not too sure about the churrasco part."

"It's marinated and then grilled. Be here in a few minutes."

Addy strolled and inspected Ryan's room. Ryan thought he should say something.

"Nice digs."

"Yes. That's one thing Dad does for us. Since we travel so much, and sometimes spend nights in the middle of nowhere, he puts us up first class when he can."

"Your dad's a pretty cool guy."

"I like to think so," she said, crossing her arms.

"No. I mean helping us and all. He doesn't have to do this."

Addy turned and continued to pace around the room. "Oh—yes he does."

"Why?"

"As you can see, he's a man of his word. That's his thing. He tells me that the most important thing to him is his connection to others, and his word is what bonds them."

"Like my great-grandpa?"

"Just like your great-grandpa. My father says he learned the power of a man's word from him. They never had contracts or agreements, just a handshake and your great-grandpa's word. That's still how Dad does business today, even with the big oil companies."

"Yeah, my grandpa did the same thing. He always told me there is nothing more important than my word and my promise."

"And you promised him you'd find these swimming monkeys?" Addy asked with a wrinkled nose.

"Yes, I—" He was interrupted by a knock at the door.

"I'll get it," she said. "That's the food."

Addy checked the peephole and opened the door. She directed the attendant in Portuguese, and instantly they had dinner served on china accented with silver and what looked like Ryan's parents' Waterford crystal glasses. After receiving Addy's generous tip, the waiter dismissed himself.

"Dinner is served," she said with a wide smile.

Ryan moved to the table and took the chair directly across from Addy.

She pulled the linen napkin tucked under her fork, snapped it open, and settled it on her lap in one fluid motion.

Ryan followed suit and began to dig into the fresh greens of his salad. Before he got the fork to his mouth he froze and asked, "Is this okay to eat?"

"Yes. The hotel ensures that all the produce is cleaned, so you don't have to worry about Montezuma's revenge."

They both chuckled and began to eat.

"So about this promise you made. Why are the swimming monkeys so special?" Addy asked.

The echo of his grandfather's warning not to tell anyone made Ryan hesitate. But since Addy was risking her life to help him, and she'd already saved his once, he was sure his grandpa would approve.

"Well, I'm not sure, but I think these monkeys are more than just monkeys. I think they are an ape-monkey hybrid. On top of that, they don't just swim; they *learned* how to swim by watching my grandpa. They communicate through drawings, and they bury their dead."

"What makes that so special?"

Ryan explained his grandfather's request and the promise he'd made.

When he was done Addy said, "So what are you supposed to do?"

"Find the monkeys—save them from the fires, and then decide if the world is ready."

"Do you think the world is ready?"

This was the first time Ryan had been asked that question. He'd thought about it himself, but now he was on the spot. His shoulders sagged under the full weight of the decision. "I don't know. There's something about the monkeys we don't know yet. Once we find out what that is, maybe I can decide. But these people are trying to kill us and destroy them—so I guess my answer is not yet."

"So what do you do when you find them?"

"Get them back to the Primate Park."

"The Webster Primate Park?"

"Yep. My grandpa and great-grandpa started the park with just a few monkeys in the early fifties."

Addy's eyes lit up. "I love that place."

"You've been there?"

"Yes. My Dad took me there several times as a kid. Said that Zachariah and his son started it."

Ryan imagined Addy as a little girl, skipping down the park's paths. Then he imagined seeing her there now.

"You'll have to come back. I'll introduce you to some of my closest friends."

They both smiled.

"Looks like I may get the chance."

The conversation stalled there, and Ryan picked up his fork and continued to eat the steak. Addy did the same.

After he devoured his steak, Ryan asked, "Did you go to college?"

Addy laughed. "Of course I did. Went to the University of Texas at Arlington."

"What did you study?"

"Criminal Justice. I was always good in school and graduated when I was twenty. Then, with Mom's help, I joined the Secret Service. Spent a year training at the Rowley Training Center just outside of DC. I came home when Mom got sick."

Ryan saw Addy's eyes change at the mention of her mother. It was a topic he wanted to avoid. "So when do you go back?"

"Soon, I hope. Just like you promised your great-grandfather, I promised Mom I'd take care of Dad when she was gone. She said she was worried about him and he was keeping something for someone. I'm worried about him, too. So I agreed to work with him for a while."

"Where did you learn that judo or whatever that was at your house?"

Addy laughed hard. "From my Mom and a few training programs. And it's not Judo."

Ryan smiled. "How did your—"

The room went dark, but Ryan could see the lights outside. He started to stand, but Addy waved him back to his seat and listened. The traffic noise outside was all Ryan heard. He was convinced they'd been found, and he'd get a bullet he'd never see coming. He stirred again, and Addy waved him back into his seat. She slipped from her chair, reached behind her back, and pulled a black Sig to her side. It was one of the same guns Thad would let Ryan shoot at the range. As Ryan watched her tiptoe to the door, he felt ashamed that a woman had to protect him. Then someone knocked. Addy pressed her back against the wall and aimed at the door jam.

"Hey, dudes … how 'bout this blackout," Thad whispered through the door.

Addy glanced at Ryan, grinned, and wagged her head. Ryan just laughed. His uncle always had impeccable timing. Addy checked the peephole and opened the door. Thad strolled in and wandered to the table. He stared at Addy's unfinished steak.

"You guys done?" Thad pointed to the plate.

"Be my guest," Addy said, holstering the gun.

Thad dropped into the chair and picked up a piece of meat with his hand.

"We leave at seven a.m. The chopper looks great and the weather looks good—still dry. I've got gear for both of you at the hangar. Just dress light—it's a jungle out there!" Thad chuckled and stuffed the meat in his mouth

"I'm headed to my room," Addy said, waving. "I'll see you gentlemen in the morning."

Ryan waved back. "See you then."

The door closed and Ryan stared at his uncle. Thad's face was already covered with grease.

Thad caught him staring. "What?" he asked.

Ryan looked back at the door and thought about the decision he'd have to make. It wasn't the decision about the monkeys and whether to share them with the world that bothered him now. It was about whether the instincts of a soon-to-be eighteen-year-old were good enough to read a twenty-three-year-old woman who could kill him with her bare hands.

CHAPTER 25

THE DEMONS ONLY came at night. The cries and the yelling from the next room made Ryan bury his head in his pillow. Maybe it was inspecting the helicopter or planning the mission that brought it on, but Ryan pleaded with God to stop it. His uncle was a good man. He'd saved many lives, including Ryan's, and Ryan wondered why God would lay such torment on a good man's soul.

Ryan ended his short prayer and made the sign of the cross as he always did. He thought about Thad and then the Godless killers on his trail. He understood how someone's doubt could grow into the belief that there is no God. At times he had his own doubts—doubts he never shared with anyone. But his mother's faith always carried him through.

As the morning light crept into the hotel room, he realized soon he'd be put between the Bible and the Godless. He hoped that whatever traits the monkeys revealed and however they changed the world's view of the evolution of man, he wouldn't let down his mother or his God.

The group assembled at seven a.m. and made their way back to the airport. On the way there, Thad told Ryan jokes and showed no ill effects from the night before. Addy and Bill rode with Paulo as before. The red-on-white Bell 412's rotors were spinning when they arrived, and after the co-pilot gave a few safety instructions outside the SUVs, Bill led them to the helicopter.

A thick mist hung over the jungle at the perimeter of the airport. The morning air smelled like a doused campfire and felt nearly liquid, as the humidity put Ryan into a sweat. He followed Addy into the rear seat of the helicopter, and she quickly donned the headphones and mike. She motioned to Ryan to do the same. He buckled the three-way safety harness, and they were in the air in less than a minute.

Addy pressed her mike button. "Did you smell the smoke from the burning?" she asked.

"How could I miss it?" Ryan shot back. "Do you think they're getting close?"

Before Addy could answer, Ryan saw Paulo turn to them from the front seat and heard another click on the intercom system.

"Our recon shows they're getting close—probably a few kilometers from the entrance to the crater. We'll set down in Coari to stage in, then head north. We'll land just to the west of the crater and avoid the smoke. We'll have to pack in from there."

Thad looked back at Ryan, gave his customary thumbs-up, and grinned. Ryan was not nearly as chipper. Hollywood images of man-eating anacondas and giant crocodiles filled his head. This was not some camping trip. This was the Amazon, a part of it few human eyes had seen.

"Are there piranhas down there?" he asked, pointing to the river.

Addy reached over and touched his forearm. "It's not what you think. It's beautiful down there."

"And besides," Thad added over the intercom, "the story of man-eating piranhas was a myth created by Teddy Roosevelt's book on his hunting expedition here. The local fishermen trapped the fish in an oxbow of the river and threw in beef to get them into a frenzy. He reported they could devour a cow—or a man—alive. Hollywood did the rest." Thad turned and laughed at Ryan. *His uncle the bookworm.*

Ryan didn't reply. He didn't believe either of them. He knew he was being hunted, and the mercenaries could be waiting. The man-eating fish and the huge anaconda were the least of his worries. He scanned the dense jungle racing by beneath him as they flew parallel to the wide, ambling river. He checked his watch—they were getting close. The chopper traced the river and then banked to the left toward the small town along its shore. A single windsock adjacent to a rusted hangar marked their target. The chopper touched down. Paulo explained they'd be on the ground for just a few minutes taking on fuel, and told them to stay put. Paulo unbuckled, jumped out, and headed to the cargo compartment at the rear of the fuselage. He reappeared with a black bag and carried it to the perimeter of the makeshift airfield, where he met two men who'd arrived in an old Land Rover. Exiting the vehicle, they dumped two black duffels at his feet. Paulo quickly unzipped the bags and appeared to be counting something. Then he pulled a compact black automatic rifle from one bag, pressed the stock against his shoulder and aimed it into the jungle. He returned the gun to the bag and tossed the bag to one of the men. The man gaped into the sack and then nodded to the other. They shook hands, and Paulo loaded the duffels into the helicopter. They were back in the air after only ten minutes on the ground. They crossed over the river and streaked north, just above the jungle's canopy.

About thirty minutes into the flight, Paulo turned back to the group and pressed his mike button.

"Okay. We'll be landing in about five minutes at a small clearing just west of the crater. The site is *not* secure." Paulo looked directly at Thad. "There are reports of some indigenous people in the area who aren't too happy with the clearing that's going on, as well as reports of squatters who are tracking the crews clearing the jungle."

Thad nodded and began to pull on a small green vest.

Paulo looked at Addy. "Thad, Addy, and I will get off first."

Addy nodded and pulled another green vest from underneath her seat.

Paulo turned to Ryan. "Do not leave the chopper until we've unloaded the gear and secured the area. I want Bill out the door next, then Ryan last. Okay?"

Addy pulled the Velcro straps of her vest tight—a bulletproof vest. Although Ryan was shivering, he broke into a sweat. His hands shook. He crossed them on his lap and held them still. He realized he was last out in case they were under fire. They were trying to protect him.

"Ryan? You okay?" Paulo asked.

Ryan could only nod.

"Hey sport, you'll be fine. Most likely there will be no problems. Just get your ass back on this chopper if all hell breaks loose," Thad said.

Paulo reached under his seat and produced two vests. He handed one to Bill and passed the other over the seat to Ryan. No instruction was necessary. As Ryan yanked the vest over his head, he heard the sound of the rotors change and felt the chopper slow. He fumbled with the side strap of the vest, but Addy reached across the seat, untangled the strap from the seat belt, and gently secured it against his side.

"You'll be fine," she mouthed without the mike.

As the chopper descended, Ryan focused on his breathing. This was it. In minutes they'd be on the ground just miles from what his grandfather called the most important discovery of the past two thousand years. And if he was right, mankind would never be the same. And neither would he.

CHAPTER 26

RYAN WATCHED THAD'S eyes trace the perimeter of the small opening in the thick jungle. Addy did the same as the chopper hovered and then dipped its nose toward the makeshift heliport. Ryan heard the pitch of the rotor get louder, and their descent slowed. He was amazed the cabin could hold together. It felt like he was in a paint-shaker. Gripping the seat's bench, he braced himself for the landing.

Both Addy and Thad were focused on the same spot. Two brown-skinned men dressed in khakis with backpacks and rifles stood at the edge of the pad and shielded their faces from the blades' wash. Ryan got a whiff of burning wood, and Thad looked up to the right and nodded to Addy. Just above the treetops, Ryan spotted the thick gray smoke drifting in from the east. The fires were now between their landing area and the crater. They were running out of time.

The chopper touched down, and Paulo shoved his door open and darted, head down, to the cargo hatch. He returned with the duffel and handed two short black automatic rifles and two magazines to Thad. Thad passed a rifle and magazine back to Addy, and she quickly jammed the magazine into the weapon and cocked it.

"An MP5," she said, patting the stock. "Stay put till we call you, okay?"

Ryan nodded. "Just let me know when you're ready."

Thad and Addy exited the chopper, and Paulo directed the two Brazilians to join them. The five fanned out in a perimeter and began scanning the jungle through the sights of their rifles. Ryan remained in the helicopter with Bill and gawked at the huge trees. The canopy reached to the sky, higher than the transplanted Amazon trees at the Primate Park that his grandfather had imported from Peru in the 1940s. He guessed the treetops were at least as high as the 150-foot radio tower they had at the park. In the setting sun, the canopy cast a long shadow across the clearing. Ryan peered into the jungle, but could only see shadows and silhouettes, some moving about in the darkness. A band of squirrel monkeys perched in the branches, watching the drama unfold from the grandstands. He wondered who else was watching. He checked the sweat rolling down his forearms and saw he was still gripping the seat.

Bill said, "Let's get ready, Ryan." He unbuckled his seatbelt, turned to the door and tightened his bulletproof vest.

Ryan let go of the seat, wiped the sweat from his eyes and followed Bill's lead, yanking the Velcro straps until the vest squeezed his ribcage. The protection felt better tight.

"I think they're ready for you gentlemen," the pilot said in a thick Portuguese accent.

Ryan spotted Paulo and Thad trotting back toward them with Addy and the other two men holding the perimeter.

"Let's go," Ryan said.

Ryan pulled the silver handle and Thad met him at the door. He exited but immediately ducked, very aware of the spinning rotors just over his head.

"Stay between me and the chopper," Thad shouted, without looking at Ryan.

The co-pilot dumped four packs on the ground. He scampered back inside the chopper. Thad guided Ryan to the packs and shoved one in Ryan's face. He slipped another over one shoulder. Paulo did the same for Bill, who grabbed the last one for Addy.

"Let's get out of here," Thad yelled as he dragged Ryan toward Addy and away from the chopper. Paulo circled his hand in the air, and the helicopter engine roared. The wind blew dry grass and dirt over their backs as they trotted to the edge of the jungle. They reached Addy and the others at the edge of the jungle, knelt, and covered their heads as the chopper rose and then faded into the distance.

Smelling smoke, Ryan noticed a haze seeping from the jungle. The reality hit him hard: He was here, on the ground, just a few miles from the legend his grandfather and his father before him had protected with their silence. Now, the fires were closing in. He didn't know if the mercenaries were waiting to stop him, but sitting in the middle of his armed entourage, he had a chance to live up to his promise.

"Okay. The guides have set up camp two kilometers to the east, just at the entrance to the jungle," Paulo said.

"What's the situation on the way? Any recon?" Thad asked.

"Yes. There are indigenous people, pipeliners, and squatters. It's hard to discern if any of our friends are among them, so we need to be careful. We'll follow the guides to camp and spend the night there. They'll take the lead, followed by Addy, then Ryan and Bill. Thad, you and I will take the rear. It's important to move as quickly and quietly as we can. Speed is our best defense. Now let's go."

Thad nodded and the guides stood and moved into the jungle. Addy slid close to Ryan and smiled.

"Looks like you're with me," she said.

"Where did you learn to do all this commando stuff?" Ryan's curiosity was getting the best of him.

Addy chuckled. "Not commando stuff—just a few tactics I learned at Rowley. Now, stay close to me. We can talk more when we get to camp."

Ryan obliged and fell in line along a thin trail through the largest collection of palms and broadleaf shrubs he'd ever seen. They were all interwoven with tangled vines that dangled from the towering canopy above and the maze of roots on the jungle floor. The band of squirrel monkeys chirped as they jumped and swung in the branches and followed the group into the jungle. Parrots perched in groups, squawking and chattering just like the parrots did at the park around sundown.

As they moved deeper into the jungle, the canopy got thick and the temperature dropped. Shafts of light illuminated the smoke as it seeped through the canopy. The sweet smell of the flora was choked off by the stench of burning wood. Ryan made a quick check behind him, and his uncle flashed a Cheshire-Cat grin back at him. Ryan forced a smile and turned back to the trail. He was surprised how easy it was for the group to move through the jungle. He couldn't believe how open it was. There was the occasional need for a machete, but he'd expected thick underbrush like in South Florida. With little daylight reaching the ground, he figured the palm saplings and green shrubbery were all that could grow. Tangled drapes of thick vines dangled above him and occasionally caused him to duck. But they were making good time. At this rate, they'd be at the camp just outside the entrance to the crater well before sundown.

"Look out, dude!" Thad yelled.

Ryan instinctively ducked and looked up at the same time. He was face to face with a giant snake dangling from one of the thick vines. Its rich green-and-white body was thick and knotted around the vine. Its huge head dangled over the path and it turned to strike at Ryan's face.

"Shit!" Ryan yelled.

"Stay still," Addy said as she ran up the trail to Ryan.

Ryan froze. Addy throttled the snake just behind its bulging jaw. It began to slowly unfurl.

"Okay, Ryan. This boa isn't quite awake for his evening meal yet. You can go ahead," she said, obviously holding back a laugh.

Ryan squatted and ducked under the snake past Addy. Thad followed. As he came face to face with Addy, a grunt escaped through his grin.

"Very funny. Thanks Addy" Ryan said.

"Don't mention it," Addy said as she released the snake and rejoined Ryan.

"Let's go, you guys. Enough goofing off. We only have a kilometer to the camp," Paulo said.

The group picked up the pace, and the light drifting through the canopy began to fade. The jungle was getting dark, and Ryan began to see an assassin in every silhouette. His shoulders and back felt the weight of the pack, and his pulse pounded in his ears. There were probably bigger snakes at night, but snakes were the least of his worries.

Up ahead, the guides and Paulo picked their way through the thickening underbrush and soon Ryan spotted the flicker of a couple of lanterns through the leaves. In just a few steps, he was standing in the center of the camp. Four tents formed a semicircle around a makeshift fire pit. The group gathered at the pit, and Paulo gave the bunk assignments. Thad and

Ryan would share a tent, so would Addy and Bill. The guides and Paulo would take the last two.

"What's the watch schedule?" Thad asked.

"You and Addy take the watch until midnight. I'll take midnight to dawn with the guides. If you see someone, don't call out. It could just be the local indigenous people checking us out. If you do confirm an intruder, call out and fire at your own discretion. Just don't hit any innocent inhabitants."

Now Ryan wasn't even entertaining the thought of sleep. Not with those instructions.

"Got it," Thad said.

"I'll take a shift." Ryan said.

"No need. We need you fresh in the morning anyway," Thad said.

Ryan knew what that meant. He stepped next to Paulo. "How far to the crater?"

Paulo nodded over his left shoulder and said, "See that glow?"

Ryan noticed the dim illumination in the distance. "Yep."

"That's the fires. The guides say the fire is five kilometers from the entrance now—burning on its own and moving slowly."

"Will it keep burning?"

"Probably. It's been a long, late dry season."

For the first time, Ryan felt concern for the monkeys. Fire was something every animal feared. Regardless of their traits, he assumed they'd either run or burn, both bad outcomes. He'd come so far and endured so much to keep his promise.

"Don't worry, dude. We'll get after it in the morning—they'll be there."

Thad's reassurance provided some relief. His uncle could read him like a book.

"Let's dump our gear. We'll have to eat MREs tonight. No fires," Paulo said.

Thad unzipped his pack and yanked out a package. "Ah, spaghetti, my favorite," he said as he headed to a tent, unzipped the flap, and tossed his pack inside. He walked to the lanterns suspended from a small tree, grabbed his canteen, and dropped onto a fallen tree. Ryan did the same, as did Addy and Bill. They shared a dehydrated dinner. Ryan tracked the guides and Paulo as they walked the perimeter. He tried to forget the reason they were searching the jungle—it would be a long, sleepless night.

CHAPTER 27

HE WAS GETTING strangled. Ryan swung his arms wildly, hoping to stop his assailant. He didn't want to go this way.

"Whoa there, killer."

He recognized his uncle's voice and opened his eyes. They burned and watered but he saw his uncle standing over him, a bandana covering his nose and mouth. The bandana pulsated as Thad panted to catch his breath.

"You were asleep. The fires are closing in. Time to get out of here." Thad tossed him a bandana. "Meet outside in five—ready to go."

Ryan bolted up, dressed, and gathered his gear. He joined the others at the center of the camp. Paulo, Addy, and Bill were talking with Thad. They all had MP5s slung over their shoulders and their faces were covered with bandanas. It looked like they were about to rob a bank.

Ryan scanned the jungle, at least as far as he could see. The air was heavy and the mist mixed with a gray-brown smoke trapped under the canopy. Despite the fact that it was after seven in the morning, Ryan could barely see the silhouette of the two guides at the perimeter of camp through the smoke. They were pointing at something and in intense discussion. He looked to the southeast and spotted the bright yellow glow of the fire front. He turned back to the group and adjusted his bandana.

"You packed and ready?" Addy asked. It was clear there was no time for cordiality.

"Yes."

She jammed an automatic rifle into his chest. "Here you go—magazine—safety—fire. Got it?" she said.

Ryan repeated the short instructions in his mind and became obsessed with the safety and where he pointed the weapon. Addy turned to Paulo, picked up her MP5, pulled it to her chest, and gave them thumbs-up. Paulo signaled the guides to take the lead and the group headed due east, deeper into the jungle. Ryan waited for Thad and Bill, but Addy grabbed his arm.

"They'll follow. We need to keep our spacing."

"Are we headed to the crater?" Ryan asked.

"Yes. The guides said the fires have not entered that area yet, and based on the surface map Dad has, we think we'll be okay once we get there."

Ryan turned to ask another question. "Are we—?"

Addy shoved him forward, hard. "No time, Ryan, we gotta get there before the fires." She nodded to the yellow glow that seemed closer already. That pissed him off—he squeezed the forearm of the rifle and picked up the pace. His throat burned as he sucked in the hot smoky air, but he kept his eyes on the guides as they trotted through the underbrush. About thirty minutes later, the guides hit a clearing and stopped. The group caught up, and Ryan gawked at the black river before them. It looked as if it was three football fields wide and ran with a strong current to the southeast, toward the fires.

"It's—" Bill choked on the smoke. "It's okay. We don't have to cross it."

He yanked a folded map from his shirt pocket and traced the river with his finger to what looked like its termination in a large lake. Thick jungle lined the river and surrounded the lake on all sides.

"We follow this river to here." Bill pointed to what appeared to be a mist rising from the termination point, concealing the ground below. "This looks like mist from a waterfall. We should be able to enter the depression right here."

"We need to hurry," Paulo said as he pointed to the glow downriver. "The fire will be there in less than thirty minutes."

"Okay. Double-time, everybody," Thad ordered, taking the lead with a machete in hand.

Thad pressed along the river, occasionally slowing to hack through tangled vines and thickets of broad-leaved plants.

Ryan noticed the smoke was getting thicker, and it was much harder to breathe. He poured water from his canteen into his hand and wet his bandana. The glow grew brighter, and Ryan checked his watch. They were fifteen minutes into Thad's charge, and he could feel the heat from the fire. He could barely make out Thad, wildly swinging the machete up ahead as the river took a meander back to the northeast. He was soaked in sweat and felt as if he was back running cross-country in Miami, except through a forest fire.

Just then, he felt the air cool, and a heavy mist began to seep through the smoke. Thad stopped and the group closed ranks. They gazed at the scene before them. Ryan looked down and watched the river fall into a thick mist and disappear. The roar of the cascading water filled his ears. The top of the jungle's canopy sloped down the side of the crater until it leveled out at least a hundred feet below. In the distance, the green canopy gave way to a large black lake. The jungle hugged it on all sides, and because of the continuous jungle, the far rim of the crater was barely discernable in the distance.

Bill patted Ryan on the back and smiled. "This is it, Ryan."

Thad rocked side-to-side, grinned, and pointed to the heart of the crater, then gave a thumbs-up. Ryan tried to reply, but nothing came out. He was finally here.

Working with the guides, Thad crept down the slope along the trail and stepped onto a rock terrace that appeared to lead under the waterfall. Thad waved the group down. As they made their way along the slope, Ryan noticed the smoke had disappeared and the air smelled like the orchids he tended back in the Primate Park. Knowing the fire couldn't get into the canyon and destroy the monkeys, he felt better. While the path was covered with vines and the going was slow, he didn't mind. They were no longer racing the fire.

Addy stepped up beside him. "Sorry about being so short with you back there."

Ryan noticed her smile was back and he grinned. "I like a woman who takes charge."

He thought he was being funny, but Addy shook her head, and he felt his face redden. She stepped ahead of him on the path. Now he felt like an idiot.

They moved behind the waterfall and the terrace thinned. The wet rock was slippery. Ryan watched as Thad and the guides crossed one by one with their backs pinned against the rock wall. They faced the roaring curtain of water dropping into the foaming lake a hundred feet down. Halfway across, one of the guides slipped and Thad pinned him against the wall with his left hand. They shared a sigh and then continued to the other side.

Once across and on firm ground, Thad motioned to Ryan. "Come on across, dude, but take your time."

Ryan looked down at the churning water. Instinctively, he leaned back and pressed his palms against the rock wall. It felt slimy, and he envisioned his boots slipping off the ledge. He tilted his head back, pressed his pack against the wall, closed his eyes, and exhaled.

Just then, Addy grabbed his hand. "We'll go together. Just don't look down."

Normally he would've been embarrassed, but not this time. He didn't care about his image; he just wanted to cross. Addy slipped in front of him and carefully slid along the ledge. Ryan followed and closed his eyes after every step. He gripped her forearm with his left hand and she gripped his with her right. As they crossed the halfway point, Ryan relaxed a little, opened his eyes, and spotted Thad rocking up and down playing an air guitar and grinning.

Just then, Addy dug into Ryan's forearm and she screamed as both her boots slipped off the edge. Her hand started to slip down his forearm. Ryan jammed his butt against the wall, swung his right arm around beside his left, and grabbed her forearm with both hands.

"I got you," he yelled as he pulled her back up on the ledge. He was surprised how light she was and even more surprised how quickly he'd reacted. He slammed his butt and backpack against the rock wall and regained his balance. His heart pounded in his chest, and he struggled to catch his breath. Addy glanced at him and smiled weakly. They slid carefully to the end of the ledge and stepped onto firm ground.

Addy locked her eyes on Ryan and squeezed his hand. "Thank you, Ryan. I—"

"Ryan. Dude. That was awesome. You rock!" Thad yelled, still grinning, and he played one more riff on his air guitar. Ryan held his gaze on Addy. She squeezed his hand and smiled; he felt the connection. He then cut his eyes to Thad, shook his head, and smiled. His uncle was crazy.

Bill and Paulo followed without a slip, and the group chopped their way to the crater floor. Once there, the heavy brush gave way to the open jungle floor.

Thad pointed to a square piece of wood mounted on a post about four feet high and jammed into the ground at the edge of the path leading through a thick maze of palms and shrubs. "Look at this."

Ryan followed the rest of the group as they gathered on the other side of the makeshift signpost. When he spotted the writing, Ryan froze. It was in English and carved into the thick wood.

Stop. Go no further.

Thad nudged Ryan with his elbow. "I told you your great-grandpa was a man of his word."

Confused, Ryan squinted at Thad. Then it hit him. He remembered the entry in his great-grandfather's notebook describing the markings on wooden markers along the trails.

"Either Zachariah taught them English, or we are not alone," Thad said.

Bill, Paulo, and Addy stared, their mouths open. Then Bill said, "You think the monkeys did this?"

"Yup. Why else would it be on this side of the sign? It's a warning for them not to *leave* the crater. I guess Zachariah could've done it, but someone would have to read it," Thad said.

"If we get to the lake, we may find more evidence that was in the notebook," Ryan added.

Thad started down the path and waved to the group. "Let's get going."

Ryan noticed the jungle had changed. It was a little thicker and full of brightly colored flowers that looked like a hybrid of giant stargazers and lilies. Every color of the rainbow was represented. The air was thick, but smelled sweet like a florist's shop on Valentine's Day. Along the path, he noted square plots of cultivated gardens growing what looked like yellow tomatoes. A few bands of squirrel monkeys and an occasional capuchin maneuvered through the overstory. The jungle was full of chirps and squawks from the parrots and other exotic birds dancing through the branches above.

The path wound for what Ryan guessed was another quarter-mile, until the jungle canopy disappeared and the lake appeared about a football field away. Arid grasses and an occasional palm covered the ground to the edge of the water.

The lake was like black glass, and a few water lilies hugged the shoreline. Ryan scanned the lake. He could easily see the opposite shoreline and well down both sides to his left. The jungle rimmed the lake, with a similar grassy clearing before the shoreline. He had a strange sense someone was watching. No one said a word as they took in the view and searched for any sign of the monkeys.

Paulo broke the silence. "What do you think about making camp over there?"

Thad turned and looked back toward the tree line. "Looks good. We'll have a clean perimeter and spot anything that approaches."

"What do you think Ryan?"

Ryan scanned the lake one more time, then looked to the site. "I doubt they'll approach us here. We'll have to go find *them*. This looks fine for now."

Thad silently polled Addy and Bill and they nodded in agreement. Paulo said something in Portuguese to the guides, and they headed for the location. In minutes they'd cleared the area with their machetes and erected three lightweight tents.

Ryan remained at the lake's edge while the others joined Paulo at the campsite and dumped their packs. He checked his watch. It was noon and the sun was baking him. He scanned the lake's edge one more time and wondered about his so-called gift. Would it work? How would the others react? Especially Addy. The last time it had cost him his friends and his school. He thought about his Labs back home, Abby and Emma, and how that bond came naturally to him. They seemed to be able to communicate with him without commands. But this would be different. He'd have to use the one thing that was all his own, developed in the seclusion of the Primate Park with the monkeys since he was a curious child—not monkeys who could swim and maybe even read. He glanced back at the lake, hoping to see one stroking along the surface. Nothing. He wiped the sweat from his face, slipped the pack from his shoulders, and headed to join the others.

CHAPTER 28

DESPITE TASTING LIKE the mystery meat they served at the cafeteria at Heritage High, Ryan gobbled two MREs in a matter of minutes. He was hungrier than usual, and he wanted to dispense with lunch and continue the search. Thad sat next to him on a rock facing the water.

"You given any thought to what you're going to do when we find them?" Thad asked without looking away from his black plastic MRE bag.

The question caught Ryan by surprise. He'd been so focused on staying alive, finding the monkeys, and impressing Addy.

"I'll try to connect with them. After that I haven't thought much about it."

Thad chuckled. "You are still seventeen. At least for one more day."

"One more day?"

"Yeah, dude. Your birthday is tomorrow. Did you forget that too?"

"I guess I did."

"Well you'll officially be able to vote, get shot at—if you volunteer to do so—and date any older woman you want." Thad grinned and looked across the campsite at Addy.

Ryan followed his eyes to her, then looked away. "Very funny."

"So, what are you going to do after we find them?"

"I don't know, Uncle T. How do I tell if the world is ready? I'm just a kid. I don't know shit."

"For one more day."

"What?"

"You'll be a kid for one more day. Did you forget again already?"

"No. But one day can't make a difference."

"You know, I used to think that, until I had a few days I'll never forget." Thad looked up from his MRE and gazed off into the distance. "It doesn't take long to figure out the right thing to do when you suddenly realize you're the only one who can make that choice."

Ryan knew he was talking about the war. He loved the stories of Thad's deeds in Iraq, including shielding an Iraqi child caught in a firefight in Fallujah, while taking heavy fire. Those wounds earned the first of two purple hearts.

"If the monkeys can swim and read, they're more like us than people thought, right?" Ryan asked.

"Yup. They'll be unique in that aspect."

"So that means if the monkeys are exposed to the world, it might prove God didn't create man—that we evolved?"

"Not only that, scientists will want to test the crap out of their DNA and maybe even their brains. They may stuff them in cages in their sterile labs and carve them up or stick them with God-knows-what in the name of mankind."

Ryan threw down his MRE and stuffed his spoon into the bag. "That's what I thought. Either way, they're screwed—and so am I."

Thad slid closer and put his arm around Ryan. "What I'm telling you is that it's just as hard to decide the right thing to do as it is to do it." Thad tightened his hug. "But I know you'll do the right thing. You always have. And the gift you have to relate to your Labs and the monkeys at the park tells me you'll connect with these guys in a way none of us can. All you'll have to do is search inside for the answer."

For some reason, Thad's words lifted some of the weight from Ryan's heart. He knew his uncle was right. For the first time, he believed that what he had was a gift, and along with that gift came responsibility. He'd made a promise, and now it was time to keep it.

Paulo approached, and Thad jumped up to meet him.

"We'll be ready in ten minutes to begin the search. I'll leave one guide here to guard the camp and our packs. Don't forget to bring plenty of water."

"Will do," Thad said, and he turned and faced Ryan. He slapped his hands together and grinned. "Let's go find us some monkeys."

CHAPTER 29

KARL HATED THE tropics. At ninety degrees and ninety percent humidity, it easily pushed his thick German blood to boiling point. He wiped the sweat from his eyes and stared at the screen of the GPS tracker. The coordinates hadn't changed in two hours. He glanced at the roaring waterfall and the slim path behind it, then back at the tracker. He was sure they were making camp, but he needed confirmation. Grandby's henchman and his two men stared at Karl with their arms crossed.

Chemo, as the Brazilian called himself, had joined Karl in Manaus. He carried his résumé on his hip. The .45 caliber H&K USP told Karl all he needed to know. Chemo was lean and muscular, and Karl knew that meant he had a deadly combination of strength and speed. His deep-set eyes were constantly moving and assessing the surroundings. Karl didn't trust him, but he needed him.

"Let's get in there and get this done," Chemo said in his thick accent. "We're running out of time. The Crusaders can't be far behind, and the fires are blocking our exit to the south."

"We wait for the call," Karl replied, not taking his eyes off the tracker. He would ignore them for now and hide his uneasiness. He was well aware he was in their jungle and using their resources. While he'd watched his two men behind him eliminate equally deadly adversaries, Chemo's home-field advantage shifted the odds of surviving below even. The bluff would work for now, but he'd sensed they'd cross them once the prize was in their hands. Chemo huffed, and Karl eyed him as he turned and huddled with the other two men. He noted the pair towered over Chemo and outweighed Karl's two men by at least twenty pounds; hand-to-hand would be rough. He scanned their jungle camo and noted the KA-BAR fighting knives and Glocks tucked tightly around their waists. His team was equal in firepower, but despite their protests, they carried light body armor, and he concluded any conflict would be best resolved with weapons at a distance.

Karl shifted when he felt the vibration of the satphone. Chemo and his men immediately spun to face him.

"Go," Karl answered.

"We camp and they gone," the voice said, struggling with English.

"Where are they relative to your location?"

"Qué?"

Karl covered the phone. "Shit!"

He looked at Chemo. He'd have to rely on his translation. He nodded and raised the phone, and Chemo closed the distance between them.

"We need to know where they are and if there's another way out," Karl said, shoving the phone in Chemo's chest.

Chemo nodded and started to jabber in Portuguese. Karl waited, not understanding a word. Chemo stopped talking and listened, then seemed to give two short orders. He handed the phone to Karl.

"The camp is empty, other than the guide. He's on the southwest side of a large lake. Only way in is through the falls, he thinks. The others are moving to the east in search of the macacos."

Karl grinned. He knew Chemo used the Portuguese name for monkeys to make a point: This was his country and his people. Karl rubbed his chin. Only one way out, and the camp was empty. They could find the monkeys at any time, but couldn't escape the crater.

"We need to go now," Chemo said.

Chemo's men shouldered their MP5s and encircled the two men. Karl's two men stepped close behind him. *Not here.* Karl knew this was not the place to take on Chemo and his men.

"We'll go to the camp and set the trap there. We can get them all at once. We leave in five," Karl said.

"Okay."

Chemo spun and led his men to the edge of the path out of earshot. He yanked a phone from his pack, dialed, and paced as he waited for the connection. Karl wondered what instructions Grandby would give him. He hoped they'd wait, just like he did.

***

The garden was his favorite spot this time of year. Charles Grandby admired nature's work. Not in the way that the masses do, marveling at the bright colors of the asters, marigolds, and wild geraniums, smelling their sweet fragrances dancing lightly on the wind and proclaiming God's wonder. He sat and admired the relentless pace of natural selection that eliminated the weaker traits and reinforced the flowers' ability to draw insects to pollinate the strong and help them multiply, choking out the weaker species. He knew Darwinian natural selection was the only answer for the complexity of life on Earth. He smiled as he read another letter in the stack on his lap from some Christian, who asked, *"If there is no God, why isn't everyone doing selfish, bad things?"* The thought of people fearing an all-knowing surveillance camera in the sky, being good simply to avoid some unknown punishment, was absurd. Darwin studied the evolution of species more than anyone of his time, and as a result, he abandoned his mother's God. Instead, he traced the complex process that created us all.

Grandby faced the sun as it emerged from the overcast and enjoyed the warmth. His servant entered the garden, phone in hand. He hoped it was good news.

"Mr. Chemo for you, sir," he said, and scampered away.

"Chemo, my friend. I hope you have some good news."

"We have them trapped in a closed crater about two hundred miles north of Coari."

Grandby grinned and leaned forward. "Good, my friend. That's very good."

"Yes sir. We're headed to their camp. They've left to search for the monkeys. We'll wait for them there. Just want to confirm my orders."

"They are unchanged. I want them alive, and as much scientific evidence of their ability as you can gather."

"Do you need the coordinates?"

"Yes. Send them through Manaus. I have a team of archaeologists staging there, and once you clear the area, they'll go in."

"Do you want me to take sole possession of the creatures?"

"Yes. Do what you must, but once we have them, we can control the flow of information. It can't be in control of the others."

"Yes, sir."

"Chemo …"

"Yes sir?"

"If you get those monkeys back to me alive, your fee will be doubled."

"I'll look forward to taking your money, sir."

"Me too," Grandby said.

"Anything else, sir?"

"No. Just let me know when it's done."

"Out."

The phone clicked off.

Grandby stood and began to plan the announcement. Surrounded by the world's most respected scientists, he'd present the missing link to the world. And that link would drag their God to the bottom of the deepest ocean, like the anchor chain on the Titanic. Finally, all of those who'd threatened and scorned him would be brought to their knees. Not to praise the God who never was there, but in awe of the power of natural selection—seen in the faces of their closest descendants.

CHAPTER 30

BLACKMON SHRUGGED TO readjust the straps of the pack digging into his shoulders. The extra weight was painful, but he knew it was necessary. It freed the four Brazilian Crusaders to carry the forty gallons of gasoline—a critical aspect of his plan. They labored to reach the falls under the weight. He knew the numbers: Each man could carry seventy pounds. The specific gravity of the fuels was about .8 and with water at 8.325 pounds per gallon, each man carried ten gallons. It would be close, but with the dry season at hand it would be just enough to get things going. The sun had drifted to the west and only a few shafts reached the jungle floor. He raised his face skyward and welcomed the cool mist from the falls on his face.

Luke, the Crusader chosen to lead the effort here, and a second Crusader trotted up the steep incline from the ledge under the falls. Blackmon noticed the Scotsman's red face had lightened a bit, but sweat still ran down his cheeks and soaked his camouflage shirt.

"Sir, Grandby's team has moved to the valley floor and is approaching the location we picked up on the GPS tracker. Their man on the inside must've made camp."

"Good. Any sign of the boy or the creatures?"

Luke looked away for a moment and appeared to be searching for the right words. "Sir, there is something you'll have to see for yourself."

"What do you mean?"

"Well, there's a signpost facing the outbound side of the trail warning someone to go no further."

"Not to leave the crater?"

"Yes, sir."

"In what language?"

"It's in English."

"Planted by the boy's great-grandfather?"

"Maybe—but who would need to read it, sir?"

Blackmon searched the Crusader's face. He looked as if he'd seen the devil himself. Then it hit Blackmon—maybe he had.

"The monkeys? You think it's for those creatures? They can read?"

"Who else could it be?"

Blackmon didn't have another answer. It was worse than his bosses anticipated. Living hominids that can read and swim like humans and God knows what else, on the wrong continent. It would be a field day for the evolutionists and the atheists—an unholy "I told you so." Blackmon paused to think through the plan. From their position at the top of the crater, he could see all four sides. He closely surveyed the perimeter.

"Is this the only way in?"

"It looks like it, sir."

"Good. Can you get us down to the floor?"

"It's just a few hundred yards down the trail. It's steep and slippery under the falls, so we'll set up a pulley line for the fuel. It will only take ten minutes or so to get across."

"Do it."

Blackmon waved the four Crusaders waiting in the shade forward. In minutes the cargo and all six men made their way under the falls and down the steep trail to the crater floor. When Luke stopped and pointed to the signpost, they all gawked at the words carved into the wood. Blackmon noted the trail led east along the water.

"How far to the camp?" Blackmon asked.

"Half a mile," Luke replied.

"Okay. Recon the area and sketch out a rough map of the crater, the lake, and any trails you encounter. And double-time it back."

Luke grabbed the only Crusader with a patrol pack and disappeared down the trail.

"Take ten, guys," Blackmon said.

Everyone dropped their packs, hit the jungle floor, and sucked on their canteens.

Blackmon pulled the satphone from his pack and stepped down the trail. "It's me."

"Did you find them?" Remington asked.

"Yes. We have them trapped in a small depression north of Coari."

"The German too?"

"Yes."

"Good."

"There's something you should know," Blackmon said.

"What?"

"We found evidence that these monkeys can read."

The phone went silent for a moment.

"Say again."

"We found a sign in English warning the crater's inhabitants not to leave."

"You mean these satanic animals can read? It's a hoax. It's impossible."

"I'm looking at the evidence right now." Blackmon waited for a reply.

"You listen to me. You and I never had this conversation, and you never saw anything. You got that?"

"I understand."

"Now, I want you to destroy everything—destroy them all, and any evidence."

"That's our plan."

"Can you trust the others to be quiet?"

Blackmon looked back up the trail to the four Crusaders watching him. He glanced back down the trail.

"I can trust one of them. The rest I can't vouch for."

"Then you know what you have to do."

"Yes, sir."

"Your Creator is counting on you now, son. Don't let him down."

"His will be done, sir."

"Report back when it's done."

Blackmon collapsed the antennae of the satphone, walked back up the trail, and stuffed it in his pack.

"We're still on plan," he said, just to cover his tracks.

The four men nodded and returned to their discussion in Portuguese. Blackmon silently asked for God's forgiveness for what he was about to do. He knew the sixth commandment applied to everyone, but God made exceptions. He was sure the thousands of Crusaders from the Holy Wars were now at his side. It was a place he'd be someday. He prayed the four men in front of him would be there too. After all, they'd die at his hands.

He heard the crackle of the dried leaves down the trail and instinctively grabbed his MP5. Luke, trailed by the other Crusader, trotted from the brush, and Blackmon lowered his barrel toward the ground.

Luke knelt, facing him, and took a long draw on his canteen. After catching his breath, he pulled a folded paper from his breast pocket. "Here's the layout, sir. The lake runs east to west." Luke pointed to the rough drawing. "We're on the south side, here. The only way to the north side is around the other end of the lake or to go across. It looks like two miles across, and there's no sign of boats, so I don't think they can get out that way. The path seems to open up closer to the camp, and heads north to the lake's edge, here. No sign of the boy or his party, so they must be moving east along the south side of the lake on their search. The German is setting up at the camp—probably an ambush. We got around the camp to here, without being detected, and the trail continues east-southeast here."

Blackmon studied the makeshift map. "Can you get two of the men to the eastern edge of the lake, here?"

"I think so."

"Okay then. You take two of these guys and start a burn across the far side of the crater. We'll get one going here. The only way out will be through us."

"Come back by yourself ..." Blackmon whispered.

Luke stared at Blackmon for a moment and then glanced over his shoulder. "You certain?"

Blackmon nodded.

"Okay, sir."

"I'll give you two hours to get into position. Contact me when you're ready to start the burn."

"Will do."

Luke started to rise. Blackmon grabbed Luke's shoulder.

"Godspeed."

"Godspeed," he replied.

Luke gathered two of the Crusaders with their gas cans strapped to their backs and headed down the trail. That left three Crusaders with Blackmon. Three good souls he'd need to terminate in the name of God.

CHAPTER 31

RYAN WIPED HIS face with the sweat-soaked handkerchief and noticed his hand was shaking. They were getting close: He could feel it. All the worry and memories of people trying to kill him disappeared into the excitement of finally encountering the monkeys. He kept pace with Uncle T as he raced along a well-traveled path drifting to the east-southeast, away from the lakeshore. Misty arcs of sunlight maneuvered their way through the thick canopy of the jungle and illuminated the wide palm fronds dangling across the path ahead. Ryan gawked at the tree trunk to his right. He'd never seen any tree in Webster's Primate Park that massive. It could easily conceal three pickups, just like his at home.

"You doing okay?" Addy asked.

"Yeah. It's just so hot. I'm sweating like a pig," he replied over his shoulder, still keeping pace. Thad stopped and studied Bill.

"Let's take five here," he said as he grabbed his canteen and chugged.

Ryan stopped and pulled his canteen from his side. He chugged the water and felt Addy pat him on the back.

"Your uncle knows we gotta get back before dark and wants to cover as much territory as he can before we have to turn around. Don't want to be caught in this jungle at night."

"I'm all for that." Ryan tried to sound confident, but he immediately searched the underbrush for anacondas. Then the haunting memory of a YouTube video of a leopard killing an anaconda darted into his mind.

"You think there are jaguars around here?" he asked.

Addy smiled. "I'm afraid so. We are in one of the thickest jungles I've seen, and we're never more than a mile from that lake. They love this stuff."

Ryan scanned the understory of the jungle. "I read in school that they're one of the strongest animals in the world."

"That's true."

"I also read that they can eat monkeys?" Ryan heard his own words as if they came from someone else.

"Don't worry. Your monkeys sound pretty smart, and after all, your great-grandfather was coming down here for years and they were still here."

Addy drew hard on her canteen, capped it, and shoved it back into its holster.

Ryan took one more drink as he remembered the fact he found most fascinating when he did the report. The jaguar's favorite method of attack was to bite through the skull of its victim and penetrate the brain—a fate he wanted to avoid.

Ryan rubbed his head. Up the trail, Thad was engrossed in a conversation with Paulo and Bill as they encircled a map and traced routes with their fingers. They all nodded and Thad broke toward Ryan and Addy.

"All right, dudes and dudette. Let's go."

Thad patted Ryan as he passed, and winked, nodding toward Addy. Ryan just shook his head.

Thad took the lead, followed by the guide. Ryan and Addy now walked together behind them, and Bill and Paulo brought up the rear. As they wound back to the south, much more sunlight reached the jungle floor. Ryan looked ahead and spotted an opening in the canopy. Thad stopped and raised his hand. The group closed around him, and he pointed to a fork in the path. The path to the left was trampled down to the dirt and cut back to the east. The right fork was clearly a pathway through the underbrush, but it was covered in long grass tilting a little forward and to the sides as if someone had recently waded through it.

Then Ryan saw it. So did the others. Another wooden sign, but this one made Ryan lose his breath. "Shit," he said.

"What is it?" Addy asked.

"I think it's a cross," he replied.

Thad nodded. "I think he's right. It's a cross."

Ryan turned to the group, and they exchanged stares.

"Do you think it's them? The monkeys did this?"

"Could be. Could've been Zachariah, but even if that's the case, who did he do it for?" Thad said. He smiled and said, "Let's go."

He started down the path to the right. Ryan followed closely behind his uncle and the rest of the group trailed after them. After sinking deeper into the jungle for a few minutes, the sunlight grew brighter again as the path wound back to the north. Still checking for snakes, Ryan scanned the thinning understory and ran into Thad from behind.

"Whoa there, dude. Have a look at this."

Ryan stepped around Thad and couldn't believe his eyes. The path ended in a clearing. Someone had removed trees, shrubs, and underbrush and cleared an area about half the length of a football field. More crosses were staked in the ground, arranged in rows spaced about ten feet apart. Thad was silent. The others gathered and looked at the clearing. Then Ryan saw the square outline of packed dirt in front of each of the crosses.

"It can't be," Ryan said, looking at Thad.

"I think it is," he said quietly.

"No!" Ryan yelled.

"What?" Bill asked, "What's wrong?"

"It's a cemetery," Thad said reverently.

"No! No!" Ryan pounded his fist into his thigh.

Addy covered her mouth.

"It may not be all of them, Ryan," Thad said, hugging Ryan's shoulders.

Ryan hoped he was right. There had to be almost a hundred graves. Then he noticed some spots were undisturbed and not marked by a cross.

Ryan pointed. "Do you see those?"

"See what?" Addy asked.

"The open gravesites," Ryan said. "They were leaving spots open. Someone is still around here."

Thad punched Ryan in the shoulder. "Dude. We're still on."

Ryan rubbed his shoulder. "What if Great-grandpa did all this? Or what if they died, and there was no one left to bury them?"

Thad calmed down.

"You don't know that, dude."

"Neither do you, Uncle T." Ryan suddenly felt tired. After everything he'd been through, he now had to face the possibility that the monkeys were all dead—gone.

"Let's just continue to search," Thad said.

"Oh shit." Ryan heard Addy cuss.

He turned around and immediately spotted the wall of smoke racing toward them in the jungle. The breeze had picked up and was blowing in Ryan's face.

"What the hell is that?" Ryan asked.

"We gotta get going," Thad yelled.

"Wait," Ryan protested. He grabbed his digital camera and snapped as many pictures as he could before Thad yanked him by the collar and dragged him back down the path. Ryan regained his balance and stuffed the camera back in his daypack. They were sprinting now, with Paulo and the guide in the lead, followed closely by Addy and Bill. Breathing hard, Ryan began to smell the smoke trapped under the canopy. Bill slowed, laboring under his age, and Addy grabbed him under his shoulder. Ryan ducked under the other. Thad hesitated and looked at Bill.

"Go. Go on!" Bill gasped.

"We got you," Ryan said as Thad pivoted and sprinted ahead.

Now Ryan felt Bill's full weight and his legs ached, but he kept running. The smoke thickened and Addy and Ryan now dragged Bill. The smoke burned Ryan's throat, and he fought off a cough. He knew he didn't have the breath.

The path made a hard turn to the right, and Ryan noticed the first sign of flames. Thad stopped. He'd reached the fork in the path and their route back to the camp was blocked by the flames. Thad spun and darted down the fork to the left. Still dragging Bill, Ryan and Addy followed and tried to keep pace with Thad, but they were losing ground. Paulo and the guide pressed them from behind. The fire had generated its own wind, and Ryan felt the intense heat against his back. The good news was the path headed toward the lake. The good news was short-lived. The path turned southeast and the jungle thickened. The smoke blocked the sun and a dusk-like darkness covered the path ahead.

Ryan's arms burned. Bill was just dead weight. Ryan glanced across at Addy, who stared down the path ahead with the commitment of a daughter saving her father's life. Ryan wouldn't quit either. He pushed the pain from his mind and kept going. They stumbled over the roots and bumps on the path. The smoke thickened. Out of the corner of his eye, Ryan noticed something moving at the same speed through the underbrush, about twenty yards off the path. He remembered the jaguars, and studied the image as he ran.

His right foot caught a root and he hit the ground face first, eating black dirt. He rolled to scramble back to his feet. Paulo and the guide sped past, and just ahead, Addy strained under her father's weight. In seconds, Ryan was back to his feet. He slipped his head under Bill's arm. Addy nodded without saying a word, and they bolted back down the path. Ryan glanced again to his right and the figure, whatever it was, was gone.

Thad had extended his lead another fifty yards on Ryan, and Ryan could barely see him in the darkness. The hot wind at his back got hotter, and sparks now blew around him—the fire was closing in. He panicked when he lost sight of Thad, but still he kept running. The smoke was thick and it was now dark on the jungle floor. He and Addy were more stumbling than running. Ryan's heart raced—still no trace of his uncle. They followed the path sharply around to the right.

"In here. Get in here now!"

Thad's voice came from a dark hole just a few feet off the path to the right. Ryan felt cool air on the right side of his face.

"Come on!" Thad appeared from the darkness and grabbed Bill. Ryan, Addy, Paulo, and the guide followed them in. Inside, it was pitch-black and cool. All the heat had disappeared.

"A cave?" Ryan shouted to Thad as they dragged Bill deeper into the darkness.

"Yes it is—saved our ass, dude." Thad slowed and then stopped, giving Ryan and Addy Bill's full weight.

Ryan heard a rustling, followed by a click, and was blinded by a light. He squinted.

"Let there be light," Thad said, "and it was good."

Ryan couldn't believe his uncle's constant sense of humor.

"Let's check you out," Thad said as he peeled Bill's shirt back a bit and traced his face with the flashlight. Bill was coughing heavily and looked half-asleep.

"How's his heart?" Thad asked Addy.

"He's been taking medication, but the doc said he doesn't need a bypass."

"I'm fine," Bill groaned.

"Sit down here and get a rest. I think you'll be fine then."

Thad swept the light around the cave and hit Ryan's face first, followed by Addy, Paulo, and the guide.

"Everyone okay?" he asked.

Everyone was okay. Ryan listened in the darkness. The sound of the group's labored breaths was suddenly drowned out as a loud hiss turned into a crackling roar outside. An eerie orange hue exploded into what looked like the flames of hell toward the mouth of the cave. They all watched the entrance in silence as the fire front raced past.

As the light from the flames lit the cave, Ryan scanned it. The walls were black and solid rock. He followed the near wall of the cave to the floor and noticed something was missing: no dirt. The floor was rock, but it looked clean, as if someone had swept it. He followed the floor past his feet and then deeper into the cave, until it melted into the blackness in the fading flickering light.

Suddenly, he saw movement. At first he thought it was the dancing shadows. After rubbing his eyes, he locked his focus on a spot deeper into the cave. Again, he saw the movement. He crept away from the group toward the darkness. The motion stopped, and so did Ryan. He leaned toward the back of the cave, taking one more step. He heard a low growl. Thad and the others heard it too.

"What is it?" Thad asked.

"Stay there. Shhh …" Ryan replied.

The growl was strangely familiar and didn't frighten him. He'd heard it before—at the park. He took another step, and the growl was louder this time, and he felt an attraction—a pull toward the sound. A calm warmth came over him. It was the same sensation he got in the park, working with the monkeys and at home with his Labs. One more step into the darkness was met with one more growl, a bit firmer than the last. He knew what he had to do.

"What is it, dude?" Thad asked in a whisper.

Ryan held up his hand. He looked at his uncle and then Addy. He thought about the ridicule of his junior high friends when he finally showed them what he'd learned. He dropped his pack and stripped his shirt. He closed his eyes and envisioned the capuchins who'd found him at the age of five, lost and alone in the park. The ones he found every day after that. He filled his mind with the feeling of friendship and began the carefully chore-ographed series of movement and sounds they'd taught him. He changed pitch, loudness, and duration of the calls exactly as he'd learned as a child. The calls identified him as the capuchins' friend.

He opened his eyes and waited. Nothing. Then he heard it—a series of faint grunts with just the right inflections. He felt the connection. But something was missing—something that linked him to Zachariah. Then he remembered. He cleared his throat and carefully recited the passage.

"Know ye that the Lord, he is God: It is he that hath made us, and not we ourselves, we are his people, and the sheep of his pasture."

Ryan finished, and a sense of joy and fulfillment swept over him. He looked back and smiled at Thad, whose eyes and mouth were wide open. He spotted Addy, who stared back in admiration and wonderment. Then it came from the darkness—the reply he knew would come.

"We've been waiting for you—welcome."

CHAPTER 32

DESPITE SQUATTING IN the shade at the perimeter of the camp, the heat choked off any benefit from the breeze and had already fouled his mood. He kept his eyes locked on Grandby's henchman and his crew.

Chemo and his men jabbered quietly with the guide the boy had left behind. They occasionally glanced over their shoulders at Karl and his men; Chemo's men's expressions made it clear Karl and his team weren't welcomed. Karl was convinced he was the topic of the conversation. He rubbed the stock of his MP5 and pondered his opponent's strategy. Clearly they were trying to recruit the guide and shift the odds to their favor by outnumbering Karl and his two men. That's what he would do.

Since he had so few, it didn't take long to sort through his options and settle on one. He nodded to his men. They leaned forward on the stock of their MP5s and turned their attention to their boss.

"Eyes on me. Be ready to react," Karl said as he pulled his Glock from its holster.

Karl's men leaned back into the shade and shifted their weight to their toes. Karl rose and marched toward Chemo's group. As he approached, they stepped back and made room for him to step between Chemo and the cornered guide. Karl stopped, stiffened, and stared at Chemo. He kept his eyes locked on Chemo, smiled, and aimed the Glock at the guide's head. Chemo's men lifted their rifles, but he was too quick. He fired. The guide's head snapped back against the tree, and he collapsed on the ground. Karl heard the two MP5s cock behind him—his men were ready.

"Now things are even again," Karl said, pointing the gun at Chemo.

One of Chemo's men targeted Karl, while the other shifted his aim between Karl's two thugs.

Chemo grinned. "You're making a mistake, my friend."

"The mistake was yours, my … friend. You don't screw with me and get away with it."

"Not screwing with you, Karl. Just interrogating a source." Chemo nodded toward the corpse on the ground.

The man who was targeting Karl pointed over Karl's shoulder and yelled something in Portuguese. Karl kept his aim on Chemo, stepped back out of reach, and glanced over his shoulder. The smoke had appeared from nowhere. It was nearing dusk and the glow from the fire illuminated the smoke cloud. Fed by the gusting wind, sparks and embers showered from the sky. Karl knew they had little time.

"We'll settle this later," he yelled, retreating to his men.

Chemo yelled something in Portuguese and gave Karl the finger. Karl ignored the gesture. He knew the fire had been set, and assumed the Crusaders had found them. They were trapped by the fire to the east, the lake to the north, and the rim of the crater to the south. He thought about the boy, the monkeys, his chance at eternal life, and he considered heading into the fire. He didn't want to face Cyrus if he failed. But some life was better than no life. Chemo appeared to draw the same conclusion, and they simultaneously headed back west down the path to the falls—it was the only way out.

The fire was on them in seconds. Chemo and his men had taken the lead and Karl trailed with his men. The flames seemed alive and jumped from tree to tree, advancing on the group. Karl felt the heat on his back and the thick smoke burned his eyes and throat. The path gained elevation and turned to the left. He felt the mist from the falls. They were close. As he passed the sign at the exit to the falls, all hell broke loose. The first burst of gunfire knocked Chemo's men to the ground. Chemo darted from the path and took cover behind a thick tree trunk. A constant hail of bullets splintered the bark of the tree. Chemo was pinned down. Karl and his men hit the deck on opposite sides of the path.

Karl scanned the falls and the perimeter of the path. The gunfire was coming from behind the falls and from the left side of the path at its entrance. Chemo returned fire, but was forced back behind the trunk by a hail of bullets. He glanced back at Karl and waved for them to advance. Karl thought about putting a few rounds in Chemo right there. It would solve his problem. But he needed his firepower right now.

He signaled to his men to advance on the flanks while he drew fire. He cocked his MP5, nodded, and opened fire. The men darted up the flanks and, once positioned, nodded. Together, they rose and opened fire. Concentrating his fire on the falls, Karl dashed up the path to Chemo. Chemo said nothing, but both men knew the next maneuver. Karl's men advanced further along the edge of the jungle as the smoke thickened and provided cover. Karl glanced back down the path and saw flames about a hundred yards out and closing fast. He nodded at Chemo, who nodded back. They waited for the covering gunfire, and when their attackers returned fire, they rolled to either side of the massive trunk and opened fire in the direction of the muzzle flashes. Karl's men closed ranks on the path and fired continuously. Karl and Chemo sprang to their feet and zigzagged toward the falls, firing constantly. Karl saw one of his men go down, but kept advancing.

The gunfire from the falls stopped. Karl and Chemo concentrated their fire on the flashes from the bushes to the left of the entrance to the falls. They were within twenty yards when Karl saw Chemo take a round to the chest. He didn't go down, but instead let out what sounded like a battle cry and kept firing until the gunfire from the entrance stopped. Karl listened but only heard the crackle from the fire behind them.

Chemo hit his knees and looked at Karl. Without a word, he fell limp and landed face-first on the path. Karl waved for his man to join him. The fire had closed in and the heat was searing his face. Karl shoved his man ahead of him onto the path and headed into the falls.

Before slipping behind the curtain of water, Karl stopped and surveyed the crater below. The crater's floor was covered in flames and smoke. Flaming embers rose in the smoke and dropped into the lake. He saw no boats and no sign of any living creature—just flames—the flames that were destroying his only chance at eternal life.

CHAPTER 33

RYAN COULDN'T MOVE. The words had paralyzed him. The response came from about twenty feet away. Thad crept closer with the flashlight and followed the cave's floor past Ryan, deeper into the darkness. Ryan locked his eyes on the beam and held his breath. The roar of the fire outside faded, along with its light, and Thad inched the beam toward the growling.

The beam froze on something. Ryan squinted and then he saw it: a brown, furry foot. Behind him, Addy gasped. Thad raised the light, and Ryan spotted them. Three large monkeys sat against the back wall of the cave, shoulder to shoulder, arms crossed. Their flat, round, button-nosed faces were framed by longer tufted hair, much like the macaques at the park, but they were much larger—about the size of a large chimpanzee. Their arms appeared to be shorter than the chimps Ryan had seen. They looked like hybrids between a monkey and an ape, just like his great-grandfather had described them. The one closest to Ryan simply stared at him. Ryan could see the specks of green reflecting the flashlight in its eyes. The second one was taller, with thicker arms, and seemed to be scowling. It guarded the third, smaller monkey with a spiked tuft rising from atop his head. The small one looked worried.

"Is Zachariah with you?" the first monkey said in very precise English.

The movement of his lips and mouth were different than any ape or monkey he'd seen, and the movement gave the monkey a human quality. Ryan turned back to Thad and the group and grinned. The light was poor, but their mouths hung wide open. They'd heard it, too: The monkey could speak.

Ryan returned his attention back to the monkeys. "My name is Ryan Barnum Webster. I'm Zachariah's great-grandson."

"Hey, Barney. He has your name," the smallest monkey said in a higher-pitched, youthful voice.

"Quiet, Taylor," the older monkey said, cutting a glance to the youngster. Then he refocused on Ryan and asked, "Is he gone? Passed on?"

"Yes. He passed on a while ago, as did my grandfather, Phineas. He's the one who asked me to come here."

The three monkeys seemed to share a look of bewilderment.

"He died after his last visit?"

"Yes."

"It's a shame your kind dies so early."

Ryan didn't know what to make of the exchange and remained silent. The monkey called Barney continued.

"Zachariah said one of his family members would return—one who is gentle and who can relate to us in the proper way. That person would be the only one we could trust. I can sense that in you, but you look so young."

"I'm eighteen tomorrow," Ryan said.

"Hey Zach," the smaller monkey said, pushing the larger monkey in the ribs, "he's the same as you."

Ryan glanced over his shoulder at Thad and waved him forward. "This my uncle, Thad."

"That means he's your father's brother, correct?" Barney asked.

"Yes, that's correct."

"Where is your father?"

"He's back home. My grandfather sent us instead."

"Where's our father, Barney?" Taylor asked.

Ryan could hear the trepidation in his young voice.

"We don't know right now, but everything will be all right," Barney answered, not taking his eyes off Ryan.

Thad shifted the light to Taylor, and Ryan noticed a glistening in his eyes, as if he'd been crying. Thad moved the light back to Barney. "We need to get you out of here," Thad said. "People are coming for you."

Barney looked at Thad but didn't reply. Ryan waited, but Barney and the others said nothing.

Thad leaned over to Ryan and whispered, "I think they'll only speak to you."

Ryan remembered his grandfather's insistence that he was the only one who had the gift.

"My uncle is right. There are men coming who would harm you, and it looks like the fire may have been set."

"Where are Mom and Dad?" Taylor said.

Zach, the muscular one, wrapped his thick arm around Taylor. "We'll find them, dude."

"I assumed that's why Zachariah's son sent you," Barney said. "He'd said you'd only appear if something was wrong or if you humans were ready to accept us for what we are. I'm guessing it's not the latter, based on the fact someone is after us."

Ryan looked at Thad. Thad tilted his head in the direction of the monkeys. Ryan thought for a moment, then said, "Are your names Taylor, Zach, and Barney?"

"You're close. This is Taylor. He's my youngest brother, sixteen dry seasons old. Zachariah is eighteen, and despite my younger brothers' insistence, my given name is Barnum."

Ryan couldn't believe his ears. He looked at Thad, who simply smiled.

"As in Phineas Taylor Barnum?"

All three monkeys smiled.

"Yes. Our parents named us in honor of that man and your grandfather. We owe much to Zachariah. He taught us about your species and how to speak one of your many languages. He also protected us from your kind at great peril to himself."

Ryan felt Thad tug on his sleeve.

"We need to get moving, dude." Thad nodded back toward the entrance to the cave.

Ryan looked back to the entrance. Addy, Bill, and Paulo remained near the mouth of the cave. Ryan could see they were still in shock. He was too. Monkey-ape hybrids that could speak. He thought about the protest from

Sarah's mother about any discussion of man evolving from ape. He'd like to see her face if she were here now.

He felt Thad's tug again.

"We gotta go. Get us all out of here."

"Where will you take us?" Barney asked.

"I can take you to the park my grandfather built. You'll be safe there."

"Where is it?"

"In Miami."

"In the United States of America?"

"Yes. That's right."

"Where the president is Jimmy Carter?"

Ryan paused. He knew from his history classes that Jimmy Carter had defeated President Ford in the elections in 1976. That was the year of his great-grandfather's last visit.

"He was the president in 1976. It's been quite a while since my great-grandfather was here. The president is Barack Obama."

Barney looked puzzled. Then he pointed to Thad.

"Why does he carry that?"

Thad looked at his right shoulder where Barney was pointing. The MP5 dangled behind him, but the barrel was visible at his side. He grabbed the barrel and showed it to the group.

"It's a rifle. It's for our protection."

"Your kind makes strange tools simply to destroy each other," Barney said.

Ryan had never thought about weapons that way.

"Can you protect my brothers and me from the rest of your kind?"

Ryan felt the responsibility crushing him again. He'd be responsible for the safety of these amazing beings, and the rest of the world would do most anything to get to them.

He scanned the cave. Addy smiled at him and nodded. He looked down at Bill and felt his encouraging gaze. Finally, he locked eyes with his uncle, who was still standing beside him. Thad nodded and patted him on his back. They were looking to him. He returned his gaze to the monkeys, and in that moment, he knew he was their only hope.

"Yes. I will take care of all of you." Ryan felt his commitment deepen with those words. For the first time, he actually believed he would be willing to die in order to protect them. It was the same way he felt about his labs.

"How do we know we can trust you and these others?"

Ryan didn't know what to say. If he couldn't convince them, it was game over. Then it hit him. He filled his mind with the comfort he'd received from the capuchins that night in the park. He remembered their message. It was as if he were in a trance. He voiced the sounds and made gestures in the order he'd learned and stopped.

Barney didn't move—he just stared at Ryan. The silence in the cave lasted for an eternity. Finally Barney leaned forward and looked to his left at Zach and Taylor. They both looked back and Ryan thought he saw a smirk on Taylor's face. Barney locked eyes with Ryan. "We will go with you and your friends."

Barney rose, and Ryan stepped back, surprised by his size. He was shorter than Ryan by a foot or so, but had a very powerful build. He could easily make quick work of Ryan.

"But what about Mom and Dad?" Taylor cried as he jumped up.

Barney walked over to Taylor, held him by each shoulder, and looked into his eyes. Zach stepped back, folded his arms, and looked at Ryan.

"They were caught in the fire trying to get to the others. They wanted us to go and be safe. It's time to be brave."

Ryan heard the young monkey sniffle.

"Okay," Taylor replied.

Barney turned back to Ryan. Zach stood next to him. Barney put one arm over Taylor's shoulder and the other over Zach's. "We're ready."

CHAPTER 34

KARL STOPPED AT the top of the crater and stared at the boot print on the damp black soil as the last remnants of sunset retreated to the west. It was an American boot-tread pattern. His men wore European boots, and Chemo and his men had worn Brazilian boots. Crusaders—and one had made it out of the crater. Based on the deep, rough edges around the print at the toe, he was moving fast into the cover of the jungle. But Karl was worried. He'd faced Crusaders before, and their commitment to the cause made them much harder to defeat than criminals and those who fought for money. He assumed it was their belief that they were on a mission from God that gave them a singular focus and commitment that outshined any fear of death or defeat. He admired them for that and wished he believed in something that much. For him, the money and the thrill of killing were simply an addiction he had to feed. Thank goodness he was so good at it.

Karl looked up from the boot print and scanned the jungle. His lone surviving accomplice did the same.

The dense jungle was nearly black. The tallest trees formed a thick canopy that choked out the last bits of dusk leaking from the cloudless sky. The smell of smoldering brush still hung heavy in the air, and the constant chatter from the squirrel monkeys and parrots faded into the white noise of the insects and reptiles that made the night their own.

Karl had covered the perimeter to the left and was scanning the path to the right when he heard it. The crackle of the jungle brush was rhythmic, as if someone was running about forty yards away through the thick maze of palm fronds and broad-leaved bushes. Then it stopped.

He reached for his pack, slipped it off his shoulders, and knelt on the path. He dipped his hand into the side pocket of his fatigues and he pulled out a night-vision scope. He slipped the scope onto his rifle and winced at the click of the mounting snapping into place. His only mercenary had dropped to his knees about ten yards behind and followed Karl's lead, installing his night-vision scope. Karl brought the MP5 to his shoulder and pressed his right eye against the soft socket of the sight. He scanned the jungle. The wind was calm and the leaves stood still. He froze on movement against a tree about thirty yards out and moved his finger to the trigger. He steadied the weapon but then pulled his finger back when he saw the anaconda's head stretch away from the trunk. He pulled away from the sight, wiped his face, and continued his scan.

Then he spotted it. It appeared to be a silhouette of what looked like a fuzzy-faced, husky smaller man facing Karl about sixty yards out. He was partially concealed by a tree trunk. Karl locked on the center of the figure and readied to fire. He saw movement and squeezed the trigger. A single shot rang out. The rustling resumed and the steps trailed off into the distance. He'd missed. He scanned the jungle for any other movement and saw nothing.

It was dark now, and Karl knew movement through the jungle would be impossible. The chopper couldn't land in the clearing until daylight. They'd have to make camp. With only two people, sleep would be difficult. A Crusader was still on the loose—they'd have to keep vigil in case he returned.

"Let's move up to the opening in the trail and set up there," he said.

"Got it, boss."

The opening was small and at a bend in the trail. From the position, they would see both directions down the path clearly and would hear anyone approaching through the thick jungle. They tied off their jungle hammocks. Karl dropped his backpack into the hammock and yanked out his satellite phone. He'd put off the call as long as he could, but it was time to face Cyrus. He punched in the numbers and waited for the connection. Cyrus answered on the first ring.

"What the hell is going on there?"

"We had a problem, sir."

"I'll say. You could see that fire from outer space. The Brazilian authorities are chattering like crazy about it all over the airwaves. Even the save-the-rainforest nuts are on it."

"We didn't set it."

"I don't care who set it. Do you have them? The kid and the monkeys?"

Karl swallowed hard. "No sir."

"No. No! Why the hell not. You had them cornered in that crater."

"We were waiting at their camp when the fire jumped us. It burned everything."

"Everything? So you're saying it burned the monkeys and the kid?"

"There was nothing living on that crater floor. I could see it on the way out."

"Did you search every inch of it?"

"No, sir. We barely made it out alive. I'm down to one man. Everyone else is dead."

"Burned in the fire?"

"No, sir. I think the Crusaders set the fire, and they were waiting for us on the trail. They killed Chemo and all his men. Got one of ours too."

"Crusaders ... where are they now?"

"We killed all but one. He's still out here somewhere."

"You listen to me carefully, Karl. You need to get back into that crater and confirm that the monkeys were destroyed. I want every inch looked at. If they're alive, I want them, and if there are any remains, we'll need them for Grandby and his people. I've invested most of my life and a good part of my fortune to get here, and I'm not going to walk away without being sure."

"I only have one man. We can't cover the whole crater. I need to get back and assemble another team."

"Did you not listen to me? The Brazilians are all over this. They'll be crawling over that crater in less than twenty-four hours, and if the monkeys are alive, they'll find them. If not, they'll get their remains. Then God knows what they'll do with them. You know how important they are to our longevity on this earth."

Karl knew he was right. "We'll head back in the morning."

"Remember to be careful. The boy and his party could still be with them."

"There's no way they survived that fire."

"You thought there was no way they would get this far. Remember Houston?"

Karl pulled the phone from his ear. He hated being reminded of his failures, especially by his boss.

"If they are with them, we'll take care of them. I promise."

"I don't need your promise. I need at least one of those monkeys. Now I've got to call Grandby and tell him his men weren't worth a shit. Get us one of those monkeys!"

The phone clicked off, and Karl tossed it into the hammock. The other man stared at Karl.

Karl stared back and said, "We're back in the crater in the morning."

CHAPTER 35

SUDDENLY RYAN FOUND it harder to breathe. Inside the cave, the air was heavy with the smell of charred wood. But Ryan knew it wasn't just the smoke: He was smothered by responsibility. After all, he was just a kid. Now he was responsible for the safety and well-being of what might be the most remarkable discovery in the last two thousand years. They stood before him—three monkeys that could not only swim, they could *talk*. He studied Barney and then glanced at Thad.

Thad looked over his shoulder to the cave's entrance. "Paulo, buddy, see if you can raise the camp."

"I've been trying for the past fifteen minutes, but I'll try again." Paulo pulled a black two-way radio from his pack, said something in Portuguese into the mike, raised it to his ear, and waited. He repeated the process twice, then pulled the radio from his ear. "Nothing."

"Think he's moved out of range?" Thad asked.

"No. Marcos wouldn't do that without making a call. He's my most reliable guide."

"Looks like we catch some z's here, folks," Thad said, as he laid his rifle against the cave wall and slipped his pack from his shoulders. He walked to the entrance of the cave. The distant glow of the fire front created an orange glow around him.

"We can't go out there?" Ryan asked.

"Don't think it's safe," Thad answered, scanning the crater. "Too hot. No telling what the fire did out there, and with no backup, we have to assume someone got to our guide."

"You don't think the fire forced him out of range?" Bill asked.

"You heard the man," Thad said, nodding toward Paulo. "He would have called in, if it did."

Addy dropped her pack. "That flashlight won't last long, and I assume all the wood out there has been burned."

Ryan looked at the monkeys. "We'll have to make camp here in the cave for the night."

"Can I get the wood from the back?" Taylor jumped forward and asked.

Ryan hesitated. Taming fire was another trait unique to humans.

"Sure you can. Get an armful and bring it here to Ryan," Barney said. He faced Ryan. "We keep it here during the wet season in case of an emergency. I think this qualifies."

Barney's lips curled into a slight smile again, and the sight haunted Ryan. Barney looked nearly human in the shadows.

"Uh … thanks. Anything you guys can do will help."

It was all Ryan could come up with at the moment. The shock of conversing with a monkey hadn't worn off yet. Taylor disappeared into the darkness, deeper into the cave. Ryan heard the logs clunking against each other, and in less than a minute, Taylor returned with his bulky arms full. Taylor curled his lips in a smile, and this time it wasn't as disturbing. It looked genuine. Ryan felt a connection and smiled back.

Ryan studied Taylor as he ambled into the light, closer to the front of the cave. He moved his long legs smoothly and without the wobble Ryan had seen in most apes. His posture was nearly straight, with his head balanced directly over his hips. He didn't waddle like a monkey or an ape—he walked like all the other guys Ryan knew.

Taylor dumped the pile of logs at Thad's feet, smiled, and returned to his brothers. Ryan checked out Addy, Bill, and Paulo. They too had their eyes on Taylor. They looked as if they'd witnessed an alien landing. Ryan couldn't blame them. It was becoming obvious these monkeys were unlike anything the world had seen. He began to feel the same responsibility his great-grandfather must have felt. He'd have to protect them: from the scientists, from the testing, and from those threatened by these hybrids creating a closer link between monkey and man. The world could easily destroy them, but Ryan wouldn't let that happen.

"Let's get this fire built. It will help keep whatever is left out there, out there," Thad said.

Ryan, Paulo, and the guide stepped in to help. Addy sat against the wall of the cave and cradled her father. Bill still didn't look well, but he definitely looked better. Ryan could see the monkeys observing *them* now. They had the same expressions the group shared while watching Taylor. They were just as curious about humans.

After the wood was formed into a campfire, Thad doused it with a little lantern fuel, stepped back, lit a match, and tossed it on the pile. The fire exploded to life and lit up the cave. For the first time, Ryan could see the three monkeys clearly; he scanned them from their feet to their heads. He locked eyes with Barney and couldn't look away. He was drawn to Barney's green eyes and felt the same gentle peace he felt when he looked at his Labs, Emma and Abby, at home. Barney smiled and nodded. Ryan returned the smile and nodded too. Ryan began to understand the gift his grandfather saw in him and silently thanked God.

"All right. Who wants the first watch? We need to get some shut-eye," Thad said.

"I will," Addy replied.

"Will Bill be okay?" Ryan asked.

"Hey, kid. I'm not dead," Bill said. "I'm right here—and I'm fine. Just a little tired."

Thad grinned. "Okay, Addy. You got it."

He plopped down in front of the fire, facing Ryan, and leaned back on his elbows. Paulo and the guide circled to Thad's side of the fire and sat down. Addy took her position at the mouth of the cave, while the monkeys stood behind Ryan and waited.

Ryan walked to the fire, sat down, and turned to Barney. "It's okay. Come join us."

Hoping he'd connected with them, he waved them forward. Taylor and Zach looked at Barney, who hesitated and then nodded. Taylor dashed to the fire and sat next to Ryan. Ryan watched the guide's eyes grow wide. Ryan glanced behind him and spotted Zach. He walked with a deliberate rhythm, like the linebackers on Ryan's school's football team. His thick arms dangled wide and swung well away from his sides. He was about half a foot taller than Barney, but still shorter than Ryan. Ryan recalled the crappy horror film he'd seen where the monster ripped off a guy's arm and beat him to death with it. Zach could easily do that to anyone in the cave. Zach hadn't smiled at all, and kept the same tough-guy expression on his face. But Ryan noticed a smirk when Zach cut his eyes to Taylor as he took his seat. Barney followed and sat next to Zach. Staring at Zach, the guide made the sign of the cross and mumbled something in Portuguese.

"So tell me how you learned to speak such good English," Ryan asked.

"I learned from my mom and dad and the films they showed us," Taylor said proudly.

"We all learned from our parents," Barney added, "and they learned from your great-grandfather. They told me he would visit for three months each dry season. He'd show up with books and pictures. He would read to them and use the pictures to help them learn. Later on, he came with a projector and reels of film. Our parents showed them to us."

Now Ryan understood how they knew so much about the world beyond the crater.

"Yeah, I love the movie about the scary shark!" Taylor said.

"Scary shark?" Ryan asked.

"Yeah. The one that was eating the people off the beaches."

Thad chuckled. "What else did you see?"

Taylor didn't answer. He just stared blankly at Thad.

"You can't talk to my uncle?" Ryan asked.

"Your great-grandfather told our parents we speak to no one except the one who spoke the verse and who has the gift. He said we'd feel it. I feel it in you and in no one else here. He said we risked death if we ever spoke to any human," Barney said.

"That's cool, dude," Thad said.

Zach smiled. Thad talked a lot like him—like someone from the seventies.

"Where do you live?" Ryan asked.

"We have a village down the path toward the lake," Barney said.

"So you live inside?"

"Sort of. We have what you call huts or lean-tos constructed."

"You built them?"

"Yeah, dude. We're not morons." It was the first time Zach had spoken to Ryan. His voice was much deeper than the others'.

"You used tools?" Ryan remembered the use of tools being unique to man.

"Yes. Your great-grandfather taught my parents and then they taught us," Barney said.

Ryan wasn't sure he understood what Barney had said. If his parents had been with his great-grandfather from the beginning, that meant they were here in 1926. That would make them at least ninety years old. He looked at Thad across the fire.

"Ask them how old their parents are," Thad said.

"How old are your parents?" Ryan asked.

Barney hesitated, and Zach and Taylor looked at him. They waited. Barney slowly eyed the group and stopped on Ryan. "Can these others be trusted?"

Ryan scanned the group too and stopped on Paulo and the guide. While he was sure he could trust Addy and Bill, Paulo and the guide were contract help and Brazilians.

"Your hesitation has answered my question," Barney said as he looked into the fire.

He stared into the flames and remained silent. Ryan wanted to hear the answer. It had to be something important for Barney to guard the information so closely. Maybe they were much older, and Ryan's great-grandfather had warned them about sharing the information with humans. In any case, Barney wasn't talking—at least not here. Ryan decided to stop the questioning for the night.

"Let's try to get some sleep," he said to the group.

Barney rose and walked into the shadows of the cave. Zach and Taylor followed. Thad lay back and rested his head on his pack. Paulo and the guide did the same. Bill drifted off, still leaning against the cave wall.

Ryan knew he couldn't sleep; how could he? Suddenly, he felt alone. He peered into the flames and thought about home. He longed for his time at the Primate Park and even the time at school. Compared to what he faced now, that was easy. He heard a rustling at the mouth of the cave and spotted Addy moving across the entrance to the other side. Her lean figure was silhouetted in the firelight. She glanced over her shoulder and caught Ryan's stare. Still, he couldn't look away. She smiled and then turned back to scan the smoldering landscape. Ryan stood, brushed off his pants, and walked to her side.

"See anything out there?" he said.

"Nothing but smoke and that fire off in the distance." She nodded to the back of the cave. "Those friends of yours are something else."

"Yeah. Can you believe it? Everything Grandpa said was true."

"You think they'll come with us?"

Ryan hadn't really thought about the monkeys making a choice to stay. "I—I think so."

"Good. I'd like to get Dad out of here as soon as we can."

"He okay?"

Addy's gaze drifted back into the cave. "I think he's fine for now. I need to get him to a doc and get checked out, though."

Ryan sensed her distress and wanted to comfort her. But he wasn't used to that. Usually he was the kid being comforted. "I can't tell you how much I appreciate everything you and your dad have done for us."

Addy looked at Ryan, and for the first time he saw an irresistible gravity in her dark-brown eyes. She reached out and touched his forearm. "By the way, happy birthday," she said.

Ryan immediately thought of their age difference: He'd never be able to impress an older woman.

"My uncle told you?"

"Yes, he did." She nodded toward the back of the cave again. "You've got quite a present back there."

Ryan smiled as he fumbled for the right words. He came up with nothing.

Addy broke the awkward silence. "You know, I think we should thank you. These monkeys or whatever they are—they're amazing. My father wouldn't want to be anyplace else other than here being a part of something so special."

"They are special. I think they're some sort of hybrid."

"Hybrid?"

"Yeah. I don't know a lot about anthropology, but these guys look a little like monkeys and are the size of the great apes. Their faces are flatter, more like ours—and they walk like us."

"I noticed that. They don't romp around like the chimps I've seen at the zoos. And their arms are shorter and their legs are longer."

"And can you believe they can talk?"

"I was shocked. They look human when they do it."

"Yeah. That's probably one of the reasons those scumbags are after us."

"From what your uncle said, you have several scumbags to worry about."

Ryan looked out the entrance of the cave. Smoke still drifted through the burned-out jagged tree trunks, backlit by a rising moon. It looked like something from an old horror film. He felt like a child, frightened by something hiding under his bed or in the closet, but he stuffed the feeling and tried to hide his fear from Addy.

"We can handle the scumbags. I just want to get those monkeys back home," he said.

"Then what?"

"I don't know. Grandpa said I'd have to decide if it was time to share them with the world. If the time was right."

"I don't know how you don't share them with the world. This is the most remarkable discovery ever."

Ryan's shoulders sagged under the weight of Addy's words. He didn't know what to say.

She seemed to sense his discomfort. She stepped closer and stroked the side of his head. "You're a remarkable young man. You'll do the right thing, whatever that is."

"You think so?"

"I know so."

Ryan inched closer, and her body's magnetism pulled him in. He abandoned his nervousness and surrendered to his hunger for her touch. He leaned in. Addy didn't pull back, and Ryan closed his eyes as their moist lips connected. It lasted longer than he'd expected, but it wasn't enough. Addy pulled back first, and Ryan thought he'd crossed the line. He stepped back and stared at the dirt.

"I'm … I'm sorry," he said.

Addy pulled the MP5 across her body and turned back out to the smoldering crater. Ryan could see her eyes glistening in the moonlight. Her dimples deepened in a smile. The silence lasted a few seconds, but seemed like a lifetime.

She kept her focus on the scorched, moonlit landscape. "I'm not."

CHAPTER 36

DAWN HAD COME quickly, although Ryan wouldn't call it dawn. He stood shoulder to shoulder with Thad and Addy, surveying the moonscape. Black jagged tree trunks jutted from the smoldering jungle floor. There were only two colors visible: black, and the brown of the thick fog that filled every space. There was no noise and no movement. Everything was dead or gone. The heavy smell of smoke made Ryan cough. When he inhaled to catch his breath, he could taste the air and feel the grit on his teeth. No one said anything. To his right, Barney and Zach appeared and stood next to Addy. They too surveyed the damage in silence.

"Where are Mom and Dad?" Taylor cried out as he ran up from behind and stood between his brothers. "Where are they?"

"We don't know," Zach said in his gruff voice. "We'll try to find them."

Zach and Barney shared a look of concern over Taylor's head. Ryan was amazed he could read their expressions.

"Let's get ready. Outta here in five," Thad said.

Ryan caught Addy's eye. She smiled and headed back toward her father. Ryan turned his attention to Barney.

"Are you ready to come with us?"

"We will be, Ryan. First we need to search for our parents."

"We'll help."

"Thank you. You indeed are of Zachariah's clan."

"I have to ask, can you eat what we do?"

"Yes. For a while. But we have Heaven's fruit, as your great-grandfather called it."

"Heaven's fruit?"

"He said they looked like yellow tomatoes."

"I've seen them along the trail."

"Fortunately your great-grandfather taught us how to dry and preserve them for travel. We've also stockpiled the seeds in anticipation of the trip."

"Trip?"

"Yes. Your trip to take us to safety—to Miami—in the United States of America, correct?"

Ryan's mind raced through the threats: Crusaders, mercenaries and customs officers. Still, there was only one place where he knew they had a chance.

"We'll take you back to my home and the Primate Park."

"The park Zachariah built?"

"That's the one."

"Ah—I'd love to see it. It sounded so beautiful when my parents talked about it."

"It is. And you'll be safe there." Ryan knew he had just lied. He didn't know for sure if they'd be safe. But it was the only place to go.

"Our things are in the back of the cave. We'll join you in a moment."

Barney followed Zach and Taylor into the cave, and they disappeared into the shadows. Ryan gathered his pack and helped Addy split the contents of Bill's pack between them. Things were different between them since last night—they were better. He could still feel their connection, but they both treated it like an unspoken secret. Everyone joined Thad at the entrance and watched as the monkeys appeared from the back of the cave, carrying what looked like old packs from the Army-Navy store. Barney's was plain khaki, but Zach's was covered with peace signs. Taylor's had a few peace signs too, but it was covered with Batman, Scooby Doo, and Yogi Bear stickers and patches. Ryan chuckled. He recognized the characters from watching the old shows on TV Land with his uncle.

Thad walked over to Taylor, leaned down, and said, "You're the coolest dude on this planet." Then he smiled and winked at Ryan. "Tell them we'll follow them wherever they want to search."

"Lead the way, Barney. We'll follow you," Ryan said, shouldering his pack and rifle.

Barney nodded and headed down the scorched path. He walked to the right, deeper into the crater and away from the exit. Ryan shrugged and waved for Thad to follow. Addy and Bill were next, while Paulo and the guide covered the rear. The downed trees and piles of smoldering ash made the path invisible, but the monkeys appeared to home in on a route. They drifted downhill and further to the east, closer to the lake.

The terrain flattened at the edge of the lake and the monkeys stopped. Ryan caught up and gawked at the sight. Despite being charred down to their frames, he could make out the structures. They looked like lean-tos and huts, just as Barney had described, and they stretched on either side of the opening for at least three football fields to the edge of the black lake. Within a larger structure, Ryan noted an old projector reel still mounted on the remnant of a projector. Singed film canisters were stacked on the ground a dozen high. A bike sat just outside the rear edge of the frame connected to a motor.

"Generator," Thad said, bumping past Ryan and nodding toward the contraption.

Zach took the lead and stalked along the path like the Terminator. The rest followed. Ryan shifted his eyes from side to side, examining the burned-out huts. Nothing was moving. Everything was charred, black, and smoldering. The brown fog began to fade, and Ryan could clearly see the lake at the end of the path.

There was something floating about fifty yards offshore. Zach and Taylor spotted it too, and picked up the pace to a trot. They dropped their packs and broke into a sprint to the water. In seconds, they were swimming the freestyle faster than any swimmer Ryan had ever seen. Zach made a wake as if he were a small speedboat.

Ryan finally reached the water's edge with the others. He could clearly see the matted, charred fur of a monkey, floating face down. Zach reached him first, gently rolled the monkey to his back, and towed him to the shore. Taylor swam at his side and helped.

As they approached shore, Ryan saw Taylor was crying. The monkey was lifeless. He thought of Taylor's parents and felt sick. Zach got his footing in the shallows and lifted the limp body with both arms and carried it to shore. He gently laid the body at Barney's feet and knelt on one knee, looking up at Barney. Ryan didn't want to, but he stepped next to Barney. Taylor stood over the body, crying, and Ryan saw a tear drop from Barney's eye.

Barney looked up at Ryan. "My father's brother."

Ryan didn't know what to say or do. He looked at his own uncle and imagined life without him. His eyes welled up. Thad stepped closer and squeezed one of Ryan's shoulders.

"Ask them what we can do," Thad said in a whisper.

"How can we help?" Ryan asked.

"You can help us search for our parents. Then we need to take him to the resting place," Barney said.

They searched for two hours. Ryan stopped every time he heard Taylor's trembling voice calling out. They found no sign of anything living in the area. When they returned to the center of the village, Barney stopped at his uncle's body.

"I'll carry him," Zach said as he scooped his uncle from the ground.

Thad grabbed Zach's pack and slung it over his shoulder. Ryan repeated the gesture with Taylor's pack.

"Where are Mom and Dad?" Taylor sobbed.

Barney knelt down in front of his younger brother, held him by his shoulders, and looked out over the lake. "They're in a special place. You need to be strong, like we talked about last night."

Taylor continued to cry and dropped his head onto Barney's shoulder. Barney was crying too, but stopped. "Okay—now let's be strong together."

Ryan heard Addy sob and looked back at her. She buried her face in Bill's chest, and Bill cradled her head with his hand. Thad stood with a blank stare. Paulo and the guide made the sign of the cross. Ryan had forgotten they were monkeys. They shared the same pain he'd felt when his grandpa had died. They were more like his family than some unique species.

Barney rose and took Taylor by the hand. The group followed Zach back up the path in silence. They proceeded past the cave and turned to the west, toward the graveyard. When they arrived, Ryan stopped and stared. The graveyard hadn't burned. He assumed that because it was cleared of all brush and trees, the fire front had bypassed it.

As the group surveyed the graves, Barney turned to Ryan and said, "You'll need to stay here, please."

The monkeys ambled to a gravesite about seventy-five yards away. Zach held his uncle's body for an hour while Barney and Taylor dug out one of the open gravesites a few rows away with crude wooden shovels. Then gently, slowly, Zach slipped his uncle into the grave. The three monkeys huddled. Ryan couldn't hear what they were saying, but they were all speaking in unison. Together, they dropped their heads and stepped away from each other, picked up the shovels, and filled the grave.

They returned, and Ryan stood up to meet them. "I am so sorry," he said. There was nothing else to say.

Barney nodded, as did Zach. Barney looked at his brothers, then back at Ryan.

"We're ready to go with you, Ryan Webster."

CHAPTER 37

RYAN COULDN'T TELL what was worse: the heat or his concerns over what waited for them outside the crater. With the canopy gone, the late morning sun beat down and heated the black charred ground below his feet. The intense heat nearly brought the damp jungle floor to a boil, and he swore he could feel the steam burning his skin. With each step, his pack cut into his shoulders under the extra weight from the contents of Bill's pack. Drenched in sweat, he could barely keep his eyes clear and focused on Paulo and the guide leading the group.

They'd left the cemetery, made their way past their old campsite, and begun the climb to the crater's only exit. With the jungle reduced to ashes, he could see all the way to the falls. The rim of the crater was singed but blended back into green jungle at the top. The fire hadn't made it out, and Ryan thanked God for that. His thanks melted into worry when he thought about the assholes who'd set the fire. They'd probably be waiting somewhere in the thick jungle leading from the crater. Ryan's group had discussed having the helicopter come to them in the crater, but the area wasn't secure and its arrival would signal to their attackers that they'd survived. He reconsidered his prayer of thanks and trudged on.

Behind him, Bill walked on his own and looked much better. He still labored in the heat, but considering the conditions, he was doing as well as anyone. Addy scanned the scorched landscape, holding her rifle across her chest. Zach and Barney followed her, with Taylor lagging behind and getting periodic encouragement from Thad, who guarded the rear.

Ryan decided to drop back and talk to Barney and Zach.

"You guys doing okay?"

Zach just looked at Ryan and grunted.

"We're fine," Barney replied. "It's just a little warm without the jungle."

"Can I ask you a question about that graveyard?"

"We call it the resting place."

"Okay. The resting place."

"What do you want to know?"

"What happened to all the others there?"

"Well, some died of old age, some had an accident, and many got very sick."

"How old is old?" Ryan asked.

Barney stopped walking, checked the distance to the others, and faced Ryan. "I'll tell you, but you can't mention it to anyone. According to your great-grandfather, it will put us in even more danger," he said quietly.

Barney resumed walking and looked straight ahead. "Between a hundred and sixty and two hundred dry seasons."

Ryan stopped. Barney kept going. Zach stared at Ryan as he and Taylor passed him.

Thad caught up to them. "You need to keep going. We're almost there."

Ryan was shocked. He didn't know of anything that old—maybe dirt.

"What? Did you see a ghost or something?" Thad asked. He passed Ryan, turned, and backpedaled up the grade. "C'mon dude."

Ryan recalled Barney's warning not to tell anyone. He could trust his uncle, always had. And Thad had never let him down. But maybe now was not the time. He began to walk and as he passed, Thad patted him on the back. "What is it? What did they tell you?" he asked.

"I'll tell you later."

Ryan picked up his pace. He passed the monkeys without comment and moved ahead of Bill and Addy just before the falls. The cooling mist rolled across his face in waves. Paulo and the guide stopped at the entrance to the ledge leading behind the falls and allowed the group to catch up.

"How do you want to do this?" Paulo asked Thad.

"You two in the front, and Addy and me in the rear. Keep these guys between us."

Paulo nodded. He checked his MP5 and disappeared behind the falls. Ryan reached back and Addy guided Bill's arm into Ryan's grasp.

"You ready?" Ryan asked.

"See you on the other side, Dad," Addy said, releasing her grip.

Bill nodded and they edged along the ledge behind the falls. The ledge was a little wider than their boots. Just behind them, Barney, Zach, and Taylor negotiated the path with no problems. Ryan couldn't believe their sense of balance. They reminded him of the fearless kids in PE who walked with ease across a balance beam.

The spray from the falls drenched him, but he welcomed the cool water. Ryan moved out of the falls onto firm ground and noticed the thick jungle had returned. Up ahead, about thirty yards into the shade of the canopy, Paulo and the guide climbed the steep incline. Ryan carefully followed, with Bill in tow. He looked over his shoulder and saw Barney and Zach emerge from the falls. Barney moved up the path and into the shadows.

Suddenly, gunfire erupted up ahead, and Ryan instinctively hit the ground. Dragging Bill, he wriggled into the brush and pointed his rifle up the path. Short bursts of gunfire volleyed back and forth ahead, then stopped. Immediately, shots rang out behind him, and Ryan looked back down the path to check on Thad, Addy, and the monkeys.

He heard more gunfire from behind the falls and rolled over, pointing his rifle down the path and flicking off the safety. He wanted to run back to help, but he had to protect Bill. The shots were rhythmic and getting louder. He watched the edge of the falls. Another volley rang out, much louder this time, and he saw a huge, square-shouldered man drag Taylor off the path while firing back into the falls. He quickly recognized the albino German from Houston. They disappeared into the jungle, but Addy emerged from the falls, aiming her MP5 at the albino. She fired short bursts and followed them into the brush. Behind her, there was no sign of Thad or the other monkeys.

The gunfire stopped. It was quiet, other than the rushing water of the falls. Ryan held his position and checked on Bill.

"You still okay?" he whispered.

Bill nodded. Ryan focused back on the falls.

Barney and Zach emerged from the edge of the jungle and returned to the path. Carefully, Ryan raised his head and checked up ahead. Paulo and the guide were on the ground, bloody and motionless.

Trembling, Ryan looked back at Barney and Zach. "You okay?"

They nodded and looked back into the falls.

"Stay here," Ryan said to Bill as he scrambled to his feet and headed down the path. "Where's my uncle?" he yelled.

"Where's Taylor?" Barney yelled back.

"They got him," Ryan said as he raced by and headed back into the falls. He carefully edged along the ledge behind the falls and barely heard his uncle's voice over the roar of the water. Thad wasn't on the ledge: His voice came from below Ryan. With his back pinned against the wet wall, Ryan stopped and listened.

"Down here," Thad yelled.

Ryan carefully leaned forward and looked down. His uncle hung by his fingers on a jagged rock about ten feet below. He wouldn't hang on long. Ryan started to slip his pack off, hoping to get to a rope in time.

"No time for that," Zach boomed. "C'mon, Barney."

In seconds, Barney slipped over the ledge, suspended by one of Zach's huge hands. Zach dropped down to a seated position and then slid over the edge, gripping the ledge with his free hand. Ryan wiped the water from his face. Zach's huge forearms bulged and his wet fur glistened. Barney climbed down Zach's torso, grabbed his foot, and reached for Thad. He caught Thad's wrist on the second try. Thad gripped Barney's forearm and in one movement, Barney pulled Thad off the rock. Thad climbed up Zach and rolled onto the ledge. Zach grunted and pulled Barney up, who rolled onto the ledge too. Finally, Zach pressed himself up and over the ledge. All four leaned against the back wall of the falls, soaked and catching their breath. Ryan was still shocked. He'd never seen such a display of strength. He stared at Zach, who grinned back, and then turned to his right and smiled at Barney. Thad panted, but gave them both a thumbs-up.

Barney leaned forward and said one word to Ryan. "Taylor?"

"The asshole got him," Thad said.

Zach snapped his head around and glared at Thad.

"I think they got Addy too," Ryan added.

Ryan had never seen the expression on his uncle's face before—it was dark and frightening—almost as frightening as the expression on Zach's face when Zach turned to Thad and said, "Let's go get them back."

CHAPTER 38

THE LOOK WASN'T quite one of panic. The urgency was there, but not the confusion. Both Thad and Zach seemed to be of one mind. Any trepidation about speaking with Thad disappeared with his rescue. Thad and Zach had quickly decided to regroup at the crest of the crater and survey the likely escape routes. Ryan scanned the area to the south and noted that the burn outside the crater the day before had cleared a swath about a mile wide in a formerly grassy savannah about a mile southwest of the trail exiting the crater. The jungle to the north and west was still thick and provided cover for the German to slip away or do God knows what to Taylor and Addy.

"Addy left the path here?" Thad asked as he pointed to the trampled palm fronds.

"Yes. She had her rifle and was firing at the German in short bursts," Ryan said.

"Then you heard more shots?"

"Yes."

Thad stepped deeper into the thicket and disappeared for a moment. He returned with bad news. "There's blood. We have to assume she was hit, and he took her with them."

"Them?"

"Yeah. It looks like the albino joined up with the dirtbag who killed Paulo about fifty yards in." Thad nodded back into the jungle. "We have to get to them before they reach a chopper. They get there, it's over."

"Where did they go?" Barney asked.

"I can't tell. I'm not a tracker, and the trail seems to disappear into the jungle. If they landed in the large clearing we did, they're headed west. But with that area to the south cleared by the fire, they could land anywhere."

Ryan eyed Barney. He was thinking, trying to reason out an answer. It was still surreal to think a monkey could do that. But Ryan no longer saw a monkey. Nor did he see the hybrid that Barney clearly was. He saw a friend. Barney raised his head and looked at Zach.

"We need help."

Zach seemed to know exactly what Barney meant. He stood and began to make a screeching call that Ryan recognized as the alarm capuchins sounded at the Primate Park when something startled them. Thad looked at Ryan, recognizing the same call, and shrugged.

After cycling through the call three times, Zach stopped and listened. The response echoed in the distance first, then grew like the roar of an approaching wave at the beach. Ryan scanned the understory, and soon there was movement in the leaves. One by one, brown and white capuchins appeared, many much larger than the ones at the park. Ryan glanced at Thad, who was watching the display. They exchanged a smile, then turned back to the show. A few of the capuchins darted from the higher branches to the underbrush. Barney and Zach moved off the path and into the brush, out of sight, to meet them. After the brief meeting, Barney and Zach backtracked to the path. The capuchins returned to the canopy and commenced a louder chatter. Then they gathered and headed due west. Barney walked over to Ryan.

"They're headed west. The young woman appears to be bleeding from her arm, but otherwise okay. Taylor is fine but his arms are bound. There are two of your kind dragging them to the west. They're moving slowly, but they have a head start. They'll be moving slower soon."

Barney nodded to the cluster of capuchins vanishing to the west.

"You can talk to those little guys?" Ryan said.

"Yes. We—"

"We need to get going," Zach said.

Thad leaned in. "You lead the way, Zach. I'll follow."

"I'm coming too," Ryan said.

"You stay here with Bill," Thad said.

"No—no way. I promised to protect them and I didn't. I'm going too."

"We could use the numbers, and Barney can take care of Bill," Thad said.

Everyone looked at Barney, and Barney agreed.

"Where do we meet?" he asked.

Bill stood up and ambled to the group. "The chopper is supposed to meet us about three kilometers down this path around noon. They'll wait one hour and then leave if we're not there," Bill said. "I'm fine. I can make it. Just go get my daughter."

"Okay. Ryan, check your ammo and drop that pack. We'll need to move fast." Thad looked at Zach and offered his rifle. "Do you need one of these?"

"While you humans are quite comfortable creating things that kill, we don't use them."

Thad pulled the gun back and slung it over his shoulders. He scampered down the path to Paulo and the guide and dropped to one knee, searching Paulo's body. He snatched two magazines and a radio and stuffed them in his pockets. He pulled two more magazines from the guide and returned, tossing them to Ryan.

"We're ready."

Zach bolted into the jungle in an instant. He moved through the thick brush as if wasn't there. His wide shoulders temporarily split the brush, and Thad and Ryan stayed close, slipping through before the openings closed. Zach's fur smelled like the Labs after an hour in the hot Florida sun. The jungle was thick and palm fronds and branches slapped Ryan in the face. Thad kept pace on Ryan's heels. Up ahead, the capuchins moved through the canopy like a wave.

About fifteen minutes into the jungle marathon, Zach slowed, and Ryan spotted the capuchins as they spread out across the canopy, then disappeared. Their chatter was still audible. Zach stopped.

"They're close. Our friends will signal the exact location."

The capuchins let out a chorus of "Eh, eh, eh" and reappeared just to the left.

"There. There they are." Zach peeled back the large green leaves, and Ryan spotted Addy. She was leaning against a tree. Blood seeped from her shirt just below the left shoulder. She was breathing heavily and looking to her left. Ryan followed her line of sight to Taylor. He was bound at the hands and had a noose around his neck. The noose was connected to the tall, thick-necked albino he'd seen in Houston. Another man chugged from a canteen nearby.

"Those are the dudes who tried to take you in Houston," Thad said. "Probably want to keep the little guy alive. Addy's usefulness will end at the chopper."

Ryan started forward with his rifle pointed at the albino. "Then let's get them."

He ran into Zach's forearm. It was like running into the cinderblock wall under the basket at Heritage High. It was the first time he'd touched one of the monkeys. Zach was solid, but Ryan sensed a gentleness: the same gentleness he'd sensed when his grandfather grabbed Ryan before he stepped into traffic as a kid.

"Wait," Zach said.

"Yeah, dude. Hang on there."

"Our friends will distract them and make it difficult to move. Then I'll get close. Can you get the first man, without ending his life?" Zach asked.

"I sure can, dude. But why not take him out?" Thad said, dropping the MP5 from his shoulders.

"Why do you humans insist on killing?"

Thad didn't say a word. Ryan knew Thad didn't have a good answer, and Zach's tone made it obvious he didn't expect one.

"I'll take care of the big one and get Taylor. You'll have to get the woman," Zach said, nodding to Ryan.

"Don't worry. I'll get her."

"Ryan," Thad whispered. "Go around to the left and make your way up from behind."

Ryan stepped aside, and Thad slipped right behind Zach. Zach crouched and disappeared into the underbrush. Thad veered right and weaved from tree trunk to tree trunk until he had a good angle for a shot. Ryan crouched and crept to his left, carefully avoiding moving the palms or bushes. Slowly, he closed the forty yards between him and Addy to ten. He could barely see Addy through the matted palm leaves and branches, but he was close. He hoped he'd be able to get to her in time. He looked to Addy's right and saw the albino and Taylor tethered with a thick rope. Taylor huffed and puffed and the noose looked tight. His eyes were wild, and he'd been crying. Ryan was sickened at the sight of Taylor being restrained like an animal. He was pissed, and he used his anger to focus on getting Addy. He carefully pulled the rifle up under his arm and waited.

Just then, the capuchins dropped down through the canopy close to the albino's lookout and pelted him with what looked like monkey shit. Their chatter rose to a peak, and, wiping the goo from his face, the lookout yelled in what Ryan guessed was German. Still screaming, he raised his gun and fired a round into the trees. When the albino turned away from Taylor to see what was happening, Zach exploded from the brush and roared. Ryan was startled. He'd never heard such a sound come from a monkey or an ape, not even from the large silverback at the park. Despite his size and strength, the albino didn't stand a chance. One swipe of Zach's meaty hand and the albino hit the ground. A shot rang out, and his henchman twisted and dropped to the ground. Thad had hit his mark. Addy struggled to free herself from the tree, and Ryan suddenly remembered that was his job. He darted from the bushes and she screamed.

"Hey. It's me."

Her face lit up. "Ryan!"

"Let's get out of here."

He pulled the knife from his belt and cut the rope from around her wrists. In seconds, they were free. He glanced back at Zach, who had Taylor in his arms.

"Go. Go," Zach yelled.

They headed toward Thad, who closed ranks. Ryan got to Thad first with Addy.

"You guys okay?" Thad asked.

"We're okay," Ryan said.

Zach arrived with Taylor.

"You all right, dude?"

Taylor didn't answer.

"He's fine. Just a little scared," Zach said.

"I'll go finish the albino," Thad said, cocking his MP5.

"No—leave him. He won't be up for a while. I promise you," Zach said.

"But he's been after us since Miami."

"He won't be after us here. No killing."

"All right. I'll just take their weapons and radios."

Thad retrieved the weapons and radios and quickly returned.

Ryan caught his attention, nodded toward the west, and looked at his watch.

"The chopper," Ryan said.

"The chopper," Thad repeated. "Hang on." He pulled a small pouch from his belt and yanked up Addy's shirt sleeve. "It's a pretty good nick, but no bone," he said.

Addy nodded and Thad deftly opened the pouch with his teeth, pressing on a thick bandage.

"Good as new," he said, grinning. Thad yanked a compass from his pocket, read it, and pointed through the jungle. "This way home."

CHAPTER 39

BLACKMON WINCED AS the last of the stitches were carefully pulled tight across the leg wound. Another inch to the right, the Brazilian doctor explained, and he would have bled out in the jungle. The office tucked in the corner of the old warehouse wasn't much of an emergency room, and certainly not sterile. Blackmon had been assured by the remaining Crusaders manning the location that the doctor could be trusted. The last thing he needed was the attention of the Brazilian authorities.

The doctor finished his dressing and wrapped the remainder of the tape around Blackmon's thigh. Then he pulled a syringe from his bag. Blackmon rolled on his side and closed his eyes. The needle felt like a bee sting in his ass, but the pain subsided immediately. Blackmon pulled his trousers up and nodded to the doctor, who nodded back and scurried out the door. Blackmon limped into the adjoining room and headed for the makeshift communications desk in the corner.

"You okay?" the black man with the headphones asked.

"Fine. I need the satphone. I left mine out there."

"No problem."

The man reached behind the flat-screen on the desk and pulled the satphone from its cradle. He handed the phone to Blackmon. Blackmon limped toward the door while the chopper pilot and another Brazilian in the center of the room winced.

"You need a hand?" the pilot asked.

He waved them off and slid through the door into the warehouse. He was down to three men, and they needed to focus on Manaus. Once outside, he stepped to the dock and dialed the number.

Remington picked up on the first ring. "I thought you were gone."

"No, sir. Still here. It got a little rough, though."

"How rough?"

Blackmon wasn't sure Remington wanted an answer. He gave one anyway. "They got four men, and I took a round in the thigh."

"The boy and his uncle?"

"No. The German."

There was silence on the other end. Blackmon knew what Remington was thinking and decided to head off the question he knew would come.

"We burned the entire crater. No one escaped except the German. No sign of the boy or his party. They didn't get out."

"But the German did."

"There were six of them and we took out four. Too much firepower. We couldn't hold them."

"Who the hell is he?"

"The team here got that report back while I was out there. Seems he works for a philanthropist in Miami, Cyrus Schultz. His father was a German businessman, part-time zoologist, and somehow knew the boy's great-grandfather."

Remington was silent for a moment. "So there is a connection."

"Yes, sir. Seems that Schultz's father tried to buy into the kid's great-grandfather's work in the sixties. Something happened, and they became competitors. The rumors we picked up about the new species came from that period."

"So one of them may have made the discovery?"

"That's possible."

"And this Cyrus may be working with Grandby and his people."

"Right. But we don't know what's in it for him."

"Where's the German now?"

"The GPS transmitter is still on his chopper. We have it headed back north to pick him up."

"Is he alone?"

"He has one other man with him."

"And you don't have direct confirmation of the death of the boy or his party—or the monkeys, for that matter?"

"No, sir. But nothing could've survived that blaze. It's dry here, and it went up fast. It scorched the entire crater."

"Still, we can't risk it. If they somehow made it and do have this new species, they could destroy all we believe."

Blackmon stroked his wound. While he didn't think anything could've survived, he knew Remington was right. Without a visual, they couldn't be sure. And if any proof got out, Grandby and his Godless friends would ensure creatures were marched around the world. They'd claim the missing link had been found and Darwin's theories were now axioms. More importantly, Grandby would attack the accounts in the Bible and tear the book of Genesis to shreds.

"I understand, sir. We'll track the German and get the team in Manaus to watch the ship and air traffic. If the boy and the monkeys are alive, they'll try to get back to the states."

"Greg, you understand we can't afford to take any chances. I've ordered more Crusaders down there to help you. If they are alive, and do get out—"

"Sir." Blackmon heard a voice behind him. He spun to see the radioman trotting toward him, out of breath.

"The chopper landed and took off again. He's probably on it."

"Jacob, I gotta go. The German is on the move and probably headed to Manaus."

"You've got to get to him and be sure he doesn't have any evidence."

"We're on it, sir," Blackmon said as he ran toward the helipad.

"Godspeed."

Blackmon ended the call and flipped the phone to the radioman as he jumped aboard the Bell helicopter. The turbines started to whine and the rotor began to spin.

"When the replacements get here, get to that crater and go over every foot, then call me in Manaus," he yelled over the roar.

The radioman nodded, gave a thumbs-up to the pilot, and backed away. Blackmon felt the chopper shudder and then lurch forward and into the air. He rubbed his thigh and offered the pain to God.

CHAPTER 40

CYRUS HAD COVERED every foot of the dilapidated warehouse. The waiting drove him crazy. They were close. Karl had taken a setback, but all indications were that the monkeys were real. The old man was right for once, and by the end of the day, Cyrus would have what he'd always wanted.

"Mr. Schultz," he heard echoing off the tin walls. He spotted a man wearing a headset waving him over. He made a beeline for the cinderblock office and slammed the door against its stop.

"Where are they?"

"In the air, a hundred miles north of Coari."

"Give me that." Cyrus ripped the headset from the man's head.

"Karl, you there?"

"Hang on, sir," the pilot said. There was a brief delay.

"This is Karl."

"You're late! What the hell is going on?"

"We found them. They're real. I repeat, they're real."

"You have them with you?"

"No, sir."

"What? You dumbass! I told you to get them and bring them here."

"Sir. I had the girl and a monkey—uh—or whatever it was. It had the fur of a monkey but with a flat face and a human nose, and it stood upright, had shorter arms. It—"

"Where the hell is it?"

"A bigger one attacked me and someone shot my man. They took him and the girl."

"You had the girl too and let her go?"

"They ambushed us. We didn't have a chance."

Cyrus took a breath. "Karl. Tell me about the monkey."

"They look like a combination between an ape and a monkey and they walk like us."

"They? How many did you see?"

"We spotted three with the boy's group. One was smaller than the others, and when we ambushed them, we got him, along with the girl."

"What else?"

"They carried packs. The one we captured had things on his pack."

"Things? What things?"

"*Aufkleber* ..."

"In English, Karl."

"Uh—stickers."

"Stickers?"

"Yes. They looked like cartoons."

"Let's try this. What was in the pack?"

"We found some seeds, a few tools, and some books."

Cyrus's interest was piqued. If they had books, that meant they could read. "Could you tell how old they were?"

"No, but the one we had looked younger than the others."

This was going nowhere. Cyrus needed the monkeys, not these trivial answers. "Where are they now?"

"I think they'll head your way. They looked like they were traveling out to meet their chopper."

"Why aren't you following them?"

"The big one knocked me out. Then they left. We just circled the area, but there's no sign of them. They're probably on the way."

"So the boy and his group have made it past you with three of the monkeys?"

"We took out two of them. They're down to the boy, the uncle, the geologist, and his daughter."

"Get your ass back here, and we'll cover the waterfront and the airport."

Cyrus threw the headset down.

"Get Grandby on the phone," he yelled to the thug in front of the laptop. The man snatched a satphone from the six sitting in their cradles. He trotted out the open door with Cyrus in tow to get line-of-sight, and dialed.

"Mr. Schultz for Mr. Grandby. It's urgent." He paused and squinted in the bright sunlight. "Hold, please."

He handed the phone to Cyrus.

"Charles. I have good news. We've found them."

"You found this new species?"

"Yes. Bad news, though, old boy. Your team is dead. Those damn Crusaders killed them."

"And your man made it?"

Cyrus could hear suspicion in Grandby's voice.

"Barely. We took heavy casualties, but the good news is they exist—and they're alive."

"You said monkeys. Are you sure they're monkeys?"

"No. As a matter of fact, my man says they're some combination of monkeys and apes, with a few human features."

Grandby said nothing.

"You still there?"

"Yes. You said they had traits of all three primates?"

Cyrus shared Karl's description. Grandby fell silent, and Cyrus could almost hear him licking his chops. He knew a little anthropology from the days he had spent with his father. Such a combination would be the pro-verbial missing link—a bipedal hominid: the last common ancestor between man and monkey. Grandby could use it like a dagger to kill the creationist arguments. After all, he'd have living proof.

"Where are they now?"

"We think they're headed to Manaus, and they're making a run for home. We need your help."

"Whatever you need."

"We need to cover the dock and airport here. I think we have enough men here for that, but I'll need your help checking the airline and cruise line reservation systems. I'll also need your help in Miami in case they get through."

"Surely they won't fly if they have the animals. You can't just buy them a ticket. The cruise line is much more likely. Easier to conceal the animals. Immigration and customs along with the CDC will be all over them if they try."

"You're right as usual, Charles. We'll focus on the docks and check all private and commercial traffic headed that way."

"My men will coordinate with your people there. I'll get the information to them as soon as possible."

"Thanks."

"Cyrus?"

"Yes, Charles?"

"They're much more valuable to me alive."

"They are to me also." But only to a point, he thought to himself.

"I'll call you when we have them."

The phone clicked off and Cyrus threw it to the man beside him. He thought about the myth his father told him before he died, and Cyrus smiled. The old man may have finally told the truth for once.

CHAPTER 41

RYAN CHECKED HIS watch for the third time in as many minutes. It was 12:18 p.m. According to Bill, the chopper would leave at one. He glanced over at Addy. Despite the bruises on her face from the beating Karl had delivered, she kept pace with him. Up ahead, Thad hacked through the thick jungle with his machete, following Zach and Taylor. Ryan envisioned Karl punching Addy's face and slammed his machete into a thicket of vines, wishing it were Karl's throat.

Addy looked over and attempted to smile, but the swelling on her cheek made her wince.

"You—you still okay?" Ryan asked. He labored to catch his breath as he hacked another vine from the path.

Addy nodded. "How are we doing on time?" she said, nearly out of breath.

"I think we'll make it at this pace."

Ryan turned his attention ahead. It was too difficult to converse, and he knew Addy was laboring just to breathe the thick humid air. Sweat trickled off his forehead and ran down his cheeks, but he wiped it with the back of his hand and did his best to ignore it.

In the distance, he heard a strange hiss. It was faint at first, and he held his breath to get a better fix. Thad stopped and craned his neck to listen too. Then it clicked—it was rushing water—maybe from another waterfall. They caught up with Thad, but fifty yards ahead, Ryan spotted Zach and

Taylor pressing forward through the jungle. They moved uninhibited by the underbrush and vines.

"What do you think it is?" Ryan asked.

"I hope it's just some falls."

"They're still going?" Ryan pointed to Zach and Taylor.

"Let's go—not much time left," Thad said, glancing at his wrist.

Thad broke into a trot. Ryan grabbed Addy's hand and followed. Zach and Taylor had stopped in a clearing up ahead, and as they closed on their position, the rushing water became a roar.

Ryan had never seen anything like it. The black water swirled and sloshed against the riverbank, but at its center it simply raced by like a speeding conveyor. It looked deep, and Ryan guessed it was more than fifty yards across, just like the outdoor double Olympic-sized pool he'd swum in at the University of Miami.

"This is not good," Thad said.

Ryan surveyed up and down river. It seemed endless. "We can't swim it," he said.

"You're damn right we can't."

Ryan looked at his watch again. It was 12:45. "We're not going to make it."

Zach and Taylor studied the water, then turned to each other and nodded.

"We can make it," Zach said.

"No way. It's too fast," Ryan said.

Taylor stepped toward Ryan, stuck his chest out, and smiled. "Not for us."

"Maybe you can make it, but we can't, dude," Thad said.

"You can with our help," Zach boomed.

Ryan looked at Addy, who shrugged. Then he looked at Thad and pointed to his watch.

"Guess we don't have a choice." He faced Zach. "How do we do this?"

Zach knelt down. He drew the shorelines in the black dirt with his finger. "I'll take Thad first. He's the largest of you three. We'll cross here." Zach looked up at Taylor.

"Then you take the woman. She's the smallest. You start further up, about here. You should end up with us, here," he said, pointing to the opposite shoreline in the dirt.

Taylor nodded. "Her name is Addy," he said, smiling proudly at her.

"Of course," Zach said. "Addy."

Ryan realized the plan left him alone on the other side of the river. He knew he'd never make it across alone.

Zach stared at Ryan. "That leaves you here, Ryan," Zach said.

"Not a good plan, dude," Thad said.

Zach raised his furry hand. "I'm not done. Ryan, you look like a good swimmer."

"I am. But I can't make it across in that current."

"But like I said, I can. I want you to jump in up here and swim as hard as you can. I'll jump in here and bring you back to shore."

Ryan studied the diagram and then stared at the racing water. If Zach missed, he'd drown for sure. He be sucked miles downstream and never reach the shoreline.

"Ryan," Zach said. He looked directly at Ryan. His deep blue eyes widened. "I trust you with my life; do you trust me?"

Ryan was thrown by the question. He'd forgotten Zach was some sort of monkey-ape hybrid. He thought of him as he would think of his other friends with the same human limits. There was something about Zach's eyes that calmed Ryan. "I do, Zach."

"Good. I'll get to you. Just keep swimming. No matter what—don't stop. I can't get you if you stop."

Ryan didn't like the sound of that. Still, he trusted Zach. "I'll try."

"There is no try. Just do it," Thad added and patted Ryan on the back.

"See you on the other side," Addy said, and kissed Ryan on the cheek. Now he was committed.

"You and Addy head upstream. Wait for me to get to the other side. When I wave to you, swim her across," Zach said.

"No problem, bro," Taylor said.

Thad extended his palm. "Be cool, dude."

Taylor slapped it and headed upstream with Addy.

Thad turned to Zach. "Let's go, dude. I'm ready."

"Lose the pack and the gun."

"Whoa—what if those guys are still out there?"

"I can't make it if you have your pack and gun. You won't need it."

Thad cut his eyes to Ryan. Ryan dropped his pack and slipped the rifle off his shoulder. Thad slowly followed Ryan's lead.

"It's two kilometers to the chopper that way," Thad said as he looked at his compass and pointed across the river. "We've got fifteen minutes." He stuffed the compass into his pocket and stepped next to Zach.

"Get behind me and wrap your arms around my neck. I'll need my arms and legs free. Just float when we hit the water."

"You're the boss."

Thad wrapped his arms around Zach's thick neck. Zach was a little shorter than Thad, but twice as wide.

"See you there, dude. Just remember, don't stop swimming," Thad said, glancing over his shoulder.

With one lunge, Zach was in the water headfirst and swimming. His powerful arms pulled at the water, but the speed of his stroke was what amazed Ryan. He noticed the wake Zach made, just as he'd seen at the lake. Despite the river pushing them downstream, Zach powered across and hit the opposite shoreline in what Ryan guessed was twelve seconds. His confidence surged. He knew the world record for the fifty-meter freestyle was just under twenty seconds. Zach had just done it in twelve with Thad on his back.

Zach pressed up on the shoreline and waved upstream to Taylor. Ryan turned his attention up the shoreline to his right. Taylor hit the water with Addy on his back about one hundred yards away, and the current pushed them past Ryan by the time they were halfway across. Taylor's stroke was even faster than Zach's. He hit the opposite shoreline and Zach plucked them both from the water with one pull. Addy looked as shocked as Ryan felt.

Now all four stood across the raging waters, waiting for Ryan. His stomach began to roil, just like it did before a race back home. The roar of the water made it impossible to hear them, but Zach waved him upstream. Ryan worked his way up the shoreline about fifty yards past where Taylor had hit the water. He was fast in the fifty. Although he'd set the state record last year at 20:25, he knew he'd have to top that here.

He yanked off his shoes and his shirt but decided to leave his pants on. Two more kilometers in the jungle and a helicopter ride to Manaus in his underwear would be too much embarrassment. He looked downriver to the other shoreline. He could barely see the group, watching intensely. He stretched his arms and shoulders and shook them out as he did before every race. Zach waved. Ryan took three huge breaths and dove in headfirst.

The water was warmer than it looked, but it shoved him to his left much harder than he'd anticipated. He pulled hard with each stroke and then tried to take a breath. When he rolled to get the breath, the current nearly flipped him on his back. He twisted back in the water but knew he'd lost momentum. He had to swim faster. No more breaths. He'd have to make it on this one. His shoulders began to burn from the pace. The river shoved him further downstream, and for a second, he envisioned being swept away. But then he heard it—they were cheering as if he were in a meet. The cheers grew louder and he channeled the adrenalin rush to his arms, pulling toward their voices. But then the cheers peaked and began to fade. He'd passed them and was being swept downstream. His lungs were burning and his arms felt as if they'd fall off. The adrenalin faded. Despite his fading strength, he clawed at the water. If he was going down, he'd go down swinging.

Just then, his wrist snagged in something and his arm was nearly yanked out of the socket. *Zach had him—Zach had him!* He smiled underwater when he heard the cheers again, getting louder. The shoreline scratched his side as Zach lifted him to safety. He didn't care—he'd made it.

Ryan sat up and coughed out some water. He cleared his eyes with his thumb and forefinger and saw Zach huffing. He wanted to hug him but he didn't have the energy. He reached out with his hand and Zach slapped it. Upstream, Thad led the charge down the shoreline as the group hooted and shouted. Thad got there first, picked Ryan up off the ground, and gave him a bear hug. Ryan rested his head on Thad's shoulders.

"You were awesome, dude. Just freakin' awesome."

Taylor hugged him around the waist. "You made it. You made it," he yelped.

Addy stood behind Thad. She looked at Ryan and smiled. She was dripping wet and her clothes clung to every line of her sleek figure. She reached out and pushed his hair back from his eyes. Ryan smiled.

Thad pulled Ryan away and held him at arm's length. "Let's get outta here, dude. We got a chopper to catch."

CHAPTER 42

THE RED-ON-WHITE helicopter sat in the middle of the tall grass, idling. Smooth waves from the rotor wash traveled along the grass tops to the edge of the jungle. Ryan felt the cooling blasts of air against his damp skin, and for the first time in days, he relaxed. They'd made it. They were going home.

As Thad led the group toward the chopper, the rear door opened and Bill stepped out, bending down in deference to the spinning blades just over his head. He waddled closer, and Addy dashed ahead to meet him halfway. She jumped up into his open arms, and he rocked her back and forth in a hug. Ryan could see the tears in his eyes. Thad and Zach walked past the pair, and Bill let go of Addy and hugged them both.

Ryan knew he looked like a shipwreck victim. His hair was still wet and dangling in his face. His side was scratched by the jagged roots of the shoreline. He was barefoot and covered in dirt. Still, Bill wrapped both arms around him.

"Thank you for getting my daughter back. Thank you." Bill released Ryan and moved toward Taylor.

Taylor stood beside Ryan and appeared to hesitate. Ryan saw his hesitation. "It's okay, Taylor. He's an old friend of Zachariah. You can trust him."

Bill smiled at Taylor, who looked at Ryan. Ryan nodded. Taylor's look of concern softened and he extended his arms. They hugged.

"And you, my friend—I'm so happy to see you," Bill said.

"Where's Barney?" Taylor asked, looking at the ground.

Bill pointed back to the chopper and Barney stepped out to meet Zach. Taylor took off on a dead run. It was an odd sight for Ryan to see a monkey sprint upright like one of his buddies. Taylor jumped into Barney's arms, nearly knocking him over. While they hugged, Zach rubbed Taylor's head.

Bill turned to Ryan. "The pilot brought some dry clothes."

Bill put one arm over Ryan's shoulder and the other over Addy's, and they headed for the helicopter together. As they got closer, Barney, Zach, and Taylor stopped outside the door. Ryan shielded his eyes against the blast from the rotors and turned one ear toward them. Still, he couldn't hear what they were saying over the constant roar of the turbines. Barney said something and they all nodded, then scanned the jungle one more time. Then it hit Ryan: This was a big step for them—they were leaving their home. Their parents were gone, and now they were putting their trust in him.

They faced the chopper and stepped into the middle bench of the helicopter. Ryan climbed into the back door, followed by Bill and Addy. He slipped on the shirt that was on the seat and pulled the headset on. The chop of the rotors got louder and they lifted off. In seconds, they were above the jungle.

"Let's make one pass over there," Thad said over the mike.

The chopper banked to the left, and Barney leaned over Taylor to look down. Tears welled in Barney's eyes. Ryan traced Barney's line of sight to the ground. They were directly over the crater. The entire jungle had been reduced to a smoldering, scorched black wasteland, from the edge of the lake across to the entire perimeter. A tear rolled down Barney's fur. Ryan thought of his own parents and wondered what he'd do if he lost them both.

The chopper banked back to the right and headed for Manaus. The crater disappeared behind them and Barney turned away from the window. Ryan now understood why his grandfather and great-grandfather protected these magnificent beings. Now it was his turn.

He leaned back against the headrest and dozed until the jolt of touch-down in Manaus woke him up. He rubbed his eyes, leaned into the window, and scanned the area around the helicopter. They weren't at the airport, but had landed adjacent to a newly constructed warehouse. A bright yellow sign with crimson letters said "Martin Exploration." It was Bill's warehouse. The reality hit him hard. He still had to get them back to Miami. How would he do that? Flying wasn't an option. Customs would surely catch them. That was why they'd landed at the warehouse.

Bill pointed to the door and Ryan pulled up on the latch. He stepped out onto the asphalt along with the others, and Bill led the group to a white steel door. The chopper lifted off. Turning, Ryan watched it disappear over the warehouse.

"Don't worry, Ryan. You won't need him to get home," Bill said as he held the door for Ryan.

Ryan entered and scanned the room. The space was clean and freshly painted off-white. Several steel desks were scattered about, and he spotted a long hallway to his right.

Bill stopped in front of the group. "All right. We're fine here for a few hours. There's a locker room down that hallway. There should be duffels there for us to get changed. Ryan, Thad, and Addy will go over the plans with me and then get cleaned up and meet back here."

"I don't know how to thank you." Ryan said, and shook Bill's hand.

Bill nodded to the monkeys. "Get them safely back to the Primate Park. That's my thanks."

CHAPTER 43

THE WARM SHOWER had washed away the sticky grime from two days in the jungle. While he'd taken a long shower by his standards, Ryan's 'don't get up until the last minute for school' motto provided shower skills that allowed him to be the first one dressed and back in the office. He walked to the large window on the far wall, used to monitor activity in the warehouse, and wondered where Barney, Zach, and Taylor had gone. He scanned the warehouse and then caught his reflection in the glass. The khaki cargo shorts and turquoise polo shirt fit surprisingly well. The Merrell sandals, Ray-Bans, and Marlins cap ensured he'd blend in well with the other tourists headed to Lauderdale. Bill had done his homework. His clothes reminded him of the trips to the ballpark to watch the games from Sarah's father's luxury box.

Miami and Sarah seemed a world away now. He hadn't called her since Houston. He checked his watch. It was 4:23 p.m. on Tuesday, and he hadn't spoken to her since Thursday night. He pictured Sarah and her mother discussing how inconsiderate he was and asking each other why she was even with him in the first place. A familiar shame crept over him, and he tried to push it from his mind.

"I feel much better now," Addy said as she entered the room.

Ryan lurched and spun around.

"Still a little jumpy, are we?"

His heart thumped hard and then slowed to a normal rhythm. She'd startled him, but he was happy to hear the strength that had returned to her voice. She tucked her wet hair into a ponytail and slipped an Astros ball cap over the knot, adjusting it just over her eyes. She'd touched up the bruises on her cheeks and the red lip gloss made the split in her lip nearly invisible. Ryan bristled at the thought of the albino German beating her. But then he remembered the kiss last night and smiled. Something wonderful swept over him. It was a new sensation, and nearly uncontrollable.

"You look beautiful." The words fell out of his mouth without ever engaging his brain.

For the first time, he saw Addy blush and drop her gaze to the floor. "You look like a good Miami boy yourself," she said as she slowly looked up and locked her eyes on Ryan.

Ryan drifted toward her. With each step, his skin heated and tingled in anticipation of her touch. She didn't move or take her eyes from his. He kept drifting closer, as if some magnetic force pulled him to her. He let the last remnants of self-monitoring fear melt away.

"I'm so glad you're okay," he said softly.

She wrapped her arms around him and pressed her body against his. "And I'm glad you came to get me."

Ryan leaned in and kissed her, long and hard.

"Hey, look at them, Barney." Taylor said, giggling.

Ryan jumped and started to release Addy, but she didn't let go. He turned to see Barney and Zach with their arms crossed, and he swore they were grinning.

Taylor was pointing at them. "You guys like each other, huh?"

"That's enough, Taylor," Zach said.

"It's fine," Addy said. "You're right, we do." She smiled and kissed Ryan on the cheek. Ryan's embarrassment faded a bit.

"I knew it. I knew I was right," Taylor said.

"Hey dudes, what's up?" Thad said as he charged into the room, rubbing his wet hair with a towel. Ryan chuckled when he checked out his uncle's wardrobe. He was sporting a pressed pair of white Tommy Bahama linen shorts and a silk floral-print shirt, finished off with a pair of Sperry topsiders. In his free hand he carried a white fedora panama hat and a pair of wraparound sunglasses. If anyone knew his uncle, they'd never recognize him. Thad wouldn't be caught dead in that outfit. He stopped rubbing his hair, held his arms out to his side, and looked down at his clothes. "What? You don't like my disguise?"

Ryan held back a laugh. "Best one I've seen."

Addy covered her mouth and giggled.

Bill entered the room, decked out in tan slacks and a lime green golf shirt and looking much better. He had a young, brown-skinned Brazilian in tow. He held the monkeys' packs including a replica of Taylor's. "Everybody ready?"

Taylor ran to meet him, snatched his backpack, and slipped it over his shoulders. "I am," he said, grinning.

"Hey little buddy, you'll need to leave those with Vicente," Bill said. "We'll be sure you get them later."

Taylor looked at Barney. "Are the seeds still inside?"

"Yes, they are. I had Vicente take some of mine and pack them in your new pack. You can't take it now." Barney looked at Taylor and nodded toward the Brazilian. Taylor frowned, stomped over to Vicente, and gave him the pack.

Bill pointed at Vincente. "Now Vicente will take the five of you to the terminal and drop Barney, Zach, and Taylor off at a warehouse just northwest of the terminal along the river, then take Thad and Ryan to the dock."

Bill stopped, sucked in a deep breath, and let it out with a sigh. "This is it, my friend," he said as he leaned in and hugged Thad. "You've made me a very happy man, and I'm sure that somewhere, Zachariah is very proud." The men patted each other on the back.

"Thanks, Bill. We can never repay you for all you and Addy have done. You guys be careful on your way back to Houston."

Bill pulled back, and with moist eyes, he looked at the monkeys. "You already have—just get these guys back safely." Wiping his eyes, Bill turned and walked up to Ryan.

"And you, young man, I think you've grown into everything a man could hope for. You're just like your great-grandfather." He hugged Ryan and it felt good. Ryan's father had never hugged him like that, but this was close enough.

"You take care, sir," Ryan said.

Bill shook his hand. "You call me Bill from now on. You've earned that."

He pivoted and walked over to Barney, taking his huge hand. "You are very special, my friend. Thank you for trusting us and for saving my life."

The corners of Barney's mouth slowly stretched into a smile and his eyes glazed with tears. He covered Bill's hand with his other hand. "You are a kind human, and I know now why you are friends with this family. Safe travels to you and your daughter."

Bill stepped back and rubbed Taylor on the head. Then he extended his hand to Zach. Zach looked down and wrapped his massive hand around Bill's, making it look like a child's. They said nothing. They didn't have to.

Barney walked over to Addy and hugged her. "Thank you for going after my little brother. I'll never forget that."

Tears ran down her face. She couldn't speak. Zach stepped over and hugged her too. Then they released her, and she bent down on one knee and stroked Taylor's head.

"You're very special," she sobbed softly.

Taylor leaned in and they hugged.

"We've got to go. It's time," Bill said.

Addy stood up and walked across the room to Ryan.

"You take care of yourself. You're a lot tougher than you think, swimmer boy." She laughed and hugged him. "See you at the park." Ryan didn't want to let her go. But over her shoulder, he saw Barney, Zach, and Taylor waiting. They were waiting on him. It *was* time to go.

CHAPTER 44

RYAN SLID FORWARD as the old white Ford panel van slowed and turned right. Gripping the seatbacks, he wedged himself up between Vicente and Thad. A quick check of his watch said they'd been on the road for just six minutes. Ryan scanned the rusting, corrugated metal warehouses on either side. Rotting crates and junk lined the road. They were either abandoned or rarely used. But the entire area looked like a junkyard, even the docks that reached out into the black river. Vicente gripped the wheel with his left hand and pointed with his right.

"There," he said, struggling with his English, "they be safe right there."

Ryan could see a doorway at the end of the warehouse to the right. The broken crates, rusted pipes, cans, and barrels were strewn to the river's edge and onto a wharf that had partially collapsed into the water. The junk was high enough to conceal anything, and it probably did. To the left, at least five football fields away, the Pacific Princess towered over the waterfront. Ryan guessed it was at least ten stories or more to the upper decks.

Vicente stopped the van and pushed his finger in front of Thad's face. "Door. They go inside door." His frustration was obvious. He looked over his shoulders and pointed to the monkeys. "They get out. Now."

"What do you think?" Ryan asked Thad.

"It looks okay, dude, but I'm not sending those guys in there without checking it out."

Thad opened the door. Ryan stepped between the seats and followed him out the door. "I'm going with you." Then he leaned back in the van and looked over the seatback at the monkeys. "You guys stay here for a minute."

He turned back in time to see Thad open the warehouse door. Ryan tiptoed between the rusted drums and broken pallets and reached the door as Thad stepped inside. The foul smell made Ryan gag. It reminded him of the bottom of his gym bag after he'd left it in his locker over summer break, blended with the foul smell of the dumpster behind the Miami seafood joint where he bussed tables in his sophomore year during one of South Florida's hottest summers.

Ryan joined Thad as he pulled his shirt over his nose and scanned the warehouse. A little daylight leaked in through the broken skylights above, but there were no lights. Rusted barrels were strewn down the left side of the warehouse. Square wooden crates stained with their dripping contents were stacked to the right. Some were broken, and sardine-like cans spilled out to the floor. Ryan pushed the door open a little wider to examine the crates closest to them. They had an outline of a fish and something written in Portuguese.

"Guess we found that stench," Thad said as he turned and pushed Ryan back out the door.

Once in the daylight, he dropped the shirt from over his nose and sucked in a deep breath.

"No one is in that shithole. Let's get them out." Ryan walked to the door of the panel van and slid it open. "C'mon, guys. It smells bad, but it's okay."

Barney stepped out first, then Zach pushed Taylor out the door.

Ryan pointed to Barney's watch. "It's almost six-zero-zero now. You need to be over there at the back of that big white ship at nine-zero-zero."

Barney studied the watch again. "Nine-zero-zero. Nine o'clock?" Barney asked, pointing to the watch face.

"You got it, buddy," Thad said. "Sorry about the smell, but if you can stay inside until you need to hit the water, it would be awesome."

Thad checked his watch and looked at Ryan. "Gotta go, dude. Gotta be in line before six."

Ryan studied Barney, Zach, and then Taylor. He remembered his promise to protect them. He looked at the black water licking the shoreline, just ten yards away.

"Don't worry, Ryan. We will make it," Barney said. "Go on."

Zach and Taylor nodded in agreement.

"Okay. We'll be ready. I promise."

The monkeys filed into the warehouse. Thad jumped into the passenger seat and closed the door. Ryan stared at the closed warehouse door. He didn't want to leave them alone. He was responsible for them. He looked back at the van. Thad rolled down the window. "Dude, they'll be fine. C'mon."

Ryan trotted to the sliding back door of the van, climbed in, and looked back at the warehouse one last time. Then he yanked the door closed, and they headed for the terminal.

CHAPTER 45

RYAN STARED IN disbelief at the chaos. From the van, he could see the tri-level riverboats jammed haphazardly along the shoreline. Used tires dangled from their decks like decorations, protecting them from the inevitable contact with the dock and each other. Small skiffs with outboard motors crowded into the tiny spaces between, carrying people or displaying their catches for sale. Along the road, vehicles meandered through the wandering clusters of people and honked their horns endlessly. It was a far cry from the Port Everglades cruise terminal in Fort Lauderdale. Despite being so tight that he squeaked when he walked, Ryan's father had taken the family on a cruise at least once a year. But not like this.

Vicente reached the main port entrance and waved to a serious-looking young man dressed in dark slacks and white shirt holding a clipboard. Several official-looking IDs dangled from his neck. Vicente pulled to the curb, shooed Thad from the passenger's seat, and bolted to the back of the van, slinging the luggage onto a cart held by the expediter. In minutes they were next to the Pacific Princess and locked in a staring contest with a clearly underpaid customs agent. He scowled at their passports and raised an eyebrow, asking for their yellow shot cards. When they produced them without hesitation, he slapped the passports closed, stuffed the yellow medical cards inside, and handed them back to the expediter. The luggage was cleared, and it disappeared with a cabin steward. In minutes they were wandering the decks.

Many had boarded in Fort Lauderdale and sailed down the east coast of Florida, made a few stops in the Caribbean, and then made their way up the Amazon to Manaus. Most of the sunburned passengers were well north of fifty and would be in bed just after sunset. Occasionally Ryan spotted a family with grumpy parents and kids shuffling their sandals and looking as if they'd been without *Entourage*, *The Hills* and *Jersey Shore* for at least two weeks. Ryan remembered the torture. After three days with his parents, he'd explored every inch of the ship. He'd found that any hope of a shipboard romance was choked out by the reality of sixty and seventy-year-olds nodding politely and calling him "sonny." He noted an occasional Marlins cap, and it bolstered his confidence in his attempt to blend in.

One long blast of the ship's horn signaled preparations were being made to depart the dock. Ryan checked his watch. It was eight-thirty.

"Seen enough of the ship?" Thad asked.

Ryan had seen enough to map out contingency plans for escape should they be discovered and cornered. It didn't take long because there were few options. He noted several hiding spots and the location of the lifeboats, and Thad had led him to the lowest deck of the ship, still exposed to the open water. He didn't plan on going overboard, but after the last week, nothing was impossible anymore.

A short jaunt up one flight of stairs landed them on deck six. They meandered down the narrow hallway to the stern of the ship and entered cabin 6091. Ryan marveled at the expanse of the two-room suite. Despite the sleeper sofa, TV, and table and chairs, the living room alone was larger than any cabin his cheap-ass father had ever rented. The bedroom had two twins and its own bathroom. Everything was decorated in white and coral blue, enhancing the view through the double sliding glass doors that opened to the balcony.

Thad yanked open the closet, pushed past the steamer trunk, and dragged one of the huge suitcases to the center of the living room. He unzipped the case and dug like a dog through the clothing neatly packed inside. "Found it," he said as he pulled the black braided nylon rope from the bag and tossed it on the floor.

Ryan noticed the knots tied about every four feet. Bill had thought of everything. Plenty of traction to pull themselves up.

"Let's check it out," Thad said as he dropped the rope and headed out on the balcony.

Ryan followed, tripped over the rope, and sprawled face first on the balcony.

"You all right, dude?" Thad said, chuckling.

Ryan pressed himself up and brushed off his shorts. "I'm fine. Nervous, I guess."

Thad leaned over the rail. Ryan stepped beside him and scanned the city. The last bits of sunlight were fading and the lights of the city were flickering to life. Through the collection of mismatched buildings and narrow streets, he recognized the hotel where he and Addy had shared dinner just four days ago. He missed her already.

"That's a long way down, dude," Thad said.

Ryan looked down at the black water. It was a long way. He hoped the monkeys could climb as well as they could swim. He looked to the open balcony to his right.

"What about them?" he asked.

"Just keep your eyes out. They're probably at dinner."

Just then, two blasts of the ships horn echoed against the city.

"Here we go," Thad said, heading for the rope.

Ryan leaned out and checked the decks below. The only windows were those of the restaurant. At nine p.m., it would be full. They'd have to center the rope on a small four-foot space between the two windows directly below them. Thad returned and tied off one end to the top rail. Carefully, he dangled the other end of the rope over the side and lowered the rope.

A wisp of wind brushed against Ryan's cheek, and he watched the rope sway as it approached the next deck. Thad paused and the rope drifted to the right. Just over one of the windows. Ryan winced.

"Careful," he whispered.

The breeze died and the rope drifted back, centering over the white metal partition.

"Okay. Go."

Thad continued to lower the rope. Slowly, it approached the water. Ryan gripped the rail hard enough for his hands to hurt. Then, the rope stopped short of the water.

"Shit," Thad said.

Ryan looked over and saw Thad empty-handed—they'd run out of rope. Thad looked at Ryan.

"It's too short."

"How much?"

Thad leaned over the rail. "I'd guess ten feet."

Ryan checked his watch—8:57. They were out of time. "What now?" he asked.

Thad looked down again and then back at Ryan, wide-eyed. Ryan didn't like the look. It wasn't quite panic, but it wasn't the cool, collected uncle he was used to.

"We need something strong enough to hold all three of them," Thad said.

Ryan thought of their tour of the ship. There had to be something. He remembered the lifeboats, but they'd never get to them in time, even if they had rope. Then it hit him.

"I got it. Be right back."

"Where, dude?" Thad yelled in a whisper as Ryan bolted for the door.

"Gym!"

The door slammed behind him, and he sprinted down the hallway, dodging passengers and hoping to avoid any crew. He passed the first stairwell and raced on to the front of the ship. Then he heard three hard blasts on the horn—they were leaving port. He lengthened his stride and made it to the second stairwell in less than twenty seconds. He bounded up the two flights of stairs to the gym and threw open the door. He put his hand against the wall when he felt the ship move forward. He leapt to the opposite wall and yanked the two jump ropes from the shelf. His legs ached and he was starving for air, but the thought of leaving the monkeys behind fueled him. He retraced his path, and at 9:01, he shoved open the door to the suite. He hoped no one had followed him.

"They're here, dude," Thad said.

Ryan bolted to the railing and looked down. He could see the prop wash churning the black water. About ten yards back, Barney, Zach and Taylor were swimming hard to keep up. He held out the ropes to Thad.

"Awesome," was all Thad said. He untied the rope and knotted the two jump ropes to the end of the nylon rope and lashed the end back on the railing. Ryan saw the other end of the rope hit the water.

"Swim!" he yelled, with his teeth clenched.

Zach seemed to dig in and split the wake. Barney and Taylor filed in behind him, and they closed on the dangling rope. Zach kept pressing closer to the stern and cleared the prop wash first. With one arm, he snatched the rope and stopped swimming. He extended his free hand and caught Barney's hand in mid-stroke. Zach pulled him to the rope, and Barney latched on. Taylor was struggling, but still closing the distance to the ship. Barney made a swipe for Taylor's arm and missed. Taylor drifted back a bit, but kept swimming. He regained his pace.

"C'mon, little dude. C'mon." Thad pounded the rail.

Taylor looked tired, and Ryan recognized the stroke of a fading swimmer. He wanted to jump in, but he knew he'd make things worse. Taylor slapped the water harder with his stroke and closed the distance again. Ryan knew this was it: He couldn't make another run. This time Zach slipped to the bottom of the rope and Barney moved above him. Zach stretched out his entire width and reached for Taylor. Taylor slapped the water and lunged for Zach's hand. Zach caught him.

"He's got him!" Thad yelled. He turned and hugged Ryan. "He's got him!"

Ryan almost cheered, but instead let out a "That's what I'm talking about" and slapped Thad on the back.

Ryan returned his attention to the rope. The monkeys weren't near the water anymore. These guys could climb even better than they could swim. They were three decks down and coming fast. They hit the restaurant windows at the divider and slipped by, but Taylor stopped, leaned over and waved, then continued on. Barney hit the railing first and rolled onto the deck. Zach catapulted over the railing and landed feet first, then pivoted and grabbed Taylor, hoisting him over the rail. Thad pulled the rope up. He threw the rope on the floor and extended a high-five. Ryan slapped it, then turned to the monkeys. Barney lay on the floor, huffing and puffing and shaking his head in disgust. Zach looked at Ryan, then Thad, nodding and smiling. Taylor put his hand up, copying Thad's high five. Thad stepped over and slapped it. Ryan did the same.

"What's wrong with Barney?" Ryan asked Taylor.

Taylor chuckled. "He hates to swim."

CHAPTER 46

"WHERE THE HELL is he?" Cyrus barked at the man monitoring the console.

"Two minutes out, sir."

Cyrus pivoted and charged the door, shoving aside the two men assigned to his personal security. The door of the cinderblock office bounced on its hinges as Cyrus marched across the warehouse through the door to the yard.

A single halogen beam lit the makeshift heliport. The rusting valves, broken crates, and corroded pipes had been pushed to a circular perimeter on the choppy asphalt. Cyrus scanned the night sky. The light from the city reflecting off the low, thin clouds made it difficult to spot the approaching chopper. He checked his watch and noted it had been two minutes since he'd left the office inside. He bristled at the thought of being so close to his prize and yet being held off by a teenager and his goofy uncle. His father hadn't lied. The hybrids existed and they could do much more than just swim. Karl had come close and failed. But now, he had them contained. Not by his men's efforts, but by a luxury cruise liner and the rules of the sea.

The sound of rotors chopping the thick air grew louder. The fog overhead began to glow and swirl, as if a UFO were making its first descent to Earth. The shaking beam from the spotlight on the chopper split the fog and illuminated the landing pad. Squinting, Cyrus shielded his face from the rotor wash.

Karl opened the door and had one foot on the skid before it touched the ground. Cyrus could see his bloodied face. Karl had an expression Cyrus hadn't seen since Karl's best friend was killed by a part-time security guard in a botched bank heist back in Germany. Karl relentlessly tracked and killed the man, going without sleep for four days. Cyrus smiled. Karl's need for revenge could prove useful.

Karl leapt from the cabin and trotted up to Cyrus. On closer inspection, the left side of Karl's face was one large bruise with a thick split of flesh stitched together with bloodied sutures.

Karl's black eyes locked on Cyrus. "Where are they?" he said, tightening his jaw.

"They got on the only cruise ship that left for the states tonight."

"How long ago?" he said through clenched teeth.

Cyrus wanted to have a little fun. "Looks like it got you pretty good."

Karl's eyes narrowed. "It's nothing compared to what I have planned for the hairy bastard."

Cyrus grinned. "You'll get your chance."

"I'll go get them now."

"Get a hold of yourself." Cyrus turned and walked toward the warehouse.

Karl bolted and blocked the doorway to the warehouse. "I'll get them and kill everyone except the monkeys. You can do your experiment, but I get to kill them, too."

Cyrus stopped. "Get out of my way, Karl."

Karl looked like a scolded dog that had suddenly recognized his master's anger, and he stepped aside. Cyrus waited, then entered through the door. Karl walked beside him and pleaded. "Why not now?"

"Too many people on that ship, and it's too difficult to board undetected. You'll have the damn Navy on your ass, and CNN will be reporting on your 'pirate attack' of a cruise ship headed to the US. I don't need that kind of attention."

Cyrus stepped to the warehouse office door and waited for Karl to open it. Always good to demonstrate who was the alpha dog. Karl got the hint and opened the door. Cyrus walked through and began to bark orders.

"Keep getting updates from the ship and forward them to the plane. Shut this place down and don't leave a trace. Tell our men not to take any action unless they leave the ship at one of the stops between here and Miami." He walked to the table in the center of the room and leaned over the large map, pointing to each location one at a time. "I want you two to take the chopper and shadow the ship to Parintins, here, Boca da Valeria, and Santarém. Then get the other jet and get to Devil's Island, Scarborough, Saint Lucia, and Saint Maarten. Don't do anything unless they leave the ship. We'll head back to Miami and set up with Grandby's people. We'll be ready for them when they get to Port Everglades—got it?"

The three men in the control room nodded, but stood still.

"Well—get going." Cyrus said.

The men scrambled and began disassembling the makeshift communication center. Karl studied the map. "That's fourteen days."

"Be patient, my friend. You'll get your chance. I promise. They created their own jail. They can't leave the ship at sea, and would be stupid to risk trying to get off at any of the other ports. The boy and his uncle are heading for the Primate Park, and we'll be waiting."

Karl crumbled the map and threw it against the wall. Cyrus grinned, then headed for the door with Karl in tow.

CHAPTER 47

JACOB REMINGTON PACED around the conference table for the thirty-fourth time. He'd been keeping count to keep his mind off of the thought of the collapse of the entire Society. The news out of Brazil was not good, and he suspected it was about to get worse. The knock on the door broke his trance.

"Come in."

Smythe led Richman into the room. "Guess we have some important bad news coming in," Smythe said, laughing.

Remington stared at him. Smythe was a dolt who rarely engaged his brain before opening his mouth. Remington tolerated him. While Smythe wasn't too bright, Remington knew he needed him. Smythe had been there longer than anyone, and the older members supported him. Some of the younger members found him amusing. Smythe finally got the hint and wiped the stupid grin from his face.

Richman circled the conference table and patted Remington on the shoulder. Remington remembered that he wouldn't be alone in his decision.

"Any more news?"

"He's calling any minute. His text was brief—just said he had more news."

Smythe had taken a seat on the opposite side of the table and yammered on about how he had read this and that report at ten or eleven o'clock, obviously thinking he'd get extra credit for working late. Remington ignored him and sat down next to the Polycom conference phone on the table. A high-pitch tone softly sounded, and Remington connected the call.

"Greg?"

"How's our jungle boy doing?" Smythe asked, folding his arms over his belly.

There was no reply.

"Go on, Greg," Remington said, staring at Smythe.

"We tracked the German. His chopper landed in a warehouse yard in Manaus. We've got eyes on them now, and it looks like they're clearing out."

"Any sign of the monkeys?"

"No, sir. Looks like he came home empty-handed."

"Where is he now?"

"We spotted a car with three people in it headed to the airport. We checked the tail numbers of the private aircraft at the terminal and one is registered to Cyrus Schultz's company in Miami. We think they're headed home."

"So, we're in the clear—they have nothing," Smythe said, looking around the room at Remington and Richman. "Good job, Greg."

Remington held up his hand and bit his tongue. "Go on, Greg."

"The helicopter was loaded and headed somewhere downriver. We also got a message from our source in one of Grandby's cells that said they were on the move—headed to Miami."

Remington felt his throat tighten. If Grandby was moving assets, then something important was headed to Miami. Remington looked at Richman, who shrugged.

"Greg, what do you guys make of that?"

"I hate to say it, but we think the boy and some of the creatures may be headed for Miami."

"So you think they're real?" Richman said.

"Yes—we do."

There was a long silence. Remington squeezed his temples between his palms. All their work was beginning to unravel before his eyes. The proverbial missing link had been found. And in a location where it shouldn't be: South America. The evolutionists would have their link and prove the theory of man from monkey. The non-believers would attack the book of Genesis and destroy the idea of the Divine Creator. He knew that would be the death knell for the Society.

"So where do you think they are?"

"Cruise ship."

"You sure?"

"I'm not certain, but if they're headed back to Miami and they have even one of those creatures, the airlines are out of the question. The only other way out would be by sea, and one just left tonight."

"Can you get on board?"

"No, sir. It's gone, and it's too dangerous to try to get on board undetected."

"Look," Remington said, "if any evidence reaches the light of day, we're done. You've got to stop them if they're on board."

"It gets worse," Blackmon said.

"Worse. How the blazes can it get worse?" Smythe said, putting on a good show.

"Grandby has dispatched a team to the crater."

"Can't you stop them?"

"Don't have the resources to plan an accident, and we can't outright kill a group of well-known scientists."

"So we cut our losses and focus on Miami," Richman said.

Remington was still stunned. Grandby's team would find evidence and quickly make it public. Then it would turn into a battle on the networks and talk shows. They'd take membership losses, but the thought that bothered him the most was his failure in his charge from God to protect the Bible.

"Jacob?"

He saw Smythe and Richman staring at him. He looked at the Polycom, and then back at the two men.

"We focus on Miami and put together a PR plan here. Greg, meet us in Miami." He looked at Richman. "And we have to play our trump card—now."

CHAPTER 48

RYAN LEANED ON the damp rail and scanned the churning water below. The constant hum of the engines had lulled the others to sleep, but not Ryan. Despite the fatigue of the past week, the decision that waited for him in Miami would not let him rest. He replayed the conversation with his grandfather over and over, and each time it came down to one request. "It's time to be sure they are safe and ensure they survive. You'll have to decide if it's time to share them with the world." Each time the comment cycled through Ryan's mind, another brick went onto the load. The weight of responsibility was crushing—and he didn't have an answer.

"Can't sleep, dude?"

Ryan snapped up and spun around. He saw his uncle scratching his crotch in his plaid boxers.

"Jeez, Uncle T. I just about jumped over."

Thad ambled over and leaned on the rail next to Ryan. "It's been some week, huh?"

"Yeah," Ryan replied as he rested his forearms on the top rung of the rail. His uncle's presence was always comforting.

Thad scanned the water. "Look, buddy, your grandpa would be very proud of you. You've done everything he asked and more. Pretty impressive for a kid who just turned eighteen."

"Thanks, Uncle T. But I'm worried about what to do when we get to Miami."

"We'll figure some way to get them to the park."

"That's not what I'm worried about."

Thad looked at Ryan. "The decision?"

Ryan wasn't surprised by his uncle's ability to read him. Ryan felt closer to his uncle than anyone, except his mother. "Yeah. The decision."

Ryan wanted to be the man his uncle was. Thad was smart, strong, and always seemed to know what to do—no matter what. Sometimes Ryan still felt like a teenage boy, striving for total irresponsibility. He hesitated, then decided to go ahead and ask. "What would you do?"

Thad rubbed his tousled hair and let out a faint laugh. "When I was your age, I would've said the hell with all this. It's not my problem, and it certainly isn't worth being killed over."

"You think I should quit—give up?"

Thad looked at Ryan. The smile had disappeared from his face. "I said that's what I would've done. But you're not me, are you? You've taken on a promise to your grandfather and put your life on the line to live up to it. You've risked everything to save those guys in there because you feel connected to them, as if they were your own brothers. No—you're not me." He looked off into the dark night. "Dad was right. You do have a gift."

Thad's admiration felt good. Ryan always thought the roles were reversed. He would've killed to be like his uncle.

Ryan glanced over his shoulder at the closed drapes on the adjacent balcony. "You know what Barney said to me back there?"

"About their age?"

Ryan nodded. "He said they can live to be two hundred years old."

"Holy shit. Really—two hundred years?"

"That's what he said."

Thad rubbed his chin. "That may be it," he said.

"May be what?"

"If that albino German knows that, it may be the reason they want the monkeys."

"Why? Other than to be the ones to say they discovered them."

"You've seen them. They walk like us, they talk like us—hell, they even make faces like us. And ninety-eight percent of a chimpanzee's DNA matches ours. Imagine how close those guys match."

"So you think he wants their DNA?"

"Don't know. For some reason, he kept Taylor alive. I'm guessing he knows they live to be two hundred years old, and has some sick plan to find out why and then transfer that trait to humans. Just imagine what that would be worth."

Ryan looked at the closed curtain on the other balcony. "I never imagined they would be so much like us."

"I've never seen anything like them," Thad said. "No one will believe a hybrid exists without seeing them. The evolutionary anthropologists will have a field day. Not only are they more like us, and in the wrong place for apes, but they're also alive—not just a pile of bones stuck in some rock."

"Yeah, Sarah's mom says there's no argument for evolution, and anyone who believes in it isn't a Christian. She says the Bible gives the account of Adam and Eve and that's how it all happened. She'd have a cow if she saw these guys."

"She's not the only one."

"I don't think she's right. I believe in God, and I think he created everything. But who's to say he didn't create the laws of science? He could have allowed evolution to happen, knowing it would lead to the first humans."

"You're getting to be quite the philosopher," Thad said, grinning.

"What do you think, Uncle T?"

Thad's attention seemed to drift out into the darkness for a moment. "I used to think that there was only one God and only one way to get to Heaven, but not anymore."

"What do you believe now—about God and all that stuff?"

"I think God is fluent in all the religions, dude—He doesn't play favorites. I saw that every day I was in Iraq. I think we're not sophisticated enough to have developed one right way of describing Him. I think I've seen his energy in the tortured, the oppressed, and the happy. I think I've seen it mostly in children, no matter where they are and no matter what their circumstances. I think it's because we haven't confused them yet with all our struggles to understand Him, and they don't try to own it or control it."

"But what about science and the Bible?"

"Well, dude, you have to decide that one for yourself. Me, I think the first law of science is that God exists in some form. You ever hear of the first law of thermodynamics?"

Ryan hadn't expected the question. He thought they were talking about God.

"I think we covered it in science."

"Well, the law says that energy can neither be created nor destroyed—it can only change forms. I think that describes the energy we sense in ourselves—some call it our soul. I think when we die, that energy goes somewhere. That's an example of a law of science being consistent with the concept of God." Thad sighed and looked up at the stars shimmering over the water.

"On the other hand, the Bible and the other books of the great religions were written a long time ago, and they were the science of the times. We had no idea about scientific laws and stuff like geology, fossils, and carbon dating. It was how we as humans could make sense of the great energy that is God. It was His way of helping us understand something we couldn't understand on our own. Then, nineteen hundred years after the Bible, we developed the ability to explain some things with science, like the first law of thermodynamics. There is one thing I think I know for sure: We will never have a perfect understanding. But the Bible got us through two thousand years."

"So why are these people willing to kill to protect the Bible and the others willing to do the same to destroy it?"

"I think some struggle with the idea of God; some battle to control it, and some abandon and ignore it—and it tortures them. Believe me, I know—I've been there. I think both groups have one thing in common: They're tormented by their frustration in trying to fully understand what can't be fully understood. They're scared. They don't want to let go of their rigid beliefs. So they lie, they cheat, and they kill in the name of their God."

"So what about the good people?"

"Good is a relative term. I like to think I was good once, but I've done some terrible things, too. When I see good, I see it in the form of a quiet confidence, a peacefulness. It's an energy I share with my family and friends, and it's something I experience when I see or do an act of kindness. It's an energy people experience when they pray in their own ways, even if they're not religious. I think it was the only energy I had left when I hit bottom, man. I learned one thing for sure: For me, understanding God is not evangelical; it's not a telethon or pulpit pounding; it's the unspoken actions I do or see that make me a believer."

Thad dropped his eyes from the heavens and turned to face Ryan. "But that's not what's on your mind, is it? You have a decision to make."

Ryan stared down into the black churning water. "Now I understand why Great-grandpa didn't want to expose them to all of this back then. It hasn't gotten any better. How can I share them with the world when people want to destroy them or put them in cages until they go crazy?"

Thad looked off in the distance. "You know, it doesn't matter what your grandpa thought, now. It doesn't matter what Sarah's mom believes, or what the assholes trying to kill us believe. It all comes down to what you believe. When the time comes, you'll make the right decision. Just take it one step at a time."

Ryan faced his uncle. Thad's words soothed him, but as he thought about the monkeys, a strange mix of sadness and obligation swept over him. "We gotta take care of them."

"We will, dude."

"No—I mean, they lost their mom and dad and their home was burned to the ground. We're it. They have no one else. We gotta take care of them."

Thad wrapped his arm around Ryan's shoulders. "We got this one, dude—we got it."

CHAPTER 49

THE THREE MONKEYS stared at Ryan. It was a question he'd never encountered. He'd used it thousands of times in his young life, and hadn't ever thought about its justification or inner workings. But now he was on the spot.

"Tell me again how it works?"

Ryan started through the explanation for the fifth time. "Like I said, you can't go outside or in the corner of the room. When you have to go, you come in here, and depending on what you need to do, you either sit or stand."

"When do you stand?" Taylor asked with a furrowed brow.

"Number one. You aim for the middle, then go."

"Then when do you sit?"

"Number two."

"Can you show me?"

"No. I don't have to go right now."

Taylor crossed his hairy arms and stroked his face. Barney and Zach seemed to be holding back a laugh.

"Then when you're done, you send it someplace else?" Taylor asked.

"You got it, Taylor. Just push this handle down and it flushes."

"Why?"

"Because you don't want it lying around, stinking up the place."

Ryan looked at Thad, standing behind the monkeys in the doorway of the bathroom. He held up his hands and shrugged. Thad was about to burst with laughter. Finally, a grunt escaped and Barney and Zach broke out in laughter at the same time. Taylor looked at the others.

"What? I don't understand."

Zach patted Taylor on the head. "We'll show you in a minute," he said, grinning.

"You guys understand it?" Ryan asked.

"We did the first time," Barney said, laughing.

"Why didn't you say something?"

"This was too much fun," Zach said as he high-fived Thad.

"All right, you guys," Thad said, still chuckling, "do your business in here, then come join us in the living room. I got some food on the way up."

Barney and Zach stepped further into the bathroom as Ryan squeezed past them.

"C'mon, Taylor, we'll show you how it's done," Zach said.

Ryan closed the door behind him. "You think they got it?" he asked Thad.

Thad put his arm around Ryan and grinned. "I think they got it on the second explanation. They'll be fine."

Ryan shook his head and walked into the living room. Three large trays covered with fruit and croissants were balanced on the round table in the corner. Two plates covered with stainless steel covers sat alone on one of the end tables.

"Can they eat this stuff?"

"Yup. Checked it out with Barney. He said they're good with fruit. I added the bread. You know those capuchins at the park love it." Thad walked to the trays atop the end tables. "And a special treat for us," Thad said as he proudly lifted the covers. Ryan smelled the cheeseburgers and fries and realized he hadn't been hungry in a week. Now he was starving. Thad dropped the covers back on the plates.

"Did you find the sweats?" Ryan asked.

"Yup. No problem. Found the sweats, sunglasses, and three pairs of size fourteens. Bill thought of everything."

"Good. Think we can pull it off?"

"I know we can, dude. Besides, we don't have a choice."

Just then, the monkeys entered the room.

"I did it. One and two." Taylor said as he raced to Ryan and hung his hand out. Ryan slapped it.

"Glad you got it," he said.

"Let's eat," Thad said, pointing to the table.

In seconds the monkeys surrounded the table. They stood and picked through the fruit, devouring all three trays, while Thad and Ryan dug into the burgers and fries. Taylor finished first and walked over to Ryan. Ryan's mouth was full of the last bite of his cheeseburger.

"What's that?" Taylor said pointing to Ryan's mouth.

Ryan chewed hard and then swallowed. "It was a cheeseburger."

"What's that?"

"It's ground beef and cheese."

Taylor cocked his head to the side. Ryan searched for the right description. "It's cooked ground beef with cheese on it."

"What's ground beef?"

"Ground-up cows."

"What's a cow?"

"It's an animal."

Taylor froze, and Ryan could see him trying to make sense of the words. Taylor's eyes grew large, and he stepped backward. "You humans eat animals?"

"Some of them," Ryan said as he stuffed a handful of fries in his face.

"I think you're scaring him, dude," Thad whispered.

Taylor kept backpedaling. "Animals like us?"

Ryan realized where Taylor's mind was going. He spit the fries out in his hand. "No—no, just certain animals. Not monkeys."

Taylor stopped backpedaling and nervously smiled.

"Taylor," Barney said, "they're fine. You remember that Mom and Dad said Zachariah ate meat, but not other humans or monkeys."

Taylor seemed satisfied with the answer and returned to the table.

"Okay, everybody," Thad started as he brushed his hands together and walked to the bags in the corner of the room. "Put these on." He handed Zach a hooded sweatshirt. "Extra-large for the big dude."

Zach grabbed the shirt and held it out away from his body.

"And large for the two of you," Thad said, handing the other two gray, hooded sweatshirts to Barney and Taylor. Barney took the shirt and studied it. Taylor immediately tried to pull it over his head. His head got stuck in the armhole, and he stuck his arm into the hood. Ryan covered his mouth to hide his amusement, then stepped over to Taylor and helped him get untangled from the sweatshirt.

"Like this, guys," he said as he carefully pulled the shirt over his head, found the armholes, and pushed his hands into the sleeves.

Barney and Zach followed him step by step. Their heads popped through into the hoods of their sweatshirts. Ryan handed the shirt back to Taylor, who did the same. The hood covered their heads and ears and extended past their foreheads. Ryan chuckled at the bright green number ten with the *Brasil* emblem on their chests. He'd seen them scattered throughout Manaus, and when he'd asked Addy, she said it was a sacred number reserved for the soccer team's best attacker. *Got that right*, he thought to himself.

"Okay, now we're gonna get cool, like this," Thad said as he slipped a pair of Ray-Bans over his ears and then pulled them off and handed them to Zach. Zach slowly opened the glasses, pushed them on, and rested them on his nose. Thad retrieved two more pairs from the bag and Barney and Taylor slid them on.

Ryan was shocked at the effectiveness of the disguise. The hood covered their foreheads and the sunglasses concealed their deep-set eyes. The tufts of hair surrounding their cheeks looked like a fashionably disheveled beard. "Holy shit, Uncle T, they look like tourists."

"Like ZZ Top on vacation," Thad added. He jammed his hand back into the remaining bag and pulled out sweatpants and three sets of loosely laced canvas tennis shoes.

"These go on like this," Thad said, slipping a pair of the cotton gray sweatpants over his shorts and stepping into a pair of the oversized shoes. He distributed the pants and shoes to the monkeys, and they followed his demonstration perfectly.

The three monkeys stood before him, transformed into something between Eminem and a hooded Duck Dynasty member. Either way, they didn't look like monkeys. They could have walked straight into one of

Ryan's swim meets without raising suspicions. Some of his friends dressed just like that.

"You guys okay now?"

Barney nodded. He looked uncomfortable.

"I'm ready," Zach said.

"Me too," Taylor said, "where we going?"

"For a walk around the ship," Thad said. He looked at Ryan. "You ready?"

"Did you notify the cabin guy?" Ryan asked.

"The steward? Yes, I did. Cool dude. He'll get in here after we leave and clean it up. Same time every day."

"Ryan and I will walk in front of you guys. Just keep up and don't talk to anyone."

"I assure you, that won't be a problem. We don't trust the other humans. We'll stay close," Barney said.

Thad walked to the suite's door and slid it open. The monkeys followed him into the empty hallway, and Ryan closed the door behind them.

"This way." Thad led them down the hallway and to the stairs, slipped through the stairwell door, and climbed up two decks. Ryan guessed the elevator would be too risky.

They emerged onto deck nine. The hallway led to an open area. A small blue slide spilled water into a pool, and a pack of kids took turns rocketing down the slide into the water below. They were greeted by a boisterous, splashing mob.

Thad stopped when he spotted them and turned around. "Let's go this way."

Ryan did his best to keep his head straight, but constantly moved his eyes from side to side, examining each passenger's reaction as they passed the group. Despite the fact that most everyone was more focused on his or her own destination, he still kept vigil. They moved to the back of the ship, and the smell of pepperoni and garlic filled the air. As they passed the grill, Ryan turned to see Taylor and Zach eyeing the slices of pizza under the hot lamps. They kept moving toward the stern and passed the soft-ice-cream dispensers. Ryan remembered his own weakness on the cruises with his family. He'd use any excuse he could to leave the family and stand in line with every other kid on the ship to hit the machine. He noted things hadn't changed. The line was still there, but there were four machines. The lines weren't nearly as long. Thad looked back at the monkeys. Zach and Taylor eyed the ice cream cones being sucked down by sugar-fueled kids.

He winked at Ryan. "Let's get one."

Before Ryan could protest, Thad was behind one redheaded five-year-old overflowing his cake cone. The kid finished, licked his hand, and Thad stepped to the machine. Ryan stood guard with his heart in his throat. This was way too dangerous. Ryan had his back to the machine and periodically checked their progress, while Barney, Zach, and Taylor watched wide-eyed as Thad distributed perfect swirls of vanilla into the cones and handed them out to the group. Ryan felt a tap on his shoulder and jumped.

"Dude. Relax. You'll draw attention to us, acting like Secret Service."

Thad handed him a cone, looked at the monkeys, and demonstrated how to properly lick the ice cream. They started toward the pool but the five-year-old had returned and stopped in front of Taylor.

"Can you help me get my ice cream?" he asked. Taylor froze. Ryan scanned quickly for the kid's parents. He spotted a couple poolside watching the young boy closely. The mother tapped the father's arm and he began to rise.

"I'll do it for you," Ryan said, stepping in. He grabbed a cone with his free hand, filled it, and glanced at the father. He was settling back into his seat.

Ryan handed the cone to the kid. "Here you go, big guy."

"Thanks, mister." The kid ran toward his father who waved at Ryan. Ryan walked a few steps, smiled, and waved.

As Taylor passed Ryan he looked up and smiled, vanilla dripping from his beard. Ryan felt a drip of cold ice cream on his hand and noticed his cone was melting. He licked the ice cream off his hand, shook his head, and followed Taylor. It would be a long thirteen days.

CHAPTER 50

CHARLES GRANDBY LOOKED out from his study and watched the black Lincoln Town Car wind along the gravel drive, past the pond and old gristmill to the front entry. Grandby yawned. It had been seven days since he'd received the news from Cyrus Schultz. He hadn't slept well since. The boy may or may not have gotten out with the creatures and, if he did, he was most likely headed for Miami. Live specimens would provide the ultimate proof, but the information that was probably left behind in the crater would solidify his arguments and finally put all of those arrogant sheep in their place. They could still worship their God, but His might and omnipotence would be destroyed. The man in the town car would provide legitimacy and proof of Grandby's claim, as well as a backup, should Cyrus Schultz fail. Grandby shook off the yawn and walked to the door of the massive library to meet him.

Doctor Eric Brunner had the world's ear. His papers on Ardi, the discovery of the earliest ancestor of the human race to split off from the great apes, had been lauded in the most prestigious journals and publications. His work at Cal-Berkeley in biological anthropology was legendary and recognized by the Royal Swedish Academy of Science with a Crafoord Prize, the closest thing to a Nobel Prize for anthropology. Now, he'd deliver an even greater prize to Grandby.

The white-gloved butler directed Dr. Brunner to the door of the library. With a thin frame, round eyeglasses, button nose, and crown of white hair circling his tanned, bald head, Dr. Brunner looked more like a grand-father than one of the brightest men in the world.

Grandby extended his hand, and Dr. Brunner shook it. "It's a pleasure to see you again, sir," Grandby said.

"The pleasure is all mine, Mr. Grandby."

Grandby relaxed a little. While Brunner was a man of high ethics, his work had led him to the same conclusion Charles Darwin had reached after his work in the Galapagos Islands: God did not create man; only the laws of natural selection did. Grandby was certain that this belief, along with the incredible evidence Grandby claimed to have, were the reasons Brunner had flown across the country on such short notice.

"Have a seat, Dr. Brunner." Grandby directed him to one of the two large, wingback chairs facing the stone fireplace. "So I trust you had an easy trip?"

"I certainly did. Thank you so much for your hospitality in sending your private jet."

"You're very welcome. Did you receive the packet of information I sent?"

Brunner leaned closer to Grandby. "If it's verifiable, it's the most re-markable discovery of our time."

Grandby smiled. "It certainly is. I'm happy to be funding the project."

"That's quite generous. Now that I've seen the information, I under-stand why you insisted on a confidentiality agreement."

"Well, Dr. Brunner, I apologize for that, but this information seemed so important that I didn't want it mismanaged, and I fear the evidence could be disturbed by any amateur with a shovel."

Brunner leaned back in his chair. "And it would certainly further your cause. I think you may have stumbled on the last common ancestor of both man and ape. Absolutely remarkable."

Brunner was as smart as Grandby had thought.

"So what do you want with my services, Mr. Grandby?"

"Call me Charles. I need someone to lead the effort and assemble a small team to uncover and catalogue any artifacts at the site."

"You understand it's in Brazil, and therefore, under their laws, belongs to them?"

"I do. But I'm interested in how quickly you could complete the project."

"These things usually take months or years, depending on the scope and the scale of the project."

Grandby hid his disappointment. He needed the information now. "How soon could you start?"

"I would need to assemble the team, which would take a few days, and then obtain the proper visas and permits from the Brazilians. I have a good friend and colleague there who'd love to lead the effort on behalf of Brazil. All in, the earliest we could be on the ground is a month or two, if we can fast-track the permits and visas."

"I need this information sooner. Is there something we could do to compress the schedule?"

Brunner raised his brow. "I'm not sure what you're asking."

"What if there was a way to gather the scientific evidence with a confidential advance team?"

Brunner got the hint. "Sir, while I respect your work, I still have a firm belief in the order of law and follow our code of ethics."

Grandby decided he'd have to take a different tack. "I'm sorry if I offended you. I am not familiar with the protocol for such a project, and I only want what's best for all of us."

Brunner straightened his thin black tie.

"So is there another way to compress the schedule?"

"Brazil has its regulations. We won't be able to get the research permit until IBAMA signs off on the environmental impacts. There's just no way to accelerate the project."

Grandby didn't want to hear it. Once the information was shared with the Brazilians, they'd surely take it over, and he'd lose control of the information. Still, if the work eventually got done, the effect would be the same. It might take a year or so to get there.

Brunner stood. "Would you like me to begin the process?"

Grandby rose to meet him. "Yes, but not just yet. I'll have to arrange the funding. I'll call you in a few weeks."

Brunner frowned. "You understand this is a discovery that needs to be shared with all of mankind. Its ramifications in the study of the origin of man will be cataclysmic."

"I understand. Thank you for your time."

"I'll await your call. Good day, sir," Brunner said. He marched out of the library without shaking Grandby's hand.

Grandby turned and strolled to the window. He watched Brunner get into the Town Car. As it drove away, Grandby thought of the boy. He hoped his luck would continue when his advanced team, minus Dr. Brunner, gathered evidence from the crater. He might not have a world-famous anthropologist, but if Cyrus Shultz was correct, in seven days the boy would deliver the most remarkable proof of man's evolution to Port Everglades.

CHAPTER 51

RYAN SPIED THE lights of Fort Lauderdale as they drifted into view and wondered if the plan would work. The black ocean glimmered and reflected the lights from shore, still two miles away. After two weeks of dodging crew members, trying to keep Taylor from draining the ice cream machine and Zach and Barney from calling room service every few hours, he was ready to get off the ship.

Ryan had worked with Thad for the last week, carefully crafting the plan. He was convinced it would work. He looked down into the churning sea. White foam from the prop wash marked their path as they sailed north to the entrance to Port Everglades. He remembered the shark attacks plastered across the front page of the Herald just a month ago. An unsuspecting tourist had given an arm to a snacking tiger shark.

He glanced back at the monkeys.

"How much longer?" Zach asked Ryan.

Ryan scanned the shoreline. He recognized the Diplomat hotel in Hollywood as it disappeared behind the corner of the balcony.

"About ten minutes," Ryan said. "You ready?"

"Absolutely," Zach replied. He stepped onto the balcony from the living room and stopped next to Ryan. "Don't worry. We'll get there. This is what we do." The corners of his mouth curled up into a smile.

Ryan glanced over his shoulder. Taylor was rechecking the plan with Thad's help, and Barney was staring off toward the shore, looking disgusted.

"He always looks that way before he swims," Zach added. "He's actually one of the better swimmers. He just hates it."

Ryan turned to face Zach. "You remember the route?"

"Off the stern, down the first channel to the left, past the lights and buildings on the left, then into the first dark cove to the wooden piers of the education facility—then wait there for you."

Zach's perfect recitation of the route helped. Still, there was the Customs and Border Patrol, the Broward County Sheriff's patrol boats, and the hundreds of closed-circuit TVs added to the port since 9/11. Not to mention the dozens of other freighters and tugs scattered around the entry to the port.

"Come here, guys," Ryan said, waving the others to join him.

Taylor trotted out, smiling, while Barney shuffled his feet and scowled at the shoreline. Thad locked his gaze on Ryan as he approached.

"What's wrong, dude?"

"Nothing, Uncle T. I just have something to say."

They stood in a circle.

"I just wanted to say, you've come a long way. You left your home in the jungle because the people chasing me destroyed it. But you've trusted me with your life, and I want you to know I won't let you down."

Ryan felt the weight of Zach's arm drape over his shoulder.

"Ryan. You saved us. If it wasn't for you, I think the other humans would have killed Taylor and the rest of us, like they killed our mother and father."

Taylor and Barney nodded in agreement. Thad just smiled. Ryan felt better, but he wasn't finished.

"You'll be in a city full of humans. You need to be very careful. Don't trust anyone. Don't speak to anyone if you're caught. Once you're at the Primate Park, you'll be safe. It will take at least two hours for us to get off the ship, so just stay at the Environmental Education Pavilion until we get there. I promise you we'll be there."

Thad pulled his head up from the huddle and looked to shore. "It's time."

"Be careful," Ryan said as he stood.

Zach's arm slipped off his shoulders, and Taylor stepped up and hugged him. Ryan thought he broke a rib. Barney patted him on the shoulder. Taylor released him, and Ryan grabbed the rope coiled on the deck of the balcony. He began lowering it, hand over hand, until it dragged in the water to the left of the prop wash. As they passed the buoy marking the channel, Ryan heard the engines slow and the ship turned toward the entrance to Port Everglades. No one spoke. They stood in the darkness and watched the ship maneuver into the narrow entrance to the port. The engines slowed to an idle, and their forward motion slowed to a crawl.

"Now," Thad said.

Zach slipped over the rail first and moved quickly down the rope. Taylor followed, then Barney, still shaking his head.

Ryan felt sick and the sweating returned as one by one they slipped into the black water and disappeared.

"They'll be fine, dude. I couldn't even see them once they hit the water."

Thad was right. But the thought of them swimming on their own through the mangrove-lined channel, past the Coast Guard office on one side and the bustling container ships on the other, had Ryan worried. It would be a long two hours.

CHAPTER 52

RYAN REACHED FOR the rail of the gangway and noticed his hand shaking as if he'd just downed three Red Bulls. It had been two hours since the monkeys had hit the water, and Ryan was running late. After re-packing the luggage and eliminating any signs of the monkeys, they'd tossed the luggage into the hallway and it quickly disappeared with a roving band of porters. He knew the next stop was customs—the last hurdle in the journey home. Despite the fact that his passport was in order, the thought of uniformed CPB agents and overactive drug dogs had him worried. The sun was warm, and he knew that even on a hot Tuesday morning in August, the beachside park would begin to fill with locals and a few wandering tourists. The chances of the monkeys being sighted were increasing by the minute.

"Dude—you need to take a deep breath," Thad said, wrapping his arm around Ryan. "Smile and look like you just had a two-week vacation."

They'd donned the tourist garb they'd worn in Manaus and blended in well. Ryan tugged on his Marlin's cap and pulled it down to the top of his Ray-Bans. He exhaled hard and shook out the tension in his arms as if he were readying for the fifty-meter freestyle. It seemed to work, and he re-checked his hands. The shaking was less obvious. Thad kept his arm over Ryan's shoulder and guided him down the gangway. His uncle still looked like he was trying out for a Jimmy Buffett impersonator contest.

The green-and-white signs overhead directed the throng to the US Customs checkpoint inside terminal two. Lines had already formed at each of the four stations enclosed in glass on three sides. The four officers wore identical uniforms and the same intimidating deadpan look Ryan had encountered at least a dozen times before when reentering the country from the so-called family vacations. They'd actually been controlled marches organized by his father, so he could scold and degrade the family members. Usually customs was a welcome sight for Ryan, but not this time. His stomach turned flips and the shakes returned. He felt the sweat running from his armpits.

"Okay, dude. Let me do the talking," Thad said as they stepped into the third line from the left, behind an elderly couple shuffling their documents.

"Don't forget to take your sunglasses off. Don't want to look suspicious," Thad said as he pulled off his shades and stuffed them in the pocket of his flower-print silk shirt.

Ryan pulled his glasses off. The elderly couple stepped forward from the yellow line and walked to the cubicle housing the customs officer. The officer was in his mid-forties, Hispanic, with a round face and thick black flattop. His biceps filled the short sleeves of the dark-blue uniform, but lacked the definition of a weightlifter's. Ryan sucked in several breaths.

"Calm down, dude," Thad scolded through his teeth, still looking straight ahead and smiling.

The customs officer examined the passports, then the old couple's faces. He didn't smile or make any conversation. It seemed to take forever. Finally he swiped the documents through a scanner, stared at the computer screen in front of him, then flipped the passports shut and handed them to the white-haired old man. Ryan felt his pulse in his throat.

The officer waved them forward, and Thad jaunted to the window. Ryan followed.

"Passports and declarations please," he said.

The officer spent a little too long looking at him. Ryan followed Thad's lead and placed the documents on the counter. The officer shuffled through the documents, matching the passports with the declarations. Then he looked up. "Nothing to declare?"

What a question. If he only knew.

"No, sir," Thad answered.

The officer looked at Ryan, and Ryan wagged his head. His mouth was too dry to speak.

The officer separated the declarations from the passports, swiped Thad's through the reader, and waited. He adjusted the screen, turning it away from Thad. Then he scanned Ryan's. He paused, and then turned behind him and waved to another chubby officer standing with a lanky man with thin brown hair and a large nose.

Ryan's face broke into a sweat and nausea twisted in his stomach. The two men approached and the officer handed their documents to the man in the white shirt. He opened the passports and read.

"Thaddeus Webster and—Ryan Webster?"

"That's us, sir. Is there a problem?" Thad asked.

"Just come with us, please, sir."

The chubby officer waited for Thad and Ryan to follow the thin man and then closed in behind them. Ryan thought his knees would buckle. Had they caught the monkeys? Had they finally caught up with Thad for the killings in California and Houston? They turned right down a short hallway and entered a windowless room with a steel desk and three chairs.

"Have a seat," the thin man said. He sat on the corner of the desk and with an open hand directed them to the two side chairs.

The officer closed the door and parked himself against the wall with his arms folded.

"Can you tell me what this is all about?" Thad said. Ryan noticed his tone was firmer than before.

"I'm Agent Dan Phillips with the ICE."

"The ICE?" Thad said.

"Immigration and Customs Enforcement. We just want to ask you a few questions."

"Ah, so you're the *man*," Thad said more aggressively, still smiling.

Phillips ignored him. "Mr. Webster, we've had a report of a monkey entering the ship."

Ryan almost choked. He held his breath.

"Why are you asking me?" Thad said.

"Well," Phillips said as he stood and started to pace, "a young girl insisted to her parents and the ship's crew that she saw three monkeys on a rope dangling in front of her as she ate her dinner while leaving Manaus. She said one even waved at her."

Ryan became queasy but held it together. The agent circled back to the desk.

"Normally I would dismiss such reports. But when we checked the registrations for the suites at the stern of the ship, your names came up."

Thad laughed and then crossed his arms. "So?"

"Well—you are part of the family that owns the Webster Primate Park. Correct?"

"Yeah, you're right there."

"So that was enough of a coincidence for my supervisors to want to look into it a little further."

Thad didn't reply. Phillips resumed pacing. "Mr. Webster, you know that smuggling in non-human primates is a serious offense."

"I don't know what you're talking about, dude. And I don't know why you're wasting our time."

Phillips ignored the protest and kept circling. "You'd lose your permit with the CDC for the park and go to jail."

"Look, Agent Phillips. I'm sorry to waste your time, but we were just coming back from a trip to check out the habitat for the squirrel monkeys in the Amazon. You see, a few years ago, Hurricane Andrew wiped out part of the jungle my grandfather imported to make the park. We need to get the understory just right and wanted to see it firsthand. We decided to take a cruise back to recover from sleeping and eating in the jungle for four days."

Phillips stopped walking and stroked his chin. "So you're—"

Phillips was interrupted by a knock at the door. The heavy-set officer opened the door, and Ryan heard a voice say, "They're clean."

The officer shut the door and shook his head in Phillips' direction. Phillips returned his gaze to Thad and said nothing. Then he shifted his eyes to Ryan. "You've been pretty quiet, young man."

Ryan froze, as if being called on in class after a catnap. "It's like my uncle said. We don't have any freakin' monkeys. Those things smell and you wouldn't catch me stuck in a cabin with one for two weeks."

Ryan was impressed with his own reply. He saw Thad grin a little.

Phillips sat back down on the desk and folded his arms. He looked at the officer behind Ryan and then back at Thad.

"Okay, Mr. Webster. You can go. Have a good day." He stood, walked to the door, and opened it.

Thad rose and Ryan followed him out the door.

The door closed, but Ryan got that feeling. The feeling he always got when he suspected his father knew he'd screwed up.

"C'mon," Thad said.

Thad led them through the hallways, following the signs to the baggage claim area, and they cleared customs. The porter stacked the luggage on a cart and looked at Thad for direction. Thad was scanning the exit and finally spotted what he was looking for. He led Ryan and the porter to the right, just short of the exit. Thad stepped close to a short, stocky, darkhaired man with a small scar on his cheek. He gave Thad a bear hug. Ryan saw tears in the man's eyes.

"Skunk, this is my nephew Ryan. Ryan, this is Skunk."

The man was tanned, burly, and a little shorter than Ryan. Ryan shook his hand. It was like a vise-grip. The man gave a quick smile. "This way, guys."

He took his first step, and Ryan immediately noticed the limp and heard the sound of steel clicking on steel: He knew the loss of the man's left leg was the connection with his uncle.

He led them down another hallway. "You doing okay, dude?" he asked over his shoulder.

"Yeah—just a psycho girlfriend who turned into a stalker."

"You always did attract the dizzy ones," Skunk said as he led them through two more hallways to a single steel door.

"How's the leg?" Thad asked.

"Good as new," he said, opening the door.

A taxi sat at the curb, idling. The porter loaded the luggage while Thad and Skunk talked about his job at the port and caught up on their buddies from their days in Fallujah. Thad tipped the porter a twenty and opened the door to the cab. Ryan jumped in and slid across the seat.

Thad hugged Skunk, then ducked in the cab. "I owe you one."

Skunk slid his index finger along the scar on his cheek. "You owe me nothing."

CHAPTER 53

RYAN SLOUCHED IN the back of the taxicab and pulled his Marlins cap even lower as they passed through the exit gate and turned left onto 17th Street. His uncle slid lower in the seat and pulled the brim of his Panama fedora over his eyes. The port was secure, and chances of an encounter with the albino German or the radical Crusaders were nonexistent, thanks to the post-9/11 security measures. But Thad said he was convinced that once they cleared the security gates, one or both of the people trying to kill them would be watching. Ryan followed his uncle's instructions and hoped they looked just like the hundreds of people exiting the port.

The taxi reached Highway 1 and turned south. Ryan peered out the window and watched the cars drift by. He raised his arm and checked the time. 10:41 a.m. He glanced at Thad and pointed to his watch. Thad nodded. It had been over three and a half hours since getting into port, and nearly five hours since the monkeys hit the water.

Ryan spotted the Fort Lauderdale Airport on his right and the traffic got thicker. He shook his head and repeatedly pounded his thigh with his clenched fist. He was late, and the summer beachgoers were beginning to make their daily trek to the coast. Soon the park would be crawling with surfers, the happily unemployed, and tourists. The chance of detection increased with each minute. The driver maneuvered through the traffic, turned left in Dania Beach, and headed down A1A. Despite Thad's earlier warnings, Ryan glanced out the back window. Just behind them was a late model SUV, probably a rental, loaded with a family of five. Behind the SUV, the road was clear all the way to the intersection they'd just left. The taxi sped up and the glare from the rental car's windshield seared Ryan's eyes. It was a typical South Florida summer day: no clouds, a hot blazing sun, and very little breeze. Ryan spun back around and watched as the cab approached the drawbridge over the Inland Waterway. To the right, he noted a sailboat approaching just as he heard the warning bell. The red lights flashed, and the red-and-white-striped gates crept down, as if defying gravity.

"Shit," he said as he punched his thigh again.

"It'll be fine," Thad whispered.

"I just hope they're still there," Ryan replied.

Thad pressed his index finger against his lips and nodded toward the cabbie. Ryan knew another five minutes waiting for the bridge meant more people at the park, and another five minutes in the steaming mangroves at the center. If the monkeys were found, he'd be forced to reveal them to the world,—if they weren't already captured and caged—and he just wasn't ready for that. He'd promised he'd keep them safe, but sitting at a draw-bridge a half a mile away, there was nothing he could do.

The gates finally lifted, and the cab sped over the causeway and looped onto the entrance to Lloyd Park. They slowed to the twenty-mile-per-hour speed limit.

"It will be here on the right in the second lot," Thad said, pulling a small note from his pocket. "A light gray Ford Expedition."

The cabbie nodded. Ryan looked to the left toward the Intracoastal Waterway. He spotted the tops of several container ships over the thick mangrove trees lining the left side of the road. Huge black cranes towered over the ships and guarded the waterway. Two were operating, but they were at least a quarter mile from the education center. The mangroves were taller and thicker than he remembered. They'd provide good cover. He re-laxed a little and kept watching the tree line. It ended at the first parking lot, but then resumed until the cab slowed at the second lot on his right. On the left, a brown wooden sign marked the entrance to the Environmental Education Center. Behind the sign, a path cut through the mangroves and disappeared at its first turn. The cab turned into the lot, and the older gray Expedition sat parked in the first space on the left, facing the road. The windows were heavily tinted to protect against the Florida sun.

Ryan smiled. If they could get to the truck, they could easily make it to the park undetected. The cabbie pulled next to the Expedition. Ryan opened the door and the thick humid air hit him. The cabbie unloaded the luggage, and Thad slipped him a fifty, refusing change. The cabbie smiled, returned to the cab, and drove away.

While they stuffed the luggage in the back, Thad and Ryan scanned the nearly empty parking lot. Three cars were parked in the same row, facing the street. Each had Thule racks either for bikes or kayaks. The kayaks would present a problem if they were drifting along the mangroves in the Intracoastal Waterway. There were no cars behind them, except for about twenty cars parked at the opposite end of the lot facing the ocean, at least fifty yards away: probably surfers. At 11 a.m., they'd be making the most of the surf and sun. Just as Thad closed the rear hatch, a Broward County Sheriff's car came into view on the left. He cruised past, and Thad waved. The officer leaned toward the passenger's window and waved back, then drifted out of sight to the right.

"We'll have ten minutes before he makes the loop to the end of the park and back," Thad said.

Ryan looked across the street to the entrance to the Environmental Education Center. "Let's go," he said.

He trotted across the street with Thad right behind him. The path immediately narrowed and took a hard turn to the right, then back to the left down to the Intracoastal Waterway. The asphalt path gave way to a wooden bridge leading to the center. The center wasn't much. Ryan had been there two times before. Once in third grade to hear a lecture about the life of the manatees in the area, and the second to hide from the cops and drink beer with Tyler and a couple of girls from Pittsburgh down for spring break. The structure was constructed of rough-cut wood coated with a thick layer of medium-brown stain. Ryan turned the corner and stepped into the room. The open-air pavilion was enclosed on three sides and covered with a steeply pitched roof. It was twice the size of his high school classrooms. A few rows of benches divided it into two sections. It was well shaded from the hot sun. Other than a few Bud Light bottles scattered on the floor, it was empty.

"So far so good," Thad said as he joined him. "Let's check out the deck."

Ryan walked across the pavilion to the exit on the other side. It opened to another short ramp that dropped down to a large round deck just above the water of the Intracoastal Waterway. A railing provided a barrier to keep the tourists fidgeting with their cameras from falling into the water. Mangroves hugged the deck on three sides, and the fourth provided an open view of a manmade oxbow in the channel. Ryan spotted a white-haired couple shuffling along the railing, admiring the view of the water and the port off in the distance.

Thad immediately went into tourist mode. "Dude, look at that," he said, pointing to the white round tower capped with a light-blue roof peeking over the mangroves. "That must be the harbor master."

Ryan caught the hint. "That's bigger than the silos back in Kansas."

Thad cut his eyes to Ryan. Ryan shrugged. The couple looked back, annoyed. The man folded their map and they shuffled back up the ramp. Once they had disappeared, Ryan ran to the railing.

Thad strolled up. "Don't be so obvious."

"I don't see them," Ryan said, scanning the perimeter of the cove.

He studied the base of the mangroves along the entire waterline, starting on the left and moving to the right. The tangled roots choked off easy access to the shoreline. Ryan's heart dropped. It was his fault. He'd told them he'd be there and he wasn't. He looked at Thad, who was bent over the rail, looking under the deck.

"I don't see them. They're not here." Ryan said.

Thad kept looking under the deck, then moved hand over hand to his right, still looking under the structure.

"What are we going to do?" Ryan asked as he followed him.

"Hey, dudes. How's it hanging?" Thad said, still leaning over the rail.

"How's what hanging?" Taylor replied.

Ryan's heart leapt. He lunged to look under the deck and started to flip over the rail.

"Whoa there," Thad said, grabbing his belt.

Ryan spotted Taylor hiding between two mangroves and a pier. "Where are the others?" he asked.

"Right here." Barney and Zach emerged from behind two other beams.

Just then, Ryan heard the rumble of outboard motors straight ahead. About fifty yards away, a white, twenty-foot Harbor Patrol boat cruised past the opening to the oxbow on the Intracoastal Waterway. Ryan could see the officer inside the air-conditioned cockpit peer into the cove. He snapped upright and tried to look casual. He heard the twin Evinrudes drop to an idle. The boat slowed. Ryan spotted a pair of long antennae extending from the top of the cabin. If he'd seen the monkeys, word would spread literally at the speed of light.

"Shit," he swore under his breath.

The boat slowly turned toward the cove. Ryan's heart raced and he felt his pulse throbbing in his throat. He readied to run, but Thad clamped down on his wrist and held him in place.

"Wait, dude. Just wait."

The bow kept turning, and Ryan saw the officer through the front windshield staring back. Thad waved, and the officer didn't wave back.

Ryan blinked as the sweat ran into his eyes. Then he heard the engines ramp up and the bow kept turning to the left. The boat turned around and roared toward the port to the right. Thad released Ryan's wrist and Ryan exhaled.

"Whew, that was close," he said.

Thad leaned over the rail. "It's clear, dudes. Let's get out of here."

In seconds, Barney, Zach, and Taylor flipped over the rail.

Ryan hugged Zach, then Barney and Taylor. "Boy, am I glad to see you."

Thad disappeared up the path and then reappeared, trotting back to the group. "It's clear, let's go."

In less than three minutes they were driving back up A1A. Ryan looked back at the monkeys. Their broad shoulders filled the entire width of the back seat. He examined their faces. They were glued to the windows, probably amazed at the clutter of mankind. He glanced at Thad, who smiled and high-fived him. Ryan stared through the windshield at the bright blue sky. He imagined his grandfather up there and smiled. If he only knew ... Ryan hoped he did.

CHAPTER 54

HIS HAIR WAS slicked back as if he didn't care what anyone thought. His tanned, narrow face came to a point at his chin, which he covered with a perfectly groomed goatee. He looked like the devil himself. He'd morphed into that persona over his twenty-two years as Grandby's assistant.

Grant Clark had been the first reader of all of Grandby's books, and because publicists willing to push Grandby's atheist agenda were as scarce as hen's teeth, he'd been acting as Grandby's point man on public relations for the past twelve years. He was connected to all the major news agencies, bloggers, and well-read supermarket tabloids. They were always hungry for controversy, and Grandby had made millions supplying it by pitting science against the myth of religion. While he reveled in the role of shooting holes in the creationists' faith, his argument always fell short because science lacked an indisputable link between man and monkey. But at noon today, he hoped that would all change.

Clark stroked his goatee and checked his watch.

"They'll call," Grandby said, looking out the window of his study.

Grandby checked his watch and noted it was 11:56 a.m. The recon team had entered the crater two days earlier. It consisted of two no-name anthropologists and two of Grandby's best men from the states. He'd hoped to have Dr. Brunner in tow, but Brunner's ethics got in the way. Grandby would send him in after swimming through the red tape of the Brazilian government, but that would be a mop-up operation. Right now, Grandby only needed a verbal confirmation from the team. That, along with the living specimens in Miami, would be all the proof Clark would need to spin Grandby's web that would snare even the most devoted believers.

Just then, the phone on Grandby's desk rang. Grandby turned and smiled at Clark. "You ready?" Clark nodded with his pen in hand. Grandby pushed the speakerphone button. "Go ahead."

"Donegan here. We have a secure line, sir, if you're ready."

"What did you find?"

"The anthropologists are still dazed. We found it all."

"Take me through it."

"We encountered an entire village, complete with structures that appear to be dwellings. Inside one of those dwellings we found an old eight-millimeter projector and cans of films from the late sixties and early seventies. Behind that structure, we found a makeshift generator with a transmission hooked to a bike."

"A bike?"

"Affirmative. It looks like one of them pedaled while the other ones watched."

Clark chuckled but kept writing.

"What else?" Grandby asked.

"The anthropologists report evidence of the widespread use of tools throughout the area."

"What kind of tools?"

"We have images we're uploading to you after the call, but they're tools used for construction, excavation, and cultivation of crops."

"What crops?"

"Anthros say it's nothing they've seen before. To me it looks like a bright yellow tomato, but these eggheads say they're not tomatoes."

"Go on."

"We also found what appears to be a graveyard."

Grandby stared at Clark. "A graveyard?"

"Yes, sir. We counted eighty-four so far. These anthropologists dug one up. They think it's some hybrid between a monkey and an ape. They wanted me to pass along that it's not a quadruped or suspensory primate. It's a bipedal hominid."

Grandby shot up and leaned into the phone. "Say again?"

"They wrote that down for me. It's a bipedal hominid."

It was better than he'd ever expected. Grandby knew that bipedalism was a locomotion trait that characterized humans. These hybrids had evolved to a form closely related to humans.

"Sir?"

"I'm listening."

"They also say they shouldn't be here. Don't know what that means, but they said it was important."

"They mean that these are the first hominids, other than humans, to be discovered in the New World—in the Americas." Grandby rubbed his hands together. "Any more?"

"Yeah. This last one is a strange one. There are signs here in English marking the paths—these guys think the hybrids can read."

Grandby leaned back and spread his arms, palms up. "Does it get any better?" he said, smiling at Clark.

"The anthros say they'll have a full report to you by end of day, along with the photos."

"Perfect. Send it to the fax on the jet."

"Will do, sir. I'll contact you again when we have more."

"All right, but be sure to leave everything in place."

"Say again?"

"I want you to leave it as you found it. We'll want to follow up through the proper channels, and I'll have those requests underway this evening."

"Ten-four, sir."

Grandby pressed the speakerphone button and dropped into his seat. "Did you get all that?"

Clark nodded. "Sure did."

"Okay. I want you to call a press conference for four p.m. today."

"Where?"

"Just outside the entrance to the Webster Primate Park in Miami."

"The Primate Park?"

"You got it. But be sure to put the word out as soon as possible."

"That's not enough notice to get everyone."

"Make your calls this afternoon and tell them we have an announcement about a significant anthropological discovery."

"That's kind of cryptic, isn't it?"

Grandby circled the desk and sat on the corner, facing Clark. "What we have there," he said, pointing to the phone, "is the missing link." He stood up and paced behind Clark. "What we have there are bipedal hominids that use tools, bury their dead, and may be able to read." He walked up and leaned on Clark's chair, his face just inches from Clark's. "And I plan on having a *living* specimen delivered to me at that Primate Park with all the world watching."

CHAPTER 55

AT THIRTY-SEVEN, WITH fifteen years of experience in investigating customs enforcement cases, Dan Phillips knew to trust his instincts. As a first-year agent fresh out of the University of Texas at Arlington's Justice Studies program, he'd made a name for himself by digging deeper into the physical evidence than anyone in the office and pursuing it to the case's end. It served him well, until he ignored a hunch and instead followed physical evidence, and twenty-two illegal Haitian immigrants were cooked to death inside a container dockside at the Port of Miami. He gave up on his just-the-facts-ma'am investigative style the instant the customs agent opened that door. He'd learned the hard way that a hunch was as important as any piece of physical evidence, and the interview with the Websters rattled in his mind. There was something about that young man that didn't seem right.

Phillips paced across the interrogation room and stopped. "You think they're hiding anything?" he asked the heavy-set CBP officer sitting at the table, sipping coffee.

The officer begrudgingly looked up. "The kid seemed a little nervous—more so than usual." He took another sip of the coffee. Phillips knew the CBP officer didn't like him crashing their territory.

"I'd like to talk to that little girl again."

The officer nodded toward the door. "You'd better hurry, agent. They cleared customs ten minutes ago."

Phillips darted for the door and slung it open. He sprinted down the hallway into the large open area between customs and the loading area just outside the front door of the terminal.

He scanned the massive lobby. The ship was on the smaller side, but still held well over six hundred passengers. The crowd was thick and looked like a sea of tropical print shirts, white shorts, and tennis shoes. He knew he was looking for a needle in the haystack.

He pushed to the right and waded through the crowd until he reached the wall of glass double doors leading to the curb outside. His eyes darted to the left and then to the right. Then he spotted her. She held her mother's hand at the curb, probably waiting for her father to retrieve the family SUV from the garage. He immediately recognized the light-brown hair in tight curls dangling from under her light-pink ball cap. With her button nose and easy smile, Phillips was sure she'd have a career on the Disney channel. He'd recognize her anywhere. He jammed the push bar and the door flung open. He sprinted to the curb but slowed to a walk as he approached the girl and her mother.

"Excuse me, ma'am," he said in his best Texas drawl, still trying to catch his breath.

"Hello, agent," she said, wide-eyed. She pulled the little girl closer and turned to face him. "Is there some sort of problem?"

"I just had a couple more questions, if that's okay?"

Her mother knelt down and wrapped her arms around the little girl. Phillips noticed the little stuffed monkey in her other hand.

"Okay," her mother said.

Phillips dropped on one knee. He looked her in the eyes and smiled. The little girl glanced at her mother, who nodded, and then the little girl smiled back.

"What's your name again?"

"Sterling. What's yours?" She seemed uninhibited, as if he were talking to a well-adjusted confident adult.

"My name is Dan. Can I ask you a few more questions about the monkey?"

She stuck the soft gray toy monkey in his face. "This is Peanut. He's a squirrel monkey."

"Oh," he said, petting the monkey, "he's very soft."

The little girl smiled and pulled the toy back to her chest.

"I'd like to ask you again about the monkey you saw at dinner. Okay?"

She nodded.

"You said you saw him climb by the window?"

"He was on a rope," she said proudly.

"What color was the rope?"

She paused and looked up at her mother, then snapped her head back to Phillips. "Black!"

"That's very good," he said.

"I remember lots of things. I even remember his two friends going by."

"Two friends?" Phillips said, looking at her mother. She shrugged.

The girl continued. "Yes. There were two bigger monkeys ahead of him. He was the only one who waved."

"What did they look like?"

"They were big and strong, they had dark-brown fur, but they had faces that looked like yours."

Monkeys that looked like him? After all, she was only five. He glanced at her mother again. Another shrug.

"How were they like me?"

"They had a nose and eyes like yours. Not like Peanut's." She showed him the monkey again.

"And where did they go?"

She pointed to the sky. "Up."

Just then, the father pulled to the curb in a white Escalade.

"Well, thank you so much." Phillips stood and nodded to the father, who'd circled the car and joined them at the curb.

"Can I ask you one question in private, ma'am?"

The woman handed the girl off to her father and stepped to the side.

Agent Phillips leaned closer. "Does your daughter have an active imagination?"

She looked offended. "She has a healthy one," she said, raising one eyebrow.

"What I mean is, do you think she really saw a monkey?"

The woman looked over his shoulder at the girl. "I'll tell you this—she's never made things up. No imaginary friends, no lies—nothing."

"So you think she's telling the truth?"

The woman stepped closer and scowled. "My daughter is no liar, I'll tell you that." She pulled back a little. "My back was to the window and so was my husband's. She's talked about it every day for two weeks—yes, I'd say she saw it." She put her hands on her hips. "Anything else, agent?"

"No, ma'am. Sorry to upset you."

She stormed toward the loaded car and climbed into the passenger's seat, slamming the door. It was just another reminder of why he'd remained single. The Escalade pulled from the curb, and as it passed, he saw the young girl wave from the security of her car seat. Then she grabbed Peanut and he waved too. Phillips waved back. Although he and his job couldn't handle a wife, he loved kids.

Phillips turned and pushed his way back into the terminal. He stopped off at the customs checkpoint and requested an officer with a dog to join him. A young wiry officer with a yellow Lab in tow followed him across the gangway, up the elevator to deck six, and back to the suite at the stern. Phillips caught the short, dark-skinned cabin steward in the hallway. He flashed his badge. "Did you clean 6091 yet?"

"No sir," the steward said in a thick accent. He looked down, as if he'd done something wrong, cutting his eyes to the dog.

"You're not in trouble. Did you see the people in the suite while you were underway?"

"Yes, sir. Mr. Webster and nephew."

"Anything unusual?"

"They were very nice people."

"No. I mean, anything unusual about their stay?"

The steward nipped at his thumb. "I remember they ate much?"

"Much?"

"They asked I clean room at same time every day. When I go in, lots of plates from room service."

"On the whole trip?"

The steward nodded.

"Can you let me in there?"

The steward looked at the dog again and then the CBP officer. He grabbed a key from his belt, and Phillips followed him to the door. He opened the door and stepped back as Phillips, the dog, and the officer entered. Immediately the dog glued his nose to the floor and darted back and forth around the entire room.

"He usually do that?" Phillips asked the officer.

"No, sir," the officer said, watching the dog with a puzzled look.

Phillips looked around. The room was clean. Too clean. He'd been in cabins before and most cruisers left behind a menagerie of shopping bags, broken water toys, old film boxes, and other useless crap. He scanned the living room: nothing except a few empty plates on the coffee table. He walked to the bedroom door and noted the two twin beds were made. He turned back to the officer, who was still watching the dog vacuum the room with his nose.

Phillips pivoted and pulled open the curtains to the balcony. He spotted the railing, opened the sliding glass door, and stepped out. It was hot and the sun forced him to don his sunglasses. He stepped to the rail and leaned over. He noted the dining room directly below and leaned back upright. Then he dropped to his knees and studied the top rail of the balcony. The rail glistened in the sunlight, except for an area about three inches wide where the finish had been scratched off. He stood back up and leaned over the scratches. He saw the outer frame of the ship split the dining room windows directly below the scratches. A rope could certainly do that.

Then he spotted it, waving in the hot, humid breeze. He reached into the right pocket of his pants, where he always carried a small evidence bag. He turned the plastic bag inside out over his right hand, reached over the rail, and pulled the thick, dark-brown hair from the rivet at the base of the railing. He carefully pulled the bag off his hand, capturing the hair inside. He zipped it shut and held the hair up to the sun. It was far too coarse for a human hair. He noted the size of the follicle attached. Again, too large for a human. He dropped the bag into his pocket and headed back into the room.

"What do you think?" he asked, pointing to the scurrying dog.

"They must have had something in here. It's not drugs because she would have alerted. I'd guess it was some kind of animal?"

Phillips nodded and smiled. "I need you to notify FWS that we may have non-human primate smuggling here."

"FWS?" the young officer asked.

"US Fish and Wildlife Service." Phillips pulled his cell phone from his pocket and pressed the number for operations. "Phillips here. I need a backup team on standby."

"What's the possible location?"

"The Webster Primate Park."

He flipped the phone shut, walked over to the Lab sitting next to the officer, and petted her on her head.

"Good dog," he said, and then he smiled and walked out of the suite.

CHAPTER 56

RYAN STARED AT Thad as they drove down the Homestead Extension of the Florida Turnpike. "Are you sure we can make it?"

"Done it before," he answered without looking at Ryan. His eyes constantly cut between the rearview mirror and the road ahead. "Besides, we don't have a choice. And with sixty acres of jungle, an electric fence, and a security system, they'll be safe for now. There's no better place we can hide them."

Ryan didn't have a better idea. He glanced over his shoulder. Barney sat on the left and stared out the window, Taylor swiveled his head from side to side in an attempt to see out both windows at the same time. Zach gazed out the right rear window.

Taylor caught Ryan's eye and pointed to the right side of the car. "This is starting to look a little more like home."

"It sure does," he said.

Taylor had already resumed his survey, and dropped his jaw when they passed the six-lane tollbooth. Ryan looked out the window. The turnpike bent to the southeast and skirted the heavily developed suburbs, just west of Miami. While a sea of orange-tiled roofs of Doral crowded the road to the left, the Everglades stated their claim to the land to the right. A thick row of cypress trees guarded its boundary and marked the edge of man's assault on the Everglades. Ryan could see the edge of the sawgrass marshes and alligator-laden sloughs. His biology teacher had pounded that ecosystem into his head, trying to make environmentalists out of the entire junior class. Now it represented a barrier they'd have to cross to enter the safety of the Primate Park his great-grandfather had built on land reclaimed from the swamp.

"Can you still find the road?"

Thad nodded. "I checked it out last year when we thought that capuchin had jumped ship. Chill, dude."

Ryan adjusted the vent and felt the cool air against his face. The lack of sleep and constant vigil over the monkeys had wiped him out. He took his uncle's advice and let his eyelids drop. He listened to the hum of the engine and faded into a shallow nap.

He was yanked from his trance when Thad exited the turnpike and headed west toward the park. Ryan pulled the visor down to shade his eyes from the blazing sun. A mile before the front entrance to the park, Thad turned north, then back to the east along a ruddy single-lane road that had been built up in anticipation of draining the marsh back in the 1940s. Ryan had been there several times as a kid after pestering his uncle so he could help check the back perimeter of the park in their small airboat.

The park's boundaries were marked by a twelve-foot chain-link fence topped with razor wire, mainly to keep humans out. An electrified inner fence ensured that the non-human residents stayed put. The fence was rarely electrified these days, since all the current inhabitants had experienced its bite and even the sight of the wire triggered a memory of the resulting shock. Ryan's grandpa added remote cameras after Ryan convinced him the technology was cheap and easily viewed from anywhere with an internet connection and a password. The swamp provided a natural barrier along the backside of the park. At four p.m. on a Wednesday, the park would be closed.

"Okay. We're here," Thad said as he pulled the Expedition onto a small turnout. "We'll have to walk it in from here." Thad shoved the SUV into park and turned to the monkeys. "You guys okay?"

"We're fine," Zach said.

"Could you share your plan with us?" Barney asked. Taylor looked a little scared.

"The park is just two hundred yards that way," he said, pointing toward the windshield. "We don't have an airboat, so we'll have to wade through the slough."

"What's a yard?" Barney asked.

"Yeah" Taylor added. "And what's a slough?"

Ryan looked at Thad, who bumped his forehead with the base of his hand.

"Sorry—it's a little over two hundred meters to the park, and a slough is a deeper swamp."

Barney frowned and crossed his arms. "Do we have to swim again?"

"Afraid so," Thad said.

Taylor giggled and looked at Zach, who grinned.

"There's one other thing you need to know," Thad said. "The swamp may have a few alliga—" Thad corrected himself. "Medium-sized crocodiles. We'll have to be careful."

Taylor glanced at Zach. "I'll watch out for you," Zach said.

"Zach can handle them," Taylor said, and smiled.

Ryan thought about the alligators. He'd seen a couple while crossing the slough with his uncle in the airboat. He wondered if Zach could look out for him, too.

"You remember the combination?" Ryan asked.

"Yup. Your grandpa let me use my birthday, since I was the one checking the rear perimeter for the past ten years." Thad nodded out Ryan's window. "Let's get going before it's dark."

Ryan looked at the sun, still well above the horizon. They'd need the time.

He stepped from the air-conditioned car and immediately broke into a sweat. The thick hammocks of southern oaks and palms blocked any breeze in the swamp. He remembered how hot the airboat rides were. The monkeys filed out of Barney's door, and Thad joined them in front of the Expedition. Thad carefully examined the break in the thick maze of sawgrass and aquatic plants in front of the SUV.

"Shuffle your feet and make just a little noise before we slide into the water. That'll give the snakes and gators fair warning."

Ryan didn't want to hear that. The gators were bad enough. He'd forgotten about snakes.

"I'll go first. Let these guys follow, then bring up the rear. Let's put the big guy here in the middle," Thad said, patting Zach on the back. "Everybody ready?"

Ryan wanted to say no, but he nodded, as did the other three. Thad slid down the small grade and shook the brush as he went. Barney was next, followed by Zach and then Taylor. Ryan checked the road one last time. It was empty and quiet. He started to shuffle through the black dirt and slid into the slough. The water was warm and smelled of old gym socks. Sawgrass sprouted in scattered areas, and bunches of trees formed hammocks that looked like a series of small, uninhabitable islands covered with tangled roots and thick underbrush. Ryan scanned the surface of the water as he waded over the uneven bottom. He could see Thad and Zach doing the same. Barney and Taylor appeared to be just focused on getting across. The trees blocked the sunlight and cast shadows across the black water. Two thirds across, Ryan could see the top of the back fence of the park.

Suddenly he heard a rustling and saw movement to the right, out of the corner of his eye, and he saw something slip into the water. He froze. Unaware Ryan had stopped, the group pulled away and was well ahead when Ryan finally found his voice.

"Hey guys," he hissed.

Taylor turned. "Hey Zach, it's Ryan. He stopped."

Ryan stayed focused on the water between himself and the hammock where he'd spotted the movement. He glanced at the others and saw Zach coming toward him, smacking the water and grunting. When he turned his attention back to the hammock, he spotted a gator surfacing about twenty feet away, but then the gator turned back. Ryan spun back around and used his arms to paddle-walk to meet Zach.

"Thanks, Zach. I didn't see him. Where did you learn to do that?"

"At the lake. Every once in a while, a crocodile would get in there. For some reason, if they hear me coming, they head the other way."

"I would, too—no offense."

Zach grunted and grinned.

Ryan and Zach rejoined the group. They reached the other side and emerged from the slough, climbing up onto firm land. Cool air drifted out of the park, and he thanked his grandfather for importing the trees and plants of the Amazon and even the massive irrigation system he cursed on a regular basis. Standing outside the chain-link fence, the monkeys scanned the makeshift rainforest. Their eyes widened as they studied the towering canopy. Ryan noticed Thad watching them too.

"You okay?" Thad asked Ryan.

"I'm cool." Ryan lied. He was happy to have them home, but knew the others could show up at any time.

Thad led them along the fence to a rusty gate secured by a combination lock. He flipped through the combination and opened the gate. Ryan heard the chatter of the capuchins, squirrel monkeys, and macaques coming from somewhere near the middle of the park. An occasional squawk from the parrots signaled their sunset ritual. Thad directed Ryan to enter, followed by Barney, Zach, and Taylor, and then Thad closed the gate.

"Okay, dudes. This is it. Your home for a little while," Thad said.

"It's remarkable. It looks a lot like the jungle at home," Barney said as he scanned the canopy again. "Are there others?"

"Many others," Ryan added. "We have more than five hundred monkeys here, but none quite like you."

"Let's get to the work room before it gets dark," Thad said, moving to the front again.

Ryan strained to see deeper into the jungle. The late-afternoon sun had dipped toward the horizon, and the thick canopy blocked most of the remaining light. Still, there was enough illumination to negotiate the jungle floor.

A howler monkey roared, warning his mates there were intruders in their territory. Several others joined in. Zach boomed out a growl, and the racket immediately stopped.

"Just like the ones at home," he said, shaking his head. "All blow and no go."

The group kept moving, and after about a half an hour, they intersected the outer trail that would lead them back to the work quarters. Thad found the gate and they entered the caged walkway that protected the park's visitors and allowed the howlers, macaques, capuchins, and squirrel monkeys to roam freely.

As they wound along the path, they passed the orangutan exhibit. Barney and Zach looked at the trench and rock barriers, then looked at each other. They repeated the looks when they passed the bonobos and the mandrills huddled behind thick black bars. Ryan wondered if they thought they were next. As the final remnants of daylight disappeared, they reached the work quarters. A fake thatched roof framed in bamboo concealed the cinderblock construction. A corrugated metal garage door at one end provided access to the garage, while a single steel door sitting just off the main path provided access to the change room, caretaker quarters, security monitors, and shop. Thad used the quarters as his second home.

"This is it, guys. We'll hole up here for the night and get you set up in the morning," Thad said as he held the door for the monkeys and Ryan.

As Ryan entered the change room, he heard a familiar voice.

"Well, well, look what the cat dragged in." John Webster leaned against the gray metal lockers on the far wall.

"What the hell are you doing here?" Thad said as he pushed past Ryan and started across the room. Just then, Ryan heard Zach growl behind them.

"Since you two didn't have any sense, I cut a deal of my own," John said.

"What the hell did you do?" Thad asked.

Ryan pivoted and the albino German stepped from the shadows. A stubby, balding man, dressed in slacks and a white sport coat, hid behind him.

The albino leveled an MP5 at the group. "It's been a long time, my little friends."

CHAPTER 57

RYAN FOUGHT PANIC at the sight of the albino pointing the MP5 at his head. He looked at Barney, Zach, and Taylor. They wanted to say something, but their self-preservation instincts were strong. They'd been taught to be silent in front of human strangers. But Ryan could read their faces. Barney stared at the albino, Zach scowled, and Taylor trembled. The stubby balding man held a pistol, drifted out from behind the albino, and stopped next to the makeshift security center where they kept the DVR and a video monitor for the security cameras. The albino circled them until he was straight ahead and stood in front of the long bench adjacent to the lockers lining the rear wall. His father wouldn't look at him.

The albino advanced until Ryan could smell his stale breath. He pushed Thad to the side with his gun barrel. "If you try anything, your nephew will be the first to die."

He had a thick German accent. Ryan remembered that from Houston. The albino stepped behind Ryan and throttled him, his thick fingers digging into his neck. Ryan thought he'd faint. He felt the cold steel of the barrel of the MP5 pressed against his cheek.

"Now, tell your friends to come in here."

"Hey, you buffoon, that's my son," John protested.

"Shut up, Mr. Webster, unless you want to be next," Baldy said.

"But Cyrus, this wasn't part of the deal."

Ryan realized this was Cyrus Schultz, the man his grandfather had warned them about—and his father knew these people. Rage filled him and he struggled to get free. He wanted to crush his father, but the albino's grip clamped down like a steel vise.

Cyrus pointed his pistol at Ryan's father. "Anything else?"

John dropped his shoulders and looked away. The albino pressed the barrel deeper into Ryan's cheek, and his teeth dug into the inside of his mouth.

"I know they do what you say."

Ryan had never been this scared. Still, he refused to give the albino the satisfaction of a whimper. He cut his eyes to Thad. Thad nodded in agreement toward the monkeys.

"Come in, guys."

Barney moved first, then Zach and Taylor.

"Tell the little asshole to close the door," the albino ordered.

"Close it," Ryan choked out.

Taylor closed the door and stepped next to Zach.

"Tell them to sit down." Ryan did, and the monkeys sat on the hard cement floor. Cyrus stuffed the gun in his belt, picked up a heavy burlap bag, and pulled out five pairs of handcuffs. He walked behind the monkeys.

"Tell them to put their hands behind them," the albino said.

Ryan did, and the monkeys complied. Cyrus clicked the cuffs on them and then walked up to Thad, who kept his hands at his side.

The albino jammed the barrel into Ryan's cheek again. "You too."

Thad stared at the albino, but slowly put his hands behind him. Cyrus clicked the handcuffs on his wrists.

"Now, hands behind your back, boy," the albino said.

Cyrus cuffed him. "Bravo, bravo boy," he said, turning to the monkeys. "Your great-grandfather trained them well."

He walked back to the bag and pulled out a long chain with thick links. He walked behind the monkeys, threaded it through the cuffs, and looped it through the water pipe that ran the length of the wall behind them. Once secured, the albino released his grip.

"Sit against the bench, next to your uncle," he said, still targeting Thad and Ryan.

Thad walked to the bench and sat on the floor, never taking his glare from the albino. Ryan followed. Cyrus walked behind them and re-cuffed them around one of the three-inch steel pipe supports bolted into the slab. The albino stepped back. Cyrus strolled over and stood in front of the monkeys. He looked at his watch. "How long until the van gets here?"

"Twenty minutes," Karl said.

Cyrus nodded. "Oh good, we have some time with our friends." He crossed his arms. "My, my—look at them. They are hybrids. Grandby will be all over this, Karl."

Karl just grinned.

"Leave them alone," Ryan said.

Karl started toward him, but Cyrus put up his hand, and Karl stopped like a trained dog.

"You'll never get away with this," Ryan said.

"Oh, I'll get away with it." He pulled the pistol from his belt and shot John in the chest. John clutched the wound and then fell to the ground.

"Dad!" Ryan yanked at the cuffs. He thought he hated his father, but not enough to just watch some asshole kill him.

"John!" Thad struggled too, but to no avail.

"You see," Cyrus said in a booming voice, "you two had a family dispute over the park that resulted in a double murder and suicide. We'll walk out of here and no one will know." He turned to the monkeys. "And I'll carve up your little carcasses and get your blood with that precious DNA."

Ryan's rage took control, and he fought wildly to break free. The cuffs clanged against the steel pipe and dug into his wrists, but he still strained harder.

"I'll kill you if you touch them, you bastard," Ryan screamed.

Cyrus turned back to Ryan. Ryan could see the madness in Cyrus's eyes as they grew wide. He was facing the devil himself. Ryan glanced at his father, lying lifeless on the floor.

Cyrus crept closer, bent down to Ryan's level, and pointed his stubby index finger in Ryan's face. "Not if I kill you first."

CHAPTER 58

AGENT PHILLIPS SPED along the turnpike, trying not to speak his mind. It wasn't that he didn't like the young Fish and Wildlife Service agent, but the kid was dead weight: just another liability that would be his responsibility if anything went wrong. But Phillips knew the ICE had agreements to operate within the parameters of several joint task forces ever since they were stuck under the auspices of the Department of Homeland Security. Phillips glanced at the fresh-faced Hispanic, who was nervously fidgeting in the passenger seat.

"So agent … ah …"

"Gutierrez."

"Right. Agent Gutierrez, what did they tell you about where we were going?"

"They said you suspected the illegal importation of multiple non-human primates."

Phillips wagged his head. The kid sounded like someone had plugged a manual into his brain. Then again, they all did.

Gutierrez's dark-brown eyes grew large as he awaited confirmation that he had it right. Phillips felt bad for the kid. "You got it. There are two suspects, both from the Webster family."

The agent jammed his hand into the breast pocket of his sports coat and pulled out his notepad. Phillips noted his trembling hand. "Yes," he said, flipping the pad open then shut. "A Ryan and Thad Webster. The nephew and his uncle."

Phillips tried to hide a smile as he exited the turnpike and headed west. "How long have you been assigned to investigations?" Phillips asked.

"Two weeks," Gutierrez said shyly. "I was a field biologist, but I want more pay."

It was worse than what Phillips had thought. He decided to try and calm the kid down. "You married?"

"Yes, sir. How about you?"

"Nope. Never."

"Kids?"

"One on the way."

Phillips nodded. "Good for you." He checked the cross street and noted the Webster Primate Park was two miles ahead. "Now when we get to the park, I want you to just follow my lead. I don't have firm evidence, and that's what we're looking for at the park. If they are smuggling monkeys, they'll keep them at the park."

The kid pulled out his notebook again.

"You don't have to write that down, do you?"

"Uh … no, sir. Just wanted to document our objective."

Phillips didn't hide the smile this time, and decided to focus on the road ahead. Two comments the young girl had made kept bouncing around in his head. "He looked like you." While he wasn't an expert on monkeys, he'd never seen one that looked like a human. She'd said the monkey had waved. It probably had just mimicked her, but still, the two comments didn't sit right.

"Hey kid. You're a biologist?"

"I was. Went to night school and have a master's in criminology."

"You know of any monkeys that have a nose and face like a human?"

"Not just like a human, but the macaques look like little old men."

"Guess that should explain it."

"Explain what?"

"A little girl on the ship said she saw the monkeys and they had a nose like mi—I mean, like a human's. Also said one waved."

"Waved?" The young agent scrunched his nose.

"Forget it." Phillips pulled into the large parking lot of the Primate Park.

"Keep your eyes peeled, kid." He drove slowly to the entrance of the park. The fence was high and topped with razor wire. A tangled thicket of green vines clung to every inch of the fence and prevented Phillips from seeing inside. He drifted by a small gate marked "employees only" and noticed it was chained shut. There was one late model suburban parked at the front gate. Phillips looped around the parking lot, passing behind the black SUV. No occupants. He pulled in next to the Suburban and gently pushed the shifter of the government-issued Taurus into park. Agent Gutierrez grabbed the door handle.

"Wait." Phillips scanned the entrance through the windshield. The entrance passed through a building made to look like a bamboo hut, complete with a thatched roof and bamboo gates bound together by fake vines. Security cameras were mounted on either side of the entrance, with a third facing out to the parking lot. If they were inside, they knew Phillips was here.

"Okay, kid. Let's go. You stay behind me."

The kid nodded. Phillips exited the car and walked to the entrance. The bamboo was actually mounted on a chain-link gate. As he approached, Phillips saw that the deadbolt mounted on a welded steel panel was open and the gate was slightly ajar. He looked back and checked on the agent, who was still right behind him. "Okay," he whispered. "Let's go in."

He slid the gate open and slipped through. Scanning the area, he noticed the only walkway into the park passed through a small building disguised as another bamboo hut. The door to the hut was closed, and he waited for the kid to join him. He could hear the faint chatter of the animals in the park, but nothing else, other than his own heartbeat.

He rapped twice on the door. "Federal agents. Please open up."

Nothing.

He tried the doorknob, and the door cracked open. As he reached for his Sig on his hip, he looked back at the kid, who was doing the same. He nodded, and then slowly opened the door. The room was lined with bamboo shelves holding maps and every trinket you could think of with a monkey on it. A counter sat along the back wall with ticket information and a cash register. Openings on either side led to a gift shop with even more jungle-related toys, games, and books. The gift shop was dark. Phillips cleared it quickly and opened the door into the park. A paved path led past a concession area, and off to the right he spotted another "employees only" sign over a bamboo archway with a thatched roof. The monkeys' chatter was now loud and clear. He looked back at the kid. The young agent's eyes were wide and his face expressionless.

Phillips carefully crept under the archway and entered a caged tunnel. The cage covered all the walkways and kept the people contained. A band of squirrel monkeys competed for positions adjacent to aluminum feeding cups dangling from chains. Suddenly, all hell broke loose above him. He pointed his Sig and nearly shot two squabbling monkeys overhead. Looking back at Gutierrez, Phillips quietly exhaled and waved him closer as he reached a cinderblock building with a heavy steel door. Since it was the only "employees only" structure in the area, he assumed it housed maintenance equipment, a business office, and probably a punch clock and a few lockers. He'd seen no other buildings except the bathrooms next to the concession area. If they were here, they'd either be inside the building or somewhere deeper in the park. If they were in the park, they'd return here soon. He knew there was no way two people could search sixty acres. If they weren't inside, he decided they'd wait for them. If they were inside, it would be an easy arrest: They had no criminal record and didn't seem like the violent type.

He glanced at the kid one more time. The kid held his newly issued Sig in one hand and nervously gave a thumbs-up with the other. Phillips grabbed the doorknob and felt Gutierrez against his hip. Phillips slowly opened the door, and leading with the Sig, he crept inside.

The room was dark, but as he opened the door the remaining daylight seeped inside. He spotted them immediately. The boy and his uncle were seated against the far wall with their hands behind them and mouths taped. Raising his Sig, he stepped closer, still targeting the uncle. Gutierrez stepped beside him and targeted the boy. Just then, he noticed the uncle's face was bright red as he tried to yell through the thick duct tape. The boy's eyes cut to the right. He spun to his right into four loud bursts of gunfire. He saw the kid go down, and Phillips felt the searing pain of a round through the arm, followed by two to his chest. As he dropped to the floor, he thought of the kid—his wife and baby—then he faded into blackness.

CHAPTER 59

KARL MOVED ACROSS the room just to the left of the door, and chuckled as he nudged agent Phillips with his huge black boot. Ryan had wanted to warn them. He'd watched the security monitor in horror as the agents made their way from the parking lot into the park, while Karl tracked every move on the monitor tied to the park's DVR system. With the thick duct tape over his mouth, he had to give all his effort to get enough oxygen through his nose. His shifting eyes and muffled yell weren't enough warning.

Blood poured out of the young Hispanic agent's leg. Ryan eyed his chest as it rose and fell with each breath he gasped. Agent Phillips was bleeding too, not nearly as much. Despite the nudge from Karl, he was still. His father had crumbled in the office doorway, and Ryan searched for a sign of life. He saw none and wondered why his father had been so selfish.

Ryan's cuffs pulled tight as Thad worked his wrists in a futile effort to break free and unleash the anger Ryan could clearly see in his reddened face. Across the room and to Ryan's left, Barney, Zach, and Taylor remained silent and stared at the agent on the ground. Ryan was certain gunfire and murder were something they'd never seen until they were exposed to man. Now, chained like circus animals, they had a front row seat, thanks to him. The mix of guilt, rage, and sadness churned in his gut, and for the first time in his young life, he wanted to kill.

Still leaning against the wall between the office and makeshift security station on Ryan's left, Cyrus asked, "You ready to finish this?" He lifted his right hand and held out the gun.

Keeping a safe distance from the monkeys, Karl walked across the room, slung the MP5 over his shoulder, and took the gun. Ryan noticed he was wearing the same black gloves Cyrus sported.

Barney's face was stoic as he studied Karl's movements. Zach seethed and stared at the albino, while Taylor gawked, wide-eyed, at the carnage Karl had wrought. Karl pivoted and locked eyes with Ryan, slowly closing the distance between them. His eyes were black, and Ryan sensed his life was about to end. Ryan shook and glanced at Thad. For the first time, Ryan saw helplessness in his uncle's face. Thad desperately swept his foot, missing Karl as he passed.

Karl smiled again. "I'll get to you in a minute." He stepped over the bench and stood behind Ryan.

Ryan didn't turn around or beg for his life; he refused to give the albino the satisfaction. He held his breath when Karl gripped his right shoulder and then pressed the barrel of the gun against his temple.

Cyrus surveyed the scene. "Him first, then the uncle, then we'll make sure on the others."

Ryan glanced at the monkeys. They knew what was about to happen. Zach rattled the chains and pulled them tight against the water pipe. Cyrus pulled another gun from his coat and stepped in front of Zach, pointing the gun at his head. "You'd better tell him to stop," he said over his shoulder to Ryan.

Karl ripped the tape from his mouth and Ryan swallowed the pain. The sweat rolled into his eyes, and he squinted to see Zach.

"Do what he says," Ryan said, his voice cracking.

Zach leaned forward and boomed, "I don't think so."

Cyrus was momentarily stunned by Zach's ability to speak, and for a split second, Ryan felt the gun barrel leave his temple.

"Drop it, big boy."

Ryan recognized Addy's voice. A single shot rang out, and Ryan heard Karl slam against the locker. Zach, Taylor, and Barney leapt up together and ripped the water pipe from the wall. Cyrus stumbled backward and fired. Ryan ducked, but kept his eyes on the monkeys. Zach freed himself and slung Cyrus against the wall. Cyrus dropped like a limp rag doll. Water sprayed from the broken pipe. Ryan couldn't wipe his eyes and the spray mixed with his sweat and burned, blurring his vision. Still, he spotted someone stepping from the garage area to his right.

"Don't try it."

Zach kept coming. He hurdled Ryan, roaring, and pinned the albino against the lockers behind him. Karl didn't have a chance.

In seconds, Addy was kneeling next to him. "You okay?"

Ryan nodded.

"Let's get these off you guys." Addy stood and looked down at Ryan. He heard Karl still struggling behind him. Addy looked over Ryan's shoulder.

"Don't worry about him," she said as she knelt down and released their cuffs.

Thad shot up and ripped the tape from his mouth. "Your timing is impeccable," he said.

Ryan pressed himself up from the floor and rubbed his eyes clear. Addy stood before him, dressed in jeans and a black T-shirt, her hair tucked tight in a ponytail.

"I heard you guys were looking for some help," she said, grinning.

Ryan hugged her and didn't want to let go.

"John!" his mother screamed as she ran from the garage area to John's side.

Addy pushed Ryan away and followed her to the office doorway. His mother knelt over his dad and hugged him. As she lifted John into her lap, Ryan noticed the blood on her bright yellow polo. Addy quickly ripped open his father's plaid shirt and tore a piece from the tail.

"Hold this here and press hard."

His mother pressed on his father's chest and cut a glance at Ryan. Tears streamed down her face, but still she gave him a worried smile, then looked back at his dad. Ryan heard the commotion behind him again and spun around. Zach had locked his arm around the albino's neck from behind.

Karl was bleeding from the right side of his chest. He flailed his arms but to no avail. The albino's arms slowed, and then he stopped flailing. His eyes dimmed and his head slumped.

Zach looked at Ryan. "Thou shalt not kill."

Zach threw Karl face-forward to the ground, and Taylor jumped on top of him. Barney stepped next to Zach and looked down at Karl. "Very impressive, I must say." Barney patted Zach on the shoulder. Zach grinned.

Ryan heard a groan behind him and remembered the agents on the opposite side of the room. He turned and surveyed the far wall. Thad crouched over the Hispanic agent and pulled a belt tight around his thigh. He was still breathing. Next to him, Agent Phillips sat upright. He yanked open his shirt and pulled at the Velcro straps to his vest. He opened the vest and winced as he rubbed the huge red bruises on his chest. He looked up at Ryan, then to the monkeys behind them. The agent's stare told Ryan everything. He'd heard Zach talk. They were caught. Thad slipped a cell phone from his pocket, dialed, and gave the 911 operator the necessary details.

"Oh no, look at this," Addy said.

Ryan looked back toward the office and saw Addy pointing to the flat-screen monitor for the security system.

"We have company—lots of it."

CHAPTER 60

RYAN COULDN'T BELIEVE his eyes. He stepped closer to the monitor perched on the desk. The monitor was set to display four cameras at a time. Each quadrant displayed a view from a camera for five seconds and then presented the next. This cycle repeated until the system cycled through all sixteen cameras. If motion was detected, that camera's view was immediately displayed. Ryan bounced his attention between the two top quadrants. He wiped his eyes as if that would help change the troubling images.

The first showed the area immediately in front of the entrance to the park. Reporters gripping microphones elbowed through a surging crowd. The throng seemed to be divided into two loosely organized herds centered on two men. The groups shouted at each other and flailed their arms. Some carried homemade signs. Some just yelled. The group on the left of the screen seemed to be led by a thin, well-dressed man, Ryan guessed nearing sixty. The second group was centered on a heavy-set man, a little younger than the first, and dressed in a gray suit. Ryan could see the reporters accumulating around each man. He quickly scanned the room. His mother was crying over his father, and Thad tended to the wounded agents. Addy stepped next to Ryan and gawked at the upper-right quadrant, displaying the parking lot camera. News vans were scattered among the cars still filing into the lot.

"What the hell is going on out there?" Ryan asked.

"I don't know, but I know how to find out," Addy said, stepping to the older color TV stuffed in the corner of the office.

She flipped it on and ran through the local channels until she hit a live feed. Ryan shifted his attention to the TV. He immediately recognized the thin, well-dressed man from the security camera. The banner at the bottom of the screen identified him as Charles Grandby. More troubling were the words drifting across the crawler.

"Grandby claims missing link between ape and man found …"

"Turn it up," Ryan asked.

Addy found the volume control on the remote and the words caught the attention of everyone in the room.

"… and we have irrefutable proof that these hybrids are bipedal hominids that use tools, bury their dead, and communicate through written English. The myth of a grand creator has been rebuked by the hard scientific facts we hold here." The man held up a file folder. "Furthermore, I believe the hybrids that survived are alive and inside this park." He pointed to the entrance of the park, and his supporters cheered and waved their hands wildly.

The reporter yanked the microphone back and pressed her earpiece hard. "Now over to Jeff, who has the other side of the story."

The picture shifted to another reporter, crammed against the second man from the security camera. Ryan recognized Sarah standing next to the stocky man in the gray suit.

"What?" he said

"You recognize someone?" Addy asked.

"It's Sarah!"

Addy pulled back and raised her eyebrows. "Your girlfriend?"

"My old one."

The reporter pressed his earpiece and shouted over the crowd noise.

"I'm here with Jacob Remington, leader of a group called the Society of True Believers, a Christian organization dedicated to the preservation of the teachings of the Bible. Mr. Remington, why are you here?"

"These claims are blasphemous, and Mr. Grandby, once again, is trying to destroy all the religions of the world. Our Lord Jesus Christ is the Creator of Heaven and Earth and all of mankind. The people inside have smuggled in non-human primates as part of this ruse. They carry the risk of serious disease and should be destroyed immediately."

"Who's behind this, sir?"

"Well, one of the criminals, Mr. Ryan Webster, is unstable and unreliable, and is well known to this young lady."

He pointed to Sarah. She leaned in and said, "Mr. Webster and I were friends until he suddenly started claiming his disbelief in God to my mother and me. Then he headed into the jungles of Brazil with his uncle to find these hellish creatures his great-grandfather *created* years ago."

Ryan felt the rage surging. "That's bullshit."

Shoved and jostled by the crowd, the reporter struggled to pull the microphone back and face the camera. "So there you have it, Mike. There are two sides to this story."

Ryan marched to the door. He reached for the knob.

"Wait," he heard Agent Phillips say.

Phillips was on his feet, but wobbly. Blood soaked the left arm of his white shirt.

"They'll kill you, son," he said, weakly pointing to the screen.

Red and blue gumball machines flashed atop the sheriff's cars weaving through the melee. Several gray-and-black Impalas rushed in with red strobes flashing from their dashes. Feds, Ryan assumed. He could see the crowd's mood settle as the officers and federal agents quickly filed from their vehicles and weaved through the mob. They set up a perimeter covering the front of the park and pushed the crowd back, forming a buffer. The TV newscaster reported the breaking news that two federal agents might be hostages inside the Webster Primate Park.

"I told them where we were headed, and when I didn't call in, they sent help. Sorry, kid," Phillips said, placing his arm on Ryan's shoulder. He looked at the monkeys on the other side of the room. "I didn't know."

Just then, two ambulances raced into frame on the screen. Ryan looked around the room. His father, cradled in his mother's blood-soaked arms, was breathing short, shallow breaths, and his eyes were now open. Thad knelt next to the Hispanic agent, glanced at the screen, then turned back to Ryan and nodded. Ryan looked at the monkeys. Taylor was still atop Karl, and he gave Ryan a gentle smile. Zach leaned against the lockers, arms crossed, looking back. Barney examined the TV, but stopped and faced Ryan. They were all waiting for *him*. This was it. Lives were at risk, and the decision he'd dreaded for so long was at hand. He thought about what the monkeys had been through so far. He thought about his grand-father and his last request. He looked back at the TV and the mob standing outside the park his great-grandfather had built. Indeed, the God he thought existed wasn't here today—the world wasn't ready.

He turned to Thad, who was still cradling the young agent's head. "You're the best, dude," he said. "I never would have made it this far with-out you."

A tear ran down Thad's cheek. His Uncle T didn't have an answer. He pulled his fist to his heart and then pointed to Ryan. Ryan repeated the mo-tion, and felt a tear run down his cheek. He wiped it away and turned to Barney.

"You know the way we came in," he said. "If you guys get to the back of the park, you can get into the glades. You'll be safe there for now." He looked at Zach, Taylor, and Barney one last time. "I let you down and I'm sorry. I'll never forget you and what you've taught me." Tears streaked down both his cheeks, and he wiped them away and sucked in a deep breath.

It was time to go. No other explanation was necessary—he'd failed and left them high and dry. He was sure they'd survive, at least for a while, in the Everglades, but they'd be alone. That bothered him the most. He studied Agent Phillips for any sign of resistance.

Phillips dropped his head. "I never saw a thing."

Ryan nodded slowly in appreciation. "I'm going out. I'll send help back in," he said, reaching for the doorknob. He opened the door.

"Wait," Zach said.

Ryan turned to see Zach standing with Taylor. Zach looked at Barney, who nodded. Then Zach checked with Taylor, and he nodded too.

Barney stepped forward. "We've got this one, as your uncle likes to say."

Zach smiled. "You've done more for us than anyone could ask. We believe in taking care of our own kind—and you are our brother."

Ryan was stunned. He felt another tear escape.

The three monkeys huddled, and then Barney said, "We'll meet you out front." Then the monkeys raced past Ryan and disappeared.

"I'm going with you," Addy said, stepping to Ryan's side and taking his hand.

Ryan looked at Thad one more time, then at his mother. He led Addy out into the park and walked along the trail to the concession stand where he'd served the park's visitors at the age of ten. He remembered what it felt like to be that young, carefree boy. He didn't feel like that anymore.

They made their way through the gift shop, and he looked at the long-armed, stuffed toy monkeys smiling back at him. He passed the cash register and remembered welcoming the thousands of people who were eager to see the primates at the park. He remembered how kind most of them were, and hoped one of them would find the monkeys. He led Addy outside. The sun was cresting the treetops, and he felt the cool air of the artificial jungle against his cheeks. He'd miss that almost as much as he'd miss Addy.

Stopping at the gate, he turned to her. "You sure?"

She leaned in and kissed him on the cheek. "Never been more sure," she said, and then pushed the gate open.

Ryan saw the line of officers with their rifles all pointed at him.

"Freeze—lock your hands above your head and get down on the ground," one yelled through a bullhorn.

By now, the crowd had grown to at least a hundred or so. Ryan was struck by how quiet it was. They all stared at him: the unstable eighteen-year-old criminal. Ryan and Addy kept their hands locked on their heads and started to kneel.

Suddenly, the crowd gasped. They were no longer staring at him, but at the gate behind him. Keeping his hands locked, he carefully glanced over his right shoulder.

The gate was open and monkey after monkey filed out. Squirrel monkeys mingled with capuchins and howlers. Macaques scampered out on all fours. The monkeys formed a loose perimeter against the fence on either side of Ryan and Addy, as if protecting the park. Most of the five hundred inhabitants of the park filed out of the gate. Finally, the procession of monkeys ended, and they all held their positions along the fence.

Ryan turned back to the crowd and noticed they were still staring at the gate. They let out another gasp, and this time they collectively covered their mouths. He glanced over his shoulder again.

Barney, Zach, and Taylor walked out, shoulder to shoulder. Taylor was grinning and almost skipping. Zach stuck out his huge chest and firmly pursed his lips. Barney marched like royalty inspecting the troops.

Ryan and Addy looked at each other. Ryan turned in time to see the officers target the monkeys. Barney stepped next to Addy, and Taylor and Zach stepped next to Ryan. All five hundred moneys along the perimeter chattered and screeched but held their positions and looked out over the crowd in full view of the cameras.

"Don't shoot," he heard behind them.

Holding his credentials in the air, Agent Phillips gingerly trotted out and stepped in front of Ryan. "They're with me."

Grandby wriggled to the front of the crowd. "I give you proof—the missing link between man and ape—and proof that your Grand Designer is nothing but a fraud, just like your religions."

Half the group erupted in cheers and then the others began to shove. Fistfights broke out at the dividing line. Bottles, rocks, and cans were launched in the air.

Barney, Zach, and Taylor stepped toward the mob. Ryan heard the rifles cock and the officer and agents took aim on the monkeys.

Suddenly, all three stepped forward. Ryan was shocked. The crowd fell silent, and the officers raised their heads from the sights of their rifles.

Then Zach said the words at the bottom of Zachariah's note.

"Know ye the Lord is God," he said clearly. "It is he that hath made us, and not we ourselves, we are his people and the sheep of his pasture."

Ryan looked over the crowd. No one moved or said a word. Grandby dropped his head and shook it. Phillips waved the ambulance crews inside. Ryan scanned the monkeys on either side and then looked at Addy, who smiled.

Agent Phillips sat down and crossed his legs as a paramedic knelt in front of him. Barney, Zach, and Taylor turned around, locked arms over each other's shoulders, and walked to Ryan. Ryan raised both hands and pulled Addy into the huddle.

Thad ran up from behind. "I'm not missing this for the world, dudes."

He ducked under Ryan's arms and joined in. No one said a word; they didn't have to. They touched heads and closed their eyes. Ryan didn't know what would happen next, but he felt the energy his Uncle T said was proof God existed. He knew he'd delivered on his promise to his grandfather, and he was sure he felt his grandfather's energy present, too. And while Ryan didn't know what would happen next, for some reason he had faith that life with the swimming monkeys would go on.

To Be Continued

ABOUT THE AUTHOR

Steve Hadden is the author of *The Sunset Conspiracy*, *Genetic Imperfections*, and *The Swimming Monkeys Trilogy*. A chemical engineer who's worked at the top of some of the largest companies in the world, Steve is always fascinated by the intersection of science, interesting people, and intriguing stories. Visit his website at http://www.stevehadden.com

Made in United States
Orlando, FL
08 March 2022

15519476R00190